Praise for

holly hepburn

'The Star and Sixpence sparkles with fun, romance, mystery
and a hunky blacksmith. It's a real delight'
JULIE COHEN

'Warm, witty and laced with intriguing secrets! I want
to pull up a bar stool, order a large G&T and soak
up all the gossip at the Star and Sixpence'
CATHY BRAMLEY

'You'll fall in love with this fantastic new series
from a new star of women's fiction. Filled to the brim
with captivating characters and fantastic storylines in
a gorgeous setting ... I want to hear more!'
MIRANDA DICKINSON

'A fresh new voice, brings wit and warmth to
this charming tale of two sisters'
ROWAN COLEMAN

'Like the dream pub landlady who always knows exactly
what you want, Holly Hepburn has created the most
delightful welcome to what promises to be a brilliant series'
KATE HARRISON

'Warm, witty and utterly charming ... It left me
with the most wonderful happy glow'
CALLY TAYLOR

'A super sparkling star of a story'
ALEXANDRA BROWN

Holly Hepburn is the much-loved author of commercial women's fiction. She lives near London with her grey tabby cat, Portia. They both have an unhealthy obsession with Marmite. Follow Holly on Twitter @HollyH_Author.

Also by Holly Hepburn

A Year at the Star and Sixpence
The Picture House by the Sea
A Year at Castle Court
Last Orders at the Star and Sixpence

To Clare Watson, who is Jude, Tom
and Shazza all wrapped up in one
dazzling goddess.

Part One

Broken Hearts at Brightwater Bay

holly hepburn

Coming Home to Brightwater Bay

**SIMON &
SCHUSTER**

London · New York · Sydney · Toronto · New Delhi

First published individually as eBooks, titled *Broken Hearts at Brightwater Bay*,
Sea Breezes at Brightwater Bay, *Dangerous Tides at Brightwater Bay* and *Sunset over
Brightwater Bay* in Great Britain by Simon & Schuster UK Ltd, 2020

This paperback edition published 2021

3 5 7 9 10 8 6 4

Simon & Schuster UK Ltd
1st Floor
222 Gray's Inn Road
London WC1X 8HB

Simon & Schuster Australia, Sydney
Simon & Schuster India, New Delhi

www.simonandschuster.co.uk
www.simonandschuster.com.au
www.simonandschuster.co.in

A CIP catalogue record for this book is available from the British Library

Paperback ISBN: 978-1-4711-7033-1
eBook ISBN: 978-1-4711-7034-8

Typeset in the UK by M Rules
Printed and bound in Great Britain by CPI Group (UK) Ltd, Croydon, CR0 4YY

MIX
Paper from
responsible sources
FSC® C020471

Prologue

November

'I can't do this.'

Merry opened her mouth to say she'd told him not to eat so much bread before their meals came, but the words died when she saw the look on his face. He didn't mean the spaghetti carbonara he was pushing around his plate; this was something bigger. Something serious.

'Alex?' she said warily, when his gaze remained resolutely fixed on the congealing food. 'What's wrong? What can't you do?'

He glanced up then, pale blue eyes resting on her before flitting away around the restaurant like a startled hare. 'This,' he said abruptly, after several long seconds of quiet. '*Us*.'

A flood of hot prickly panic washed over Merry. '*Us*?' she repeated, and the word stuck in her suddenly dry throat. 'What are you talking about?'

'You and me. Our relationship.' He took a deep breath. 'I just can't pretend anymore.'

And now the heat gave way to icy coldness, like an Arctic wind had blown in from nowhere. 'I don't understand,' she said, as numbness stole over her. 'What can't you pretend?'

There was a long silence during which Alex didn't look at Merry. 'That I still love you,' he said finally.

The air gushed from Merry's lungs as though she'd been punched. Surely she must have misheard – this was Alex, after all; her boyfriend of more than half her life, who worshipped her and called her a goddess and promised he'd always be at her side – her soulmate. Of course he loved her, Merry decided with an incredulous shake of her head, as much as she loved him. She sucked in a ragged breath, only dimly aware of the wheezing croak that accompanied it, and tried to gather her scrambled thoughts together enough to formulate a reply.

'I've been bottling it up,' Alex went on, in an oddly detached tone. 'But I just can't do it anymore. I'm sorry.'

It was the flatness with which he uttered the last sentence that broke her. As though he'd smashed her favourite mug instead of her heart. Her eyes swam. 'You're *sorry*?'

The words were louder than she intended, and thick with emotion. His eyebrows furrowed in alarm as he looked at her. 'Don't cry,' he said, as the woman at the neighbouring table fired a covert look their way. 'For God's sake, Merry, you must have known this was coming. Don't make a scene.'

Her jaw dropped a little as she stared at him, his features

shimmering through the tears that were threatening to cascade down her cheeks at any moment. *Don't cry* – had he really just said that? When he'd taken all her hopes and dreams for the future and casually crushed them as though they were nothing?

Blinking, she swallowed hard, trying to dislodge the lump that had formed in her throat. 'How am I supposed to have known?' she managed in a hoarse half-whisper. 'We've been together since we were sixteen years old. You said you wanted to marry me.'

He flapped a hand. 'Maybe that's the problem. Fifteen years is a long time – we're not the same people we were back then.'

'Of course we're not,' Merry said, with a fresh wave of bewildered hurt. 'We've grown up – evolved into adults.' She took another ragged breath. 'Adults who fit together perfectly.'

Alex let out a long sigh. 'We used to. But lately – well, you have to admit it hasn't been easy. Especially not since . . .'

He trailed off but Merry didn't need to hear the rest of the sentence to know what he meant: the writer's block that had sucked the colour from every aspect of her life. At first, she'd put it down to the bone-weary exhaustion that had been creeping up on her for months, born from the never-ending whirlwind of meetings and lunches and launch parties that came with the territory when you were a *Sunday Times* best-selling novelist. But she'd always been able to escape into her writing and find solace in the worlds she created for others;

Holly Hepburn

even when the real world was too much, her characters never let her down. Until the day she'd opened up her laptop and the words hadn't come.

She'd tried not to panic – told herself it was a temporary thing. Her writer friends were supportive, if unsurprised.

'Bloody hell, Mer, you've delivered two books a year for the last five years,' Jess had said when Merry had confided in her. 'Cut yourself some slack – take some time off. Your deadline isn't for months.'

Except that the deadline came and went, and still Merry was paralysed by the inability to write. Her publisher was understanding, but it gnawed away at her self-confidence and stopped her sleeping. Even the thought of sitting down at her laptop flooded her with anxiety; the blank screen made her feel sick. And, inevitably, it had affected her relationship with Alex. She hadn't realized just how much until now.

'You said you understood,' she said across the table. 'You said you'd do whatever it took to help.'

'I tried,' Alex protested, sounding injured. 'I listened when you wanted to talk, suggested you see a counsellor, and hardly dared to breathe while you were locked away in your office trying to write. It's been seven months of treading on eggshells, Merry, and I'm not sure what else you expected me to do short of writing the bloody book for you.'

His resentment was unmissable and Merry thought she knew why. Alex had been so proud of her high-flying career, had always basked in the light of her success and boasted about her awards and sales figures. There wasn't much to

6

boast about when there were days that even getting out of bed was too much for her.

'I didn't expect you to give up,' she said quietly. 'The Alex I love would never do that.'

He sat back, dropping his fork onto the plate with a clatter that rang with ominous finality. 'Like I said, we've both changed.'

There was a barely concealed snort from the woman at the neighbouring table. Alex cleared his throat. 'I think it's best if I move out. A clean break all round.'

The thought of living alone in the Chiswick flat they'd always shared caused yet another jolt of unreality to wash over Merry. 'But where will you go? This is madness, Alex – can't we try to work things out? I – I love you.'

He shook his head. 'That's the thing – I don't believe you do, not like you used to, anyway. And maybe that's part of the reason you can't write about love anymore. You've forgotten what it feels like.'

The words were like a blade slicing into her heart. 'Don't tell me what I feel. I know what love is. If anyone has forgotten, it's you.'

'I've found a flat-share in Greenwich,' he said. 'Signed the paperwork a few days ago.'

It wasn't a spur-of-the-moment decision, Merry realized with dull comprehension. He'd been planning this for a while, weeks or even months, and had chosen this specific restaurant to deliver the final blow because it was new to them both and held no special memories. At least he hadn't done it in the living room at home, where she'd be forced to relive it over and over again; at least he'd thought about that. Or perhaps he'd cynically calculated that she'd be more likely to hold it together in public – less likely to break down. She honestly didn't know; the Alex sitting across from her suddenly felt like a stranger. There was only one thing she did know: there was nothing she could say or do to change his mind. He was leaving her. 'When will you go?' she managed, fighting to preserve what little dignity she had left.

Alex puffed out his cheeks. 'Now.'

'*Now*?' she echoed, gaping at him. 'But you haven't got any clothes.'

'I'll buy more,' he said, with a careless shrug that caused a fresh trickle of pain to run through her. 'It's better this way, believe me.'

Looking up, he caught the waiter's eye and made the familiar little 'Can we get the bill?' gesture Merry had always found faintly ridiculous, although she'd never told him so. Moments later, the waiter stood at their table, his eyes carefully averted from Merry's stricken expression. She watched in frozen silence as Alex paid and pushed back his chair. 'Will you be okay getting home?'

The roaring in her ears made it hard to focus on what he was saying. Taking a long deep breath, Merry tapped one finger against her wrist, counting the beats and forcing the flood of anxiety down. 'Yes,' she mumbled. 'I'll be fine.'

He hesitated, as though there was something more he

wanted to say, then nodded once. 'Text me when you're there. We'll talk tomorrow.'

She watched him until he was through the door and gone, fighting every instinct to stand up and call his name. Around her, the other diners continued with their meals in blissful ignorance; Merry expected at least some of them to be goggling at her with avid fascination but the truth was that hardly anyone seemed to have noticed. She fixed her gaze on the white tablecloth and battled for control of her thudding heart and racing thoughts. She took a swig of wine, hardly tasting it as she swallowed. Alex would come back, she comforted herself, once the reality of sharing a flat with a stranger sunk in. They'd never spent more than a few weeks apart – he'd realize he still loved her and he'd be back, begging for her forgiveness. Merry dug her fingernails into her palms and let out a shaky breath. He had to.

The woman at the adjoining table leaned across, sympathy etched across her face. 'Look, I know it's none of my business and I can see it hurts like hell right now, but one day you're going to be glad you didn't marry him.'

At that, Merry's brittle self-control shattered, and she burst into howling sobs.

WANTED – WRITER IN RESIDENCE!

1st February – 31st August

The Orkney Literary Society is pleased to announce a six-month residency opportunity. Open to published authors from the UK, we are offering full accommodation in a traditional Scottish croft, transport and a stipend of £5000. In return, we expect the chosen author to promote reading for pleasure in and around the Orkney Islands, working with our thriving library and bookshops to deliver a series of public events throughout the year. The author must also produce at least one new artistic product during the residency, featuring Orkney and the neighbouring islands.

This residency would suit a writer who seeks time and solitude to work in a beautiful and magical place.

For further details on the application process, please email: **Niall.Gunn@Orkneylib.gov.uk**

Closing date for applications: 30th November

Chapter One

Three months later

'First time on a wee plane?'

Merry opened her eyes to peer at the elderly woman in the seat next to her, then closed them again quickly as another burst of turbulence sent her stomach lurching. She didn't trust herself to speak and instead managed a curt nod.

'*Och*, it's not normally like this,' the woman said, and Merry heard the rustle of cellophane. 'Can I interest you in a bullseye at all? Take your mind off things, mebbe?'

It was going to take a lot more than a boiled sweet to distract her from the horrible certainty that they were all going to die, Merry thought, but the woman was trying to be kind so she opened her eyes and did her best to smile. 'Thank you.'

She unwrapped the sweet and popped it into her mouth. At least she'd have minty fresh breath when she died, she told herself as the plane wobbled and bucked again. Her fingers gripped the armrests and she offered up a prayer to any god who was listening; of all the writing retreats in all the world, she had to choose the one that started with a death-defying flight.

'So, if you've not been on one of these wee planes before, this is very likely your first trip to Orkney,' her neighbour observed, with an openly appraising look. 'Are you on your holidays?'

'No, I'm visiting for work,' Merry replied, surreptitiously crossing her fingers. The advert for the writing residency had promised solitude and magic; was it too much to hope that they would somehow cure her writer's block, and that time might heal her still-raw heart?

The woman eyed her thoughtfully for several long seconds, clearly taking in her neatly styled dark hair and perfect make-up, then her face lit up. 'I know who you are! You're the new Writer in Residence, staying at the old Dougal croft.'

There was no point in denying it, Merry reasoned, although how her neighbour had deduced her identity was a mystery. 'I am,' she replied. 'Who's Dougal?'

'He was the shepherd who used to own the croft. Wrote poems too, mostly about the sea, and when he died, he left everything to the Literary Society.'

Merry absorbed the news, picturing a cottage overlooking the ocean. It was nice that her home for the next six months had a writing connection. Perhaps that would help her too. 'Did he ever have anything published?' she asked.

Her neighbour snorted. '*Och*, no. They were terrible poems – far too obsessed with describing the sea as a woman, all soft, rounded curves and deep, mysterious crevices.' She looked sideways at Merry. 'He didn't have much luck with the ladies, if you know what I mean – I think it was the beard. A bit too sheepy.'

'Oh,' Merry said, struggling to keep a straight face. 'Well, I can see how that might not help.'

The woman thrust out a hand. 'I'm Bridget McGinty. Pleased to meet you.'

'Merry Wilde.'

Bridget squinted thoughtfully. 'Is that your writing name? I'm not sure I've read anything by a Mary Wilde.'

Merry hid a wry smile; if she had a pound for every time someone had cheerfully admitted they'd never heard of her, she'd be a lot richer than she was now. 'Almost – I use my full name, which is Merina.'

'Merina Wilde,' Bridget said, rolling the name around before shaking her head. 'No, I've definitely never heard of you.'

'Well,' Merry said, summoning up her usual good grace. 'You have now.'

'Aye,' Bridget replied, rustling another bullseye wrapper. 'And I'll be hearing your name a lot more over the next six months, if Niall Gunn has anything to do with it.'

That was a name Merry certainly knew. Niall was the librarian at Orkney Library and he'd been her main point of contact for both her application for the residency and all the admin that had followed. He was due to meet her at the airport when she landed. *If* she landed . . .

As if on cue, the plane lurched again and the contents of Merry's stomach swooped. She pressed her lips together tightly, praying she wasn't going to throw up all over Bridget's sensible shoes – that wouldn't do much to preserve her glamorous author reputation, although she suspected Bridget had already seen through that. As if reading her mind, the older woman patted her hand and smiled. 'Not long now, dearie. And just think, you can write it all into a book – it's all copy, isn't that what they say?'

It was all Merry could do to nod – and wonder if she'd made a calamitous mistake in running away to Orkney.

Bridget had clearly decided that her new acquaintance needed looking after, because she waited while Merry collected her suitcase from the tiny luggage carousel and escorted her through to Arrivals with the proud air of someone doing their official duty.

'There's Niall,' she said, and pointed to a tall, dark-haired man waiting in front of the floor-to-ceiling glass windows, holding a sign that read *Merina Wilde*, albeit upside down.

He spotted them a second later; his eyes locked onto Merry and he smiled, causing her to slow a fraction as the impact hit her. She didn't really know what she'd expected him to look like, but she hadn't anticipated he'd be so . . . well, so Clark Kent. The mental image she'd built up while reading his meticulously detailed and grammatically perfect emails had been of someone older and grey-haired, who took the time to sharpen their pencils to precise points and brewed their tea for 23.3 seconds precisely, not of an undercover superhero with a million-watt smile.

'Would you look at that sign,' Bridget tutted, casting an apologetic glance Merry's way. 'He's a good lad, but a wee bit away with the fairies at times. Comes from reading all them books, I shouldn't wonder.'

'Probably,' Merry said dryly.

She used the time it took them to cross the Arrivals hall to study Niall Gunn more closely. He wore a dark grey suit with a crisp white shirt and polished black shoes, all of which she found distinctly un-librarianish. The black-rimmed glasses were entirely on brand, however, and as she came to a halt in front of him, she saw they framed sea-blue eyes lined with thick dark lashes that most women she knew would kill for. She wouldn't mind betting that there were one or two library users who came not to borrow books, but to gaze at the librarian instead.

'Hello, Merina,' he said, with another flash of a smile. 'Welcome to Orkney.'

Merry opened her mouth to reply but Bridget beat her to it, clearing her throat in the most meaningful way and staring pointedly at the sign Niall held. His smile faltered a little and he looked down. A hot red stain crept up his neck as he realized his mistake and he turned the cardboard up the right way. 'Sorry.'

He looked so mortified that Merry couldn't help feeling it rub off on her; an answering blush warmed her own cheeks and she hastened to put him at ease. 'Don't worry. I speak Australian.'

As soon as the words left her mouth, she started to cringe – Bridget was giving her the oddest look. But Niall's mouth twitched and he broke into a wide grin that made Merry's embarrassment subside. They stood smiling at each other for a few seconds, then Bridget cleared her throat again. 'I'll leave you to it, then. Lovely to meet you, Mary, dear. I look forward to finding out all about your books.'

She nodded to Niall, her disapproval still evident, and beetled for the exit. Niall studied Merry, a quizzical expression in his eyes. 'Did she just call you Mary?'

'Happens a lot,' Merry said. 'I usually shorten Merina to Merry, but people often struggle with it and Mary is a much more sensible name. Still, it's better than the Christmas jokes I used to get at school.'

Niall raised a sympathetic eyebrow. 'Only at school?'

'And occasionally at book signings,' she admitted with a good-natured sigh. 'Usually from older men accompanying their wives, all of whom think they're the first person ever to make the joke.'

He nodded. 'So, what would you prefer me to call you? Merina?'

She liked the way it sounded with his gentle Scottish burr – slower and softer than with an English accent – but it was far too formal for everyday use. 'Merry is fine.'

'Welcome to Orkney, Merry,' he said, holding out a hand. 'Thank you for agreeing to be our Writer in Residence.'

She took his outstretched fingers, which were long and perfect for running along the spines of books, and shook them. 'Thank you for allowing me to come. I can't tell you how much I'm looking forward to my time here.'

He let go of her hand and tucked the sign under one elbow before reaching to take one of her suitcases. 'I hope you're going to like it. I think it's one of the most beautiful places in the world, but I suppose I'm biased, having been born and raised here.' Pausing, he fired an enquiring look her way. 'Ready to see the croft?'

Merry smiled, remembering Bridget's description of the cottage and its previous owner. 'Ready.'

He led her out of tiny Kirkwall Airport towards the car park. Merry shivered in the chilly February air and pulled her scarf closer to her neck; the weak winter sun was doing nothing to lift the temperature and it somehow felt much colder than London despite the temperature being only a degree or so lower. Perhaps it was the freshness of the air, she thought; there was a crispness to it that caught in her lungs when she took a breath. Whatever the reason, she was going to need a bigger coat.

'It's about a thirty-minute drive to Brightwater Bay,' Niall explained, as he negotiated the exit and followed the signs for Kirkwall. 'I thought you'd like to settle in this evening, so I've taken the liberty of buying a few essentials – milk, bread, cheese, that kind of thing.' He hesitated, then cast an enquiring glance her way. 'And I know it's Sunday tomorrow, but the library will be closed and I'll have some free time, so I thought I could give you the grand tour, if you like? Help you get your bearings.'

'Thank you,' Merry said, tearing her gaze from the passing scenery to smile at him. 'That all sounds great. Although I could wait until Monday if you'd prefer – I'd hate to make you work on your day off.'

'It's no bother,' he replied easily. 'I'm happy to do what I can to make the island feel like home.'

Home, Merry echoed in her head, and forced down the faint stir of uneasiness the word created deep inside her. Home had always meant Alex and although she'd gradually adjusted to his absence in London, it felt strange to think of somewhere new in that way. But Niall was right – this was her home now, at least for the next six months. The sooner she started thinking of it that way, the better. 'Well, thank you,' she said again. 'I appreciate it.'

Niall nodded. 'The croft is a little bit remote, on the west coast up near Marwick, but you've got a few neighbours nearby in case of emergencies. And, of course, I'm only a phone call away – you've got my mobile number.'

She had – it had been in one of the many emails he'd sent and she'd saved it in her contacts as Niall the Librarian. But she couldn't imagine what kind of emergencies he expected her to have between now and the morning. The long journey from London had started early and taken its toll on her, especially the terrifying final leg. Merry was planning a hot bath and an early night, both of which she anticipated would be entirely emergency free. But she knew he was just trying to be a good host and put her at ease in a strange new place, and for that she was grateful.

'Thanks,' she said. 'It all sounds wonderful. I can't wait to see more of your beautiful island.'

His beaming smile told her it had been exactly the right thing to say.

The next thirty minutes zoomed by as Niall pointed out landmarks and places of interest from the car windows, all illuminated by the slowly setting sun.

'I love this time of day,' Merry said, during a brief lull in the conversation. 'The last hour before the sun sets is pretty extraordinary – everything shimmers with gold and nothing seems dull or mundane.'

'There's not much about Orkney that's mundane,' he said and, once again, Merry detected the pride in his voice. 'If you're looking for the extraordinary, you've come to the right place.'

The sun was very low on the horizon when they arrived at the croft but the view from the cliff still took Merry's breath away. She barely glanced at her new home; all her attention was taken by the amber and pink skies over the gunmetal grey waves that were only a stone's throw away from the tiny cottage, and the orange-red sun hovering on the edge of the world. She walked towards the wooden fence that ran along the clifftop as though drawn by an invisible thread, her gaze fixed on the beauty laid out before her. The only sounds were the cries of the guillemots circling overhead and the crash

21

of the sea as it pounded against the sandstone cliffs. Light danced across the rolling waves and she could see how the bay had got its name; the water sparkled and burned beneath the sinking sun. It was a world away from Chiswick, with its busy coffee shops and endless traffic, Merry thought, and for the first time in for ever, she felt a sense of peace creep over her frayed and jangling nerves.

Seeming to sense she wanted to be alone, Niall immediately vanished inside the stone cottage and she was barely aware of the car doors opening and closing as he retrieved her cases and whatever he deemed as essential to her settling in. It was only when the last of the sun's rays had died away and darkness was stretching out its fingers that he approached her, carrying a torch to light the bumpy grass under their feet.

'Sorry,' she called, once he was near enough to hear her. 'I'm afraid I got swept away by the gorgeousness of that sunset.'

She saw his teeth flash in the gathering gloom. 'Completely understandable,' he said, and his voice was warm. 'It gets me like that sometimes too. Are you ready to come inside now, or should I give you a few more minutes?'

A puff of wind blew up out of nowhere, and Merry realized the temperature had dropped again. She shivered. 'No, I'm ready to go inside.'

Niall pointed the torch towards her feet. 'I've lit the fire and made a pot of tea – I hope you don't mind?'

Merry laughed. 'Not at all! I wouldn't have the first clue how to get a fire going – it's not a skill I've ever really needed. And tea is always welcome.'

Light spilled from the windows and open door of the croft, outlining it with an inviting glow against the velvety-blue dusk. There was no danger of light pollution here, mused Merry; the stars would be spectacular when they came out. She was looking forward to taking them in. Once upon a time she'd taken herself off to sleep in a tower in Norfolk to learn the names and positions of all the constellations, because a character in a book had been a cosmologist and she'd needed to know. That was back in the days when writing was something that filled her with joy, when the mere thought of creating a new world didn't cause her heart to flutter inside her chest like a trapped bird.

Niall shifted beside her, causing Merry to cringe. What must he think of her? First, she'd walked off to stare at the sunset without a single word of explanation and now she was standing gawping at the croft like she'd never seen a building before. 'Sorry,' she apologized again. 'I don't mean to be rude. It's just I'm—'

'Taking it all in?' he suggested, and his tone was gentle. 'Don't worry, I know the feeling well. But the tea will be stewed if we leave it much longer and I don't want you to describe me as a complete heathen to your friends and family.'

She did her best to smile, although she wasn't at all sure he could see it. 'The fact that you've lit the fire and made the tea at all makes you a hero in my book,' she said, blowing on her chilly fingers to warm them up. 'But you're absolutely right, it would be a waste to let it stew.'

Inside, the cottage was as snug as she'd expected, but the

atmosphere was warm and homely. The door opened straight into the tiny living room; its floor was made of heavy grey flagstones and spread with thick, brightly coloured rugs, and the walls were bare stone. It should have radiated cold but that seemed to be kept at bay by the roaring flames in the fireplace that lined one wall. Merry glimpsed a radiator under the burnt-orange brocade curtains that covered the window and felt a quick flash of gratitude that she wouldn't be reliant on her non-existent fire-starting skills for warmth in the mornings. A small, two-seater sofa faced a flat-screen TV and a tall bookshelf stood against the inner wall, carrying row after row of books. Merry couldn't resist a quick glance across the spines, instinctively looking for her own titles, even though she knew it was unlikely they'd be here.

Niall saw her looking. 'Just a random selection of the second-hand books that get donated to the library,' he said, half apologetically. 'You might have seen similar bookshelves by the seating areas at the airport gates – I like to give people the opportunity to pick up a book whenever they can.'

Merry smiled. 'I'm sure they're grateful. I know I am.'

A look of unmistakable pleasure tinged his face. 'The kitchen is this way.'

He led her through to a small hallway with doors that she assumed opened into the bedroom and bathroom. The kitchen was even smaller than Merry had anticipated; she took in the basic appliances and obvious lack of storage space and breathed a sigh of relief when she spotted at least a slender dishwasher. It might not be as well-equipped as her own back in Chiswick, but it would do. And best of all, steam drifted from the spout of a teapot dressed in a red and blue knitted tea-cosy, which sat in the centre of the round kitchen table, flanked by two pottery mugs and a jug of milk.

'Is that . . . a Captain America tea-cosy?' she asked with a curious sideways glance. Admittedly, she didn't know much about the croft's previous resident, but he hadn't sounded much like an *Avengers* fan.

Niall looked simultaneously pleased and embarrassed that she'd recognized the design. 'It is – my granny knitted it for me. She's a big Marvel fan – a bit like me. Anyway, I've got plenty of others if it's not to your taste.'

Merry licked her lips, suddenly thirsty, and realized she'd had nothing to eat or drink since leaving Aberdeen. 'God, no, it's perfect,' she said, reaching for the teapot. 'Do you mind if I pour? I'm desperate for a cuppa.'

As they sipped the tea – still piping hot – Niall did his best to describe the layout of the island. Merry listened, trying to picture the scattered towns and landmarks he mentioned; she recognized some from her own research, but others were new to her. Eventually a yawn escaped her. 'Sorry – it's been a long day.'

He drained his mug and placed it on the table, before getting to his feet. 'Of course it has. I'll leave you to get some rest.'

'Thank you,' Merry said. 'You've been so kind and generous with your time.'

'Not at all,' he said, tipping his head. 'What time would

25

you like me to collect you tomorrow? You have your own car in the shed, of course, but it would be easier if I show you round a bit before expecting you to find your way on your own.'

'I'd like that,' Merry said, grateful all over again for his thoughtfulness. 'Is ten o'clock okay?'

'Perfect,' Niall replied, smiling. 'See you in the morning, Merry. Sleep well.'

The cottage felt very empty once he'd gone, uncomfortably reminding Merry of the way the flat had been in the early days after Alex had left. She pushed the thought away, reminding herself that this was a fresh start, and turned the large iron key in the lock of the door, although she doubted she needed to – who was going to come rattling the door handle all the way out here? Then she set about exploring the rest of her new home.

Niall had placed her cases in the bedroom, which also contained a comfortable-looking double bed with a surprisingly soft tartan throw, and whitewashed wardrobes set into the wall. It was the bathroom that pleased her the most, however, with its claw-footed bathtub that was entirely impractical in the small space and the most welcome sight she'd seen all day, alongside the tarmac at Kirkwall Airport. Merry twisted the hot tap and was gratified to see a plume of steaming water gush into the white enamel depths. Then her stomach chose that moment to remind her she hadn't eaten for hours; she left the bath running and went to see what food Niall had given her.

The fridge held butter, cheese, milk and a brown paper bag filled with assorted vegetables. She discovered bread and eggs on the worktop next to the tea and coffee, along with a bottle of Highland Park single malt whisky with a hand-written label that simply said 'Enjoy!' It was a thoughtful gift and one Merry decided it would be rude not to sample before she went to bed.

She threw together a quick omelette, eaten with doorstep wedges of crusty fresh bread and butter, and allowed herself an hour-long wallow in the bath. Then she pulled on her pyjamas and poured a generous measure of Scotch into a glass, before flopping onto the sofa in front of the warm glow of the fire. Her laptop sat on the coffee table, unopened since she'd left London. Pushing down an all-too-familiar surge of guilt, Merry covered it with a *Discover Scotland* magazine and reached for her phone instead to check for messages. There were three from her best friend, Jess, each one increasing in urgency.

I miss you already. Let me know when you get there x

How's the journey? Met any hot Scottish lairds yet? x

Have you fallen off the edge of the world? Been eaten by a polar bear? Text me to say you're OK! x

Smiling, Merry snapped a photo of her glass silhouetted against the fire and sent it back with the words:

Still alive. No polar bears so far but I do have whisky. Cheers! X

Jess responded instantly.

Does that mean there are hot lairds? x

Merry shook her head in wry amusement; Jess had been

insistent that the best way to get over Alex was to get *under* someone else but Merry had resisted all her best friend's well-meaning encouragement to start dating again. It was too soon and, besides, she was only on Orkney for six months; the last thing she needed was another doomed love affair.

None at all. Sorry to disappoint! x

Placing her phone on the table, she nestled into the squashy cushions behind her. It was weird to think it would be months before she saw Jess again, she thought, raising her drink and savouring the bitter heat as it flowed across her taste buds. And weirder still to think of all the book launches and parties Jess would go to without her. Merry had been so absent from the publishing merry-go-round since the break-up that she doubted many of her fellow writers would even notice she'd vanished to Orkney, but she was going to miss the social side of her career. Jess had kept her in the loop; there'd always been something going on – the safety net of something she could go to, if she chose to.

Merry tipped her head, listening to the lazy crackle of the fire and the utter silence beyond it. She was in the middle of nowhere here, with no friends and no party invitations, but wasn't that the point? She'd come to Orkney to escape publishing, to get away from her old life and rediscover what made her feel alive. More importantly, to find out whether she'd lost the thing that had always made her feel most like herself: her ability to write. And maybe, just maybe, to mend the gaping hole where Alex had once been.

'No regrets,' she told herself firmly, just as her phone

vibrated to tell her she had a new message. It was Jess, of course.

Give it time. No regrets? X

The coincidence made Merry smile. It was the kind of thing that happened all the time between her and Jess – they'd been known to finish each other's sentences and crack the same joke at exactly the same time. Her fingers moved swiftly across the screen:

No! Not yet anyway x

The yawn overtook her just as she was swirling the whisky around her glass, admiring its amber glow in the firelight. She was exhausted, she realized, suddenly barely able to keep her eyes open. With a sigh, she downed the last of her drink and made her way to the bedroom, where she pulled back the heavy woollen throw to slide beneath the thick goose-down duvet. She closed her eyes with a long, weary sigh as sleep came to claim her. And for the first time in months, she didn't mind the emptiness on the other side of the bed.

Chapter Two

The noise from overhead sounded like feet stomping on the roof. Merry squinted upwards, disoriented and confused by what she heard. How could anyone be on the roof, she wondered blearily, and how could she hear them if they were? Her flat was on the first floor, not the top ... and then the low ceiling over her head came into focus and she remembered where she was. Did the birds wear boots in Orkney? It sounded like it.

When curiosity overcame her disinclination to swing her feet out of the warm bed and onto the much chillier floor, she hopped across the floor to pull on her dressing gown and headed for the door that led outside. She tugged on the boots she'd left there the night before and ventured into the crisp morning air.

The sea breeze snatched her breath and she gasped as her lungs contracted from the cold. But the view across the clifftops was more than enough to compensate: a forget-me-not sky dotted with cotton-wool clouds and sunlight dancing upon the white-crested waves. The light had a different quality to that of the sunset the night before, but it was no less incredible.

I could definitely get used to this, Merry thought, as a smile curved her lips. Then a shrill bleat shattered the peace. She leapt out of her skin and whirled around, seeking the source of the sound, and blinked in disbelief. There was a goat on the roof of the croft.

She gaped at it for a moment, her brain struggling to process what her eyes were telling it. The first issue was the roof of the croft itself, which wasn't tiled with slate or terracotta as she'd assumed: it was grass. Long green grass that was actually growing and waving in the wind.

What kind of lunatic covers the roof of a house with grass? Merry asked herself incredulously. *Just how bonkers had this Dougal been?*

And then a vague memory tugged at her brain: an episode of *Grand Designs* featuring an earnest, ecologically sound and entirely non-lunatic homeowner, who'd explained why soil and grass made great insulation materials, as well as helping the environment and increasing biodiversity. Except Merry was pretty sure he hadn't envisioned a snowy-white goat with a frankly insolent stare as part of that biodiversity.

The goat bleated again, as though demanding to know who she was. Merry waved her hands in a shooing motion. 'Get down from there. Get down!'

It regarded her without blinking, its yellow eyes fixed on

her for several long seconds in goaty contemplation. Then it dipped its head and pulled up a mouthful of grass, chewing slowly as it studied her once more.

'Hey, stop eating my roof!' she objected, taking a step closer. 'There's plenty of grass down here for you.'

Predictably, the animal ignored her. Merry looked around in desperation; where had the stupid creature come from? Had it strayed from a nearby farm? She scanned the empty horizon and frowned. Where *was* the nearest farm? Then her gaze came to rest on a metal-framed yard to the left of the croft, with a gate that was open and a food trough in the middle. There were unmistakable footprints in the dark brown mud – unmistakably cloven footprints . . .

A horrible suspicion presented itself to Merry. She glanced at the goat again and saw it was still watching her with detached interest. 'Oh no,' she said, shaking her head fast. 'Don't tell me you come with the accommodation.'

The goat bared its teeth and bleated a reply. Merry pressed her lips together and glared at it – she must be wrong. There'd been no mention of livestock when she'd applied for the residency and Niall hadn't said anything about any animals when he'd dropped her off. 'Don't get too comfortable,' she told the goat, folding her arms across her dressing gown in defiance. 'I definitely don't need a housemate.'

Back inside the croft, she checked the time: just after nine o'clock. Niall was due to arrive in less than an hour and there was nothing to be gained by ringing him to demand an explanation before then. She'd just have to hope there was some roof left by the time he turned up, she decided as a faint bleat filtered through the ceiling, and that he'd be able to put her goat-sitting fears to rest.

'Good morning,' he said when she opened the door an hour later. 'How was your first night on Orkney?'

He smiled and, once again, she caught a flash of Clark Kent, although he was dressed much more casually today. Merry could see the collar of a red-checked shirt poking above his battered navy Barbour coat and his legs were clad in blue jeans. She wondered which was his normal work-day wear, the suit or the jeans. And then she wondered why she was even thinking about it and gave herself a hefty mental shake.

'I slept well,' she told him, summoning up an answering smile. 'Thanks for the whisky.'

'Ah, you're welcome. I wasn't sure you'd be a whisky drinker, to be honest, but thought it was worth leaving a bottle, just in case.'

'It was very much appreciated,' Merry said, as the memory of the smoky amber liquid danced on her tongue. 'I've already recommended it to a couple of writer friends.'

Niall laughed. 'The distillery is here on the Orkney mainland. I might have to start charging them commission.' He paused to study her. 'Are you ready for your tour? It's a beautiful day.'

Merry hesitated, wondering whether to mention her run-in with the goat. She'd gone out to check on it after her shower and there'd been no sign of it. Surely it couldn't have come back in the meantime – Niall would almost certainly have commented if it had climbed up there again. But maybe it wasn't an unusual sight on Orkney, she thought. Maybe it was entirely normal and a goat on the roof was worth two in the yard, or something equally unfathomable . . .

'Definitely ready,' she said, pushing the whole ridiculous idea out of her head. 'Where are we going first?'

'It's a surprise,' Niall replied, as she pulled on the woollen baker hat Jess had given her as a farewell gift. 'But I'm quietly confident you'll like it.'

Merry couldn't help a quick glance at the roof as they walked to the car; just as she'd suspected, there was no goat there now, or anywhere nearby, and no sign of anything untoward. The grass looked perfectly normal, or as normal as it could while growing on top of a house, and it appeared to be entirely unravaged by teeth. In fact, if she hadn't spotted more tell-tale hoofprints in the mud outside the door, Merry might have been inclined to believe she'd dreamt the whole encounter. Even so, she decided not to say anything to Niall; novelists had a reputation for eccentricity at the best of times and Merry knew it was a fine line between having a few quirks and being several tiles short of a Scrabble set.

He'd obviously noticed her glancing up, though, because he gave her an enquiring look as the car nudged along the rough track that led to the main road. 'Are you curious about the grass roof?' he asked. 'It's a tradition that probably came from Scandinavia, but you'll find roofs like it dotted all over Scotland. A lot were thatched, and slate tiles are more common now, but the previous owner of this croft insisted on keeping the grass and Orkney Literary Society decided to honour his wishes when we inherited it from him.'

'Yes, I heard a bit about Dougal from Bridget yesterday,' Merry said, suppressing a smile as she recalled the older woman's observations. 'He sounded colourful.'

'He was,' Niall said, nudging the car out onto the smooth tarmac of the main road. 'In fact, he wasn't a million miles away from the kind of character you might dream up for one of your stories. A bit like old Jorge in *Separate Lives*, actually, but not quite as funny.'

Merry shot him a startled look; it hadn't occurred to her that he might have read any of her books. Niall caught her looking and raised both eyebrows. 'I'm a librarian, remember? And I always try to read at least one book by the authors we offer the residency to, but in your case, I didn't need to make a special effort. I'd already read and enjoyed most of them after we stocked them in the library.'

It wasn't the first time a librarian had told Merry they were a fan of her work, so she didn't really know why she felt a blush start to creep across her cheeks. 'Oh. Well, thank you. I'm glad you liked Jorge – I've got a bit of a soft spot for him too.'

The conversation turned to other favourite fictional characters and Merry was so engrossed that it wasn't until they pulled into a car park a few minutes later that she realized where Niall was taking her. 'Oh!' she squeaked, both hands flying to her face in delight. 'It's Skara Brae! I've always wanted to come here, ever since we learned about it at school.'

He parked and nodded towards the sign that welcomed them to the famous Neolithic village. 'I thought you'd like it – writers usually do. There are so many stories here – even the way it was discovered is thrilling.'

Merry cast her mind back to the research she'd done before coming to Orkney. 'It was uncovered during a brutal storm, wasn't it? Back in the nineteenth century?'

'So the story goes,' Niall agreed. 'But there are those who say the village was an open secret long before then, it was just that no one really gave it much thought until the storm damage revealed a few of the houses in 1850. Even then, it took another 75 years and another storm to uncover just how much of the village had been preserved beneath the ground.'

Excitement fizzed in the pit of Merry's stomach. 'I can't wait to see it.'

'Then let's go and take a look,' Niall replied, obviously gratified by her enthusiasm. 'I've genuinely lost count of the number of times I've been here but it never gets old, especially when there's someone new to share it with.'

He greeted the middle-aged woman at the ticket office warmly and introduced Merry. 'It's so lovely to meet you at last,' the woman said. 'I love your writing – it's a real thrill to know you're staying on Orkney and exploring our treasures.'

'Elspeth has been counting down the days until you arrived,' Niall said solemnly, causing the woman to turn bright red. 'I think she's hoping you might write her into a book.'

'What a thing to say,' she said, shaking her head and tut-ting, but Merry thought she detected a tiny bit of hope in her eyes too. 'Although I am a big fan. Now, I'd offer you the guidebook but Niall has been here so many times that he knows the patter off by heart – he's the best guide you could have.'

And now it was Niall's turn to look embarrassed. 'I wouldn't go that far.'

Elspeth smiled. 'No need to be modest.' She turned to Merry. 'There's not much about Orkney that he doesn't know. I sometimes think he's like a walking version of Google.'

'I'll be getting my head jammed in the doorway on the way out if you don't stop,' he said. 'I'm hoping it's not too busy yet – no coach tours?'

'We've only been open fifteen minutes so not yet.' Elspeth reached below the counter and withdrew two small white bundles. 'I take it you'll be needing these?'

He took them with a grateful nod. 'We'll be careful.'

The exchange baffled Merry, but there was no further explanation. Instead, Niall tipped his head in appraisal. 'Ready to go back in time, Merry?'

His words caused another frisson of excitement to run through her. 'Absolutely.'

Just outside the ticket office, Niall paused. 'There's a rep-lica of how the houses might have looked, but I sometimes think it's better to visit the real thing first, to draw your own conclusions. What do you think?'

Merry considered the question; on one hand, she could understand how it might help visitors to interpret what they were seeing if they'd visited the replica first, but what she really wanted was to allow her own senses to tell her the story of the people who'd lived there five thousand years earlier. She nodded at Niall. 'Let's come back here afterwards.'

The path to the ancient village was dotted with stone markers that helped create the illusion they really were travelling backwards through time. It was the one that mentioned the Pyramids that really caught Merry's imagination, though; the houses she was about to see had been in place longer than one of mankind's greatest feats of engineering. But even that couldn't prepare her for the sense of history she felt when she and Niall finally reached Skara Brae.

As Elspeth had indicated, only a few hardy souls were exploring the site so early on a cold Sunday morning in February. There were eight single-room buildings set into the ground, so that visitors could look down into them from the grassy mounds and raised modern walkways surrounding them. Some had stone pathways running around the outside, but several signs politely asked for people to keep their distance and stay off the grass where possible. In London, there would be ropes and alarms and probably several stern-looking stewards to keep visitors under control, Merry thought, but the lack of any real physical barriers here created the illusion that she could stroll into one of the houses whenever she liked.

As though reading her mind, Niall pulled the two white bundles from his Barbour pocket and smiled. 'Want to go inside?'

It was the most unnecessary question she'd ever been asked. 'Of course,' Merry gasped. 'Can we?'

He tugged at one of the bundles and it fell apart into two white shoe covers. 'We can if we wear these and make sure no one copies us.'

Merry didn't need to be told twice; she took the proffered mesh covers and pulled them over the soles of her sturdy boots. With a quick glance around, Niall climbed carefully down to the pale gravel floor of the nearest house and held out a hand to Merry to help her to follow.

She felt it almost as soon as she reached the ground: the essence of people long gone that seemed to emanate from the grey stone walls. Spellbound, she took a moment to gaze around in silent awe before walking through the narrow door that led into the nearest house. Her fingers trailed along the lichen-covered stones and she wondered who might have done the same thing, thousands of years earlier, coming home or leaving forever. It was a privilege and an unbeliev-able thrill to stand in that place, at that time, and feel the echo of their lives.

'On the surface, it looks as though they had quite a simple lifestyle,' Niall said, not far behind her. 'They lived in one room, fished in the sea and farmed the land. The houses are all the same, which suggests no one was more important than the others, but there's one building which seems to have been used to make tools and jewellery. So they were actually quite a sophisticated people, by the standards of the day.'

He sounded more like an archaeologist than a librarian, Merry thought, hiding a smile. Then she recalled how Elspeth had described him as a walking Google, and Merry understood exactly what the other woman had meant; she had the definite feeling she could ask Niall anything about Skara Brae and its people and he would be able to give a full and knowledgeable answer.

'Why did they leave?' she asked, remembering that experts believed the villagers had abandoned their homes in a hurry.

'No one knows,' Niall replied simply. 'There might have been some catastrophic event, like a storm, that forced them to run for their lives. The buildings were filled with sand when they were uncovered, which is why there's such a fantastic level of artefact preservation.'

Merry half-turned to look at him and she saw his face was alive with enthusiasm. It made him look younger, although she was suddenly aware she had no idea how old he actually was – perhaps a year or two older than her, which would make him mid-thirties, but he might just as easily be in his late-twenties. She watched him as he talked, explaining other possible theories for the abandonment of Skara Brae, and found herself idly wondering what Jess would make of him. 'Hot,' she heard her friend's voice say in her head. 'Hot, passionate and very into books – what's not to love, Mer?'

Merry felt her face grow warm and she hurriedly silenced the voice and gazed around them as she tried to focus on what Niall was saying. But she was very aware that part of her brain was in complete agreement with the imaginary Jess and for the first time, Merry was grateful to be nursing a broken heart – because if she hadn't sworn off men for the foreseeable future, and certainly for the duration of her residency, she might find herself developing quite an inconvenient crush on the librarian of Orkney.

He stopped talking and it took her a moment to realize he'd posed her a question. Trying not to panic, she spooled back mentally and established he'd asked if she'd ever considered writing a historical story. 'Not really,' she said after a second or two of consideration. 'I'm not sure my publisher would like it for a start – the contemporary books I write sell pretty well and I can't imagine they'd be up for a total change of genre.'

Niall looked surprised. 'Oh, I'd always assumed a successful, well-established author like you could write whatever they chose. Are they really so strict?'

Merry smiled. 'Strict isn't quite the right word,' she said, and hesitated, thinking of the way her publisher had bent over backwards to help when she'd finally admitted there was a problem. 'It's more that the readers don't always like it when an author shifts to writing another kind of book. And that makes the publisher's job harder, because it's tough to come back from a book that hasn't sold well. I suppose it's just a risk.'

'I can see that,' Niall said slowly. 'But what happens when you get an idea that doesn't fit into the way you write now?'

'That's never happened,' Merry answered, and shifted uneasily from one foot to the other. The conversation was going in an unexpectedly uncomfortable direction; she wasn't sure she wanted to talk about writing at all. 'But you never know – maybe Orkney will inspire me.'

He grinned. 'That's an absolute given. Let me show you the rest of the buildings.'

They stopped in the replica house on the way back to the visitor centre, and Merry could see what he meant when he'd described Skara Brae's people as sophisticated. The room was clearly divided into living and sleeping areas, with a stone dresser in pride of place that would have displayed all their high-status goods like pottery and jewellery. The craftmanship was incredible considering the tools they had available, Merry marvelled as she gazed around. What on earth had happened to make them abandon their apparently comfortable lives here?

Elspeth beamed at Merry when they arrived back at the ticket desk and handed over the shoe covers. 'What did you think?'

'I think it's amazing,' Merry replied warmly. 'Really extraordinary. And you were right about Niall knowing everything there is to know. I feel as though I've attended the best lecture ever.'

The other woman laughed as Niall threw Merry a look that was both pleased and embarrassed. 'Careful now or his head really won't fit into the car. I'm glad you've enjoyed your visit and I'm looking forward to seeing you again at the Meet the Author event on Friday.'

For a moment, Merry frowned, then she remembered one of Niall's emails had mentioned a small wine and nibbles party at the library, with a few guests to ease her into her residency. But it definitely hadn't been described as a Meet the Author event – that sounded a lot bigger than Merry had anticipated.

'Actually, I need to talk to you about that,' Niall said, his tone sheepish. 'We've had so much interest in you from the locals that we thought it might be a nice idea to upgrade to a properly ticketed event. So they have to pay to attend, but the price includes a glass of fizz and a copy of your most recent novel, which we thought you might like to sign. I hope you don't mind.'

'Interest is always good,' Merry said, a touch warily because she'd been involved with too many library events when only an old man and his dog had turned up. 'How many people are you expecting?'

Please don't say four, Merry thought anxiously, resisting the urge to shut her eyes. The librarian pushed his black-rimmed glasses onto the bridge of his nose thoughtfully. 'I think at the last count it was a hundred and twenty-two, but I'll have to check.'

Merry felt her eyes widen. 'A hundred and twenty-two?'

Niall shrugged. 'I daresay it'll be more by the time Friday comes and word gets around that you're actually here. Like

I said, there's been a lot of interest and we've a strong community of book lovers on Orkney.'

Behind the ticket desk, Elspeth rubbed her hands in anticipation. 'I've got my ticket. I can't wait for you to sign my copy of the book – I've held off buying it ever since Niall announced you were our new writer in residence so I could get a personally signed one.'

Her enthusiasm was so obvious that Merry had to smile. 'I'm looking forward to it already,' she said. 'See you on Friday, Elspeth.'

'Lunch?' Niall asked, as they made their way back to the car. 'There's a wonderful fish restaurant overlooking the bay in Kirkwall.'

'Sounds perfect,' Merry said, suddenly ravenous. 'And thanks for giving me such a special tour of Skara Brae – I can't tell you how lucky I feel.'

'No problem,' he said easily. 'As I said earlier, most authors like it here. But I don't give everyone a behind the scenes tour – I save that for the ones I know will really appreciate the experience.'

He busied himself with opening the car door, leaving Merry to wonder exactly what it was about her that had told him she'd be thrilled. She knew he'd read some of her books – perhaps he'd seen something deeper than she'd expected in her carefully crafted sentences. Or it might have been the way she'd drunk in the sunset over Brightwater Bay the night before, savouring every last drop of wild beauty until it had all gone. Whatever the reason, Merry was glad he'd chosen to give her a glimpse of Skara Brae's secrets. It was a memory she would treasure forever.

She climbed into the car beside Niall and thanked her lucky stars she'd taken the plunge back in November and replied to the Orkney Literary Society's advert. From the outside, she knew it had looked like a knee-jerk reaction to the bombshell Alex had dropped on her, but there'd been more to it than that; her subconscious had somehow known that the islands would be a balm to even her deepest wounds and had prompted her to grab the opportunity. And although Merry had come a long way since those devastating days after Alex had left, she'd still been looking forward to the six-month residency. It was early days but so far, the experience had exceeded her expectations. In fact, she was beginning to believe Niall's claim that everything about Orkney was extraordinary. If the islands managed to carry on impressing her at this pace, she'd have a new problem at the end of the six months. She wasn't going to want to leave.

Chapter Three

The restaurant was every bit as delightful as Niall had suggested, and not only for its spectacular views over Kirkwall Bay. On his advice, Merry ordered the sea bass and it was sublime. The sticky toffee pudding she had for dessert was even better; she scraped up the last morsels and ate them with a sigh of deep contentment. It was a good thing she wouldn't be eating like that every day, she thought as she placed her licked-clean spoon back on her plate, or her writer's arse would be more of a problem than her writer's block.

The conversation had flowed as smoothly as the waves in the bay; they'd covered everything from the best James Bond to Jane Austen's finest moment and Merry was enjoying herself enormously until Niall steered the conversation round to the life she'd left behind in London.

'Do you think you'll miss home?' he asked. 'Orkney's beautiful, but it's a big adjustment from a city like London.' He paused. 'There's no Deliveroo for a start.'

Merry allowed herself to smile. 'My waistline will be thankful for that.'

'And, of course, you'll miss Alex.'

The blood pounded in Merry's chest as she stared at Niall. There'd been some brief email chat about her family situation when she'd first accepted the residency – enough to establish that it would be just her staying at the croft – but she was sure she'd never mentioned Alex, either in passing or by name. Why would she?

Niall must have read the confusion on her face because his ears turned suddenly scarlet and he shifted uncomfortably in his seat. 'That is your fiancé's name, isn't it? You mentioned him in the acknowledgements of your last book.'

Of course she had, Merry thought with a dull thud of recollection; she'd mentioned Alex in the back of every book she'd ever written. A couple had even been dedicated to him, back when she'd thought he'd always be with her. And now she faced the excruciating prospect of telling Niall that she'd been painfully and devastatingly dumped, of seeing pity and embarrassment blossom in his eyes as he put two and two together and worked out the real reason she'd come to Orkney. The thought was almost more than Merry could bear. Then it occurred to her: she didn't have to explain anything.

'Yes,' she said, nodding slowly. 'That's his name.'

'Didn't he mind you coming here for six months?' Niall asked, raising a curious eyebrow.

'No,' Merry replied, grateful she hadn't had to lie. The

truth was that she had no idea what Alex might think about her escape to Orkney, because she hadn't told him she was going.

If Niall thought there was anything odd about her curt response, he was tactful enough to hide it. 'London's loss is our gain,' he said, with such genuine warmth that Merry felt her awkward embarrassment start to fade. 'There was something I wanted to flag up, actually. It's about the event on Friday.'

'Oh?' she said, relieved that she seemed to have avoided outing herself as tragically broken-hearted.

'It'll be a fairly relaxed evening – sort of an "in conversation" thing – but we thought it might be nice for you to do a reading.'

Merry nodded. 'Of course. I'll read a chunk from my last book.'

'You could if you wanted to,' Niall said, and he leaned forwards, his eyes keen. 'Or we thought maybe you'd like to write something especially for the event. Something about Orkney.'

Instantly, Merry's mind spiralled into panic. She took a deep breath, fighting for control, and her ears buzzed. 'Something new?'

'If that's okay?'

Merry's heart thumped as she tried to calm down long enough to think of the best way to answer. One thing was for certain, she couldn't tell the truth; 120 people were coming to hear their new writer in residence talk – the last thing they needed to know was that she'd gone there on false pretences, that she wasn't a real writer. Not anymore. No, her writer's block had to remain a closely guarded secret. Niall couldn't find out about it or he might conclude that she wasn't the best person for the role and demand that she leave; what good was a writer who couldn't write, after all?

She pushed the thought away and forced herself to smile. 'Of course. I'll start thinking about it right away.'

'Brilliant,' he said, as his expression lit up with enthusiasm. 'I can't wait to see what you come up with.'

And Merry, picturing herself staring at a blank sheet of paper in front of one hundred and twenty people, broke into a cold sweat. 'Yeah. Me too.'

Niall offered to drive back to Brightwater Bay via the Standing Stones of Stenness, suggesting they might arrive in time for sunset, but Merry's head was already fluttering at the thought of having to write something good enough to read aloud on Friday; all she wanted now was the peace and solitude of the little cottage overlooking the ocean.

'Another time,' she said, hoping he wouldn't take her refusal as a sign she wasn't interested.

She did accept his suggestion that they stop at a supermarket to top up her food supplies, because the thought of an evening alone with only a crust of day-old bread to eat was not appealing. 'And now you know where it is, so you'll be able to pop in whenever you need to,' he said as they loaded her bags into the boot of the car. 'I can drive past the library if you like, so you know where to find that too?'

He sounded so keen to show it off that Merry didn't have the heart to say no, and she soon understood the source of his pride. Far from the small, underfunded council building she'd expected, Orkney Library shared its premises with the local Archive offices and was a modern, triple-fronted construction of glass, steel and stone, with a pleasant wide courtyard out the front and a curving arch over the quadruple doors that led inside. It might be silent now, but Merry could imagine it must be popular with the local book-loving community. And this was where she had to come on Friday, to meet them and introduce them to her writing. If she managed to produce any writing . . .

Once again, the sun was on its way down when they arrived back at the croft. Merry allowed Niall to help her carry her shopping inside but declined his offer to help put it away. 'I'll find a home for everything,' she told him. 'And I've taken up far too much of your day already – I'm sure you have better things to do than unpack my shopping.'

He read between the lines, as she'd hoped he would, and left her with a reminder that she'd find the car in the garage off to one side of the house. Merry secretly thought that it was more of a lean-to than a garage, but she was pleased it was there at all and, more importantly, that it contained a car; she didn't have much in the way of expectations for a luxury drive, but it made a big difference knowing she had her own wheels for independent travel. However, it would have to wait until morning, she decided as she viewed the rapidly darkening sky. Goat or no goat, she didn't plan to investigate in the dark.

What she ought to do was open her laptop. It sat on the coffee table, where she had hidden it underneath a magazine so that its mute accusation was out of sight. But even the thought of it caused a shiver of uneasiness that she preferred not to make worse, so she slid it under the sofa and turned her attention to the bookshelf she'd noticed the night before. She ran her fingers along each shelf, smiling when she saw a book by someone she knew. Niall had been correct in his prediction that she wouldn't find one of her own books there, but she didn't mind that. And she was genuinely gratified to find a title by Jess – one of her early bonkbusters, before the genre had fallen out of favour with the book-buying public. She studied the hot pink and gold cover fondly and snapped a photo to send to Jess, who immediately responded by ringing her.

'Where in god's name did you find that?' she demanded, her New Zealand accent made all the stronger by her obvious amusement. 'The local charity shop?'

Merry smiled. 'The bookshelf in my cottage. In between *The Wasp Factory* and *To Kill a Mockingbird*.'

Jess laughed. 'Perfect. I bet neither of those features a threesome with two male models.'

Merry's mood lifted a little. It was good to hear her friend's voice. 'I don't imagine so, no. How are you, anyway?'

'Oh, bearing up,' Jess said with a dramatic sigh. 'Missing my best friend since she ran away to the most remote location in the entire country.'

'Actually, Orkney is very well connected,' Merry pointed

out. 'There are ferries and buses and planes running to the mainland all the time.'

'You know what I mean,' Jess replied. 'It might as well be Everest Base Camp for all the chance I have of seeing you. But it's far too late to moan about it now – tell me what you've been up to instead.'

Merry did her best to describe Skara Brae but left out the part where she'd lied to Niall about the current status of her relationship with Alex. Instead, she focused on telling her friend about the horror of having to write something to read out at the Meet the Author event.

'You can totally do it,' Jess said, the moment Merry had finished talking. 'Just treat it as a writing exercise – tell yourself it doesn't matter. No one is ever going to see it.'

'But they are,' Merry objected. 'At least a hundred and twenty people will hear it. And then it will almost certainly be put on display somewhere so that the next writer in residence they appoint can laugh at how terrible I was.'

Jess was silent for a moment. 'You do realize that's rubbish, don't you? I know you're still struggling with your novel but that's hardly surprising, given the circumstances – how can you expect to write wall-to-wall romance when you've given up believing in love?'

Merry started to speak but her friend cut her off. 'You're one of the most talented writers I know, Merry. And deep down, I think you know you've got this. So what if it's not perfect? You can edit to make it better. But you can't edit a blank page.'

'But what if I write something that's terrible? What if they decide I'm not good enough to be their Writer in Residence?'

'Then you come home, move in with me and we have the time of our lives as the world's best flatmates,' Jess said. 'Job's good.'

There was no doubt about it, Merry reflected after chatting for a few minutes more, her mood was definitely calmer for having spoken to Jess. And then everything changed.

'I saw Alex,' Jess said.

Merry froze. 'Where?'

'In the pub on the High Road.'

'In the George?' A frown tugged at Merry's forehead. 'He lives in Greenwich now, what on earth was he doing in Chiswick?'

'Having a pint with some old friends, he told me,' Jess went on. She paused. 'He asked about you.'

That was something, Merry supposed. In the early days after the break-up, when she'd been raw and hurting and wondering how she would get through the next hour without Alex, let alone the rest of her life, she'd messaged him a lot. He replied at first – terse, matter-of-fact responses that did nothing to alleviate her pain. And then, when it became clear she wasn't coping or adjusting to the situation, he'd gone silent. The messages remained unread, leading Jess to gently explain that he'd almost certainly blocked her. That had hurt too – did he hate her so much that he couldn't bear to see her name in his message list? – but she eventually came to see that it was the best thing he could have done; without any way of contacting him, short of turning up outside his work, she was forced to face the brutal truth that their relationship was over. Alex was never coming back. So hearing that he cared enough to ask Jess about her was a balm to her still-sore heart.

'What did you tell him?' Merry asked Jess, trying her hardest to sound detached even as her chest thudded in anticipation.

'The truth, of course,' Jess said, and Merry thought she sounded pleased with herself. 'That you answered an online advert from a man you'd never met and have since moved to Orkney.'

'Jess!' Merry spluttered, unsure whether to be amused or angry. 'You didn't!'

Her friend sighed into the phone. 'Okay, I might not have phrased it quite like that, but you get the idea.'

Merry was silent for a moment, trying to imagine how Alex might have reacted. Was it too much to hope that he'd be spurred into wild jealousy and come tearing up to Orkney to tell her it had all been a horrible mistake? Probably. That kind of thing only happened in novels. 'What did he say?'

Now it was Jess's turn to be silent. 'He said he hoped you were happy,' she said eventually. 'I'm only telling you this because I know you're still harbouring a crazy hope that the weasely little prick will come back to you. And I think you need to know he's moved on. Which means it's time for my weekly reminder that you should too.'

It wasn't anything Jess hadn't said before, but the words still stung. 'I don't want him to come back,' she objected.

'Liar. You're forgetting that I know you, Merina Wilde.'
Jess paused, and when she spoke again, her tone was gentle.
'Look, I get that it's easier to pin all your hopes on Alex
instead of getting back out there and taking a risk. But just
keep an open mind about meeting someone new. It doesn't
have to be Mr Right, just Mr Right-For-Now.'

She made it sound so easy, Merry thought wistfully,
probably because it *was* for her. Jess was a master at dating –
she knew the best apps, always kept her options open and
was never short of a date. The only man Merry had met on
Orkney so far was Niall and he – well, even if Merry had
been ready to start dating again, she was far too professional
to mix business with pleasure. But with her usual uncanny
ability to see inside Merry's brain, Jess had already inter-
preted the silence. 'What about the librarian guy – you said
he's nice? Who knows – maybe he's read the *Kama Sutra*!'

The thought made Merry's cheeks burn even as she
laughed. 'Jess!'

'What?' her friend protested. 'It's just something to bear
in mind, that's all. Promise me you will, okay?'

It was exactly the kind of advice she would give if the shoe
were on the other foot, Merry thought. But Jess didn't know
that Merry had already clanged that door shut by pretending
to still be in a relationship with Alex. And Merry was quite
happy for her not to find out. 'Of course, I'll bear it in mind,'
she lied cheerfully. 'Author's honour.'

'And keep me updated,' Jess went on. 'I want written
progress reports. And photos. *Lots* of photos.'

'Okay,' Merry said, hoping Jess would let the subject go if she pretended to go along with things. 'I'll see what I can do.'

There was a brief pause. 'Don't worry about the reading, Mer. You've got this, babes. Get yourself out exploring, let the scenery inspire you and give yourself the freedom to write something different. You can do it.'

Merry forced herself to sound positive. 'Good idea. Thanks, Jess.'

After she'd hung up, Merry spent several long minutes avoiding looking at the edge of her laptop sticking out from beneath the sofa. Jess was right, she could do this. But it didn't have to be tonight. She'd get up early, jump in the car and go in search of inspiration. And then she'd write something that would make the Orkney Literary Society proud.

She thought of Elspeth's excited expression when she'd talked about Merry signing her book, and Niall's trust in her ability; she couldn't let them down. No matter what, she'd write something for Friday evening.

She just hoped it would be something good.

Chapter Four

The cries of the guillemots woke Merry early on Monday morning. She lay still for a moment, listening to the ebb and flow of their calls and picturing them floating on the breeze above the cliffs, then pushed back the covers and headed for the kitchen. She was determined not to waste any time, determined to make this the day she wrestled her writer's block into submission. And she wouldn't do that by staying in bed.

Armed with a strong cup of coffee, face muffled by her hat and scarf, she slipped outside into the still-dark morning and made her way to the fence that ran along the cliffs. Someone – presumably Dougal – had placed a stone bench a little way to the left of the croft and Merry sat there now, with her back to the bay, waiting for the sun to come up. She sipped her coffee, savouring the heat and the bitterness, and let the sounds and smells of the morning wash over her.

The air was salty – she could taste it on the rim of her cup – and had that hyper-freshness that she'd noticed when she'd first arrived on Orkney. The cold was biting; it stung her eyes and prickled her skin. Instinctively, she hunched into her coat, shoulders bunching together in an effort to preserve her body warmth. She took a deep, freezing breath in and forced herself to relax, accepting the cold and making it part of her. She was only a few feet away from the croft, there was no danger she'd succumb to hypothermia and so she might as well allow the icy air to wake her up.

The first blush of dawn grew like a bruise on the horizon. Merry forced herself to be still, breathing slowly and deeply as the light suffused the clouds with dim greys and purples. Next came pink, with a hint of orange, and then tentative tendrils of yellow heralded the arrival of the golden sun itself. She shaded her eyes against its brilliance as it washed the land with pale amber light and gazed in silent wonder as the clouds turned from candyfloss to cotton wool. And with the sun came a sliver of hope, because no writer could fail to be inspired by beauty like this, day in, day out.

Maybe everything would be all right after all.

Eventually, Merry sighed and stretched, feeling the muscles in her back complain about being still for so long. A quick glance at her watch told her it was almost nine o'clock: time to go in search of her transportation. Empty mug in hand, she headed for the garage.

She wasn't sure what she'd expected to find – an ancient rust-bucket that ran on hope and prayers, maybe, or a trusty second-hand Ford that had been around the block a few times – but she certainly hadn't anticipated a shiny, cherry-red Mini Cooper. She stood for a few seconds, blinking at the gleaming car, then backtracked into the house to rummage in the drawer for the key. Of course, if she'd bothered to seek it out earlier, she'd have known just from looking at the fob exactly what kind of car it was.

The goat was there when she stepped outside again. It stood directly in her way, staring at her with yellow and black eyes, unblinking. Merry stopped and let out a huff of disbelief. 'So, I didn't dream you. What do you want, Mr Goat?'

It didn't reply. Obviously.

'Go home. I don't have any food.' She could have sworn its eyes swivelled briefly to the grassy roof. 'And don't get any ideas about climbing up there again – I need it more than you do.'

She was just about to consider going in search of a broom to shoo the animal away when she heard a shout ring out. Glancing around, she saw a white-haired woman marching along the clifftops towards her. 'Hello!' the woman called, waving an arm cheerfully in Merry's direction. 'And a very good morning to you! I see you've met Gordon.'

Merry felt herself sag in relief; surely this must be the goat's owner coming to reclaim him? 'Yes, he's been eating my roof. Is he yours?'

In a few more purposeful strides, the woman was standing in front of Merry. 'Goodness, no. He belongs to the Watson farm, a few miles that way.' She fired a severe look the goat's way. 'Have you been making a nuisance of yourself again, Gordon? You ought to be ashamed.'

The goat let out an unconcerned-sounding bleat and wandered towards the clifftop to snatch at a tuft of grass. The woman shook her head and thrust out a hand. 'I'm Sheila, your next-door neighbour.'

Now that she was nearer, Merry could see that she was older than her brisk walking pace suggested. Her face was brown and wrinkled beneath her shock of coarse white hair and her eyes were the faded blue of overwashed denim. *She must be seventy if she's a day*, Merry marvelled as she shook her hand. 'I'm Merry. The new Writer in Residence.'

'I know. Bridget McGinty told me.' Sheila cocked her head. 'But it's Merry, is it? As in Merry Christmas, not the Virgin Mary?'

'As in Merry Christmas,' Merry confirmed. 'But I'll answer to Mary if needed.'

Sheila snorted. 'Well, you shouldn't. Names have power, girl – never take them for granted.' She lifted an arm and Merry saw she was carrying a sturdy canvas bag. 'I brought bannock for breakfast. It goes best with plenty of butter and a cup of tea.'

She fired a meaningful look towards the open door of the croft and Merry realized with a sinking heart that she was going to have to invite her in. 'That's very kind of you,' she said, summoning up her most professional smile. 'Would you like to come inside?'

Sheila contrived to look surprised. 'That'd be lovely. If you're sure you're not too busy with the writing?'

Merry's smile dimmed a little. 'I haven't actually started yet. Your timing is perfect.'

Once inside, Sheila's gimlet gaze roamed over every surface. Merry left her examining the bookshelves and went to put the kettle on. She'd had no idea what a bannock was, but it turned out to be an oval fruit loaf that was still warm and smelled utterly delicious. She cut four thick slices and spread them with butter, before placing them on a tray with Niall's tea-cosy in pride of place.

She found Sheila with Jess's paperback in her hand, peering at the writing on the back with avid interest. 'Jessie Edwards. I don't think I've heard of this author before. Is she good?'

Merry didn't trust herself to look up from the tea tray without spilling. She concentrated on sliding it safely onto the coffee table before answering. 'Yes, she's brilliant.'

The older woman turned the book over and stared at the cover, which featured a bikini-clad blonde with bubble-gum-pink lips hovering suggestively around a lollipop. 'It looks a wee bit trashy.'

'It is,' Merry agreed, knowing that Jess would be the first to concede that her books were a long way from being literary in style and content; they had a plot, for a start. 'Bonkbusters usually are. But I guarantee you won't be bored.'

Sheila sniffed and put the book back on the shelf. 'So how are you enjoying Orkney so far? I hear you've been exploring Skara Brae.'

A wry smile tugged at Merry's lips. She shouldn't be surprised that word had got around; every aspect of island life she'd encountered so far suggested a close-knit community that was totally different from what she was used to in London. 'Yes, Niall showed me round yesterday.'

'He's a kind one, right enough,' Sheila said. 'Totally useless with anything practical, but his heart is in the right place.'

Merry almost frowned; Bridget had said something very similar at the airport but that hadn't been Merry's impression at all. Niall was obviously clever and bookish, but he'd managed the logistics of her arrival on Orkney with impeccable attention to detail that suggested he was very capable on a practical level as well as intellectually. But she didn't want to argue so she took a bite of bannock instead. It was melt-in-the-mouth delicious. Sheila watched her eat with obvious pleasure. 'What are you hoping to write while you're here?' she asked, once Merry had washed down the cake with a mouthful of tea. 'I'm sure you've got professional commitments to meet, as well as taking inspiration from the islands.'

The question raised the usual storm of anxiety in the pit of Merry's stomach. 'I've got a novel to write,' she said vaguely, keeping her eyes on her plate.

The older woman nodded. 'What's it about? If you don't mind me asking, that is.'

I do mind, Merry thought, as her nerves started to jangle. *I mind very much.* But she couldn't think of a way to politely fob Sheila off, so she decided to stick with vagueness. 'Oh, it's early days. I'm still finding my way with the story.'

'Is that how it works, then?' Sheila asked, raising her eyebrows. 'Only I heard your next novel is due out in

November – I don't know much about these things but that doesn't feel very long away for a book you're still finding your way with.'

The mere mention of November made Merry's ears roar. Ten months away. And before then, the book had to be edited, and copy-edited, and proof-edited and subjected to a final read-through to catch any final typos or errors before it was printed. Ten months was no time at all – not when she hadn't written a single word of it.

The mug shook in her hand and she was forced to put it on the table.

'Merry?' Sheila's voice sounded as though it was coming from a long way away. 'Are you okay, lovey?'

She dug her fingernails into her palm, forcing herself to focus on the sharp pain, and counted slowly to twenty, taking long deep breaths in through her nose and letting them out through her mouth. And gradually, the panic lessened its grip on her. Merry opened her eyes to see her neighbour was watching her in alarm.

'I'm fine,' she said, dredging up a brief smile. 'Sorry. I had a bit of a panic attack then.'

Her eyes strayed to the laptop, which was now in plain view. Sheila followed the direction of her gaze and understanding dawned on her face. She busied herself with topping up the tea and flashed a businesslike smile Merry's way. 'You know, I find going for a run very helpful when things get a bit much. The scenery along the cliffs certainly helps get things into perspective.'

It was the last thing Merry had expected her to say. 'A run,' she repeated, staring at the old woman beside her on the sofa. 'Along the cliffs? But you're – I mean, can you . . .'

'Out with it, lassie,' Sheila said, but her expression was amused rather than insulted. 'Don't beat around the bush.'

There was nothing for it, Merry decided, she'd have to just say it. She squared her shoulders. 'Isn't it a bit risky running along the cliffs at your age?'

Sheila inclined her head. 'You sound like my daughter. But, as I always tell her, I've been running around this island for the last seventy-nine years, ever since I first learned what my legs were for, and it hasn't killed me yet.'

Merry felt her jaw drop open. 'Seventy-nine?'

'Aye,' Sheila replied, unperturbed. 'Eighty in June. You should come to the party.'

'Wow,' Merry said, still trying to get her head around the idea of an almost-octogenarian racing along the cliffs in all weathers. 'I'm impressed.'

The old woman leaned towards her and patted her hand. 'My point is that it's very good for your peace of mind. Helps me sort out all kinds of problems. And maybe it would do the same for you – what do you think?'

Merry nearly laughed, until she saw the determined expression on her neighbour's face. 'Oh no. I couldn't. I can't run – I'm not even a member of a gym back in London.'

'Hush, woman, of course you can run. You just put one foot in front of another. Come out with me one morning and I'll show you how it's done.'

'I couldn't,' Merry repeated, more firmly. 'Thank you for the kind offer but I'm really not a runner.'

Sheila sat back. 'Maybe you're right, but it's like most things, isn't it? You don't know what you're capable of until you try.' She glanced at the laptop, and then back at Merry. 'Let me know if you change your mind.'

She drained her tea and got to her feet. 'I'll just put this in the kitchen, shall I?'

'Let me,' Merry said, taking the mug and placing it on the tray. By the time she returned from the kitchen, Sheila had her coat on and was standing by the front door.

'Lovely to meet you, Merry,' she said. 'Thanks for the tea and the chat.'

Merry smiled. 'Lovely to meet you too. And thank you for the cake.'

'Bannock,' Sheila corrected. 'I'll see you at the library on Friday evening if I don't see you before.'

It wasn't until Merry had loaded the dirty plates in the dishwasher and got herself ready to try her luck with the Mini that she noticed Jess's book had vanished from the bookshelf. Smiling, she made a mental note to tell Jess she had a new reader. And then she went out to explore the island.

Niall was delighted to see her at the library that afternoon.

'Merry, you made it!' he said, when he arrived at the front desk. 'Let me give you the tour. Or perhaps you'd like a cup of tea first?'

It was obvious he was bursting to show off his domain so Merry shook her head. 'Tour first, tea afterwards.'

He beamed at her and led her through the stacks, taking time to linger in the bright and inviting children's department and pointing out the display that proudly declared she was Orkney's Writer in Residence. Once again, Merry was struck by the deep pleasure he so obviously took in showing her around, and by his heartfelt love for his job. Yesterday, she'd wondered whether he might have made a good archaeologist; today, she was certain he was a librarian through and through.

'This is the room where we'll hold your event on Friday,' he told her, pushing back a folding door that opened into a large hall. 'As you can see, we've got plenty of space for a decent-sized audience.'

'It's perfect,' she said, smiling. 'And well done for enticing so many bums on seats.'

Now it was Niall's turn to smile. 'That's down to you, not me. All I've done is present the opportunity; it's you they're coming to see.'

He rounded off the tour with a visit to the Orkney Archive rooms, which held the thousands of records relating to the islands dating back centuries. It was quieter here than in the library; Merry had to force herself not to tiptoe, and the air was filled with the smell of old paper.

'Tea?' Niall whispered, as they returned the way they'd come in.

'Yes, please,' she murmured back.

It wasn't until they were sitting in his cluttered but orderly office with steaming mugs of tea that he asked how her morning had been.

'It started well,' Merry said, and described the glorious sunrise she'd seen. 'And then I met a couple of interesting characters.'

Niall slapped his forehead when she told him about Gordon. 'Of course! I should have mentioned him. A few of the previous writers have had similar trouble – months can go by and no one sees him and then he seems to take a shine to one of you and you can't get rid of him.' He gave her a rueful look. 'Sorry.'

'I don't really mind, now that I know he's not my responsibility,' Merry said. 'I just had visions of being expected to look after him, and you could write what I know about looking after goats on an extremely small postage stamp.'

'Me too,' Niall said. 'But let me know if he becomes too much of a nuisance and I'll have a word with the Watsons. I'm sure they'll find a way to keep him away.'

'Thanks,' Merry said. 'I also met one of my other neighbours – an older lady called Sheila.'

'Ah, yes,' Niall said. 'I didn't think it would be long before curiosity got the better of her. Did she behave better than Gordon?'

Merry laughed. 'She didn't jump on the roof and start eating the grass, if that's what you mean. But she did try to persuade me to go running with her.'

Niall raised his eyebrows. 'Did she now? You should be

honoured – her daughter has been trying to get her to take a running partner for years, but she's always refused.' He paused and gave a little huff of amusement. 'She must think you'd be able to keep up with her.'

Merry thought back to her near panic attack and shifted uneasily. 'I wasn't actually planning on joining her,' she said. 'I don't run.'

'Oh, I see,' Niall said, with a puzzled frown. 'Well, who knows what her reasons were. But you'd have a friend for life in her daughter, Grace, if you kept Sheila company. I know she's fretting her mum will have a fall while she's out and it might set her mind at rest if she knew she wasn't alone.'

Merry felt a sinking feeling in her stomach and pushed it firmly away. She wouldn't be guilted into a kamikaze running mission along the cliffs in the dead of a Scottish winter. She wouldn't.

'I visited the cairn at Maeshowe too,' she told him, changing the subject. 'The Neolithic people really knew how to bury their dead, didn't they?'

'They did.' Niall's expression was filled with familiar boyish enthusiasm as he agreed. 'You should visit in midwinter, when the setting sun lines up just right to light up the inside of the tomb. It's incredible – quite a spiritual experience.'

She looked at him then, wondering whether she should tell him about the moment she had almost been able to picture an ancient funeral procession making its way along the low, narrow passageway that led to the stone-clad chamber.

The scene had been so clear that she'd pulled out a scrap of paper from her bag and scribbled some hurried notes so she didn't forget the details. It was as close to spiritual as she'd ever been.

'I can imagine,' she said carefully. 'Maybe I'll have to come back in December.'

There was a knock at the door and a young, red-haired woman poked her head into the office. 'Sorry to bother you, Niall, but the server has gone down again. No one can log in.'

He glanced at Merry and pulled a face. 'Duty calls – sorry.'

'No problem,' she said, standing up. 'I've taken up too much of your time again. I'll stop being a pest once I've settled in properly.'

'Not at all,' he replied. 'It's been lovely to see you – drop in any time.'

He walked her to the entrance doors and smiled. 'I'll be in touch with more details and final numbers for Friday but, basically, it's due to start at six-thirty, so if you can get here by six o'clock, that would be perfect.'

Merry nodded. 'Six o'clock. Got it.'

'And if you want a jaw-dropping journey home, take the road that takes you past the Stones of Stenness. Google Maps will try to take you the shorter route but you should be able to change it.'

She made a mental note of the name. 'I will. Thanks.'

'Drive carefully,' he said, as she headed through the doors. 'And don't let Gordon bully you!'

Chapter Five

The standing stones were every bit as impressive as Niall had promised. The road he'd recommended wove its way between two lochs and the three Stones of Stenness stood to attention, six metres tall and visible long before she got close enough to appreciate them. Merry pulled the Mini into a layby at the side of the road, which seemed to serve as a car park, and got out. There were a few other visitors wandering in between the stones. Merry made her way through the kissing gate and paused to read the information on the signs, marvelling at the feats of strength and engineering that had got the enormous slabs into place. Originally, it was thought there had been twelve stones forming a circle around a vast hearth, and Merry couldn't help wondering what the people who placed the stones did there. Was it a sacred place? Somewhere they came to dance and celebrate? The equivalent of a town hall, where rules were made? Perhaps it was all three – the possibilities were endless. But at last, mindful of the time and wanting to be back at the croft before darkness fell, Merry dragged herself away from daydreaming about the past and got back into the car.

She resisted the temptation to stop at another, more complete circle of stones just a few minutes north of the ones she'd just left. Niall hadn't mentioned those. He probably hadn't wanted to spoil the surprise, she decided, as she slowed the car to gaze out of the window. And it was just after she'd passed those stones that she felt the steering wheel pull in a strange, sharp jolt and heard the unmistakable *whomp whomp whomp* of a flat tyre.

'Shit!' Merry muttered, flicking on the hazard lights and wrestling the car to a stop as close to the side of the road as she could manage. The car behind her beeped, as though she was being inconsiderate by suffering a mechanical mishap, and she resisted the temptation to make a rude gesture. Apart from anything else, she was on Orkney in a professional capacity and it would be just her luck for the driver of the beeping car to be a fan of Merina Wilde.

She got out of the car and surveyed the driver's side tyre; as she'd suspected it was flat. She stared at it helplessly for a moment, cursing her bad luck, before wondering what to do next. Was there a breakdown service she could call? Niall would know. She reached into her bag and pulled out her mobile. After listening to the phone ring and ring, Merry concluded he must still be dealing with technical issues at the library; besides, really, she ought to be able to solve a problem like this on her own. As long as that didn't involve actually changing the tyre herself.

She'd just looked up breakdown recovery on her phone when another car slowed and beeped its horn. Mumbling another rude word under her breath, Merry ignored the driver and focussed on her phone. Then she realized the car had stopped.

'Excuse me, miss,' a male, charmingly accented voice called. 'Do you need some assistance?'

The accent certainly wasn't Scottish – it sounded Scandinavian or perhaps Nordic – and was so out of place that Merry looked up instantly – and nearly dropped her phone. Gazing at her from the open window of a battered Ford pick-up truck was the most beautiful man she'd ever seen. He had untidy blond hair that flowed past his shoulders, a slightly darker beard that was much longer than the fashion in London, but no less neatly trimmed, and a smile that made her almost forget her own name.

'Sorry?' she managed, in a tone that was more of a squeak than anything else.

He leaned one muscular forearm in the space where the window should be and fired her a look of friendly concern. 'Are you in trouble? How can I help?'

'Oh,' she said, waving vaguely in the direction of the car. 'I've got a flat tyre. But don't worry – I'll just call a garage.'

Immediately, the pick-up truck pulled over and parked in front of the Mini and Merry found herself torn between happiness – because she'd get to look at this extraordinary man up close – and irritation because he'd evidently decided she needed to be rescued.

And then he got out of the car and all coherent thoughts left her brain.

He was a Viking, she decided faintly as he walked towards her, plucked from history and wrapped up in modern packaging, but there was no disguising heritage like his. There was his height, for a start – he must be 6'5" at least. And his physique was equally impressive; there were muscles rippling as he walked that his black t-shirt and jeans did nothing to hide. He looked like the cover model from an epic Norse saga. He looked like he could out-Thor Chris Hemsworth.

'My name is Magnús Ólafsson,' he said. 'I'm at your service.'

Merry caught herself staring at his eyes, which were an even deeper green than her own. 'Merina Wilde,' she said, preferring not to wonder why she'd given the more alluring version of her name. 'Thank you for stopping.'

He nodded and glanced down at the Mini. 'Do you have a spare?'

'I have no idea,' Merry confessed. 'This isn't my car and today is the first time I've driven it. I haven't even opened the boot, much less checked whether there's a spare tyre in there.'

Magnús smiled, but there wasn't so much as a hint of condescension on his face. 'No problem, I'll take a look.'

He walked to the back of the car and opened the boot. Merry knew she should follow, but she was rooted to the spot. She'd never met someone whose appearance had affected her so drastically; was it very wrong that she wanted to stare at him for the rest of her life?

Moments later, Magnús's tousled head appeared above the Mini as he straightened up. 'Bad news – no spare tyre.'

Merry felt a wash of disappointment and it took her a few seconds to understand why: from the moment Magnús had stopped his truck, she'd been subconsciously looking forward to watching him heft the old tyre from the car, possibly by lifting the Mini up with one hand, and replace it with a new one. And now that pleasure had been taken from her. 'Okay, thanks for checking,' she said, hoping she didn't sound as regretful as she felt. 'I guess I'd better ring the garage after all.'

'I'll wait while you call,' Magnús said.

'Oh, I'm sure you have much better things to do,' Merry exclaimed, hoping he'd disagree.

He didn't let her down. 'Not at all,' he said, flashing her an easy smile. 'I'll wait.'

'Hopefully this won't take long,' she said.

Except that the first three garages she tried didn't have the right tyre to fit the Mini.

'She'll have run-flat tyres, miss, and I don't keep them in stock,' the first mechanic told her. 'I could mebbe get you one by Wednesday morning?'

It was the same story at the next two. Eddie's Repairs in Kirkwall had the right tyre but no one to come out and fit it. Merry thanked him and hung up, discouraged. 'I don't know what to do,' she told Magnús. 'The only garage who has the right tyre can't come out and fit it.'

He shrugged. 'Then we will go and collect it.'

She stared at him, aghast. 'I can't ask you to do that – it's all the way back in Kirkwall.'

Magnús regarded her quizzically. 'It is only twenty miles. And really, I don't see that we have a choice.'

We, Merry noted and, far too late, it occurred to her to wonder whether she ought to have been more reticent about accepting help from a strange man by the side of the road, no matter how handsome he was. But it was hard to imagine his charming chivalry hid anything sinister and he was right about one thing: short of abandoning the Mini and walking all the way back to Brightwater Bay, she really didn't have a lot of choice. 'Are you sure you don't mind? I'm happy to pay for your petrol.'

He waved the offer away. 'I was only going home, so no, I don't mind. And I am happy to help – I have a sister back in Reykjavik and I hope that someone would do the same for her if she needed it.'

Merry's imagination whirred – any serial killer worth his salt would almost certainly invent a sister to reassure his victim before luring her into his car. And then she gave herself a serious mental shake and forced the ridiculous idea out of her head, imagining what Jess would say if she was there. *Get in the damn truck*, probably. Closely followed by *and find out if he's single.*

'Okay,' Merry said, taking a deep breath. 'Then I accept. Thank you.'

Magnús walked around to the passenger side of his truck and opened the door. 'I'm afraid it's not very clean. I wasn't expecting any company.'

'Don't worry,' Merry said. 'I won't mention it in my review.'

His forehead crinkled. 'Review?'

'Like Uber,' she explained. Then, when his expression stayed blank, 'Or Trip Advisor?'

'Ah, yes,' he said, and grinned. 'Very funny.'

It would have been funnier if she hadn't had to explain, Merry thought, but it was her own fault for assuming Uber might have reached the far north of Scotland. Or maybe Magnús had never needed to get home drunk after a night out – she had no idea.

'So, Merina Wilde, what brings you to Orkney?' he asked, once he'd turned the pick-up around and pointed it back along the road to Kirkwall.

He was the first person she'd met since arriving who hadn't known who she was and why she was there before she'd so much as opened her mouth, Merry thought. It made a refreshing change and she half-wished she didn't have to spoil things by telling him the truth. Most people were fascinated when she told them what she did for a living, and some were even a little star-struck; she quite liked the idea of hanging onto her anonymity for a little while longer. But there was always the chance that he'd see the posters at the library or dotted around Kirkwall and work it out for himself, and then he'd wonder why she'd lied.

'I'm a novelist,' she told him. 'The library hosts a Writer in Residence scheme and I'm the lucky writer. It means I'll be here for the next six months, doing events and talking about books to anyone who'll listen.'

He glanced sideways, his expression animated. 'But this is amazing! In Iceland, we are all book lovers – we even have a tradition devoted to giving each other books on Christmas Eve. It's called Jólabókaflóð.'

It was a word Merry had only ever seen written down before and he pronounced it *yo-la-bok-a-flot*, so it took her a moment to make the link. 'I've heard of that,' she said warmly. 'It sounds wonderful.'

He fired an admiring look her way. 'Authors are like rock stars in my country. Although obviously, we have rock stars too.'

The conversation flowed easily between them. Merry discovered Magnús had left Iceland in his early twenties and had spent a year travelling the world before taking a summer job on Orkney and eventually settling there. He now ran a boatyard in Kirkwall, building and repairing boats for the local fishermen and residents, and, during the summer months, he skippered a tour boat, running excursions around the coast for whale watching, or taking tourists to the other islands in the archipelago. It was all so fascinating that Merry was more than a little disappointed when they pulled up outside Eddie's Repairs.

'Magnús,' a short, round-bellied man called, when they hovered in the doorway of the garage. 'What brings you here?'

'A mission of mercy,' Magnús replied. 'This is Merina. She called about a tyre for a Mini earlier.'

'Please, call me Merry,' she said, as Eddie stuck out an oil-stained hand. 'And yes, I did call you. Would it be possible to collect the tyre now?'

Eddie rubbed his chin. 'Aye, that's no bother.' He glanced up at Magnús. 'And I suppose you'll fit it? Do you have a jack and a spanner and all that?'

Merry felt a tingle of warmth in her cheeks as she once again pictured Magnús hefting the car aloft with one hand as the wind sent his long hair streaming. *Good grief*, she thought and gave herself a sturdy mental kick. *Get a grip, Merry.*

'I was hoping you might be able to lend us the tools we need,' Magnús said, mercifully oblivious to Merry's over-heated imagination. 'I'll be able to return them tomorrow.'

'Of course,' Eddie said, and he glanced at Merry again. 'Anything for our Writer in Residence, eh?'

He went to fetch the tyre. Magnús leaned towards Merry and grinned. 'See? You're a rock star here too.'

She laughed and tried not to blush further. 'Believe me, there's nothing rock and roll about sitting up until four o'clock in the morning, wondering whether your main characters are ever going to kiss each other.'

'Are they the kind of novels you write – kissing books?' he asked.

Merry hesitated as a sly inner voice reminded her that she currently didn't write *any* kind of novel. 'Usually, yes,' she managed. 'At least I try to.'

He nodded. 'Then I will keep an eye out for them. Maybe you will even sign one for me.'

'That's the least I can do,' Merry said, 'given that you've just driven twenty miles out of your way to help me and will have to drive another twenty *and* change a tyre before you can escape.'

Magnús shot her a look that made her stomach swoop in a lazy arc. 'What makes you think I want to escape?'

Eddie chose that moment to reappear, which gave Merry some much-needed breathing space. How could Magnús have this effect on her when they'd only just met? She needed to calm down and remember why she was on Orkney in the first place: to mend a broken heart. The last thing she ought to be doing was harbouring impractical fantasies about a man she barely knew, no matter how much he looked like a Viking.

'Here's your tyre,' Eddie said, lifting the black circle into the bed of the pick-up truck. He vanished back inside the garage momentarily, then returned with a jack and spanner set. 'And here's everything else you need. There'll be locking wheel nuts in the car, I imagine. Which just leaves us with the bill.'

Merry winced as she paid the astronomical cost of the new tyre but told herself it was a small price to pay for her freedom around Orkney. And then Eddie was waving them off, with a firm promise that he'd see Merry at her event.

'You are giving a talk?' Magnús asked, once they were back on the road.

'At the library,' Merry said. 'On Friday.'

'Then that is perfect,' Magnús said. 'You can sign a book for me there.'

Merry felt embarrassment crawl over her. 'Oh, don't feel you have to come. It's just going to be me wittering on about books.'

Magnús smiled. 'I can't think of a better way to spend an evening.'

And Merry forced herself to look out of the window, in case the warmth of yet another inappropriate mental image gave her away.

The Mini was exactly where they'd left it, looking somewhat lonely by the side of the road. Merry watched as Magnús tucked his long golden hair into the perfect man bun and expertly changed the tyre, although a treacherous little voice inside her head whispered that he might have done an even better job if he'd removed his t-shirt ...

She had her runaway imagination firmly under control by the time he'd finished and was able to thank him without blushing. 'I don't know what I'd have done without you.'

'Someone else would have stopped,' he said modestly. 'There are many good people on these islands.'

'Well, I'm glad it was you.' The words were out of her mouth before she could stop them and a hot rosy glow washed over her.

'Me too,' he said, then hesitated. 'But it occurs to me that if you don't know many people here yet, you might like to go for a drink one evening. Or perhaps even dinner?'

It was a tempting offer, and Merry could practically hear Jess's voice screaming at her to say *YES YES YES!* But hadn't she just told Niall she was still in a relationship with Alex? How would it look if she went out for drinks or dinner alone with the incredibly good-looking Magnús? Even if his offer had been platonic rather than romantic, people would be bound to talk and the last thing Merry wanted was to be the subject of gossip, especially not since she was on Orkney in a professional capacity.

Regretfully, she shook her head. 'It sounds like a lovely idea but I'm afraid I can't.' She paused, wondering whether it was presumptuous to assume he found her as attractive as she found him, and decided it was safest to fall back on the same story she'd given to Niall. 'I'm . . . I've got a boyfriend, back in London.'

Magnús accepted the rejection with a gracious smile. 'Of course you have. Forgive me for even asking.'

'I'll just have to come up with another way to repay you for your kindness,' Merry said, trying to ignore the hard knot in her stomach that was suggesting she'd just made a mistake.

'That won't be necessary – it was entirely my pleasure to help.' He waved a hand and climbed back into his truck. 'Take care, Merina. Perhaps I'll see you on Friday.'

Merry watched the road until he was nothing more than a speck in the distance. Then she climbed into the Mini with a weary sigh, noting that it was almost four-thirty and that the sun was dipping in the west once more. 'So much for getting back before nightfall,' she muttered, starting the engine.

But she couldn't help smiling a little as she drove along the winding roads that led to the croft. The flat tyre had been inconvenient and expensive, but it had brought her an unexpected adventure with a stunningly good-looking and generous man. She'd just have to make sure Jess never found out that she had turned down the opportunity to get to know Magnús Ólafsson better.

Chapter Six

The next morning was wet. Merry spent a restless hour or so watching the rain patter against the windowpane, occasionally gazing beyond to the dull grey sky that barely differed in shade from the sea, avoiding her laptop and trying not to daydream about Vikings. Eventually, she decided enough was enough; if she didn't get out of the croft soon, she might spontaneously combust. She flicked through the folder of tourist leaflets that had been thoughtfully tucked among the books, disregarding anything that sounded too outdoorsy. Finally, she found something that caught her eye: a printed webpage about a chapel built by Italian prisoners of war during the Second World War. It was completely different to the Neolithic monuments she'd visited so far. Perhaps that was what tugged at her imagination and made her want to go.

The chapel was on the uninhabited island of Lamb Holm, just off the southern tip of the Orkney mainland. It was accessed by driving across the Churchill Barriers, which Merry read had been built in the 1940s as a naval defence after a German U-boat attack. The barrier didn't look much now, she thought, but at least it provided a road link between the islands – and meant she didn't have to work out how to catch the ferry.

The sea was calm, despite the torrential rain, and that was something else Merry was grateful for: there were no crashing waves to contend with as she drove across the narrow strip of tarmac that topped the barrier. She'd have to keep an eye on things while she explored the chapel – the last thing she wanted was to need another rescue, especially since she didn't think she could rely on Magnús to magically appear again.

The chapel itself stole her heart even before she'd gone inside. From the front, it was designed to look like an Italian church, complete with gothic pillars and a bell tower over the portico door, and if Merry hadn't already known it was a façade attached to a pair of Nissen Huts, she wouldn't have guessed. But it was the interior that really made her gasp. The rain, combined with off-season, had kept the tourists away and Merry had the building to herself, which allowed her to stop in the doorway and take in the scene laid out before her. The walls and ceiling were domed, following the rounded shape of the huts, and covered with intricate decorations: imitation brickwork that climbed into the illusion of a vaulted ceiling, frescos of angels and cherubim, and an altarpiece that showed the Virgin Mary cradling her infant son. A deep crimson carpet rolled down the centre of the chapel, flowing to the ornate ironwork rood screen and gates. Beyond that stood an altar, flanked by two *trompe l'oeil* stained-glass windows. All that was missing was the heady scent of candles and incense that Merry usually associated with Catholic churches.

She walked forwards, shaking her head in wonder at the skill of the men who'd created such a thing of beauty using whatever they could scavenge from their immediate surroundings: corned beef tins and car exhausts and wood rescued from wrecked ships. It was an astonishing testament to the ingenuity and talent of the Italian prisoners, and the generosity of their guards, all so that they could practice their faith and be reminded of the homes they'd left behind to fight for their country. There was an almost tangible sense of peace here, similar to the one she'd felt in the burial chamber the day before and, to a lesser extent, in the shadows of the Standing Stones. Merry didn't know whether it was the monuments and buildings that exuded calm, or the islands themselves, but the tranquillity was wonderful.

She sat on the low wooden bench that lined one of the walls and listened to the silence. There were stories captured here too, moulded into the metalwork and carved into the wood and painted onto the fabric of the building – labours of love that spoke of a deep longing for the familiarity of home, of the fear and isolation of being a prisoner in a strange land, and of the comfort that their faith could bring. Merry smiled softly as she looked around; it seemed as though everywhere she turned on Orkney, there was another story waiting to be uncovered.

The door opened and a woman of around thirty tumbled noisily inside, shaking an umbrella and muttering under her breath. She stopped when she saw Merry, her eyes widening in apology. 'Sorry to disturb you. I thought I'd have the place to myself on such a miserable day.'

'Don't apologize,' Merry replied. 'I was just soaking up the atmosphere and thinking. It's so peaceful here.'

The woman smiled. 'That's why I'm here too. Well, that and sweeping the floor. Unfortunately, God doesn't believe in doing his own housework.'

Merry laughed. 'No, I don't suppose he does. Let me get out of your way, then.'

'*Och*, don't let me chase you away,' the woman said in dismay. 'Take your time, I'm in no rush. It's nice to have the chance to sit down for a while, without the kids nagging for this and that.'

'How many do you have?'

The other woman crossed the floor, pulling off her rain-soaked coat, and sat on the bench beside Merry. 'Just the two, although it feels like more most days, especially since it's just me and them. Do you have kids yourself?'

Merry shook her head. She and Alex had talked about raising a family someday but it had always been a distant plan, something they'd do eventually. And now she was glad of that distance, because the thought of single parenting on top of the pain and stress of breaking up made her shiver with anxiety. 'I have nieces and nephews.'

'That's nice. All the fun and none of the fights.' The woman gave Merry a sideways look and frowned. 'You look a wee bit familiar. Have we met before?'

'I don't think so,' Merry said, studying her in return. 'I've only been here a few days. I'm Merry.'

'Helen,' the woman said. 'But I'm sure I know you from somewhere. Have you got family on Orkney?'

Again, Merry shook her head. 'No. I'm here for a few months to write a book.'

Or try to, anyway, she thought. Beside her, Helen snapped her fingers in triumph. 'That's where I've seen you before – there was a piece in the Orkney news about you!' She fired an admiring glance Merry's way. 'The famous romance novelist, Merina Wilde.'

A bubble of laughter escaped Merry. 'I wouldn't go that far.'

'You're famous on Orkney,' Helen replied. 'I bet everyone you've met so far has known who you are, am I right?'

Merry cast her mind back to the day before and her meeting with Magnús. A rueful smile tugged at her lips. 'Almost.'

Helen sighed. 'Having an imagination like yours must be a wonderful thing. Where do you get your ideas from?'

'From everywhere,' Merry said, and waved a hand at their surroundings. 'In fact, before you came in, I was thinking about the men who built this chapel – who they were, what they felt, what happened when they returned to their families after the war. There's inspiration in everything, if you know where to look – I suppose writers just pay more attention than most people.'

'My grandfather was one of those men,' Helen said. 'He was taken prisoner in occupied France and brought here to help build the Barriers. My grandmother met him by chance when he briefly came ashore to the mainland and it was love at first sight, by all accounts, although they weren't allowed to fraternize or even speak. But he was able to find out her name and, when the war was over, he wrote to her from Italy. Eventually, he came back to visit – they were married the following month and together for fifty-two years.'

Merry clapped her hands in delight, tears of joy stinging the backs of her eyes. 'How wonderful! Oh, that's exactly what I mean – there are love stories in the unlikeliest of places. They might not all end as happily as this one, but they're there.'

Helen gave her a wry smile. 'It certainly gives me hope that there's someone out there for me, although I hope it doesn't take a war for me to meet him.'

'Thank you for telling me,' Merry said, and something rustled faintly inside her brain, trying to get her attention. She felt an accompanying stab of anxiety and forced herself to focus on Helen. 'I'm sure there's a good man for you just around the corner.'

The other woman sighed. 'Maybe. God knows I've met a few bad ones along the way. But listen to me blethering on and taking up all your time. I'll go and find something else to do while you do your thinking – the sweeping can wait until you've finished.'

'No need. I think I've got everything I came for.' Merry got to her feet and smiled. 'It's been so lovely to meet you. And thanks again for sharing the story of how your grandparents met – you have no idea how much it helps to be reminded that, sometimes, love does conquer all.'

There must have been a hint of heartbreak in her voice, because Helen gave her a long look, then pressed a hand to her arm. 'You're welcome,' she said, the words warm with sympathy. 'If you want to know any more details, you'll find me here every Tuesday and Friday around this time. I'm afraid I can't come to your event at the library – I've no childcare in the evenings.'

'I understand,' Merry said, making a mental note to bring a signed copy of a book for Helen the following week. 'But I have a feeling I'm going to be a regular visitor here over the next few months. It's so calming.'

'Well, that's something to look forward to, although it might not be so quiet next time,' Helen said. A squall of rain rattled against the metal exterior of the chapel. 'Mind you don't drown on your way home!'

The rain died off by mid-afternoon, giving way to blue skies and sunshine, so Merry decided to take Sheila's advice and try exercise as a way to shift the anxiety she felt about Friday's event. Usually events like this were easy and fun, almost like having a chat with a friend that just happened to have an audience, and she always enjoyed meeting readers afterwards. But the knowledge that she had to write something to read aloud gnawed at her stomach like a nest of rats. And the overwhelming sense of pressure made her head spin.

The wild beauty of the cliffs helped, along with the bracing sea air. By the time she returned to the croft, windswept but glowing from her exertion, she felt calmer, and settled on the sofa with one of the novels from the bookshelf. But she found it hard to concentrate on the words – an image of the Italian chapel kept drifting into her mind; the almost-tangible sense of tranquillity, coupled with the genuine delight she'd felt when Helen had told her the story of her grandparents, gently tugged at her imagination until she knew she'd have no rest unless she did something to settle her thoughts. Her laptop was still on the coffee table but even the thought of opening it made her flinch. Instead, she rummaged in her case for the half-filled notebook she'd brought from London in the hope that one of the old ideas inside might inspire her. Turning to a blank page, she began to jot down some notes about the chapel. That was straight-forward enough. Encouraged, Merry added the other places she'd visited so far, and the people she'd met. But the moment she started to try to think of things in terms of a narrative, her brain baulked and ground to a halt. Facts were okay, it seemed. Fiction was not.

Even so, she battled against the block for the best part of two hours, carving out sentences with her pen as best she could. Most of them were about Magnús – she seemed to be able to write endless sentences describing him – but many were about Skara Brae and the other ancient monuments she'd seen. Maybe that was what she should write – a travelogue detailing her thoughts and impressions of Orkney so far. Her nose wrinkled in disgust, picturing the bewildered faces of the audience as she described sights they'd been seeing their entire lives. But it was better than nothing, she reminded herself. She couldn't cast any spells from a blank page.

She was about to call it a night when her phone vibrated on the coffee table. Expecting to see a message from Jess, she opened the screen and checked the name.

It wasn't Jess. The number didn't have a name attached but Merry recognized it immediately. It was Alex.

Immediately, Merry started to shake. Nausea rolled up from her gut and she found it hard to breathe. Alex, after all the months of silence. What on earth could he possibly want?

There was only one way to find out. With trembling fingers, she swept the screen.

I hear you've moved to the other end of the country. Hope you're happy x

It was the kiss that caught her eye. In all the years they'd been together, on countless Valentine's Day cards and birthday cards and texts, she'd never known him to add a kiss. It wasn't his way, he'd said, when she'd asked him once, and she'd never questioned it again. And here he was, adding kisses where they shouldn't be. What the hell did it mean?

She closed the message and dropped her phone onto the

sofa, staring at the flickering flames of the fire. It was obvious that meeting Jess had prompted him to get in touch, but she wasn't sure why. Was it simple curiosity? Or a subconscious fear that maybe Merry was finally starting to get over him? If he was a character in one of her books, Merry knew which one it would be. And she wasn't sure how she felt about that.

Jess was altogether more forthright with her feelings and she fired back instantly:

WHAT A KNOB. He can't bear that you might be happy without him.

Although she knew exactly what Jess would say, Merry responded with:

What should I do?

Her reply was almost instantaneous, exactly as Merry had predicted:

Delete it. Do not reply. I say this as your friend, because I love you – no good can come of this xxx

She was right, Merry knew; there was no way she could continue to get over Alex if the possibility of messaging him was there. It would eat away at her thoughts until she persuaded herself that one little message couldn't hurt. And then she'd be back to square one, staring at her phone and wondering why he hadn't replied.

Another message from Jess popped up.

Have you done it?

Merry couldn't help laughing. Jess knew her too well. Taking a deep breath, she brought up Alex's message and pressed the delete button.

Done x

GOOD! I'm proud of you, babe. Keep on keeping on x

It felt good to reclaim a little bit of power from Alex, Merry discovered. In fact, it felt better than good – it felt *great*. Smiling to herself, she reached for her notebook once more and read over what she'd written. Then she pressed her pen against the paper and started to write again.

Chapter Seven

'I hope you packed some sturdy trainers when you left London.'

Merry stared at Sheila, who was standing on the doorstep of the croft in full waterproof running gear with an expectant look on her face. 'Sorry?' she managed after a few seconds had elapsed. 'I mean, yes, but why do you want to know?'

'Isn't it obvious?' Sheila said, with unconcealed impatience. She waved an arm at the pale blue sky and gentle glow of sunrise. 'It's the perfect day to start your running journey.'

'Oh no,' Merry exclaimed, taking a step back into the living room. 'I'm sorry, Sheila, but no.'

The older woman walked forwards, herding Merry backwards like an errant sheep. 'Oh yes,' she said, with steely determination. 'You couldn't ask for a more beautiful morning. Besides, I need you.'

The indignant refusal that had been forming on Merry's

lips died as she gazed at her neighbour. 'What do you mean, you need me?'

Sheila let out a huff of irritation. 'My daughter thinks I'm too old to run on my own. She thinks I need a . . . a *babysitter* to make sure I don't fall over and graze my knees, like some kind of toddler. And she's roped in the doctor.' She fired a grumpy look Merry's way. 'So I'm afraid you've really got no choice in the matter. You're coming running with me.'

Merry couldn't help it: she laughed. 'Well, since you asked me so nicely . . .'

The old woman had the grace to look a little embarrassed. '*Ach*, you're right. Let me start over. Merry, it would be a great personal favour if you would consider keeping me company on my run today.' She paused and wrinkled her nose in disgust. 'Because I'm obviously so elderly and infirm.'

'It was going so well until that last sentence,' Merry said with an amused grin. She studied Sheila for a moment and her amusement faded. Underneath the prickly exterior, she thought she detected a quiet desperation and she cast her mind back to Monday, when her neighbour had talked about the way running helped her mental health. And then Merry thought about how she might feel, if something she loved doing was suddenly snatched away, and she gave an inward sigh. 'Okay. Give me some time to get changed.'

It only took a few minutes of running before Merry realized she'd made a terrible mistake. Not only had Sheila set off at a blistering pace, she was also keeping up a stream of constant conversation and questions that required Merry to snatch an already elusive breath to answer. Even so, she did her best to keep up with both the running and the chat, until her thudding heart forced her to concede defeat. 'Sheila, slow down!'

Her neighbour stopped and turned around, a look of crafty surprise on her face. 'Oh, I thought a young thing like you would have no bother keeping up. Sorry.'

'Just a bit slower,' Merry puffed, bending over and placing her hands on her knees. 'This is the first time I've run for years.'

To her credit, Sheila waited until Merry had caught her breath, even though she was clearly impatient to be off. And when they did start again, the pace was much gentler. It took a while, but eventually Merry found that her lungs had adjusted to the exertion and breathing became easier. It helped that Sheila now seemed content to run in silence and soon they were both lost in their thoughts.

Merry had no idea how much distance they'd covered when the idea came to her. She'd been thinking about her writing the night before – her description of how she'd felt able to sense the stories of the people who'd lived on Orkney thousands of years earlier – and the image of a woman had popped into her head. She was dressed in animal skins, with a fine beaded necklace around her neck and a circlet of metal on her golden hair, and she carried an axe high in one hand. Her face was bared into a snarl that was half fury and half fear. She was so real that Merry

felt she was standing on the path in front of her, silhouetted against the sea. And she knew straight away that this
woman lived in Skara Brae.

She held the image in her head, cradling it as her feet
pounded along the path, terrified it would disintegrate before
she could absorb it fully.

'How much longer, Sheila?' she puffed, and her neighbour
glanced over one shoulder in surprise, as though she'd forgotten Merry was even there.

'You can go back now, if you like,' she called. 'I know
my way home.'

'But what about your daughter?' Merry replied. 'I don't
want to leave you on your own – what if you fall?'

Sheila threw her a withering look. 'Do I look unsteady
to you? Besides, what Grace doesn't know won't hurt her –
I'm sure you're not going to tell anyone you couldn't keep
up with me.'

She really is incorrigible, Merry thought, with a burst of
indignant laughter. Torn between the desire to do the right
thing and a sudden burning need to explore the character
floating in her mind, she ran for a few more paces before
reaching a decision. 'Will you knock as you go by, to let me
know you're okay?'

'Of course,' Sheila said. 'See you later. And mind *you* don't
fall, now. I don't need that on my conscience!'

Back at the croft, Merry didn't even stop for a shower.
Panting, she kicked off her trainers at the door and threw
her lightweight jacket into a heap on the floor before making

for the kitchen to grab a pint of water. Then she made a beeline for the sofa, gulping down water as she walked. And as the sweat cooled on her skin, before her brain could register a complaint, she wrenched open the laptop and started to type.

Merry didn't think she'd ever felt more nervous than she did while driving to the library in Kirkwall on Friday evening. She'd spent the rest of Thursday in a writing frenzy, pausing only when her ravenous stomach forced her to swallow down a few slices of Sheila's bannock cake. When her eyes grew too gritty to see, she gave in and went to bed, only to wake up at five o'clock to continue writing. She had no idea whether what she was creating was any good, she only knew that it was a compulsion, something she had to draw out of herself before it withered away to nothing. By Friday lunchtime, the first draft was done and Merry finally took herself off for a much-needed shower, grateful that there was no one else in the croft to comment on how she smelled. And by the time she had to leave to reach the library for her event, she had something that she hoped might not cause Niall to rescind her residency on the spot.

'How have you been?' he asked when she arrived at the front desk, struggling to keep a lid on her anxiety. 'Had any adventures over the last few days?'

Merry thought about Magnús, her visit to the Italian chapel, and her kamikaze run along the cliffs with Sheila, and some of her anxiety lessened. 'You could say that.'

He grinned. 'I can't wait to hear about it. The kettle's on, unless you fancy something stronger?'

The temptation to ask for a dram of whisky to steady her nerves was strong, but Merry reluctantly shook her head. The reading was going to be difficult enough, without the added stress of slurring her words. 'Tea would be perfect, thanks.'

'Come this way,' he said. 'The audience has started to arrive already so you can hide away in my office, just in case they decide to stampede.'

She laughed. 'How many tickets did you sell in the end?'

'Two hundred and forty-three,' he said, sounding pleased. 'That's the best turnout we've ever had.'

Merry blinked; events in London were never that well attended, not even with massive-name authors. If Niall ever tired of being a librarian, she thought faintly, he could probably get a marketing job at a publishing house. And then the reality of such a decent crowd set in, and Merry hoped even more fervently that the story she'd written was going to hit the mark. Two hundred and forty-three people who knew the story of Skara Brae well ... 'That's brilliant,' she managed, after a second or two. 'Great.'

Something of her anxiety must have carried in her voice because Niall slowed and looked at her. 'Is everything okay? You sound a bit ... I don't know ...'

She forced herself to smile. 'Just a bit of pre-event nerves. Don't worry, I'll be fine.'

Niall shook his head. 'I'd have thought you've done so many of these things that they're second nature to you now.'

He threw her a sympathetic look. 'It's quite reassuring that you're nervous – reminds me that you're a human being rather than a superstar author and all-round goddess.'

Merry wanted to say that she'd never felt less like either, but they arrived at his office and the moment passed. He ushered her inside and busied himself making tea.

'I have to go back downstairs to make sure everything is running smoothly, but no one will bother you up here,' he said, once the tea was brewed. He checked the clock on the wall. 'I'll be back to collect you at six-twenty and we'll get you miked up so you're good to go. Then you and I will have a lovely chat, following the questions I sent over yesterday, and we'll finish up with your reading. Sound okay?'

It did, apart from the fact that she'd been so engrossed in her writing that she hadn't checked her emails and had no idea what questions he'd sent her. 'Fine,' she said, crossing her fingers that he hadn't asked anything too out there. 'Sounds perfect.'

'And afterwards all hell will break loose, but we'll cross that bridge when we come to it.' He paused to flash his Superman smile and Merry felt her nerves settle a little more. 'Don't worry, they already love you.'

She managed to maintain her smile until after he'd closed the door, at which point she sagged into her chair. They might love her now, Merry thought unhappily, but would they still feel that way after she'd trampled all over their history?

*

'And what was it that first drew you to writing?'

Summoning up a practised smile, Merry launched into the answer she'd given so many times that she didn't even have to think about the words. So far, the event was going well; the hall looked great, with two squashy armchairs on a raised stage and well-placed spotlights to light them. Niall was an easy and professional host, allowing her the time and freedom to answer, and following up any interesting points she made with intelligent questions she knew wouldn't be on the list he'd compiled. The audience was attentive, listening in rapt silence and laughing at exactly the right moments. All in all, it was that rarest of things – a dream author event – and Merry was able to almost forget what was coming at the end.

'You're often quoted as saying love stories are what make us human,' Niall went on. 'Is that why we're so obsessed with finding our happy ever after, Merry? Even when our hearts get broken and we have to pick ourselves up and start all over again?'

The question made her hesitate. Was this really a question she could answer when she wasn't sure she still believed in happy ever after? Niall waited patiently as the seconds ticked by, but she could see his concern growing when she didn't answer. And then the clouds in her mind cleared, and she knew what to say. She took a deep breath.

'I suppose, in a way, that is what makes us human. Our response to heartbreak, I mean. Because on one hand, we're conditioned to evolve and learn when we encounter physical pain, so that we don't get hurt that way again. But that doesn't seem to apply where love is concerned.' She paused and gazed out at the audience. 'When someone we're in love with breaks our heart, it feels like the end of the world – we feel as though we'll never love anyone that way again. But eventually, if we're lucky, we'll meet someone new and fall for them. Our hearts don't remember how much it hurt before – they only know what they want. And that's why we'll always chase our happy ever afters, because it's who we are. What else can we do?'

A smattering of applause broke out around the hall, followed by self-conscious laughter when not everyone followed suit. Merry smiled. 'I see we have some hopeless romantics in the house. You guys are my tribe.'

Niall's gaze met hers and a flash of something passed between them. 'Mine too. Now, what can you tell us about the book you're writing now?'

And there it was, the question she'd been dreading. She stared at him, like a deer in the full beams of an oncoming lorry, and blinked hard. 'Actually, I'm not going to tell you anything at all.'

She watched his smile slip a little and hurried to reassure him. 'From the moment I arrived on Orkney, I've been seeing stories. That's not so unusual – I'm a writer, after all – it's my job to find them. But there's something magical about this place.' She stopped to gather her thoughts and fired a fleeting glance Niall's way. 'You described these islands as extraordinary and it's a word that has come into my head over and over as I've been exploring. There's nothing ordinary about Orkney – it's a place that has stories woven into its very fabric – and that's what I want to talk about. Not the novel I started to write long before I came here.'

He nodded in understanding. 'So, would now be a good time to ask you to read something you have written since you arrived on Orkney?'

A surge of adrenaline burst through Merry, almost paralysing her with its intensity. *No*, she wanted to say, *there'll never be a good time to read this story*. But the moment for backing out was long gone. Besides, she had nothing else to read, other than the godawful travelogue she'd scribbled in her notebook, and she was determined that was never going to see the light of day again.

She squared her shoulders and lifted up the pages she'd printed on the surprisingly modern printer at the croft, hoping the audience couldn't see the paper shaking in her hands. 'This is something I wrote after visiting Skara Brae.' She stopped and fired a nervous look Niall's way. He held her gaze firmly and gave her a barely perceptible nod of encouragement. 'It's called *The Woman with Eyes of Gold*.'

The audience settled in expectation. Merry shifted slightly in her seat so that she was facing them and took a moment to cast her eyes across the sea of faces. She spotted Magnús near the back, head and shoulders above the rest of the crowd, and her spirits lifted again at the sight of him; she hoped he wouldn't be too offended that she'd used his heritage as inspiration. Taking another deep breath, she began to read.

'They came before dawn – men with burning swords

and murder in their hearts. She saw them long before they saw her, and smelled them even before that. Even so, there was barely enough time to send a warning around the village, and no time at all to gather more than a handful of precious belongings. If the invaders found them when they stormed the houses – if Fen could not get her people away fast enough – then she knew unimaginable slaughter would follow . . .'

It felt as though Merry read for an age, although she knew it wasn't more than ten minutes. Total silence reigned as her voice died away and she glanced nervously across at Niall, who was looking at her with such rapt admiration that she almost blushed. He lifted his hands and began to clap, which seemed to startle the audience into remembering its responsibilities; applause broke out and Merry even picked out a few cheers. Then she heard the scraping of chair feet and saw, to her utter astonishment, that some people were on their feet. The applause went on and on, so much so that it took Niall several seconds of standing and appealing for quiet before the crowd gave in and settled down again.

'I think I speak for all of us when I say that was an incredible piece of writing,' he said, glancing at Merry once more. 'We're going to take a short comfort break now and then Merina will be happy to sign your books. But before that, I'm sure you're all going to want to put your hands together and thank her for a fascinating, very enjoyable chat.'

Once again, clapping and cheering filled the hall. Merry smiled and waved her own thanks, still overwhelmed with relief that no one had booed. After a few more seconds, Niall leaned towards her. 'Let's get out of here. It sounds like they'll cheer all night if we let them.'

He led her off the back of the stage and she took refuge in the staff toilets, leaning her flushed face against the cold mirror and waiting for the post-event energy to die down a little. She always felt wired afterwards, and sometimes had trouble sleeping, but she knew she'd need this feeling to get through the next few hours of signing. As much as she loved meeting her readers, it often left her exhausted.

It was lovely to see some familiar faces in the queue. Elspeth beamed in delight as she watched Merry scrawl her signature, and clutched the book to her chest as though it was precious. Sheila and Bridget McGinty came together, and Merry saw the corner of a hot-pink book in Bridget's bag as she tucked Merry's on top. Sheila caught her eye and winked. 'I do like to share a good read,' she said. 'And there's quite a waiting list for that one.'

Magnús towered over the table as he held out three copies for her to sign. 'One for my mother, one for my sister, and one for me.'

A flurry of loud sighs broke out among the women nearby and Merry had to hide a smile. 'I would have given you a signed copy for free,' she said. 'To thank you for rescuing me from flat tyre hell.'

'And that would have been very kind of you,' Magnús said gravely. 'But the ticket came with a book and so here we are.'

His eyes met hers and she suddenly wished there weren't

a hundred people in the queue after him, so that she could talk to him properly, the way they had on the journey to and from Kirkwall. And then she remembered that she'd told him she was with Alex, and the thought withered away. 'Well, thank you anyway. Happy reading.'

It took another seventy minutes for her to work her way through the queue. Niall brought her two cups of tea, both of which went undrunk, and hovered at her side, managing the queue and gently hurrying anyone who seemed inclined to monopolize her time. By the time the last book was signed, Merry was so tired she could hardly lift her pen.

'Whisky?' Niall offered, as the last audience member left the hall.

Merry leaned back in her chair and rubbed a hand over her eyes. 'Fresh air,' she said.

'Follow me.'

It turned out that the courtyard in front of the library was still full of people, so Niall herded Merry back into the stacks of books before she was seen. 'We'll wait here. I'm sure they'll drift off in a few minutes – it's too cold to linger.'

The smell of old books and paper surrounded them. Merry took a deep breath, savouring one of her favourite scents, and wondered whether Niall would think she was weird if she took down a book and buried her nose in its pages.

'You gave me a few scary moments in there,' he whispered, smiling in the half-light. 'Kept me on my toes, I can tell you.'

He meant the question about love, Merry supposed, and her refusal to talk about the book she was meant to be writing. 'Sorry about that. I should probably admit that I hadn't even looked at the list of questions you sent over.' She gave him an apologetic look. 'I was too busy writing about Skara Brae.'

Niall tipped his head. 'I don't blame you. And I'm sorry for asking you about the novel you're working on. I should have realized you wouldn't be allowed to talk about it in public.'

'No, it wasn't that . . . ' she trailed off as another wave of weariness washed over her.

Niall waited, his expression quizzical, and Merry was filled with a sudden urge to tell him the truth. It was a risk but at least now she'd proved to both herself and Niall that she hadn't lost her touch entirely; it was early days but maybe – just maybe – she could find a way past the block that had plagued her for longer than she could remember. She gazed into his eyes, battling a rising tide of nausea at the thought of confessing the truth, but the calmness she found there helped. He'd understand. She knew he would.

'There's something I need to tell you,' she began, feeling the heat of shame crawling up her neck. 'I've . . . I've got writer's block – that's why I didn't want to talk about my current novel. I failed to deliver it when it was due and my publisher gave me a generous extension and I missed that too. And it was starting to take over my life – I couldn't sleep, I couldn't eat, I couldn't function because of the crippling self-doubt. I didn't know what to do, until I saw your advert. It felt like a sign so I fired off an application, even though I'm pretty sure it was tantamount to fraud.'

She summoned up the courage to look at him then, expecting him to be angry, but instead she found his gaze was warm with compassion. 'There's no shame in that. You wouldn't be the first person to seek refuge here and I definitely don't think you're a fraud.' He shook his head as though astonished she might even think such a thing. 'I've read your work, remember? And if your reading tonight was anything to go by, you haven't lost your touch.'

Merry took a deep breath. 'That's the first piece of fiction I've written for almost eighteen months.'

The look he fired her way was filled with horrified sympathy. 'I would never have known,' he said quietly. 'To me, it was beautiful and haunting and so good that I almost asked you to read it again immediately. You could have heard a pin drop in the silence after you'd finished, and believe me, that's no small achievement in a roomful of Orcadians.'

A surge of relief flooded over Merry. 'Thank you,' she said, blinking back the unexpected tears that prickled her eyes. 'I was so nervous – I couldn't tell if it was any good, or if I'd done the story justice.'

'Oh, you did,' Niall reassured her. 'It was like we were there when Fen and her people fled and the storm hit.'

The words gave her a further buzz, this time of delighted satisfaction. 'Then I can definitely say that being here has helped with the writer's block. I don't know whether that means I'll be able to make any progress with the novel I have to write – I can't even bear to think about it right now – but just knowing that the ability to write hasn't completely deserted me helps.'

'Let me know what I can do to help,' Niall said. 'I've been told I'm a pretty good listener, especially over a glass or two of whisky.'

'I'll bear that in mind,' she said gratefully. 'Thanks for understanding.'

'No problem,' he said, with a lopsided smile. 'If there's one thing you can rely on a librarian for, it's reading between the lines.'

He glanced over his shoulder then, surveying the now empty courtyard. 'Looks like it's all clear now. I'll give you a few minutes, shall I? I'm sure you're desperate for that fresh air by now, along with a few minutes of alone time.'

It was probably the understatement of the year but Merry appreciated his perceptiveness. She puffed out her cheeks and rubbed her aching shoulders. 'You could say that.'

It was a clear and cloudless night. The library was still lit up, and the glow stretched upwards as well as outwards, but it wasn't enough to dim the stars that glittered against the blue-black sky. Merry gazed upwards, hugging her arms close to her chest and sucking in slow lungfuls of air as she let her tiredness take hold. It had been an adrenaline-fuelled few days: first running with Sheila, then the desperate compulsion to tell Fen's story and lastly this evening. She was going to pay for it all tomorrow, she knew. It might be better not to bother getting out of bed.

The faint crunch of gravel made her turn around and she saw Magnús was standing a few feet away. The light caused a halo to dance around his golden hair and she was reminded fleetingly of the angels she'd seen painted on the walls of the Italian Chapel. 'Hello again,' she said, managing a worn-out smile. 'I thought you'd gone.'

'I was on my way,' he replied. 'And then I saw you were heading for the courtyard too and I must confess that I loitered, in the hope of spending a little more time in your company.'

Merry thought back to the signing queue when she wished for more time to speak to him and couldn't prevent a flutter of pleasure that he'd evidently felt the same way. 'So here we are,' she said, echoing his words to her.

He smiled and the skin around his eyes crinkled in a way that made Merry's own mouth curve into a matching smile. 'Indeed,' he said. 'And I am sure you must be very tired so I will not keep you for long. I simply wanted to extend my hand in friendship once more. I know what it is like to live in a strange place, knowing few people.' He paused and gave her a rueful look. 'Although it is apparent from this evening that you have many friends and admirers already, so perhaps you don't need another.'

Merry felt something constrict inside her; of all the things she'd left behind in London, she supposed it was friendship she missed the most. Jess couldn't offer more than phone support; it would be nice to have someone to go for a drink with occasionally, Merry thought, and she couldn't rely on Niall all the time, no matter how kindly he'd offered. Would it be so very wrong to accept Magnús's friendship, safe in the knowledge that he thought she was in a relationship?

'No, you're right,' she admitted, hesitating for another second or two before making up her mind. 'I don't really know anyone and I could use a friend. So if that offer of a drink is still open ... ?'

He beamed at her with a mixture of surprise and delight. 'Of course! Tomorrow evening? I will pick you up at seven-thirty, yes?'

Squaring her shoulders, Merry nodded before she could change her mind. 'I'd like that. Yes.'

Merry woke late on Saturday morning with the memories of the night before dancing in her head. Had she done the right thing in accepting Magnús's offer of friendship? But she could hardly take it back now – what was done was done. And as Jess would no doubt tell her, it was only a drink. That would have been much easier for Merry to believe if she hadn't had a distinctly non-platonic dream about Magnús just before she'd woken up ...

Pushing the thought away, she got out of bed and wandered through to the kitchen for a cup of tea, wincing as her legs protested after her run two mornings ago. Mug in hand, she headed for the sofa and idly reached for her laptop, intending to go through the emails she'd neglected on Thursday and Friday, but instead her gaze landed on her open notebook, with its page of notes about her visit to the Italian chapel. *That story of Helen's was lovely*, she thought, imagining the moment her grandparents' eyes had first met, perhaps outside a café in Kirkwall. The picture in Merry's mind was so real that she felt she could almost hear the clinking of coffee cups and murmur of conversation. She tapped at the keyboard, easing her way into the scene. The sun was shining. A motorbike might zoom by, sending up a little flurry of dust that neither of Helen's grandparents noticed. And before she knew it, she'd written half a page of words.

She swung her feet onto the sofa and tapped a few more thoughts. Two hours later, her tea was untouched. And Merry had the start of a new story.

Part Two

Sea Breezes at Brightwater Bay

Orkney Literary Society presents

A Writing Workshop with Writer in Residence: Merina Wilde

Is there a story you're longing to tell but don't know where to start?
Maybe you've made a start but don't know what happens next?
Or perhaps you've reached 'The End' and need help to make your story shine?

If any of this sounds like you, why not get inspired by internationally bestselling author Merina Wilde as she shares the tips that catapulted her to the top of the *Sunday Times* bestseller list!

Saturday 4th April
10am–4pm at Orkney Library

Booking essential.
Email: Niall.Gunn@Orkneylib.gov.uk

Chapter Eight

There was snow at Brightwater Bay.

Merry didn't realize immediately; the thick curtains in the bedroom of the croft were drawn for protection against the winter chill, rather than the sun, which, in February on Orkney, didn't rise until long after eight o'clock. A quick glance at her phone told her it was just after seven, so she closed her eyes, burrowing beneath the thick bedcovers once more. It took a moment or two longer for the curious silence to register, and when it did, it caused Merry to frown. Brightwater Bay was hardly King's Cross, but there was a pattern to the sounds she normally woke up to: the distant crash of the waves as they pounded the cliffs and the faint cries of the birds freewheeling over the bay. But today everything seemed muffled, as though she'd spent the night at a loud gig in a tiny club. Merry hadn't been to a club in months, so what was causing this weirdly stifled sense of sound? It was almost as though . . .

A fizzle of excitement ran through Merry as she sat up in bed. There was only one rational explanation, although she'd hardly dared to hope it might happen during her stay. Scotland had more than its fair share of snow, but the Gulf Stream that flowed past the islands meant Orkney escaped the kind of freezing conditions that affected the Scottish mainland. And on a practical level, Merry had been relieved to learn that heavy snowfall was unlikely – the last thing she needed was to be snowbound in a remote clifftop cottage. But the part of her that was a writer, the part of her that was still eight years old, couldn't prevent the thrill of anticipation that coursed through her at the thought of a winter wonderland waiting right outside her front door. Swinging her legs over the edge of the mattress, Merry reached for her dressing gown. There was no point in hiding under the duvet, wondering. The only way to be sure was to investigate.

The blast of cold air that hit her as she opened the front door of the croft confirmed her suspicions: several centimetres of white powder covered the ground between the front door and the edge of the cliff some fifteen metres away. Beyond the meagre puddle of light from the hallway, the skies over the bay were still dark, but Merry knew dawn would soon break over the roof of the croft. And when the sun rose high enough, she'd have a clearer picture of just how much snow had fallen.

The sea was loud now that she was no longer insulated by the snow-laden cottage; in fact, it seemed more furious than ever amid the other-worldly silence. A gust of freezing wind hit her, bringing with it a flurry of sharp flakes laced with a familiar salty tang, and Merry shivered in her dressing gown. As tempting as it was to reach down and brush the snow with her fingers, the sensible thing to do right now was close the door and dress in the warmest clothes she had.

An hour later, full of tea and toast and wrapped up against the cold, Merry ventured over the threshold of the croft. Weak sunlight now sparkled on the freshly decorated landscape; the clouds were leaden, but patches of blue still peeked through. Snowflakes no longer tumbled from the sky, but the wind had thrown those that had fallen into drifts against the cottage wall. Wellies crunching, she picked her way across the expanse of white that led to the fence marking the cliff top. The bench where she usually sat to contemplate the spectacular view was buried, and the cliff walls themselves glistened as though speckled with diamonds. It was almost like being in Narnia, Merry thought, if Lucy Pevensie had emerged from the wardrobe beside the sea instead of into a forest.

She stood for a while, listening to the roar of the Atlantic and allowing her senses to take in the newness of her environment. If her best friend Jess had been there, they might have made a snowman, or at least exchanged a volley of snowballs. Originally from New Zealand, Jess was no stranger to snow and often complained that even in the depths of winter London rarely managed enough to make an ice cube, let alone a snowball – although it was usually enough to bring the transport system to a halt.

She'd be in her element now, Merry thought fondly.

She gazed around until her nose started to run and her toes felt numb, then reluctantly went back inside. Her phone was flashing on the coffee table as she knelt to light the fire, and when she checked the screen she saw there was a message from Niall, the librarian who was her main point of contact as Orkney's Writer in Residence.

Everything OK? We don't have much snow in Kirkwall but it might be different in the wilds!

Merry smiled as she tapped out her reply – it was so thoughtful of him to check on her.

That's because it's all here. It's a good job I planned to spend the day writing because I don't think I'm going anywhere! Thanks for checking on me, though.

Niall's reply was instant:

Happy writing! Let me know if you need anything.

She watched the flames as they began to lick the logs, then padded to the kitchen to make a scalding cup of coffee. When she returned, the fire had started to warm the small living room and her toes had almost defrosted. Settling on the sofa, she reached for her laptop and focused on the words she'd written the day before.

The throaty rumble of an engine outside interrupted her train of thought. She frowned; the croft wasn't exactly on the beaten track – who on earth could it be? And then there was a hearty knock on the door. Pushing her laptop aside, she went to find out.

The man on the doorstep was tall, his features partially

obscured by a thick tartan scarf and a black woollen hat. He tugged the scarf down to smile at Merry.

'Good morning. We've been sent by Niall to make sure you're not snowed in. I'm Hugh Watson.' He waved a gloved hand in the direction of the Land Rover that was parked beside the croft. 'And getting out of the car is my wife, Clare. We're responsible for the menace that is Gordon, among other things.'

Gordon was the goat Merry had found eating the grass roof of the croft the day after she'd first arrived, and he'd been a sporadic visitor since, generally contemplating her with a mildly judgemental expression every time he saw her.

'Lovely to meet you,' she said, as Clare slammed the car door and trudged through the snow to join them. 'I'm Merry.'

'Can you believe this weather?' Clare said in an accent that hinted at Essex roots. The pom–pom on her bobble hat wobbling as she glanced around. 'I haven't seen this much snow for years.'

Merry shook their hands. 'It's very kind of you to take the trouble to come.'

'It's no bother,' Hugh said. 'We've been meaning to drop by and say hello since you arrived, but the farm has kept us busy.'

Clare flashed a smile Merry's way. 'The weather just gave us an excuse.' She bent down to lift a wooden basket from the ground at Hugh's feet. 'And we brought some emergency supplies. I've got bread, milk, eggs and cake.'

The kindness of the gesture touched Merry. 'Thank you. Won't you come in for a cup of tea?'

'We'd love to,' Clare said promptly, but Hugh was gazing at the snow piled up against the doors of the shed housing the car that was part of the Writer in Residence package.

'It's a Mini, isn't it?' he asked her.

She nodded. 'That's right.'

Hugh squared his shoulders. 'Not ideal for this kind of weather, but better than a push bike. The temperature is set to stay low for the next few days so I'll clear you a path to the road, just in case you need to get out and about.'

'Oh, you really don't need to—' Merry started to object.

'It's no bother,' Hugh said again. 'It'll take less than twenty minutes – just long enough for you to make the tea. I'll have two sugars, please.'

He was already heading back to the Land Rover so Merry decided to give in gracefully. She stepped back to let Clare inside. 'How about you – tea or coffee?'

'Tea, please,' Clare said. She pulled the hat from her head, revealing silky blonde hair, and gazed around inquisitively. 'You know, I think this is the first time I've ever been in here.'

Merry took her coat and hung it by the front door, then led her through to the kitchen. 'Oh? You've never visited any of the other writers who have stayed here?'

Clare lowered the basket to the small square table and began to unpack the contents. 'No.' She pulled a conspiratorial face. 'Between you and me, they've tended to be a bit stuffy, and I've never been a fan of their writing anyway. You, on the other hand . . .'

She trailed off and offered Merry a look that was a mixture

of embarrassment and admiration. 'Well, let's just say I've read all your books. Maybe more than once.'

'Thank you,' Merry said, a pleasing glow washing over her. 'It's always lovely when someone says that. Makes up for all the times I've wanted to throw my laptop out of the window.'

The other woman laughed. 'I've never thought of it like that. Being a writer sounds like a dream job, but I suppose it's still hard work.' She gave Merry an openly curious look. 'Is your next book going to be set on Orkney?'

Merry hesitated. Her next book – the one she'd agreed on with her editor, which everyone was expecting her to deliver in two months' time – was currently gathering metaphorical dust in a file on her computer, and she hadn't so much as looked at it since arriving on Orkney. The book she was actually writing, the story that kept her awake at night long after she should have been asleep and had her fingers itching for her keyboard almost from the moment she woke up, was most definitely *not* agreed on with her editor. It wasn't the kind of book Merina Wilde was famous for. It was uncharted territory; a story she really didn't have time to tell. And no one knew she was writing it, not even Jess.

'I'm certainly finding the island inspirational,' Merry said carefully, after a few seconds of thought. 'How could anyone fail to fall in love with such a beautiful place?'

If Clare noticed that Merry had dodged her question, she didn't show it. 'There's plenty of inspiration here, especially for a romance writer.' Her eyes danced. 'And speaking of romance, I hear you've been out and about with Orkney's very own answer to Thor.'

Merry couldn't stop the tide of crimson that flooded her cheeks. 'Do you mean Magnús Ólafsson?' she asked, as much to buy herself time as anything, because there wasn't anyone else Clare could mean – at least not that Merry had met.

'I do,' Clare said. 'Now *there's* a romantic hero just waiting to be written about.'

Merry focused on filling the teapot, but a mental image of Magnús still flashed up in her head: tall, rugged, with shoulder-length golden hair and a magnificent beard that would probably have inspired drinking songs in the kingdoms of his Viking ancestors.

Magnús had stopped to rescue her when the Mini had got a flat tyre in the middle of nowhere, and he'd convinced her to go for a drink with him by way of a thank you. He'd taken her to the Fisherman's Friend pub in Stromness and they'd spent the evening bathed in the glow of the wide stone fireplace. Magnús had been funny and charming and attentive, and the hours had flown by in a blur of laughter – helped by several whisky cocktails on Merry's part. He'd given her a lift back to the croft afterwards and there had been a moment as he'd walked her to the front door that she'd imagined climbing up on tiptoes to kiss him. But he'd stepped back and the moment had passed, leaving Merry both grateful and a tiny bit regretful that she'd made it impossible for things between them to be anything other than platonic. All of which meant she had to agree with Clare's analysis – Magnús Ólafsson did have all the hallmarks of the perfect romantic hero. But that wasn't a conversation she was ready to have with someone she'd only just met, no matter how lovely she seemed.

'No romance there – we're just friends,' she told Clare, striving to keep her tone light. 'I think he felt sorry for me, not knowing anyone here, and took me under his wing.'

Clare raised her eyebrows. 'Lucky you. I know several women who have been trying to get under that wing for years.'

Determined not to blush, Merry summoned an awkward smile. Now was the time to mention Alex, her childhood sweetheart, whose existence gave Merry a ready-made excuse to avoid romantic temptations during her six months on Orkney, with Magnús or anyone else. The fact that she and Alex had split up the previous November was another of Merry's secrets, along with her inability to write the book she was meant to be writing. 'Well, I don't suppose Magnús is short of admirers but, as I say, he's a friend. I'm . . . I've got a boyfriend. Back in London.'

Perhaps it was the way she stumbled over the words or something in her tone, but Merry suspected the look Clare sent her way was knowing. 'That doesn't mean you can't write Magnús into a book, does it?'

'No, it doesn't,' Merry had to concede, although it wouldn't do much for her overactive imagination to think of him that way.

Clearing her throat, she loaded a tray with the teapot and mugs, before reaching for the cake. 'This smells wonderful,' she said, unwrapping the waxed cloth to release the sweet scent of citrus mingled with sugar.

'Lemon Madeira,' Clare replied. 'I wish I could say I slaved over a hot oven to make it myself, but I'm the world's worst baker. It came from the Italian bakery in Kirkwall – have you visited yet?'

Merry's ears pricked up. She'd seen the bakery from a distance but hadn't found the time to visit. And of course it made sense that it would be Italian – many prisoners of war had been kept on Orkney during the Second World War and not all of them returned home once the fighting had stopped. She knew of at least one love affair that had bloomed as a result.

Could there be a connection? she wondered.

'Italian bakery?' she repeated. 'No, I haven't been there yet, but it sounds like my kind of place.'

'Rossi's is everyone's kind of place,' Clare said. 'It's a family-run business, which is often the way on Orkney, with three generations working there now. And the result is cakes and desserts to die for. Morag insists on Sicilian lemons for this Madeira, which means it's like a little slice of sunshine on a plate.'

It sounded heavenly to Merry and she made a mental note to visit as soon as the snow had melted. 'Thanks for sharing it with me.'

'You're doing me a favour,' Clare said ruefully. She patted her stomach. 'If it's in the house I'll only eat it, and you know what they say – a moment on the lips . . .'

Merry lifted the tray and carried it through to the living room. 'I'm amazed Sheila hasn't recruited you to keep her company on her clifftop runs,' she told Clare, conjuring up a mental image of her wonderful but slightly terrifying 79-year-old neighbour, who liked nothing better than a kamikaze run along the coast. 'I'm still not sure how she convinced me to join her, but it's definitely helping with my writer's backside.'

'Sheila knows me too well to even think of asking me,' Clare said cheerfully. 'But you're fresh meat. And too polite to say no.'

There was some truth in that, Merry thought, remembering the way Sheila had bulldozed her into that first early morning run. And the unaccustomed exercise had been hard – she'd thought her lungs might burst as she'd tried to keep up with the formidable older woman pounding the path ahead of her. But the next run had been easier, and the one after that had almost been enjoyable, and now, just three weeks later, Merry found herself looking forward to the peculiar exhilaration she'd come to associate with pushing her body into keeping up with her neighbour. 'I might have caught the bug,' she admitted to Clare.

'Don't tell Sheila that,' Clare advised in mock horror. 'She'll sign you up to the Orkney half-marathon in a heartbeat.'

'Not a chance,' Merry said firmly.

They sat on the sofa and Merry steered the conversation round to Clare's life on the farm. It wasn't that Merry didn't like talking about herself, more that she found other people fascinating and she never knew when she'd hear something that might spark an idea for a story. And she liked Clare already – she was funny and self-deprecating and it was no hardship to listen to her talk, especially when she mentioned the llamas she and Hugh kept for their wool.

'If you think Gordon is a handful, you should meet Rosie,' she told Merry with a wry shake of her head. 'We only got her to help protect the livestock from predators, and somehow she's now the matriarch of a whole herd.'

'So that's your business now? Llama wool?' Merry asked.

Clare nodded. 'We still keep the sheep and cows, but farmers have to move with the times and there's a huge market for llama and alpaca fibre. We get it spun into wool and ship it all over the world.'

There was another heavy knock on the door, which made them both jump. 'Sorry,' Clare said. 'Hugh's not known for a delicate approach to anything.'

His face was ruddy as he stamped his feet on the doormat and stepped into the croft. 'All done. Just take it slowly, keep the car in a low gear, and you'll reach the road no trouble.'

Merry smiled. 'Thank you so much. I really appreciate your help.'

He took the mug of tea she gave him and tipped his head in thanks. 'We look out for each other here, as you've no doubt discovered.'

Merry's eyes met Clare's. 'I have,' she said, and they both

smiled. 'Now, how about a slice of cake? Because I've got to be honest, if I have to wait any longer, I might drool on the carpet.'

Chapter Nine

The snow lingered for two days before rain washed in overnight and melted every trace. Merry was sorry to see it go – it might have made life a little more complicated, but the beauty it brought more than made up for any inconvenience. And really, there'd been very little of that; thanks to Hugh, she'd known she could venture out if she needed to, but she had taken the opportunity to hide away and write.

Niall wasn't the only one to check up on her. Jess had video-called the moment Merry's photo of the snow had reached her, demanding that Merry go outside and share the magic.

'Looks pretty secluded,' Jess had observed when Merry panned the camera around to show her the snow-covered landscape. 'Seems to me that what you need is some company.'

Merry laughed. 'I'm perfectly fine on my own. I have everything I need.'

Jess shook her head. 'I think you'll find you're running

out of logs for your fire, Mer. You need a big strong man to come and chop some more.' She left a meaningful pause. 'If only you knew one.'

'Jess—'

'Don't *Jess* me,' her friend said impatiently. 'This is a solid gold opportunity for you to get some sizzling Viking action and I would be failing in my best friend duties if I didn't point that out. I bet he's got an enormous axe.'

'Jess!'

'I'm just saying.' Her voice softened. 'As I've told you a million times already, it's high time you forgot Alex, babes. Why not see if Magnús can help you do that?'

All the usual objections crowded into Merry's thoughts: it was too soon to date again, she was on Orkney in a professional capacity, there was no point in starting a relationship when she'd be leaving in less than six months' time … But by far the biggest obstacle was that Merry had already lied about her relationship with Alex. And Jess had no idea she'd done so. 'I—I'll think about it.'

'I'm not suggesting you marry him,' Jess said. 'Just have some fun. And maybe some hot sex. Why not invite him over and see what happens?'

'I'm sure he's busy,' Merry replied, thinking guiltily of the solicitous message Magnús had sent that morning; he'd taken some persuasion that she didn't need him to drive over to keep her company.

Jess sighed. 'Don't make me come up there and play matchmaker, Mer. Because I will, if that's what it takes.'

The thought filled Merry with a longing to see Jess that was so strong she almost suggested she caught the next plane north. Except that would cause more problems than it solved, she thought, which probably meant Jess could *never* visit her on Orkney. 'I'll think about it,' she repeated, crossing her fingers.

And then the snow had gone, taking any temptation to act on Jess's instructions with it, and Merry had been glad about that, even though she missed the wintry view across Brightwater Bay. She could only hope Jess's determination to matchmake would melt away too.

The clouds had cleared by the time Merry backed the Mini out of the shed beside the croft on Thursday morning. Carefully, she trundled to the main road and pointed the car towards Kirkwall. The blue skies made the journey even more of a pleasure than usual and she found herself slowing the car as she passed the tall stones of the Ring of Brodgar, marvelling as she always did at the feats of human endeavour that had put them there. Niall had once told her that there was nothing ordinary about Orkney, and it was a sentiment Merry found herself agreeing with almost every day. It was unlike anywhere else she had ever been.

She found Niall in his office at the library.

'This is an unexpected pleasure,' he said, his face lighting up when he saw her in the doorway. 'How are you? Did you enjoy the snow?'

Merry's first impression when she'd met Niall was that he must somehow be related to Clark Kent; he had the same combination of dark hair and blue eyes, and the slightly pre-occupied manner that suggested he was only half paying attention to the world around him. That changed the moment he smiled. Merry was sure she couldn't be the only one to have noticed a definite Superman vibe there. And he was different when he was talking about something he felt passionate about, like the abandoned Neolithic village of Skara Brae, or some other aspect of Orkney, or a book he'd read and loved. That was when his enthusiasm shone through and Merry wondered how on earth he was still single when half the women on Orkney must see what she saw when she looked at him.

'I'm fine,' she told him. 'And the snow was amazing. I wanted to thank you for sending Hugh and Clare to check I was coping, and to see if you wanted to grab an early lunch.'

If Niall was surprised by the invitation, he didn't show it. 'Always. What's the occasion – or isn't there one?'

Merry smiled. 'Research trip . . . kind of. I've heard great things about Rossi's.'

'Excellent choice,' Niall observed, getting to his feet and reaching for his coat. 'Although I think we both know you had me at *early lunch.*'

Rossi's occupied a double-fronted sandstone building with glorious arched windows that held a mouth-watering array of baked treats. Golden cannoli packed with fresh cream and raspberries nestled beside lobster-tailed shells of crisp *sfogliatelle*, rainbow-coloured macarons and meringues filled another shelf, and row after row of croissants and other delicious pastries lay below those. The other window was dedicated to savoury treats: glistening sausage rolls, delectably stuffed pasties and soft floury rolls that almost begged the onlooker to tear them apart. Inside, Merry could see an old-fashioned glass display counter promising more tasty treats, and tables covered with gingham-checked cloths, most of which were occupied. And behind the counter, she saw a familiar face: Helen, the woman she'd met in the Italian chapel a fortnight or so earlier, who had shared the romantic story of how her grandparents had met and fallen in love. The story Merry hadn't been able to stop thinking about ever since.

Niall pulled open the white wooden door and gestured inside. 'Shall we?'

Helen spotted them immediately and her face broke into a delighted grin. She dropped the tea-towel she was holding and hurried out from the counter. 'How lovely to see you again!' she said, beaming at Merry. 'I've been wondering how you've been getting on.'

'I'm fine,' Merry answered, returning her smile. 'Niall has been looking after me very well.'

Helen nodded in approval. 'He takes his work seriously.'

'Always,' Niall said solemnly. 'Especially when it comes to showing our visitors the best place for tiramisu.'

Helen laughed as she gave Merry a sideways glance. 'And we don't even pay him to say that. Are you here to shop or for lunch?'

Merry's gaze was drawn to the counter display and felt her mouth water a little. 'Erm . . . both?'

'Then let me find you a table,' Helen said. 'My grand-mother is going to be so excited you're here. I told her all about meeting you the other week.'

Ushering them to an empty table, Helen gave each of them a menu, promising to be back in a few minutes. Niall studied the menu for a moment then glanced at Merry. 'So, I'm curious – you said back at the library that this is a research trip. How did you mean?'

Merry paused. She wasn't ready to tell anyone about the idea that was growing in her head; apart from anything else, she wasn't exactly sure what it was, let alone whether she could actually write it. But she didn't want to rebuff Niall either, so she kept her eyes on the menu as she answered him. 'I'm fascinated by everything about Orkney. And I can hardly write about the islands if I haven't explored them in detail, can I?'

Niall clearly read between the lines, as she'd expected he would. 'I completely get the need for authenticity – isn't there some age-old rule about writing what you know?'

'There is,' Merry said, wryly aware that if the rule was true, she should be writing about misery and heartbreak right now. 'But like most writing rules, there's a balance to be found. Some people spend so much time on research that they never get around to the writing part.'

'Well, in the interests of authenticity, I think you should definitely visit the Highland Park whisky distillery,' Niall said.

Merry raised an eyebrow, thinking of the bottle he'd left

in her welcome box; it was almost empty. 'That's not a bad idea,' she said slowly. 'I mean, I wouldn't want to be remiss in my duties as Orkney's Writer in Residence. I really should explore every aspect of the culture here, including the time-honoured tradition of making whisky.'

'You should,' Niall said, his expression innocent. 'And I should come with you, to make sure you properly understand the significance of whisky to the islands and their people.'

'Good point,' she agreed, trying not to grin. 'When shall we go?'

'I've got the day off on Saturday if you're free?'

Merry spooled mentally through her diary, which was the emptiest it had ever been: no book launches for author friends, no publisher lunches, no drinks with Jess in Chiswick . . . The only firm commitment in her diary at the moment was the creative writing workshop at the beginning of April. 'I don't think I've got plans,' she told Niall.

'Excellent,' he said, looking pleased. 'I'm sure they'll be delighted to show you round. Leave it with me.'

Helen materialized beside them, notepad and pen poised. 'What can I get you?'

Merry chose the fresh minestrone soup with black olive ciabatta, while Niall ordered a mozzarella and prosciutto panini, and Helen took the order through the checked curtain to where Merry assumed the kitchen was. She gazed around the café, drinking in as much detail as she could; every effort had been taken to reproduce the atmosphere and charm of an Italian café and she wondered whether Helen's grandfather had opened the business when he'd returned after the war in search of the woman he'd fallen in love with. It couldn't be a coincidence that his wife and daughter and granddaughter all worked together in an Italian bakery in the middle of Orkney, could it?

'A macaron for your thoughts,' Niall said, cutting into her musings.

Merry smiled. 'Deal. I was just wondering how this bakery came to be here, that's all.'

Niall tipped his head. 'Because it's Italian, you mean? I daresay Morag and Agnes will tell you themselves, but I think it was Giovanni's way of putting down roots; making a life here by bringing a taste of Italy to his new home.'

Merry smiled, her suspicions confirmed. She should have anticipated Niall would know the history of Helen's family – the Orkney community was incredibly close-knit, as she supposed island communities often were, and she'd seen first-hand how fascinated Niall was by the past. Maybe she should tell him about the seeds of the story that was growing on her laptop, but she wanted to run it past Helen first. It wasn't that she needed permission, exactly – she wasn't using their story – but Helen's tale of her grandparents' love affair had inspired Merry to create characters of her own and she wanted to make sure the family knew what she planned. She hoped they'd be pleased.

'That makes sense,' she said to Niall. 'It must have been hard, leaving Italy behind and starting a new life here.'

'He wasn't the first person to come to Orkney and fall in

love – both with the islands and the people. It's why we have such a rich heritage,' he replied, and his mouth twisted into a smile. 'Although in Giovanni's case, there was a special someone who captured his heart.'

Merry felt something stir inside her head, a faint tickle that she'd come to associate with the writing part of her brain. Maybe the story she was building wasn't as far removed from her other books as she'd thought; maybe it was just a different kind of love story – one that embraced different kinds of love: the love people had for their homeland, or other places that touched their hearts. The love they felt for their family and the bonds that held them together when circumstances tried to tear them apart. And perhaps even the love the land had for its people. A shiver danced across Merry's shoulders at this last thought, and it took her a moment to place the cause – it was the sensation of dots being joined in her imagination; an electric fizz of the kind she'd hardly felt in the last year or more. But Orkney seemed to have the power to inspire her. She had felt that same fizz after visiting Skara Brae with Niall, when she'd almost been able to touch the characters she had created, and it was happening now, when she thought about all the different things love might be.

Forcing herself to focus, Merry smiled at Niall. 'Of course. Although Orkney casts such a powerful spell that I can't imagine anyone ever wants to leave.'

'You'll get no argument from me,' he said, making no apparent effort to hide his pleasure. 'Does that mean the magic is working on you too?'

She saw no reason to lie. He'd heard her read the story she'd written after her visit to Skara Brae and knew she'd been inspired by the mystery of the village and its people. 'Do you know, I think it might be.'

'Excellent,' Niall said, his eyes shining, and Merry had the distinct impression he was resisting an urge to clap. 'And there's plenty you haven't seen. We'll make an Orcadian out of you yet.'

She laughed. 'Do you say that to all your Writers in Residence?'

His cheeks reddened slightly, but he didn't look away. 'No, not all of them.'

Merry thought back to Clare's comments a few days earlier, when she'd hinted that some of the previous writers had come across as stuffy. It was hard to imagine anyone staying that way in the face of such friendliness and charm – everyone she'd met so far had been both kind and interested in her, and in the way she interacted with their treasured stories and history. It was, she decided, both an honour and a responsibility. 'Well, I'm pleased you think I'd fit in.'

Whatever Niall had been about to say in reply was lost as Helen arrived with their drinks and some grissini. She flashed an apologetic smile as she hurried away to serve another customer.

'Bookings for the writing workshop are going well,' Niall said as he reached for a breadstick. 'In fact, I think it's going to be a sell-out.'

'That's wonderful news,' Merry replied, and forced down

the uneasy thought that she couldn't inspire a roomful of writers if she hardly wrote herself. 'I'm looking forward to it.'

Niall paused as he chewed. 'I hope you're ready to meet some of our more eccentric residents. I recognize some of the names on the delegate list and at least one has a very high opinion of his own talent.'

Merry's heart sank into her boots. 'Oh?'

'He's written one book already – a semi-autobiographical account of growing up on Orkney,' Niall said, then sighed. 'He asked me for advice on getting it published and I tried to tell him I didn't think it was quite ready for submission to publishers, but that wasn't what he wanted to hear.'

She offered a sympathetic grimace; she'd met plenty of writers who were so keen to send their work out into the world that they weren't prepared to make them the best stories they could be.

Niall went on. 'Eventually, after many rejections, he self-published and has sold a fair few copies to locals – enough to convince him that traditional publishing is run by short-sighted idiots who don't recognize his brilliance.'

Merry tried not to groan. 'Is he working on another book?'

'So I understand,' Niall said. He gave her a rueful smile. 'Although he hasn't asked me to read it, what with me being one of the idiots who doesn't appreciate him. Anyway, I thought I'd give you the heads-up.'

'Thank you,' Merry replied, and wondered who else she might encounter on the course. She had no doubt there would be some talented writers – there always were. Just as there was often one who came along not to learn, but in the expectation of being discovered . . .

And then Helen was back with their food, which caused Merry to push the thought of the writing course to the back of her mind as she inhaled the mouth-watering scent of freshly baked bread and piping hot soup.

'Enjoy,' Helen said, as she backed away. 'Let me know if you need anything else.'

Both the soup and the bread were as delicious as Merry anticipated. She asked Niall about his work at the library as they ate, and he told her about the new computer system that allowed users to access ebooks on their smartphones and other devices much more efficiently than before. 'It's perfect for those readers who live on the more remote islands, or those who can't get to the library as often as they'd like,' he explained. 'They can download an ebook from home and read it, or even pick it up on audiobook, and at the end of the loan period, it simply vanishes from their device. No more worrying about late fines.'

Merry noticed Helen glance over several times as she ate, with a curious gaze that was half professional curiosity and half impatience. She didn't neglect the other customers, but she was there the moment Merry laid down her spoon and pushed the empty bowl away with a satisfied sigh.

'Everything okay?' Helen asked, reaching for the bowl.

'More than okay,' Merry replied. 'It was the best, freshest minestrone soup I've ever had.'

Niall nodded. 'Mine was delicious too. Compliments to the chef.'

Helen threw a delighted look back at the checked curtain. 'I'll let my grandmother know. Now, can I tempt you with the dessert menu?'

Merry smiled and exchanged a look with Niall. 'I think it would be rude not to look, wouldn't it?'

She had the tiramisu, on Niall's recommendation, and had to concede it was better than any she'd tasted in London. By the time they'd finished eating, the lunchtime rush seemed to be dissipating and the bakery was much quieter. Helen asked whether Merry might spare a few minutes to pop into the kitchen to meet her mother and grandmother.

'Of course,' Merry said. 'I'd love to.'

She could see the family resemblance from the moment she stepped into the bright, airy kitchen. Morag Rossi might be white-haired and almost bird-like in old age, but her chin was strong and her blue eyes lively, just like those of her grand-daughter. Agnes had brown eyes – inherited from her father, Merry assumed – but her smile was identical to Helen's as she greeted Merry and Niall.

'It's so wonderful to meet you,' Agnes said. 'Helen has been raving on about your books non-stop and we've all read them.'

Merry smiled. 'It's very kind of you to say so.'

Morag nodded at Niall. 'You made a good choice with this one. She's got the magic touch.'

'Thank you, Morag,' Niall said gravely. 'I think you're absolutely right.'

'I'm delighted to be here,' Merry said, feeling her cheeks start to burn. 'Orkney is a special place.'

'It is,' Morag said. 'Especially for those with the imagination to appreciate it. I hope you find some good stories here.'

Merry knew an opening when she saw it. 'It's funny you should say that. Helen told me the story of how you met your husband and – well, I haven't been able to stop thinking about it.' She paused and took a deep breath, deliberately not looking Niall's way. 'So, I wondered if you'd mind very much if I used it as inspiration for a story of my own.'

The words hung in the air for a moment, long enough to convince Merry that she'd made a terrible mistake. Then Morag let out a surprised-sounding huff of laughter. 'Goodness, I wouldn't mind at all.' She fixed Merry with a twinkling gaze. 'Although I'm sure your hero will have a wee bit more gumption than my Giovanni. I loved him dearly, but I think if I hadn't told him I was going to marry another man he'd never have found the nerve to come back to Orkney.'

Agnes stared at her mother open-mouthed. 'I didn't know that. I've always thought Dad came back because he couldn't stay away from you.'

Morag dipped her head. 'Well, doubtless there was a bit of that too. But he'd got settled back in Italy after the war, remembered how much he loved the warm weather, and I was worried we'd become nothing more than pen pals.' She nodded at Niall. 'So, I hatched a plan with Niall's grandfather and I told Giovanni he'd asked me to marry him.'

'Mum!' Agnes said, aghast, but Morag simply smiled.

'It worked,' she said. 'He came over on the next boat and marched straight round to Ian's house to tell him I wouldn't be marrying anyone but him.'

Merry couldn't believe what she was hearing. 'Without asking you first?'

'Without so much as a by-your-leave,' Morag replied. 'So, naturally, I told him I wouldn't marry anyone who hadn't even the manners to ask me if I would.'

'And that's when he proposed, down on one knee, by the harbour. With all the fishermen looking on and cheering,' Helen breathed.

'With an engagement ring he'd bought in Italy before catching the boat,' Agnes added in a fond tone of voice that told Merry that this part of the story at least was family legend.

Morag sighed. 'I suppose I should have played hard to get,' she said, with a sideways glance that encompassed both Helen and Merry. 'Isn't that what you young ladies do now? But I knew I loved him – had done since the first moment our eyes met – and it didn't seem fair to keep him waiting. So, I said yes. And we were married for forty-three years.'

'It sounds to me like Giovanni had plenty of gumption,' Merry said, smiling. 'Although perhaps not quite as much as you.'

'I was only nineteen, but I knew I couldn't leave it up to him to come back of his own accord,' Morag said. 'Men have their uses, but they're simple creatures and easily distracted.

They need a kick up the backside sometimes to make them see what's in front of them.'

'Gran!' Helen said, firing an embarrassed look Niall's way, but his mouth quirked into a wry little smile.

'*Och*, don't mind me,' he said cheerfully. 'Everyone knows I'm a total disaster when it comes to romance. Maybe I need you to take me in hand, Morag.'

The old woman shook her head. 'Someone certainly needs to,' she said. She glanced at Merry. 'Anyway, I hope that helps with your story. I look forward to reading it when it's ready.'

Merry smiled in gratitude. 'Thank you. I'll make sure you're one of the very first readers.' She looked at Agnes and Helen. 'You too. I'd love to hear what you think, when the time comes.'

'And me,' Niall said. 'I want first dibs too.'

Merry laughed. 'Of course. I've never written a historical novel before – you're going to be my right-hand man for all things Orkney-related.'

Helen clapped her hands, her gaze sparkling. 'This is amazing. A Merina Wilde story inspired by my very own family! I can't wait to read it.'

And Merry smiled in response, trying to ignore the little voice in the back of her head telling her she was a fool to even consider stepping outside her comfort zone. 'And I can't wait to write it.'

Chapter Ten

'Am I keeping you up?'

Merry finished her second yawn and gave Sheila an apologetic look across the living room sofa, even though the words had clearly been tinged with amusement rather than annoyance. 'Sorry. I was up late with a book Niall gave me.'

Her neighbour placed her mug on the coffee table. 'Sounds like a page-turner. Anything I might have read?'

Merry gave the question some consideration. As far as she could tell, Sheila's reading tastes varied from Ian Rankin to Jill Mansell, and she had, since Merry's arrival on Orkney, developed an almost insatiable taste for Jess's early bonkbuster novels, which she'd shared with her book club. Niall had mentioned he'd had to put in a special request for additional copies from other libraries to keep up with demand. But Merry had no idea whether Sheila's range might incorporate a non-fiction account of the Second World War and its effect on Orkney. Perhaps she had read it, given it concerned her home turf.

'It's called *Orkney's War* by Alison Johnson. Do you know it?'

Sheila nodded. 'I do – the author came to the islands a few times doing research and suchlike. It's not my kind of thing, though. I like a good story to sweep me off my feet and it doesn't feel quite the same when you know it really happened.' She paused and pulled a face. 'Especially not when you're related to some of the people who feature.'

Merry thought back to the chapter she'd read the night before, which had been about the terrible sinking of HMS *Royal Oak* by a German U-boat at Scapa Flow in 1939. The ship had been swallowed up by the sea in just minutes, taking 834 men with it. The loss had prompted Winston Churchill to order the construction of permanent barriers to prevent future attacks and the project had taken four years to complete. Helen's grandfather, Giovanni, had been one of the Italian prisoners of war put to work on the barriers. Did that mean Sheila might have Italian ancestry too?

But Sheila shook her head when Merry asked the question.

'My father worked as an engineer for Balfour Beatty,' she said. 'They were in charge of getting the work done, although he always used to say there was no point in shutting the stable door after the horse had bolted.'

There had been no more U-boat attacks, at least, Merry thought, and the barriers served a useful purpose in connecting the previously isolated islands. She'd used one of the causeways to visit the chapel on Lamb Holm; it was where she'd first met Helen.

'They're still an impressive bit of engineering,' she said to Sheila. 'It must have been very satisfying to be involved with the construction of something that helps so many people every day and has stood the test of time.'

'I've never thought of it that way,' Sheila admitted, after a moment's reflection. 'But you're right – Dad should have been proud and so should I. Thank you.'

'I'll keep an eye out for his name as I'm reading,' Merry said.

As she sipped her tea, she saw Sheila cast a covert look around the croft's living room. It wasn't the first time she'd done so in the thirty minutes she'd been sitting on the sofa, and Merry couldn't imagine what was sparking the older woman's curiosity.

A moment later everything became clear. Or at least slightly less puzzling.

'How's your young man in London?' Sheila said. 'Andy, isn't it? Have you had a wee tiff?'

Merry felt a rush of blood to her cheeks. There was no possible way anyone on Orkney could know the truth … *was there?*

She took another sip of tea, hiding behind the rim of the mug to regain some of her composure. 'It's Alex. He's fine and, no, we haven't argued – what makes you say that?'

Sheila shrugged. 'My husband always gave me a card on St Valentine's Day, even after thirty years of marriage, and sometimes he even managed flowers. I know it's been almost a week since the fourteenth, but I used to leave the card up for a good few days.' She gave Merry a shrewd-eyed look. 'And it strikes me that someone who deals in romance for a living might be the type to expect her man to show how much he loves her, but mebbe you're not the sentimental type.'

And now Merry's cheeks flamed even more, because Alex *had* always made an effort on Valentine's Day and she'd felt his absence keenly this year. Not that she'd expected a card – he didn't even have her address on Orkney – but there'd been no message on her phone, nothing to indicate she was still on his mind. After fifteen years together, she might have expected something . . . but she knew that was wishful thinking. Nothing in the way Alex had behaved since their break-up suggested he felt anything for her, apart from the single message he'd sent a few weeks ago to confirm she'd left London. Jess was right – it was time she got over him. But she wasn't sure she wanted Sheila to know the truth about Alex. She wasn't sure she wanted *anyone* on Orkney to know.

'No card or flowers,' she said, forcing herself to sound light. 'We used to do all that in the early days, but not anymore.'

None of it was a lie, she told herself, but Sheila wasn't buying it for a second. 'Not even when you're hundreds of miles apart?' she asked, arching her eyebrows.

It was the only flaw in Merry's explanation, because that was exactly what most loving couples would do – seek to prove their love to their partner through the time-honoured traditions of the day. 'Not this year,' she said and hoped her smile wasn't as brittle as it felt.

The other woman studied her for a moment, looking as

though there was something she very much wanted to say. Instead, she sighed and folded her hands in obvious disapproval. 'Well, I suppose it's your business.' She fixed Merry with a purposeful stare. 'And I didn't come here to poke my nose into your love life – there was something else I wanted to discuss.'

'Oh?' Merry said, suddenly even more wary.

Sheila's eyes gleamed. 'As you know, my daughter refuses to believe that I'm as fit as I've always been and perfectly capable of running the odd mile here and there.'

Merry hid a smile. Sheila's idea of the odd mile tended to stretch to five, along the edge of the clifftops that lined the coast, with no deference to the weather or time of year. 'She worries about you, that's all.'

'She *fusses*,' Sheila replied, with an indignant sniff. 'But I will say she's been much better since I started running with you. And what with it being the Orkney half-marathon soon—'

And there it was, Merry thought. She held up a hand. 'Let me stop—'

'—I wanted to let you know I signed us both up,' Sheila finished, as though Merry hadn't spoken. 'As a gift from me to you.'

The sheer brazenness almost took Merry's breath away. 'A *gift*?'

'Aye,' Sheila replied. 'Just think of all the plotting you can do during our training runs. You'll thank me one day.'

A half-marathon, Merry thought faintly. Thirteen miles

of undoubted pain and suffering when the furthest she'd ever covered was three. It didn't seem possible she'd ever be able to run that far but, then again, she hadn't known she could manage three, and it had got easier every time she ran. Maybe she'd be able to do it, given enough time to prepare . . .

'When is it?'

'Saturday ninth of May,' Sheila said. 'Plenty of time.'

Merry did a quick calculation in her head. 'That's less than three months,' she said, staring at her neighbour's complacent expression. 'You can't be serious!'

'Of course I am,' Sheila said. 'What's the point of being alive if you never challenge yourself?'

Ordinarily, Merry would agree with the sentiment, but this seemed impossible. 'Eleven weeks, Sheila. That's not a challenge, it's a death wish.'

'Hush now,' Sheila said, frowning. 'You sound like my daughter. No one is saying you'll set a blistering pace, but imagine the sense of satisfaction you'll feel when you cross the finishing line.'

'*If* I cross the finishing line,' Merry pointed out. 'If running thirteen miles doesn't actually kill me first.'

'Naturally,' Sheila said. 'Would it help to think of it as part of your Writer in Residence duties?'

Merry cast her mind back to Niall's email containing the formal terms and conditions of her role: she was fairly certain it hadn't committed her to kamikaze death runs along Orkney's peaks and troughs. 'How?'

'Contributing to the local community,' Sheila said. 'You might inspire me to try my hand at writing something.'

Suddenly, an idea popped into Merry's head. 'I'll make you a deal. You come along to my creative writing course in April, and I'll agree to run this half-marathon.'

The older woman held out a hand. 'Deal.'

The alacrity with which she accepted the offer made Merry suspicious, but she knew there was no way Sheila would let her back down now. She took the older woman's hand and shook it once. 'I hope I'm not going to regret this.'

'Like I said, you'll be thanking me,' Sheila said. 'Preferably with a mention in the acknowledgements of your next book. Or maybe you could name a character after me.'

Merry couldn't help laughing. 'I'm sure that could be arranged.'

The conversation moved on as they finished their tea. Finally, Sheila got to her feet with a sigh, and reached for her coat. 'So, I'll see you in the morning for a run, yes? A nice four-miler should get the blood pumping.'

Merry agreed, although she fully intended to stop when she felt she couldn't take any more. She followed Sheila to the door. 'See you in the morning.'

Her neighbour was several paces away when she turned back. 'I hear you've been stepping out with Magnús.' She paused and fired an innocent look Merry's way. 'Now *there's* a man who knows how to send a Valentine's Day card.'

She was gone before Merry could reply, which was almost certainly a good thing. Sheila's attitude bore a striking resemblance to Jess's; in fact, if Merry didn't know better, she might suspect the two women were working together to push her towards Magnús. And a sly little voice in Merry's head reminded her that maybe she wouldn't mind if they succeeded.

Niall insisted on picking Merry up for their tour of the whisky distillery on Saturday.

'No point in visiting if you can't sample the goods,' he told her over the phone on Friday evening. 'And believe me, you're going to want to try the whisky. I get the impression they're laying on a few special treats in your honour.'

He arrived at 11.30 on the dot and raised both eyebrows at the face Merry pulled as she bent to do up her boots. 'Bad back?' he asked as she straightened.

'Bad everything,' Merry replied, trying not to groan. 'Sheila made me run for what felt like a hundred miles yesterday and my muscles are making their dissatisfaction known.'

'Ah,' Niall said, perfectly straight-faced. 'Has she talked you into the half-marathon, by any chance?'

Merry reached for her coat and wondered, not for the first time, why her arms were aching just as much as her legs. If the next eleven weeks were going to make her feel this bad, maybe she ought to quit now. 'How did you guess?' she said with a sigh.

He laughed. 'I've known Sheila all my life. When she's determined to do something, she doesn't let anything stand in her way. And she's already worked out you're a soft touch – she probably didn't even ask you, just presented you with a *fait accompli*.'

'Right again,' Merry admitted. 'She even suggested it was part of my job as Writer in Residence, although I did persuade her to come to the creative writing workshop in return.'

The look Niall flashed her on the way to the car was one of amusement laced with pity. 'Excellent work. I suppose I shouldn't mention that Sheila was one of the first bookings we took, along with Bridget McGinty.'

It took a moment for Merry to grasp the implications of his words. 'You mean I didn't persuade her at all? She was already coming?'

Niall started the car. 'Don't feel bad,' he said kindly. 'Sheila and her pals are famously crafty. There are times when I think even Machiavelli could have learned a thing or two from them.'

Merry managed a rueful laugh. 'So I'm beginning to appreciate. I can't wait to see what they write!'

The Highland Park distillery was just outside Kirkwall, which meant their route took them past the Brodgar standing stones. The sky was iron grey, with dramatic dark clouds and a definite threat of rain, and Merry had been looking forward to seeing the ring of tall monoliths out-lined against the spectacular backdrop. But the view was nothing like the one she'd been anticipating; the stones were hidden by serious-looking trucks and a multitude of smaller vans that filled the makeshift car park and grass verges. There were a couple of executive coaches parked by the side of the road and it was almost impossible to see past to the stones at all.

'What's going on?' she asked.

Niall's gaze flickered to the trucks and then back to the road. 'Location filming for some movie or another. It happens fairly often around the islands, although it's hard to get permission to film at the stones themselves.' He glanced across again. 'This must be a Hollywood blockbuster or something equally big budget.'

Merry craned her neck to stare as they passed and thought she caught a glimpse of a camera swinging around on a crane over the stones. 'I wonder what the film is.'

'I could probably find out,' Niall offered, as the stones receded behind them. 'The crew will be staying locally – someone is bound to know what's going on.'

Merry shook her head. 'No, don't worry. I'm just curious.'

Niall gave her a sideways look. 'I'd have thought you'd have seen loads of film sets, what with living in London. It feels like every movie made has a scene set there these days.'

'I'm a writer,' Merry reminded him solemnly. 'I don't get out much.'

The rest of the journey was uneventful, until Niall pulled into the car park next to the grey stone buildings of the distillery. 'I'll leave the car here,' he said, as Merry got out and stretched her grumbling muscles. 'Pick it up tomorrow. But don't worry – I've arranged transport for later.'

As usual, he'd thought of everything, Merry observed. It

was going to be a shock when she eventually went back to London and had to start thinking for herself again.

Iron lanterns glowed invitingly against the gloomy skies, even though it wasn't long after midday, and lit the doorway to the visitors' centre. Merry followed Niall inside, where he was greeted with a broad smile by a curly-haired, russet-bearded man in a navy blue checked shirt.

'Good to see you, Niall,' the man said, moving from behind a solid-looking cash desk to extend a hand. 'And this must be Merina.'

'It is,' Niall said. 'Merry, meet Andrew Driver, master craftsman and one of the most intimidating men I've ever met.'

Merry laughed. 'Pleased to meet you,' she said as she shook his hand, noticing the rough skin and calloused fingers. Whatever his role at the distillery, she was willing to bet he didn't spend much time behind the cash register.

'And you,' Andrew said. 'So, I hear you're a whisky drinker?'

'I am,' she answered, wondering what else Niall had said. 'Although I'm embarrassed to admit I've only just discovered Highland Park.'

'Better late than never,' Andrew said. 'And you're about to discover a whole lot more. I hope you brought your drinking boots.'

Merry opened her mouth to reply, but Niall beat her to it. 'We talked about this, Andrew. Remember what happened the last time you said that?'

'Not really,' Andrew said cheerfully. 'But I know a very good time was had by all.'

'Until the hangover the next day,' Niall said, grimacing.

Merry glanced from one man to the other with some amusement. 'I'm looking forward to learning about the process of distilling whisky too,' she said. 'If there's time in between the sampling.'

Andrew smiled. 'We're giving you the full Orcadian Vintages tour, which usually takes around three hours and includes some parts of the distillery not usually open to the public. It finishes up in front of an open fire, with some of our finest vintages to taste.'

Niall gave her a pained look. 'And that's where things started to get hazy last time. But I'm sure you'll be more sensible than me.'

'We encourage everyone to drink responsibly,' Andrew said, shaking his head at Niall. 'But some of us are more responsible than others.'

This was a different side to Niall, Merry thought, as she followed the two men through a door in the stone wall. So far, he'd been the consummate professional in all his dealings with her, but she sensed he was more relaxed – more off-duty – today. It was almost certainly because of Andrew, who was obviously a good friend, but Merry liked to think it was a sign that he was starting to consider her a friend too, rather than part of his job. She had no intention of over-indulging on whisky, however. No matter how good the vintage samples were.

She found everything about the tour fascinating, from the aged barrels in the warehouse to the smoky scent that filled the air as they neared the rooms with the kilns. Andrew talked as they walked, explaining that the distillery officially dated back to 1798, but there had been an illegal operation selling contraband on the site long before that.

'And the techniques we use are even older,' he said, with more than a touch of pride. 'Most of the senior staff have Viking ancestors and we work hard to preserve the knowledge and skill that's been handed down for centuries, whether that applies to the whisky itself or the way we craft the casks that hold it.'

'It sounds wonderful,' Merry said, admiring the fierce orange glow of the wide kiln. 'Is that peat you're burning there?'

He nodded. 'From Hobbister Moor, a few miles away from here. It's around four thousand years old and is what gives our whisky its rich, unique taste. If there's one thing Orkney isn't short of, it's peat.'

'Have you noticed there aren't many trees?' Niall asked Merry. 'Our climate is mild, but we're open to the elements and the winds can be pretty fierce. There are a few woodlands tucked away here and there, but you won't find the views obscured by swathes of forest.'

'Which is ironic, considering we're an island nation with a strong tradition of boatbuilding,' Andrew said, grinning. 'Do you suppose that's got something to do with the lack of trees?'

'Well, the peat smells amazing,' Merry said, knowing the aroma would linger on her hair and clothes for days. 'No wonder your whisky wins so many awards.'

'Speaking of whisky, I think it's high time we drank some,' Andrew said. 'Let's head back to the warehouse and you can try some straight from the cask.'

He led them back through to the warehouse, where he introduced them to a shaven-headed man called Jamie. 'He's in charge of the 100,000 or so oak casks we keep on site and I'm pretty sure there are some that only he knows about,' Andrew said, as Jamie shyly shook Merry's hand. 'We'd be in deep trouble if he ever left us, which is why he gets paid more than me.'

Jamie laughed. 'I wish!'

Andrew tipped his head. 'I thought Merry and Niall could try one of the 2015 casks – might be a nice contrast with the older vintages they'll be sampling later?'

'Aye, that's a good idea,' Jamie said, and thought for a moment. 'I've got just the ticket. Follow me.'

The sheer number of casks made Merry's head spin; row after row of dark brown barrels that all looked the same. She'd known Highland Park whisky was good, but she'd had no idea just how big the distillery's range was. But Jamie obviously knew his way round the labyrinth of barrels and after a brisk minute's walk, he stopped beside a row that appeared to be exactly the same as its neighbours. He placed a hand on one of the casks. 'This one is still maturing – it won't be ready for a few years yet. We taste a sample from each cask on a regular basis, to make sure the flavours are developing in the way we're expecting.'

Merry frowned. 'Why wouldn't they?'

Jamie shrugged. 'We're careful about the casks we use – only the best US and European oak. Our staff are pretty knowledgeable about wood and the art of barrel-making – we even consult with a boatbuilder in Kirkwall from time to time, to draw in more expertise.'

Merry's ears pricked up at that. *How many boatbuilders could there be in a place the size of Kirkwall?*

She could only think of one.

Jamie continued to speak, oblivious to the curious look she sent his way. 'But occasionally we get it wrong,' he went on. 'If a cask isn't stored in the right way or the wood is too green, that might affect the flavour of the whisky.'

'And sometimes it's the peat,' Andrew said. 'The acid levels have to be just right for the smoky flavour to permeate the barley in the way we need it to.'

Niall leaned towards Merry. 'Distilling whisky is a dark art,' he said solemnly. 'Wait until they tell you about the full moon sacrifice.'

Reaching behind the cask, Jamie pulled out a cluster of small tasting glasses and filled them one by one from the cask. Amber liquid danced in each glass as he handed them round.

Andrew inhaled deeply above the rim of his glass. 'You'll notice the peaty smell is strong – it hasn't had time to mellow.'

Merry watched Niall breathe in the aroma and followed his lead. Andrew was right, the scent from the whisky in her glass was earthy and strong – she thought she detected more than a hint of moss too, although she had no idea if it was just her imagination. And then Andrew took a sip, rolling the liquid around his mouth for several long seconds before swallowing.

'Coming along nicely,' he told Jamie. 'In a few more years it'll be smoother than your head.'

Jamie rolled his eyes. Merry hid her smile with the rim of her glass and took a warming mouthful of the golden liquid. Her tongue tingled with sudden heat and immediately, she understood what Andrew had meant: the whisky was good, but it wasn't a patch on the bottle Niall had given her when she'd first arrived on Orkney. It was rougher, somehow, and lacked the aged quality and polish of the whisky she had back at the croft. It felt unready.

She swallowed, and felt the liquid burn its way down to her stomach. 'It's still wonderful.'

Jamie put his empty glass down. 'Aye, it's not bad. But I'd be interested to hear what you think once Andrew has stunned your taste buds with the vintage malts.'

'And on that subject,' Andrew said, passing his glass back to Jamie. 'Let's head that way now. We've got a private tasting room all set up – not that we really need it today, since there aren't any Saturday tours running at this time of year, but there's a lovely open fire in there that should be just about roaring now.'

'Perfect,' Merry said, with a grateful smile. She'd have to find a way to thank Niall for organizing this; it was a wonderful way to spend a Saturday afternoon.

She was just about to follow Andrew's lead out of the cask labyrinth when she saw a familiar mane of hair swish by the end of a row. Stopping, she peered after its owner. 'Magnús?' she called, blinking incredulously. 'Is that you?'

There was a brief silence, then a tanned face appeared around the line of casks, framed by long golden hair that almost glowed like a halo under the lights. Green eyes stared at Merry for a moment, then the face split into a delighted beam. 'Merina! This is a most unexpected pleasure.'

She couldn't help smiling in return. 'It is. How are you?'

Andrew turned back to see what was happening and gazed back and forth between them. 'Ah, I see you two have already met. Magnús is the consultant boatbuilder Jamie mentioned earlier.'

'I wondered if it might be,' Merry admitted. 'You did say most of your staff were Vikings.'

Andrew grunted. 'Although none of us look the part quite so heroically as Magnús here.'

It was true, Merry had to concede; even in jeans and a white t-shirt, Magnús somehow managed to look as though he'd stepped straight from the ninth century. It was the long hair and impeccable beard, she thought, not to mention the chiselled features and unavoidable muscles and towering height. Magnús made every other man in the room look ordinary, including Niall and he was practically Superman.

'How are you enjoying the tour?' Magnús asked. 'Is this book research or purely for fun?'

'Both, probably,' Merry said honestly. 'There's definitely

a story or two here and I'm sure a bottle or two of whisky will be coming home with me later.'

'I recommend the Valkyrie,' Magnús said. 'And not just because I can totally imagine you swooping into Valhalla on a winged steed, sword in hand like a glorious avenging angel.'

The flattery was so outrageous, and the overall image so unlike her, that Merry almost blushed. 'I don't know about that – the last time I met a horse it tried to eat my dress.'

Andrew shook his head and sent a dry glance Jamie's way. 'Forget your bald head, I think we should aspire to making our whisky as smooth as Magnús's chat-up lines.'

Everyone laughed as Magnús accepted the obviously familiar teasing with good grace, although Merry had the fleeting impression that Niall's laughter was less enthusiastic than the others. His gaze met hers for a moment, as though gauging her reaction and she wondered at the slight coolness she saw there. But then he looked away and she decided she must have imagined it; there was no reason for him to be anything other than amused by the banter between Andrew and Magnús.

'And I agree that the Valkyrie would suit Merry very much,' Andrew went on. 'But we've several vintage whiskies to try, and I'm under strict instructions from Niall not to get anyone drunk, so perhaps we'll save it for another time.'

'Of course,' Magnús said, firing an easy smile Merry's way. 'You're here for six months – plenty of time to work your way through everything on offer.'

He only meant the whisky, Merry told herself, but she

couldn't prevent a tiny fizzle of excitement at the thought of trying some of Orkney's *other* Viking temptations. And then she gave herself a stern mental shake. This was Jess's doing, she decided – Jess and Sheila's. All their talk of being snowed in and grand romantic gestures had turned her head, encouraging her to see more than was actually there. She cleared her throat and sought a reply that covered all the conversational bases. 'I'm looking forward to trying everything.'

There was a momentary silence, during which Merry had the horrible suspicion she'd somehow managed to say the wrong thing, then Niall stepped forward with a brisk smile. 'In which case, we really should get on.'

'Of course,' Andrew replied. 'Follow me.'

Merry only had a few seconds to say a hurried goodbye to Jamie and Magnús before Andrew ushered them back the way they'd come. He kept up his stream of fascinating information about the distillery as they walked and Merry asked the occasional question, but Niall was quiet, listening without comment. She glanced at him once or twice, wondering whether she was imagining the set jaw and tension around his eyes. It must be her writer's imagination, she decided, as they entered a tastefully lit room with a glorious fire crackling in the hearth. A low table sat in front of four winged armchairs, with a tray of black, silver-stoppered bottles and glasses that sparkled in the firelight. Music played quietly in the background, an acoustic melody that Merry guessed was probably a traditional folksong, and the atmosphere was so inviting that she almost wanted to move in.

'This is the Eunson Room,' Andrew said. 'Named after the distillery founder, Magnus Eunson, who was quite a character by all accounts.'

Another Magnús, Merry noted, and wondered if this one was descended from Vikings too – probably, with a name like that. The cathedral in Kirkwall was called St Magnus, after the Viking Earl who had been martyred in the 12th century, and she was sure that had something to do with the popularity of the name on Orkney, although the Magnús Merry knew had been born in Iceland. She imagined the name was pretty popular there, too.

Andrew waved Merry and Niall towards the chairs and proceeded to pour the first of what would be several generous measures from the array of bottles. He explained what they could expect from each vintage as they went, but Merry was still surprised by the subtle differences in flavour; her favourite was the oldest vintage they tried, from 1968, but she didn't dare ask how much a bottle would cost. More than she would be willing to pay, even in the warm and slightly tipsy glow of whisky good enough for Odin himself.

'Good, isn't it?' Niall said, after draining the last dregs from his tasting glass. 'It almost makes me want to give up being a librarian and get a job as a taster here instead.'

Merry gave him a half-smile. 'Some people say you should never turn your passion into a job. Not if you want to stay passionate, that is.'

She'd heard it said of writing – that making it into a career killed the love – but it had never been that way for her and

Holly Hepburn

she was sure it wasn't the reason for her writer's block. She'd just grown tired and each story had become harder to write, and taken longer, until at last she found she had no energy to write at all. That was when her problems had really started. But those dark days seemed to be behind her, thanks to the breath-taking wonder of Orkney.

Beside her, Niall shook his head. 'I've been a librarian for ten years and I'm as passionate about books as I've ever been. I can't see that changing.'

'No, I know,' Merry replied. 'But books are different – there will always be authors who take a well-worn idea and make it fresh again. Whereas whisky . . .' She paused to take a breath and ploughed on. 'Whisky doesn't have quite the infinite variety that books can offer. It might lose its appeal after a while.'

She glanced across at Andrew, hoping she hadn't accidentally insulted him. But he simply smiled, raising his glass in the firelight to swirl the vibrant gold-hued liquid around the glass. 'It hasn't yet,' he said, and tipped his glass in her direction. '*Skál!*'

Dusk was falling when Andrew finally conceded they had tasted enough and allowed them to leave the distillery, on the understanding that they came back again soon. Merry held up the bag containing her purchased bottle of Valkyrie, plus the souvenir tasting glass and bottle of ten-year-old Viking Scars whisky that Andrew had presented to her as a gift. 'Just as soon as I've worked my way through this!'

The night was cold as Merry and Niall waited for their

taxi. Andrew had wanted them to stay inside, but Merry's head was woozy with whisky and she found herself craving fresh air. Not that it was helping her to feel any less woozy; if anything, her sense of woolly but warm well-being had increased now that she was outside.

'S'freezing,' she said to Niall as they leaned against his car, staring up at the first stars of the evening.

Niall nodded. 'The taxi won't be long.' He gave her a concerned look. 'But we can wait inside if you like?'

'No,' she said, and took another deep breath of bracing air. 'No, it's nice to be outside. I had a lovely time today, by the way. Thank you for organizing it.'

'It was my pleasure,' he said, then grinned. 'It actually was – I love visiting the distillery. Thanks for giving me an excuse.'

'I'm not surprised – your friends seem like a lot of fun,' she said. 'And I think I could listen to Andrew talk for hours.'

Niall raised his eyebrows. 'Believe me, he'd let you. But they're a great bunch.' He paused and when he spoke again, his tone had a strange stiffness to it. 'Just be careful around Magnús. I know you've become friends but I get the impression he's ... that he ...' He puffed out a long breath that clouded in the cold. 'That his intentions are not entirely platonic.'

Merry knew without having to look that he was blushing. This was because of Alex, she thought; because she'd led Niall to believe she had a relationship to go back to in London. It had made sense at the time, but now, with several glasses of whisky running through her veins and dulling her thoughts, she couldn't really remember why she'd stretched the truth. Something to do with professionalism, she decided, and keeping life simple. And she'd told the same lie to Magnús, so at least she could reassure Niall on that point. Even if she was starting to accept that her own intentions towards Magnús weren't platonic either.

'No need to worry about that,' she said, as stoutly as she could. 'He knows about . . . that I'm not—'

She stopped as a sudden urge to come clean washed over her. It was stupid to maintain the lie, especially since it meant giving Alex space in her head – space he no longer deserved or had a right to occupy. It was time she moved on and she couldn't do that if she was pretending to still be in a relationship with someone who'd made it clear he didn't want her. Merry gazed blearily up at the stars and willed herself to think clearly. It was also true that Magnús wasn't a long-term prospect but, as Jess had pointed out, she didn't have to marry him, just have some fun. But that definitely wasn't an option if everyone thought she wasn't single . . .

'There's something I need to tell you,' she said, reluctantly turning her head to look at him.

By the light from the wrought-iron lanterns, Merry saw he was frowning. Doubt made her hesitate; was this something she ought to admit while not entirely sober? Maybe she should wait for a better opportunity, one when she wasn't tipsy. But then she might lack the courage to say anything at all.

Reaching a decision, she opened her mouth to speak again, but a flash of car headlights made them both stare at the car park entrance as a taxi swung in through the gates.

A second later, Niall turned back. 'Merry?' he said. 'What were you going to say?'

But the moment had passed and the compulsion to come clean had gone with it. Merry reached for the bag that held her whisky and shook her head. 'Nothing important. Come on, let's get out of the cold.'

Chapter Eleven

Merry woke up the next morning, head pounding, with no real memory of going to bed. Her mouth was sour with the taste of whisky and she knew the bedroom must reek of it. She lay still, wincing at the throbbing around her temples, and tried to piece together events from the night before. There had obviously been more whisky after she'd left the distillery – she hadn't been drunk enough to cause a hangover this bad. She remembered getting into the taxi, recalled saying goodbye to Niall as he got out at a very nice cottage on the other side of Kirkwall. Then she'd arrived home, had managed to light a fire in the hearth, and her memories started to become less clear.

It had seemed like a good idea to open the bottle of Valkyrie, she thought slowly. At some point, there'd been dancing, followed by some terrible singing to old Christina Aguilera songs. She'd been on the phone too – who had she called? And her eyes felt hot and gritty, suggesting there might have been tears. Merry turned cold and sat up fast, groaning at the agonizing burst of pain in her head. She grappled with her phone, not wanting to look at the list of calls made but desperate to know the truth. *Please don't let it be Alex*, she thought as she brushed the screen with trembling fingers. Then a worse possibility occurred to her: *please don't let it be Niall . . .*

It was eleven-thirty and she had three missed calls from Jess, plus six unread messages. The call log supplied the details her memory could not and she slumped against the pillow when she saw the numbers she'd called the night before. Not Alex. Not Niall. Just Jess. She breathed a sigh of relief that caught in her throat as her eyes focused on the final call made.

And Magnús.

Merry closed her eyes, trying to dredge up the details of what she'd said. The call had lasted four minutes and fifty-eight seconds – plenty of time for her to embarrass herself to an order of magnitude greater than any she'd previously experienced.

Magnús, she thought weakly. She'd almost have preferred Alex.

Her phone vibrated in her hand, causing her eyes to snap open in a way that hurt all the way to the back of her skull. The screen told her it was Jess, and she considered ignoring it, except that she knew it wouldn't do any good. Sooner or later, she'd have to face her best friend.

She accepted the call. 'Don't raise your voice above a whisper or I'm hanging up.'

'Are you kidding?' Jess's voice was louder than a foghorn. 'I'm just glad you're alive. I had visions of you throwing yourself over the cliff.'

A tsunami of shame washed over Merry. 'Oh god. Was I really that bad?'

Jess sighed. 'Worse. I haven't known you to be that incoherent since the night we emptied that bottle of tequila at Christmas. You sang the whole of "Fighter".'

'Sorry,' Merry said miserably.

'Hey, it's me you're talking to.' Jess's voice softened. 'You don't ever have to apologize to me, Mer. Maybe to Christina Aguilera, but not to me.'

Merry felt the ghost of a smile tug at her lips. 'Okay.'

'Especially not when you spent so long ranting about what a dick Alex is,' her best friend went on. 'It's taken a ridiculous amount of time, but I think you might finally be getting over him.'

And now Merry allowed the smile to take hold. 'Maybe.'

'There's no *maybe* about it – you told me in pretty explicit terms what you wanted to do to that hot Viking of yours.' There was a definite element of glee underlying the words *hot Viking*. 'And I wholeheartedly approved of your plan.'

The smile vanished. For a moment, Merry thought she might actually throw up. 'Which was?' she croaked.

'You were a bit hazy on the specifics, but I approved on general principles.' Jess paused. 'Why?'

'Guess who I called straight after I got off the phone to you?'

'Oh.'

Merry sighed and ran a hand over her puffy eyes. 'Yeah. *Oh.*'

There was a brief silence. 'Do you remember what you said? Any of it?'

'No.'

Another pause, and then Jess rallied. 'Well, let's hope for the best here. Maybe you laid out your wicked plans and he hotfooted it over to your place. Are you sure you're alone?'

That was a suggestion that sent Merry spiralling into an even deeper maelstrom of panic. She lowered the phone and listened: nothing. Getting out of bed, she tiptoed to the door, ignoring the sudden shiver caused by cold air hitting her alcohol-frazzled skin. The bathroom was empty, and so were the kitchen and living room.

'I suppose he might have left already,' Jess mused, when Merry passed on the absence of anyone else in the croft. 'Any evidence that you weren't alone?'

Merry edged closer to the coffee table, with its still-open whisky bottle and single empty glass. There was a plate with a half-eaten cracker and a lump of cheddar. Her laptop was open; she didn't want to even look at whatever it was she'd written. 'I don't think he was here,' she told Jess. 'I feel sure I'd remember.'

'But you don't remember what you talked about?'

Merry sat heavily on the sofa and wished she was still unconscious. 'No.'

'Well, there's only one way to find out,' Jess said, sounding more cheerful than Merry found helpful. 'You're going to have to ask him.'

'I can't!' Merry said, aghast.

'You can,' Jess replied. 'And besides, what else are you going to do – avoid him for the next five and a half months?'

'I could come home,' Merry said. 'Say I've got a family emergency and just never come back.'

'Or you could send him a message and ask. Grasp the nettle. Lance the boil. Drain the wound.'

'Yeah, I get the idea,' Merry said, as her stomach churned ominously.

Jess's voice was warm with sympathy. 'Sorry, babes. You know I'm right.'

The problem was that Merry *did* know: the only way to deal with something this toe-curlingly bad was head-on. 'Fine. I'll message him.'

'Good girl. Ring me as soon as you have details,' Jess instructed.

It took Merry ten minutes to compose her two-sentence message to Magnús:

Hey, how are you? Think I owe you an apology!

His reply was almost instant:

Not at all! How's the head?

Merry gnawed at a fingernail. How to respond in a way that might encourage him to offer up some glimmer of what they had talked about?

It's been better. But I'm sorry for bothering you. I hope I wasn't too annoying?

This time, there was a slight pause before Magnús replied and Merry wondered whether he was trying to come up with a tactful response.

You weren't annoying at all. Luckily, I am a big Destiny's Child fan and your singing voice is quite charming.

She couldn't type fast enough:

My singing voice?

Merry saw the blue ticks that indicated the message had been read and then her phone buzzed. Magnús was calling her.

Feeling sicker than ever, she answered. 'Hello.'

'I thought it might be easier to explain over the phone, rather than messages,' he said, and Merry couldn't prevent an image of him, hair blowing in the breeze, from popping into her head. It was a shame she couldn't ever see him again, not after the extreme mortification of today.

'Uh – okay,' she managed. 'Thanks.'

'I must admit I was surprised to see your number appear on my phone last night,' Magnús said. 'But I assumed you were still with Niall and Andrew. And then I answered and realized you were not.'

Merry wished a plume of magma would spurt up from one of the long-dead volcanoes under her feet and incinerate her where she stood. 'No.'

'And then I was disappointed to realize you hadn't meant to call me at all,' Magnús went on, his tone cheery. 'In fact, you weren't aware that you had. Unless you meant to sere-nade me with an extremely heartfelt rendition of "Survivor".'

The relief was like balm to her jangling nerves. If she hadn't known she was calling him, maybe she hadn't said anything too embarrassing. 'I *sang* to you?'

'You did,' Magnús confirmed. 'Although as I say, you didn't know you were singing to me. So, I listened for a short while, in case I was mistaken, and then I did the gentlemanly thing and hung up.'

Four minutes and fifty-eight seconds, Merry thought and swallowed. Probably the whole song and then the start of something else – Kelly Clarkson or Gloria Gaynor, she supposed. But at least she hadn't said anything regrettable. Surely, he would tell her if she had . . .

'I still owe you an apology,' she insisted. 'No one needs to hear me sing, least of all when I'm a bit the worse for whisky.'

He laughed. 'As I said, your voice was charming. And quite emphatic. But if you really feel the need to make it up to me, you can meet me for a drink tomorrow night.'

She let out a mirthless bark of laughter that made her head feel as though it might topple from her neck. 'I'm never drinking again.'

'In which case, you can drive,' he said, apparently unperturbed.

Merry sighed. She couldn't say no, not when he'd asked in lieu of an apology. 'Okay – where?'

'The Sword and Thistle, north of Kirkwall,' he said promptly. 'They have a music quiz that I've always wanted to try. There's a round on girl bands that you might be good at.'

'Ha ha,' Merry said, and then realized she really was

smiling. 'Okay, you've got a deal. Let me know the time and where to pick you up.'

'I will,' Magnús said. He paused. 'And just so you know, if I were Alex, I would definitely have put a ring on it.'

He hung up, leaving Merry to stare at her phone in bewildered mortification. She could only hope that the comment had been in reference to her Spotify playlist. Because really, what else could it mean?

The pub was busier than Merry had been expecting. They arrived a few minutes before 8pm and all the tables were taken. There were a number of customers leaning on the bar, pens and papers in hand, and Merry was about to suggest she and Magnús do the same when a shout rang out and an arm waved in their direction.

'Some friends,' he explained, and began to thread his way through the tables. 'I hope you don't mind if we join them?'

How could she mind? Merry thought. Her stomach had lurched and fizzed in the usual way as she'd watched him walk down the path from his house and she'd had to forcibly remind herself this wasn't a date. The presence of his friends helped to reinforce that. It was a pub quiz with some people he knew – all above board. Nothing to feed Merry's feverish imagination.

She stopped dead when they reached the table where his friends were sitting. She didn't know four out of the five occupants. But the fifth was very familiar indeed.

'Nick!' she cried, as he looked up and noticed her.

His face lit up in recognition. 'Merry! What the bloody hell are you doing here?'

She grinned and hurried around the table to kiss the tall, dark-haired man on both cheeks. What were the chances of running into anyone she knew from London in a pub on Orkney? Furthermore, what were the chances that the person she ran into would be Nick Borrowdale, the actor who was the darling of the BBC's Sunday night flagship show, *Smugglers' Inn*?

'Never mind me, what are you doing this far north?' she demanded, with a quick glance at his companions to make sure she didn't recognize anyone else. 'You do know you're not in Cornwall, right?'

'Filming,' he said, 'and not *Smugglers' Inn*.'

The penny dropped in Merry's head. 'So that's why no one can see the Ring of Brodgar for trucks and camera rigs,' she said. 'It's you!'

Nick flashed his trademark lazy grin and Merry was sure the entire room sighed. 'I'm afraid so. But it's not just me – let me introduce you to Elspeth Connor, the Oscar-nominated director of *The Islander*, which is the epic blockbuster we're filming right now.'

Merry smiled at the petite, blonde-haired woman and kissed both cheeks in greeting. 'Lovely to meet you. I'm Merina Wilde – Merry, for short.'

'And this is Sam Silverton, our producer,' Nick went on. 'And beside him, the world's best stuntman, Kiki Braun, and our sound engineer, Polly Jones.'

Once Merry had said hello to everyone, she turned to introduce Magnús to Nick, but it soon became obvious he knew him already.

'Magnús has been advising our production department for months,' Elspeth explained with a smile. 'Apparently, you can't make an authentic Viking boat without consulting him, and I'm told he's a whizz with a circular saw.'

Merry glanced at Magnús, who had the grace to look sheepish. 'Is there anyone you don't know?'

'Not on Orkney,' he replied. 'Or in Reykjavik.'

'Never mind that,' Nick interrupted. 'I still don't understand why you're here. The last time I saw you was in that pub in Richmond.'

Merry filled in the blanks, carefully omitting any mention of splitting up with Alex.

'Merry is a massively successful novelist,' Nick explained to the rest of the table. 'So, if we get any literature questions, she's our girl.'

Merry laughed. 'I think it's a music quiz, so I'm afraid I'll be no use at all.'

'And has Alex made an honest woman of you yet?' Nick asked.

Merry swallowed. 'Not yet.'

Nick rolled his eyes. 'Now there's a man who doesn't know how lucky he is.'

She felt someone staring at her. When she turned her head, she saw it was Magnús, his forehead crinkled into a puzzled frown as he studied her. She opened her mouth to ask what was wrong, but Sam Silverton was leaning across the table. 'What kind of novels do you write, Merry?'

That was a very good question, Merry thought, as she pushed Magnús's odd look to the back of her mind and tried to work out a passable answer to Sam's enquiry. 'I usually write romantic fiction,' she said carefully. 'Love stories – the kind that make people smile and generally feel happy.'

Sam didn't miss a beat. 'Usually?'

Merry hesitated but saw no harm in explaining a little more; only Magnús had any local interest and she was itching to bounce the idea off someone else creative, especially someone in the business of stories. Normally, that would be her agent, but Phoebe didn't even know Merry was writing this particular story . . .

'I'm working on something a little different right now, a historical story inspired by an epic, real-life love affair here on Orkney during the Second World War.'

From the corner of her eye, she saw Magnús watching her again and ignored him. Sam's face came alive with interest. 'Sounds fascinating. How far have you got?'

She paused again, wondering how much more to reveal and decided it didn't really matter. 'I've got a working outline and the first 15,000 or so words. It's still early days.'

Sam looked as though he was about to say more, but there was a crackle from the overhead speakers and a booming voice announced the start of the quiz. Magnús handed her the answer sheet and a pen. 'You're the only writer here – it stands to reason you'll have the best handwriting!'

It soon became clear that some of the other teams were taking the quiz very seriously. Merry got a few questions right, but mostly concentrated on writing down the answers her team-mates gave her. At the end, they discovered they'd come respectably mid-table, which Kiki said was probably all for the best. 'We don't want to make enemies among the locals,' he said, with a wink.

Once the winners had been announced, Magnús went to the bar for drinks and Merry caught up with all Nick's news. He was still single, but claimed to be enjoying the bachelor lifestyle, and set to start filming the final series of *Smugglers' Inn* that summer.

'And then what?' Merry asked.

Nick shrugged. 'No idea. I think there are a few movies in the pipeline, but I haven't accepted any new roles yet. I'll see if any of them catch my eye first.'

'What he means is, he'll see if any of the leading ladies catches his eye,' Kiki said, and everyone laughed.

'That's not fair,' Nick objected, although his tone was mild. 'I'll have you know I'm a one-woman man. I just haven't met the right woman yet.'

When Magnús returned, Merry found herself on the opposite side of the table to him and opportunities to talk were limited. She chatted to Sam instead, listening to his description of *The Islander*, which was a time-travel blockbuster about a Jacobite soldier doomed to relive the bloodiest battle of the war until he worked out how to save the life of his childhood sweetheart. Needless to say, Nick was playing the role of the tragic hero and Sam had every confidence the film would be a smash hit as a result. 'He's box office gold,' the producer said, firing a contented look Nick's way. 'The screen lights up every time he's on it.'

And then the pub was closing and it was time to head out into the night. Sam pressed a business card into her hand as she said goodbye. 'Your new novel sounds like my kind of story. Send me that outline when you're ready.'

Merry stared at him, stunned, then pulled herself together. 'I will. Thanks, Sam.'

She barely listened as Nick promised to let her know next time he was in London so that they could meet up for dinner, but his parting comment brought her back down to earth. 'Maybe I'll give Alex a nudge at the same time,' he joked, planting a kiss on each cheek. 'Tell him it's about time he got you down that aisle.'

Her head was whirling as she navigated the way back to Magnús's home. He was uncharacteristically quiet too, although he answered politely enough when Merry asked about his plans for the following day. But he spent much of the journey gazing out at the darkness beyond the window. When Merry pulled up outside his house, he sat in silence for a moment, then turned to her with the same puzzled expression she'd noticed earlier.

'There is something I don't understand,' he said, after a few more seconds of quiet. 'Why did you tell Nick you were still with Alex?'

The inside of the car lurched crazily, making Merry think

for a split second that they had been hit. Then she realized the car hadn't moved at all, it was simply her shocked reaction to a question she hadn't been expecting. 'Sorry?' she said. 'I don't think I understand.'

'Yes, you do,' Magnús said slowly and patiently. 'I asked why you told Nick you were still in a relationship with Alex, when you and I both know it is not true.'

A roaring started in Merry's ears. How could he possibly know? No one on Orkney knew. Unless . . . her mind flew back to her drunken phone call on Saturday night, and Magnús's parting shot the next day: *if I were Alex, I would definitely have put a ring on it* . . . Her insides contracted in horror as she stared at him. What had he overheard?

'How do you know?' she asked through lips that didn't feel like her own.

The car was dark apart from the glow of the streetlight, and Magnús's face was shrouded in shadow. Even so, Merry could see the sympathy in his eyes as he studied her. 'Once you'd finished singing, you became upset,' he said. 'I only listened for a moment or two, but I heard enough to understand that Alex had ended things some time ago.'

Blood rushed to Merry's cheeks and she was grateful for the cover of darkness so Magnús couldn't see her embarrassment. She swallowed, trying to work out how to respond and then realized it was far too late to try and save face. She had to tell the truth. 'It was last November. You'd think I'd be over it by now.'

'Not at all,' he said. 'There's no rule book for getting over a broken heart – it takes time.'

She said nothing, staring out of the windscreen at the dimly lit street and cursing her own stupidity for lying in the first place. 'It's part of the reason I came here,' she said, after what felt like an age had passed by. 'I wanted a fresh start, somewhere I wasn't constantly reminded that he wasn't there anymore. And there was the small matter of not being able to write in London.'

'Perfectly understandable.'

His voice was so gentle and encouraging that Merry felt the walls she'd been using to block off all the hurt and disappointment and anxiety of the last year and more start to crumble. For a moment, she considered shoring them up and telling Magnús with a bright smile that everything was fine really. But she was weary of pretending, tired of hiding behind Alex, and so, with an effort that cost her more than she'd expected, she let the walls collapse.

The world didn't end. Magnús seemed to sense she needed time to gather her thoughts and waited patiently for her to be ready, even though Merry thought it must have been more than a minute since she'd last spoken. 'I didn't set out to lie about Alex and me,' she said finally. 'I just wanted to keep things simple and, well, I thought it would be easier to do that with a fiancé back in London. And ... I suppose there was a part of me that wanted to still believe it was true.'

She stopped speaking and waited for the tears that should accompany so heavy an admission. They didn't come; her eyes remained dry and her heart didn't feel as though it might crack again. She probed further, pushing into the corners where her deepest sorrow usually hid, and was surprised to find nothing there. No pain, no aching loss, no longing for the comfort of knowing Alex would always be there. The space where her unhappiness had been felt empty and clean, as though the walls hadn't been holding her up but keeping all her sadness in.

Merry let out a tiny incredulous huff. Jess had repeatedly told her she needed to let go of the past but she hadn't really understood what her friend meant – until now. 'Wow,' she said, in a voice that was shaky with amazement. 'I feel so much . . . lighter.'

Magnús smiled. 'Perhaps now your fresh start can really begin.'

A bubble of giddy laughter eddied up inside her and forced its way out. Merry clamped one hand over her mouth; Magnús might be understanding now, but he was going to think she'd lost the plot if she gave in to this almost uncontrollable urge to laugh out loud. She waited until the desire had subsided to remove her hand and answer him. 'Perhaps it can.' On impulse, she reached across and squeezed his broad forearm. 'Thank you.'

His gaze was soft. 'I didn't do anything.'

'You made me admit the truth,' she replied. 'And that meant I had to step out from Alex's shadow once and for all.'

'Then I am glad I was able to help,' Magnús said, and reached for the car door.

'Wait,' Merry said as another, less gratifying, thought occurred to her. 'Is that why you invited me to the quiz, even though you already planned to go with friends? Because you knew about Alex and felt sorry for me?'

'No. As I told you yesterday, I wanted to check out the quiz and asked you to join me. Then Sam and Nick found out about it and suggested we go as a group.' He paused and smiled. 'I thought it might do you good to spend time with some other creative people. And I was right.'

'So, it wasn't a pity date, then?' Merry pressed and then cursed her own stupidity – it hadn't been a date at all – but Magnús didn't seem to notice.

'I promise that whatever I feel for you, it's not pity. The truth is, I just wanted to spend some time with you. Everything else came after.'

Whatever I feel for you . . . What was that supposed to mean, she wondered as her head began to whirl once more. 'Well, good,' she managed eventually. 'That's fine, then.'

He waited for a moment longer, as though expecting her to say something else, then pushed the handle and opened the door. 'Sleep well, Merry. Let's speak again soon.'

She sat still after he'd gone, her hands resting on the steering wheel as she tried to process everything that had just happened. And then she turned the Mini towards the croft and went home to Brightwater Bay.

Chapter Twelve

Merry kept herself to herself for the next week. She answered messages from Niall and Magnús and Jess, went running when Sheila demanded, and chivvied Gordon the goat off the roof of the croft on three separate occasions, but, for the most part, she spent the seven days after her climactic conversation with Magnús on her own.

She'd made a conscious effort not to think about it too much, preferring to lose herself in the world she was creating for her new story, but the truth was that Alex barely crossed her mind. Her heart still felt raw, but she had the sense that it was raw in the way a healing wound might be: pink and sore, with the promise of wholeness ahead.

By the following Tuesday, Merry was forced to face another unexpected revelation: she'd lost weight. The almost daily runs she was doing with Sheila meant the jeans that had been snug around her waist when she'd arrived on Orkney were now loose, and her pyjamas hung around her hips. She was going to have to go shopping.

She spent a happy few hours browsing the boutiques in Kirkwall, delighted to discover some beautiful designs and outfits she would never have found online. Laden down with bags, she called in to Rossi's for a mid-morning pastry and was pleased to find Morag sitting behind the counter.

'Helen's little boy is a wee bit poorly,' she explained when Merry commented on her granddaughter's absence. 'She'll be here for the lunchtime rush, though, if you wanted to see her.'

'No, I just thought it would have been nice to say hello,' Merry said, as she paid for her delicate *sfogliatelle* pastry and latte. 'But it's lovely to see you too. How are you?'

'Better for seeing you,' Morag replied, her eyes twinkling. 'Tell me, how's the story coming along? Do you need any more inspiration?'

Merry didn't – the story was taking shape almost effortlessly on her laptop – but it was obvious that the old woman was desperate for an opportunity to reminisce about the past and revisit her youth, and it felt like the least Merry could do to listen.

'I am always open to inspiration,' she told Morag, who waved to the young waitress making her way among the tables.

'I'm going to take a short break,' she said, when the girl hurried over. 'Let me know if you need help.'

The girl glanced shyly at Merry and nodded. 'Of course, Morag. Can I get you anything?'

The older woman asked for a pot of tea and led Merry over to an empty table in the window. 'This used to be Giovanni's favourite seat,' she told Merry. 'When the doors were closed for the evening, he'd sometimes set it up like a street restaurant in Rome, with candles and roses and such-like. We'd sip red wine and pretend we were looking out at the Trevi Fountain.'

Merry smiled. 'It sounds wonderful. So romantic.'

Morag sighed. '*Och*, he knew all about romance. For my birthday one year, he borrowed a car from my uncle and loaded it with blankets and a hamper and champagne so that we could have a midnight picnic under the Merry Dancers.'

'The Merry Dancers?' Merry repeated, frowning in thought. 'Are they more standing stones?'

'Goodness, no,' the older woman said, her blue eyes sparkling. 'Although I admit, that would have been romantic too. No, the Merry Dancers are what we call the aurora. You might know them as the Northern Lights.'

Of course, Merry thought. She'd read that the aurora could often be seen during the winter months on Orkney but somehow she'd forgotten. 'That sounds wonderful,' she told Morag. 'But weren't you cold?'

Morag's gaze clouded over as she visited the memory. 'Not really – we had love to keep us warm.' Her eyes sharpened as they came to rest on Merry once more. 'And a lot of very thick blankets – because he might have been romantic, but my Giovanni was also practical. He thought of everything.'

Merry pictured the scene and smiled. 'The perfect man.'

'When he wanted to be,' Morag agreed. 'So, you've not been aurora-hunting yourself?'

'No,' Merry said. 'It hadn't even occurred to me.'

Morag sniffed. 'It wouldn't, I suppose, what with you being a Londoner and all. But I'm surprised Niall hasn't suggested it.' She gave Merry a sideways look. 'Or Magnús.'

There was definite hint of subtext that Merry chose to ignore. 'I'll ask them. It sounds like an unmissable sight.'

'It is,' Morag confirmed, and leaned across the table, lowering her voice. 'And if you've a handsome man by your side when you see them, so much the better.'

She winked and Merry couldn't help laughing. *Was everyone on Orkney an incorrigible matchmaker?* 'I'll see what I can do.'

Morag had plenty of other stories to share, but it was the image of the midnight picnic, spread beneath a blanket of ethereal dancing light that stuck in Merry's mind as she drove home. She deposited her shopping in the bedroom and settled on the sofa, phone in hand. That she wanted to see the aurora for herself was a given, but who should she ask to take her? Both Niall and Magnús would be willing to help, she knew, and she liked them both immensely. But one was business and the other was – well – not exactly pleasure, but he did cause a shiver of excitement to ripple through her whenever she saw him. Not that she wanted anything to happen between them – she was still determined to keep her time on Orkney as uncomplicated as possible. But as she was sure Jess would remind her, that didn't mean she had to live like a nun.

Reaching a decision, she messaged before she had time to change her mind.

It was another week before Magnús deemed the weather promising enough to go aurora-hunting. Merry didn't mind; her head was so full of the book she was writing that she barely knew what day it was and had to read his message twice when it arrived because she'd forgotten she had even suggested it.

Tonight, at 10pm. Dress warmly and plan to be out until the early hours. Don't forget your camera!

Stretching, Merry closed the lid of her laptop and went to dig out the thermals she'd bought in preparation. It would do her good to get out of the croft, she decided. Other than her ever-increasing runs with Sheila, she hadn't left the cottage for days. She was on first-name terms with the Tesco delivery driver now, and whole days sometimes slipped past without her even noticing the hours go by. It was like old times, when the words had flowed from her fingers and onto the screen almost like witchcraft, and she felt something sing deep inside her as she watched the story grow.

She hadn't told Jess about running into Nick Borrowdale, mostly because she anticipated her friend's first question would be whether he was single, but also because she wanted to keep the knowledge of Sam Silverton's interest in her new book a secret. It would probably lead to nothing – she'd lost count of the times a studio or producer had made all the right noises about turning one of her novels into a film or TV drama and it had never happened yet. Practically every writer she knew had a similar tale to tell; the ones that made it onto the screen were few and far between. But perhaps it was the magic of Orkney, where stories seemed to have more power, or maybe it was simply the right story at the right time; whatever the reason, she had a good feeling about Sam's interest, a sensation in the pit of her stomach that simply said *yes*.

She had sent the outline, anyway, along with the first 25,000 words, and tried not to feel guilty that he was seeing it before her agent. *It would all come to nothing*, she told herself whenever the uneasiness raised its head. And if anything did happen, she could cross that bridge when she got to it.

The skies were clearer than she'd ever seen them when Merry stepped outside the croft just after ten o'clock that night. She stood beside Magnús and gazed upwards, craning her neck as far back as it would go as she took in the myriad stars shimmering against the black velvet sky, with the merest crescent of moon hanging nearby.

'Amazing,' she breathed. 'They feel so close. Are they always so bright?'

Magnús nodded. 'On clear nights like this. Obviously, there's very little light pollution here, which helps.'

'I could look at them all night.' She stared for a moment longer, then glanced at Magnús. 'Although catching the aurora would be cool too.'

He grinned. 'Let's get going, then.'

She reached into the croft to grab her rucksack and holdall that contained everything she thought they might need. Magnús took the holdall and blinked in surprise at the weight. 'What have you packed in here?'

'Just some essentials,' Merry said, waving an airy hand.

'Essentials. Right,' Magnús said, hefting the bag onto the rear seat of the jeep. 'Did I mention it's a two-mile hike to the best aurora-watching spot?'

Merry felt her mouth drop in dismay. 'Two miles?'

Magnús grinned again and climbed into the driver's seat. 'I'm kidding. There's a car park just below the clifftop.'

The journey took twenty minutes, during which Magnús did his best to manage Merry's expectations. 'There's no guarantee we will see anything at all,' he warned, as he nego-tiated the black road that led to the northern tip of the island. 'There's really no predicting when the aurora will dance, but the moon is in her first phase so moonlight shouldn't be much of a problem. And obviously, the weather is in our favour.'

The clear skies meant it was cold, however, and Merry was glad of both her woollen hat and the thermals she wore underneath her clothes. The walk from the car park to the top of the cliffs was enough to get her heart pumping, but nowhere near long enough to warm her for long, especially with the biting breeze that was blowing inland from the sea. The view was uninterrupted but it came at a cost; Merry suspected her nose would be as red as a cherry within min-utes, if it wasn't already. So much for romantic; the young Morag had clearly been made of sterner stuff than Merry, she decided.

It transpired that Magnús had a rucksack and holdall of

his own, so they made two trips from the car. And Merry laughed out loud when he produced a waterproof picnic rug and laid it on the grass. 'Great minds think alike,' she said, pulling a similar rug from her own rucksack. 'Have you brought hot chocolate too?'

He shook his head. 'I've gone one better,' he said, and refused to elaborate further.

Surely it couldn't be champagne, Merry mused, although at least it would be perfectly chilled. They settled down, wrapped in thick blankets, and Magnús pointed out some of the constellations. 'There's Venus,' he said, pointing to a particularly bright star. 'And if you squint a bit, you might just be able to make out the Andromeda galaxy – see?'

He leaned closer and pointed so she could follow the line of his finger. The breath caught in her throat; the dense swirl of lights might be tiny and distant but it was more beautiful than she could have dreamed possible, a glistening opal surrounded by a forest of diamonds. She stared at it for a long time, forgetting about the cold, forgetting about Magnús beside her, imagining the far-off galaxy and the secrets it held.

'Do you suppose they look at our cluster of planets and wonder what it is, the way we do with them?' she asked eventually.

He spread his hands. 'Who knows? But I find it a comforting thought that we are not alone in the universe, don't you?'

'Of course,' she said. 'I used to make up stories about other planets when I was a child. Too much *Star Trek*, I suppose.'

'Even then, you were a writer,' he observed.

'Even then,' she agreed, and smiled.

It took an hour for the first lights to appear, and they were so faint that Merry wasn't sure Magnús was serious. She peered at a faint grey smudge on the horizon, watching as it flickered and vanished. 'That's it?'

'Patience,' Magnús said. 'We're going to have a very good show tonight – I can feel it.'

They sipped at the hot chocolate Merry had brought and munched on the pastries she'd collected from Rossi's earlier that day. And slowly, before their eyes, the aurora unveiled its brilliance.

The colours were more muted than Merry had anticipated but the curtain of shifting light was still a sight to behold. Magnús let her gaze at it for a while, then touched her arm. 'Now I'm going to let you into a secret. Did you bring your camera?'

Tearing her eyes away from the sea of greens, blues and pinks that bent and arced in the sky, Merry rummaged in her bag until she found the SLR camera she'd rarely had time to use. Switching it on, she handed it to Magnús. He knelt behind her and positioned the camera so that it was pointing at the sky where they could both see it.

'Watch,' he said, opening the flip screen.

The viewer exploded with colour and Merry couldn't prevent a gasp of pure astonishment. It was the same view, with the intensity turned up by a million; the columns of light flexed and turned, dancing upwards and downwards across the screen with a shimmer Merry simply couldn't pick up when she looked past the display to the sky itself. The blues and greens and pinks split into turquoise and cyan, emerald and lime, cherry blossom and bubble-gum, and yellow chased peach through the centre. She sat there, mesmerized by the sight, until at last Magnús sighed and lowered the camera.

'I'm afraid I can't feel my toes,' he said, shifting away from her and getting to his feet with obvious regret. 'I am sorry.'

Merry laughed and arched her back, suddenly aware of her own stiffening muscles. 'It's okay,' she told him. 'I should probably take some photos, anyway – my friend Jess won't believe I actually did this otherwise.'

She stood up and took the camera, snapping off picture after picture, marvelling all over again at the incredible colours that showed on the screen.

'The lens picks up more than the human eye,' Magnús said. 'Most aurora watchers view them through a camera screen.'

Once she'd taken plenty of photos with the camera, she pulled out her phone and snapped a few using that, so that she could send them easily to Jess. And then she saw the time – 12.40am.

'I had no idea it was so late,' she said, surprised to note she didn't feel in the least bit tired. 'Or is it early?'

'The night is young in terms of the Dancers,' he replied. 'The best displays often happen in the early hours. But we can go any time you like.'

'Not yet,' she said, turning back to the curtain of dazzling colour. 'I'm nowhere near ready to leave yet.'

'In that case, it's probably time for this.'

Magnús opened his rucksack and produced two tin mugs from inside. Then he pulled out a thermos flask and unscrewed the lid. A waft of whisky-laden steam hit Merry's nostrils, with a hint of lemon and cinnamon beneath it.

'A hot toddy!' Merry said, beaming at him. 'My grand-mother used to swear by that to ward off a cold.'

'Then we should certainly honour your grandmother's wisdom,' he said, pouring some of the steaming liquid into one of the mugs.

Merry took it gratefully and noticed he poured himself a much smaller measure. It was a shame he had to drive, but there was really no alternative; there were no handy night tubes to hop onto when it was time to head home. Wrapping her gloved hands around the hot metal mug, she took a sip and savoured the smoothness as the whisky mingled with the honey and caressed her taste buds. Magnús lowered himself to the rug next to her and they sat, side by side, sipping their drinks and watching the ever-shifting horizon.

'Some people think my ancestors believed the aurora was a bridge that led to the gods,' he said, after a while. 'Others say they thought the lights were the glow reflected from the armour of the Valkyrie as they rode above the great battles and decided who would have the great honour of dying.'

It didn't sound like much of an honour to Merry but she knew the Vikings had set great store in going down in a blaze of battle-fuelled glory. 'I've heard the idea about the bridge before. It was called the *Bivrost*, wasn't it?'

The look he gave her was impressed. 'That's right. It means "moving way" in Old Norse. How did you know?'

She smiled. 'I've seen the *Avengers* movies,' she said, her tone teasing. 'But, actually, I must have read it somewhere. Authors are like that – we collect snippets of information and store them in our brains in case they ever come in useful.'

Magnús nodded. 'That makes sense. So which theory appeals most to your imagination – a bridge to the gods or a symbol of the awe and the might of the Valkyrie?'

Merry considered the question. 'Both are good, from a writer's perspective – plenty of scope for conflict and drama. But I think I'd go for the bridge – gives the potential for a nice climax where our heroes ascend and finally meet the gods.'

'Good answer,' Magnús said approvingly.

The admiration in his voice made Merry feel warm in a way that no amount of hot toddy could manage. 'How about you?' she asked, as much to cover the blush that was creeping up her cheeks as anything. 'Which theory do you prefer?'

'I have a weakness for the Valkyrie,' he said, with a self-deprecating smile. 'There's something about a strong, powerful woman who never shies away from battle that appeals to me. Probably because I was raised by my mother and my sister and that description fits them to a tee.'

Merry thought back to his compliment in the distillery, when he'd likened her to an avenging angel. He'd got that wrong, she decided with a little inward sigh; she couldn't even cope with the death of her relationship, let alone choose who lived or died on the battlefield. 'They sound awesome,' she said out loud.

Magnus smiled. 'Who, the Valkyrie?'

'I meant your mum and sister, but the Valkyrie are cool too,' she said, swatting his arm because he'd known exactly what she'd meant. 'I'd quite like to channel some of their strength and confidence, that's for sure.'

He took a long, thoughtful sip from his mug, then sent a quizzical look her way. 'You don't think you are strong or confident? I beg to differ.'

He stretched out a hand to tuck a curl behind her ear. 'You're strong, resilient, talented and resourceful, not to mention intelligent and beautiful. In fact, I've never met anyone quite like you.'

The breath caught in Merry's throat as his fingers brushed her skin and she almost forgot to feel embarrassed at the compliments he'd just paid her.

'Thank you,' she managed. 'I don't feel any of those things, except for maybe when I'm talking about writing, and even then I worry that people will think I'm a fraud. Especially since I haven't written anything for so long.'

'But you have written,' he objected with a frown. 'I've heard you read a story that kept an entire hall of people spellbound, and I know you're working on a new idea now. That takes talent and whatever it was that stopped you writing doesn't seem to be there anymore. Wouldn't you agree?'

There wasn't much she could say to that, she decided, and

gave a reluctant nod.

'And the fact that you've come through it, plus coped with the end of a long-term relationship, shows strength and resilience. Coming up with new story ideas suggests you're resourceful, and turning them into something everyone wants to read takes intelligence.'

Now Merry's cheeks were burning even more fiercely than the aurora. 'Stop,' she protested, lifting a gloved hand to fan her rosy face. 'You don't have to do this.'

He shrugged and went on as though he hadn't heard. 'I can't prove that you're beautiful, since that's in the eye of the beholder, but would it help if I said you're one of the most stunning women I have ever met?'

She stopped breathing. Had Magnús really just called her stunning? 'I—'

'I'm not telling you this because I have any kind of agenda,' he interrupted before she could voice her objections. 'I know you're still healing after Alex and I have no intention of being anything more than a friend to you. And as a friend, I am telling you all this because you clearly have no idea how extraordinary you are.'

Merry sat in silence, struggling to take in everything he'd said. Had Alex ever described her like that – as a strong, resilient, extraordinary woman? She was fairly certain he hadn't and definitely not in recent years. And of course she knew that Magnús was simply being kind, trying to bolster her confidence because he knew it had taken a knock, but it still felt good to know he saw some positives in her, in spite of her slightly erratic behaviour around him.

'Thank you,' she said in a low voice once she was sure she had control of herself. 'It's very nice of you to say so.'

He waved her thanks away. 'I'm only telling you the truth. One day you will come to accept it.'

'Maybe,' she said. 'And thank you for bringing me out here too. I can't believe how incredible it's been – there's no one I'd rather have shared it with.'

The words were out before she could stop them but even as she spoke, she realized it was true. On impulse, she leaned across to plant a kiss on Magnús's cheek, just as he turned his head her way.

His lips were warm against hers. For one horrified moment, she didn't move, then started to pull away, framing an apology even before she'd moved. But his hand cupped the back of her head, gently holding her a centimetre or two away, and his breath caressed her skin. The temptation to edge forwards until their lips touched again was overwhelming but Merry didn't dare. Hadn't he just told her he saw her as a friend? And yet he'd stopped her from pulling away.

Her eyes met his and she saw her own confusion mirrored there; he had no idea what to do either. The sensible thing would be to ease gradually apart and laugh it off. Except neither of them seemed to be moving.

'Do you want me to let go?' he whispered.

Merry thought for a second and carefully shook her head. 'No.'

His gaze was steady on hers. 'Are you sure?'

She didn't nod and didn't speak. Instead, she leaned into him until her lips grazed his. The pressure was so gentle that it was almost like being brushed with a feather, but her body reacted with a fierceness that took her breath away. She let out a tiny involuntary moan that clearly was not lost on Magnús, because he pressed a fraction harder, his mouth soft but insistent, and Merry had to fight the urge to tear off his hat and sink her fingers into his long hair. Slowly, he eased her lips apart and explored the inside of her mouth. She tasted whisky and salt and the cool, indefinable essence of the night air. And then she stopped trying to notice what she could taste and gave in to the kiss.

It felt as though hours might have passed before they broke apart, but Merry could see the aurora still dancing on the horizon. Her lips tingled where his mouth had been, and she raised a gloved hand to touch them. Morag had been right: a picnic under the lights *was* romantic, even when the temperature was barely above freezing.

Magnús seemed similarly shell-shocked because he was staring as though seeing her for the first time. 'That was ... unexpected,' he said at last. 'Are you okay?'

'I think so,' Merry said, and her voice sounded peculiar to her ears. 'Are you?'

He gave the question serious consideration before nodding. 'Yes. A little surprised, but in a good way.' There was a brief pause, during which he regarded her with serious eyes. 'Although it occurs to me that we probably should not have done that.'

She couldn't argue; it was far too soon for her to be kissing anyone, no matter how tempting it was. And yet Jess's voice was echoing in her ears: *just have some fun.* And Merry had to admit, kissing Magnús had been fun. Not least because he was the first man she had kissed who wasn't Alex.

She sighed. 'No, we probably shouldn't. It complicates things.'

'It does,' he agreed. 'And you need time to get over Alex.'

That was true too, although Merry couldn't help feeling that kissing someone else might help that to happen faster. But clearly Magnús didn't feel the same way – he'd practically said he wasn't interested in kissing her again, and that was probably all for the best, given that everyone she knew on Orkney thought she was still engaged to Alex. Kissing Magnús did complicate things and she didn't need complication. No matter how much she might have enjoyed the moment itself.

Her restless gaze came to rest on the distant dancers. Was it her imagination or were they flickering and fading away?

'Perhaps the show is over for tonight,' Magnús said, cutting into her thoughts.

And Merry felt a sudden wave of tiredness sweep over her, a bone-weary exhaustion that went deeper than her body. 'Yes,' she said with heartfelt regret. 'I think it is. We should go home.'

Chapter Thirteen

The creative writing workshop rolled round faster than Merry would have thought possible. After agreeing with Magnús that kissing each other had been a bad idea, she'd done her best to force the memory from her head and had succeeded largely by throwing herself into writing. The result was that she'd spent huge chunks of the ensuing month bent over her laptop, when she wasn't out running with Sheila, and had become something of a recluse. And now it was Saturday 4th April and she was finding it something of a shock to have to dress in proper clothes and venture into civilization. She wasn't at all sure she remembered how to hold a conversation.

'Hello, stranger,' Niall said, when she arrived at the library just before nine o'clock. 'I was beginning to wonder whether you'd grown bored with us and done a moonlight flit back to London.'

'Sorry,' she said, even though they had been in regular

contact via email and she knew he was only joking. 'Call me old-fashioned, but I got the impression that a Writer in Residence should actually do some writing. So that's what I've been doing.'

'I know,' he said, tapping the side of his nose. 'I've got spies everywhere.'

Merry grinned as she followed him up to his office. He meant Sheila, she supposed, who was as subtle as an elephant when trying to uncover what Merry was working on. 'And Robbie, your Tesco delivery driver,' Niall said, when she mentioned Sheila's name as a possible spy. 'He keeps me up to date with how you're doing, whether you're getting your five-a-day, that sort of thing.'

'As you can see, I'm in perfect health,' Merry said, spreading her arms.

Niall looked at her more closely. 'You are. Does this mean the training is going well?'

She nodded. 'It is, although I think Sergeant Major Sheila would like me to work harder. But it's good to get out of the house – I need someone to make me exercise when I'm deep into writing a book.'

He concentrated on making her a cup of tea before speaking again. 'So, it's coming along? The book, I mean.'

Merry considered the 75,000 words of story on her laptop and felt the usual cautious bubble of excitement when she thought about how well it was knitting together. It would need an edit, of course, and she had no real idea whether it would all make sense when she read it back, but it was definitely taking shape. At her current rate of work, she'd finish it by the end of April, which was coincidentally the time when she was meant to deliver the book her agent and publisher thought she'd been working on. But she'd face that problem when she reached it.

'I think so,' she said to Niall. 'I'm enjoying writing it, anyway.'

He nodded. 'And have you told your publisher you've decided to switch genre and write a historical Second World War novel?'

'No, because I'd quite like to keep enjoying the writing and if I tell them, they might want me to stop,' she said. 'As a wise person once said, it's easier to ask forgiveness than seek permission.'

Niall pursed his lips thoughtfully. 'Wasn't that Ron Weasley?'

Merry laughed. 'I have no idea but it works for me.'

'And you don't think they'll mind that you're working on this book, rather than the one they're expecting.'

It was a question that had kept Merry awake on more than one occasion, but there was no scheduled publication date for the novel she ought to have been writing; her agent hadn't wanted to create any false pressure on Merry and her editor had agreed. Even the delivery date of the end of April was more of a guide than a hard deadline. 'I'm hoping they will just be glad I'm writing again.'

'A story inspired by Orkney, too,' Niall said. 'How could they not be glad?'

Merry hoped he was right. 'How is the delegate list look-ing for today?' she asked, changing the subject before he could ask any more uncomfortable questions.

He handed over a sheet of paper and grinned. 'You've got a full house – twenty eager writers, all set to soak up everything you have to teach.'

She took the list and read the names. As she'd expected, Sheila was there, along with her partner in crime, Bridget; they'd be a handful but nothing Merry couldn't cope with. And George Armstrong's name was there too; he was the self-published author Niall had previously warned her about, who thought he knew all there was to know about writing already, but she'd dealt with that type before too. She was surprised to see Clare Watson's name on the register and said as much to Niall, who told her Clare had signed up after meeting her and was looking forward to the day immensely. And then, right at the bottom, she saw another name she recognized: Magnús Ólafsson.

'What?' she muttered, blinking in disbelief.

'I have no idea,' Niall said, when she asked if he knew why Magnús had enrolled on the course. 'Maybe he thinks he has a novel in him too, like at least half the population.'

Merry squared her shoulders. It would be awkward seeing him – they hadn't really talked much since their ill-fated kiss under the aurora borealis – but he had as much right as anyone to attend the day if he wanted to polish his writing skills. It might even give them the chance to clear the air and get back to being friends, she thought wistfully.

Because although she'd been wrapped up in writing for the past month, that didn't mean she hadn't missed his messages.

'There was something I wanted to ask you,' Niall said, as they made their way downstairs to inspect the room where Merry's workshop would take place. 'How well do you know the author Jessie Edwards?'

Merry stopped on the stairs. 'Pretty well,' she said cautiously. 'Why?'

'We've had several requests to invite her to Orkney – she's built up quite a fanbase here over the last few months – and I wondered whether you might like to do an event together, that's all.'

'I'd like that a lot,' Merry said, beaming at him. 'She's one of my very best friends.'

'Ah,' Niall said, and gave her a pleased look. 'I'll get in touch, see if she'd like to come and visit.'

Merry thought back to the many times Jess had threatened to come up to Orkney and matchmake. 'I can honestly say she'd like nothing better,' she said ruefully, and realized she'd have to come clean about her relationship with Alex before then. The last thing she needed was for Jess to drop the truth on an unsuspecting Niall.

'Excellent,' he said, and pushed open the door to Merry's classroom for the day. 'Now, is there anything you think you'll need?'

The workshop was going well, Merry thought as she gazed around the room just before lunch. The delegates had varying levels of experience: some hadn't written since school, others had dabbled but never made anything stick, and others, like George Armstrong, saw Merry as his ticket to the kind of million-pound book deal he assumed all authors got these days. She'd been tempted to explain the realities of publishing to him – that million-pound book deals were usually the domain of celebrity authors, whose fame could command sales in huge numbers, but she doubted he would listen. So, instead, she focused on offering what advice she thought he might take. Right now, all the delegates were engrossed in an exercise involving the Three Act Story Structure and she hoped they were enjoying it. Sheila and Bridget seemed especially enthusiastic and Merry suspected the story plan they were giggling over owed more than a shade to Jess's outrageous plots.

By contrast, Magnús had been the perfect student and, once Merry had got over the treacherous surge of lust she'd felt when standing near enough to read his work, she'd been pleasantly surprised by the lyrical quality of his writing. He hadn't tried to engage her in conversation, had been respectful of her role in leading the workshop and had worked hard. But then, once she'd got over the surprise of seeing his name on the list of attendees, she hadn't really expected anything else.

Niall appeared just before midday to inform them all that a buffet lunch had been provided in the main hall. Merry wrapped up the session and told them they would start again in an hour. She watched them all file out and smiled when Niall told her he'd taken some food up to his office.

'I know you'll want some alone time,' he said, with a sympathetic smile.

'Thanks,' she said gratefully.

She was just about to head upstairs when she saw Magnús waiting nearby, clearly trying to catch her eye. 'You go up,' she told Niall. 'I'll be there in just a minute.'

Her insides lurched on cue as she got near to Magnús. 'Good work this morning,' she said, doing her best to squash the sudden burst of attraction that threatened her composure. 'You've got a real talent for writing – have you done much before?'

'Some,' he admitted. 'But not for many years. It's surprising how quickly the knack for inventing stories comes back. I can see why you love it so much.'

She lifted her eyebrows. 'It's certainly kept me busy over the last month. How have you been?'

His green eyes met hers. 'Fine. I've been busy too, working.' He cleared his throat and she thought he looked almost nervous; it was such a departure from his usual confident manner that Merry found herself staring. 'So, anyway, I've been thinking and I know you said you don't want any complications and that's fine – I don't either – but I can't help thinking about that night when we . . . under the aurora, and I wondered maybe if you might like to give things a go. As in go on a date. With me.'

And now Merry stared even more, because not only was

he not acting like the Magnús she knew, but he didn't sound like him either. 'I thought we agreed that was a bad idea,' she said slowly.

He shrugged, and she thought she caught a glimmer of his old confidence. 'We did. But here's the thing – life is short and I try to live it so that I can look back at the end with no regrets.' He hesitated, as though trying to work out what to say, then plunged on. 'And I think I would very much regret not taking this opportunity to get to know you better, Merry.'

She almost didn't catch the last sentence because she was distracted by his lips and the memory of kissing them. The trouble was that she wanted the same thing – to get to know him better – but she had the horrible feeling that the more she got to know him, the harder it would be to leave at the end of her time on Orkney. And she was doing so well with her writing – did she really want to risk derailing her progress by indulging in a romance that was doomed from the start?

'Magnús—' she began but was distracted by the sudden buzz of her phone in her pocket.

'Don't decide now,' he said quickly. 'Think about it for a day or two and let me know.'

But Merry wasn't really listening; she was staring at her phone and wondering why on earth her agent was calling her, on a Saturday of all days. It had to be something serious for Phoebe to interrupt her weekend with work.

'Sorry,' she told Magnús in a preoccupied voice, 'I need to take this call.'

She hurried outside to the courtyard at the front of the

library, where a couple of delegates were smoking. Finding an empty corner, Merry answered the phone.

'Hi, Phoebe, how are you?'

'I'm not bad,' her agent replied, in a tone that somehow managed to sound irritated and excited at the same time. 'I've just had a very strange conversation with a film producer from LA. Can I ask exactly when you were going to tell me you'd written a historical novel set on Second World War Orkney, Merina?'

Merry felt her blood run cold. 'Oh.'

'Yes,' Phoebe said. '*Oh*. Because I was under the impression that you were busy working on the book you are contracted to write. The one your editor is expecting to receive at the end of this month.' There was a pause, during which Merry wanted to vanish into a hole in the ground. 'Does this mean you won't be delivering that book?'

'Probably,' Merry said, wincing. 'On the plus side, I think my writer's block is better.'

'I'm very glad to hear that,' Phoebe said dryly. 'It might have been nice to talk about this change of direction before you went hell for leather after it, don't you think? And it might have been better if I'd actually heard about it from you, rather than from a total stranger.'

Merry closed her eyes. She had no defence, absolutely none, other than the certain belief that nothing would ever come of Sam Silverton's interest in her story. 'I'm sorry,' she said in a small voice. 'I was going to tell you, but it was all going so well and I didn't want you to tell me to stop.'

There was a long silence and then she heard Phoebe sigh. 'I'm on your side, Merry. I want you to get better and write things you're passionate about. But you need to keep me in the loop. I can't fight your corner if you keep me in the dark.'

She was absolutely right, of course. 'No, I know,' Merry said. 'Sorry.'

This time, Phoebe's sigh was more impatient. 'Stop saying you're sorry. Luckily for you, it seems this producer wants to option the book, based on the outline you gave him. He's been sounding out studios and has one on board already, pending all the usual legal stuff.'

Merry almost dropped the phone. 'What?'

'And the reason that's lucky is that a potential film deal will obviously make your publisher very happy and might soften the blow that you're not actually writing the book they think you are.'

'*What?*' Merry said again, unable to believe what she was hearing. 'Did you really just say Sam wants to option the idea? And that he's got a studio on board *already*?'

'Apparently,' Phoebe said. 'Look, I'm sorry to drag you away from your island retreat, but I think we're going to have to do some damage limitation with your editor. Why don't you come down to London for a couple of days and I'll set up lunch so we can lay everything out for them?'

Her head still whirling with the implications, Merry found herself nodding. 'Okay. As long as it doesn't clash with the Orkney half-marathon.'

There was a sharp intake of breath in her ear. 'A half-marathon? But you're not a runner.'

'I am now,' Merry replied. She squared her shoulders. 'But yes, I'll come down and we'll tell them everything.'

'And you will let me read this new book at some point, will you?' Phoebe asked. 'Before the meeting, I mean.'

Merry laughed. 'Yes, of course. I'll send it to you as soon as it's finished. Which will be around the end of the month,' she said, before Phoebe could ask.

'Fabulous,' her agent said, and her voice softened. 'Congratulations, Merry. I know it's been a tough couple of years but maybe this is exactly what you need to get everything back on track. And if you tell anyone I said this, I'll deny it, but well done for taking a risk – on Orkney and on this new novel. It sounds brilliant.'

Merry felt the backs of her eyes prickle with unexpected tears. Phoebe had never been anything less than supportive, but hearing her say such kind things was like a warm hug on a gloomy day. 'Thanks. I hope you're going to like it.'

'I love everything you write,' Phoebe said simply. 'Now go and get a wee dram to celebrate, or whatever it is they drink up there in the arse end of nowhere.'

She hung up and Merry was left staring at her phone, wondering whether she'd dreamt the whole conversation. She was still there a few minutes later when Niall appeared, a look of concern on his face.

'Merry? Are you all right? I thought you were coming up to have some lunch.'

She blinked hard and stared at him, still half in shock. 'I was, but my agent called. She's found out about the historical book.'

Niall's mouth dropped in understanding. 'Ah. Is everything okay?'

'I think so,' Merry said, and then the full impact of Phoebe's call sank in. 'In fact, I think I might have a film deal! Or at least the start of one.'

'For the historical?' Niall said, his face lighting up with excitement. 'That's incredible news – congratulations!'

It was, Merry thought, and reached out to grab Niall's arm. 'I think this calls for a celebration, don't you? Give Andrew a ring – we're going to need a bottle of the 1968 vintage tonight!'

'Excellent plan,' Niall replied with a grin. 'I'll call him right now.'

He hurried inside, leaving Merry alone with her thoughts once more and Phoebe's words echoed in her head – *well done for taking a risk*. Perhaps, she mused, it was worth taking another risk. As Magnús had pointed out, it was better to try and fail than regret never having tried at all.

Maybe she hadn't fallen out of love with love after all, Merry told herself as she went inside to find Magnús. Maybe there was hope for her heart after all.

Part Three

Dangerous Tides at Brightwater Bay

Orkney Literary Society presents

An Evening of Conversation with: Merina Wilde and Jessie Edwards

Join our celebrated Writer in Residence, Merina Wilde, as she chats to special guest, Jessie Edwards, about her life and career as an internationally bestselling author. Expect surprises, secrets and a sprinkling of sauciness as these two superstar novelists reveal why we just can't help falling in love with love stories.

Saturday 13th June
6.30pm at Orkney Library
Booking essential.
Email: Niall.Gunn@Orkneylib.gov.uk

Chapter Fourteen

Merry thought she was going to die.

Her lungs were on fire, her heart was thudding and her legs – well, her legs felt as though they belonged to someone else. She was eleven miles into the Orkney half-marathon and it felt like eleven thousand.

Why had she ever thought she could do this, she wondered as her muscles burned with built-up lactic acid. She could be safely tucked away in her clifftop croft right now, working on a story with a mug of steaming coffee, instead of wondering whether she was going to need CPR from one of the paramedics she'd seen at intervals along the sidelines. The burst of euphoria she'd felt at seven miles felt like a distant dream, and it didn't help that her practically octogenarian neighbour, Sheila, had abandoned her shortly afterwards, declaring her 'a wee bit too slow'. And it helped even less that her other running buddy seemed to be taking the ridiculously hilly course completely in his stride – although the fact that he was a 6'5" Viking probably gave him an advantage.

Merry puffed her hair away from her damp forehead and glared at Magnús. 'Are you actually human? How come *you* don't look like a sweaty tomato on legs?'

'Nobody looks like a tomato on legs,' he replied, in an even-breathed tone that suggested he was out for a Sunday stroll instead of a gruelling half-marathon. 'And I am sweating – you just can't see it under my beard.'

She fired a disbelieving glance his way. His long blond hair was tucked into a smooth man-bun and his golden beard was glistening in the May sunshine. It could be perspiration that made it seem as though he was glowing with health and vitality, she thought as she forced her legs to keep pounding the unforgiving tarmac beneath her feet. Or it could be some god-like power he was keeping to himself.

'You're doing so well,' Magnús said encouragingly. 'Just a little bit further.'

Biting back a rude response, Merry dug deep and tried to focus on keeping a steady pace. When she'd first agreed to join Sheila on one of her runs along the clifftops around Brightwater Bay, she'd had no idea it would lead to this madness. Yet, somehow, she'd found herself going for longer and longer, supposedly to keep Sheila company, but her neighbour was a lifelong runner and often left her behind, and before Merry knew it, she'd been entered into the Orkney half-marathon. Now here she was, with burgeoning blisters on both feet, despite her moisture-wicking socks, and a toenail that felt suspiciously loose. Magnús was probably right, there might only be a comparatively short distance to go, but it felt like it would take forever. And she was fast running out of energy. Her legs were leaden and every step was like wading through treacle. Her pace was definitely dropping.

She fumbled in the tiny pocket of her running trousers and dug out a handful of jellybeans. The enormous bowl of porridge she'd had before the race had been burned up miles ago and she knew her body must be craving more fuel. Beside her, Magnús adjusted his stride to match hers.

'This is the worst bit,' he said. 'But look – there is the twelve-mile marker. Only just over a mile to go.'

A wave of heaviness washed over Merry; a mile was still a long way. She'd been stupid to think she could do this – she was a writer, not a runner. And surely no one would blame her if she stopped now. It wasn't supposed to be this hard.

'I remember my first big run,' Magnús went on, his tone irritatingly conversational. 'It was a marathon around Reykjavik and I clearly recall thinking it would be the death of me.'

Merry gritted her teeth. Did he have to sound so cheerful when talking about impending death? 'Obviously it wasn't.'

'No, it wasn't,' he agreed. 'But at around twenty-three miles, I hit the wall and almost gave up. My legs ached, my head hurt and I had a most uncomfortable case of nipple chafe.'

The last few words were so unexpected that Merry

laughed in spite of herself, a hoarse, wheezy gasp that turned into a snort. At least she didn't have chafed nipples to contend with, thanks to the some fairly rigorous sports-bra research.

'I'd just decided enough was enough when I realized someone had started running beside me,' Magnús continued, as though she hadn't reacted. 'It was an old man – or at least he seemed old to me at the time. I found out later he was sixty-one. He didn't speak or try to make eye contact, he simply ran next to me in silence for about five minutes while I puffed and grimaced and struggled with every step. And then he glanced over and said, "I hope you don't mind me joining you. I find this part of the race especially hard and having someone to run with helps me get through it."'

Merry wanted to roll her eyes but wasn't sure she had the strength. 'That sounds like exactly the kind of mind-games Sheila would try,' she managed. 'Are they related?'

Magnús smiled. 'Part of me knew what he was doing, of course, but it gave me something to cling to; a reason to keep going. And before I knew it, we'd passed the twenty-four-mile marker and suddenly the fog seemed to lift. I found some energy and my legs felt lighter – although my nipples still rubbed.' He gave her a sideways look. 'My companion told me to use Vaseline next time. It turned out that it was his forty-second marathon.'

The tightness in Merry's calf muscles made her feet drag as she battled to keep moving forward. No doubt Magnús meant well by sharing evidence that he'd once been a mere mortal, but having him there to witness her humiliation and failure wasn't helping at all. She was a sodden mess of pain and perspiration; even her eyeballs were sweating, for god's sake.

'If this were any kind of a decent story, he'd have vanished as you crossed the finish line,' she panted, licking her parched lips. 'And you'd have discovered he'd died the night before but wanted to complete one last race before joining his ancestors.'

'That would be a better ending,' Magnús conceded. 'But instead we went for a post-race drink and I woke up the next day wearing someone else's coat, with no idea how I'd got home. My finishing medal was hanging from a tree outside.'

Once again, Merry couldn't help a huff of wheezing laughter. 'Sounds like a good night.'

'It was. Although I don't really recommend it as a general warm-down.'

A drunken night out was the last thing Merry had planned for when she finished the race. The only things she wanted were a cold shower, followed by a long bath and her bed. If she ever finished . . .

'And look,' Magnús said, holding up his wrist to show her the fitness tracker he wore, 'there's just half a mile to go. You can do this.'

Half a mile, Merry thought, and wanted to cry. It didn't sound that far, not when there were twelve and a half miles behind her, but she was so tired and sore. Sheila would have finished ages ago; perhaps she was impatiently scanning the other runners as they finished, wondering what was taking Merry so long.

The idea that Merry might not make it to the end wouldn't even occur to her. Failure wasn't something Sheila seemed to be familiar with, reflected Merry, as tears of self-pity stung her eyes.

But, for Merry, it was something she'd come to Orkney to escape. And up until now, she'd been doing quite well. She was writing again, at least; she had unexpectedly fallen in love with the islands and been inspired by the stories she'd heard. Her heart was healing too; it no longer ached when she thought of her ex, Alex, and the life they would never have together. Meeting Magnús and becoming friends had helped ease the lingering hurt, of course, but it was more than that. Being on Orkney, away from London and all its memories, had given her perspective. And, when she wasn't gasping for breath and wishing for death, it had also shown her she was stronger than she'd known.

The realization brought a sudden surge of determination that caught her by surprise. Magnús was right – she *could* do this. Half a mile was no distance – she could walk if she needed to. It didn't really matter if she crawled across the line, although it was Sod's Law that the local press would catch the image for posterity if she did.

'Tell me another story,' she gasped to Magnús. 'I don't care what it is – just talk.'

And Magnús did. He described the town he'd grown up

in back in Iceland, and made Merry smile with his obvious affection for the people who had shaped his youth. She'd heard him mention his family before – the mother and sister who'd raised him on their own after his father had left – but only in passing, as part of other conversations. She loved his assertion that single mothers were viewed very differently in Iceland than in the UK; there was no stigma attached to raising children without a man and many women deliberately chose to solo parent.

'Icelandic women see no need to settle for a partner who does not honour and support them,' he said. 'They would rather be independent, and our society admires their strength instead of judging or condemning them.'

Even distracted by her weariness, Merry couldn't help noticing the pride in his voice and, she thought, a touch of homesickness for the land of his birth. She could hardly blame him; the more she heard about Iceland, with its dramatic landscape and refreshingly egalitarian attitudes, the more appealing it sounded. She vaguely recalled reading that it ranked highly in the World Happiness Report too. All of which made her curious about why Magnús had left as a young man and never gone back.

'It felt too small to me then,' he told her when she asked. 'Everyone knew everyone and I found it a little ...' He paused to find the right word. 'Stifling.'

'And yet you settled on Orkney,' she pointed out between gasped breaths. 'Which is even smaller.'

Magnús shrugged. 'I'd travelled by then and got a taste

for lands that were not my own. When I was eventually ready to settle somewhere, Orkney was the perfect place – it reminded me of home in many ways and yet was unlike anywhere else I'd been.' He flashed her a smile and waved a hand at the road ahead. 'And look, there is the finish line, waiting for you to cross it.'

It was the most welcome sight Merry had ever seen. A reasonable-sized crowd waited on either side of the silver barriers that lined the approach; friends and family of runners perhaps mixed up with those who'd already finished, she assumed, although her vision was too blurry to pick out any individual faces. Whoever they were, a loud cheer went up when they spotted Merry and Magnús.

'What do you think?' Magnús asked, eyeing her speculatively. 'Got enough left in the tank for a sprint finish?'

'Ha ha,' she managed, then realized he wasn't joking. 'No. I've barely got enough left to plod.'

'You're stronger than you think,' he said, which made Merry want to hit him. Hadn't he spent the last mile encouraging her not to give in to her fatigue? And now he expected her to find some hitherto undiscovered seam of energy to race for the line, as though she was Wonder Woman instead of a desperately drained novelist.

Her rising indignation caused her feet to hit the ground harder. Before she knew it, her pace had increased as her muscles seemed to forget how tired they were. She fired a suspicious look at Magnús; did he have a Voodoo doll of her somewhere on his person, forcing her legs to move? Or was it some kind of mind-control, like a fitness-obsessed Derren Brown? Whatever the reason, she was definitely running faster. Gritting her teeth, Merry dug deep and let an unexpected burst of adrenaline power her forwards.

If Magnús was surprised, he didn't show it. Instead, he matched her speed and stayed with her. She couldn't look at him now – all her attention was fixed on finishing. Her lungs burned and her heart pounded and she thought her legs might fail her, even as she powered over the line. She let out a loud, ragged sob that was half elation and half exhaustion, and told her weary body it could stop.

Her legs wobbled as she slowed. One foot landed unevenly, sending her lurching to the side and forcing her spent muscles to tighten as she tried to stay upright. With a sick surge of panic, Merry realized she was going to fall.

Magnús caught her before she crashed to the tarmac. 'Steady,' he murmured, his voice full of concern. 'Just hold onto me. I've got you.'

The temptation to do just that – to throw her arms around him and let his strength keep her upright – was almost too much for Merry, but then she caught sight of Niall coming towards them. He held two foil blankets in his hands and wore a studiously neutral expression on his face. She forced herself to step unsteadily back, hoping her legs weren't about to betray her again. 'I'm okay,' she wheezed at Magnús. 'Just a bit . . . knackered.'

And then Niall was at her side, handing one silvery blanket to Magnús and draping the other around Merry's shoulders.

'That was quite some finish,' he said, shaking his head in admiration. 'Well done!'

She hadn't thought it possible to turn any redder, but Merry felt her cheeks grow even hotter. 'Apart from the bit where I almost face-planted onto the road,' she said, trying to get her breathing under control. 'I bet the photographer would have caught that.'

Niall pulled a bottle of water from his pocket and unscrewed the lid before offering it to her. 'I didn't even notice,' he said. 'No one did.'

His blue eyes didn't quite meet hers and Merry knew he was just trying to make her feel better; he'd seen her stumble and so had anyone else who'd happened to be watching. Just as he'd seen Magnús catch her, which wasn't a problem in itself except that it had probably looked as though she'd thrown herself into Magnús's arms in celebration. And that was a problem for two reasons: firstly, Merry had led Niall to believe she was still in a relationship with Alex, and secondly, she knew he suspected Magnús wanted more than just friendship from her. She took a long sip of water and wondered what he'd say if he knew she and Alex had split up over six months earlier. She wondered what he'd say if he knew she and Magnús were already more than just friends.

'I'm just glad it's over,' she puffed, wiping her mouth with the back of her hand. 'And that I never have to do it again.'

Niall glanced over his shoulder. 'I think Sheila might have other plans. I heard her mention the London Marathon earlier.'

'Absolutely not,' Merry said, and she'd never felt more certain of anything. 'I'm not entering another race in my life.'

'Wait for the endorphins to kick in,' Magnús said, grinning. 'You'll feel like you can do anything then.'

And she knew what he meant; there was a definite buzz creeping over her worn-out limbs, a sense of well-being that was totally at odds with how she'd felt for the last few miles. She fixed Niall with a stern look. 'Don't let me agree to anything, okay? I'm a writer, not a runner.'

'No reason you can't be both,' Magnús said.

Niall gave him a sidelong glance and raised his chin. 'She doesn't have to do anything she doesn't want to.'

Merry watched their eyes meet and something about the way they stood reminded her of stags squaring up to each other – Magnús was suddenly taller and more Viking, and Niall had an air that was distinctly more Superman than Clark Kent.

'Where do we collect our medals from?' she asked, as much to distract them as anything.

There was a brief moment when she thought they might ignore her, then both of them seemed to stand down. 'I'll show you,' Niall said.

Sheila materialized from the crowd as they walked. 'Well done,' she said briskly, and Merry couldn't help noticing the older woman looked as fresh as a daisy. 'You did well, all things considered. Now—'

Merry held up a hand. 'I'm not running a marathon, Sheila. Forget it.'

The other woman gave her a look of twinkly-eyed surprise. '*Och*, I'd never dream of suggesting such a thing! I was going to tell you to have a nice long bath and an early night, that's all.' She squeezed Merry's forearm. 'I'll see you for a run on Tuesday morning.'

Merry could only watch as her neighbour turned neatly around and vanished into the crowd. 'I'm less than half her age and somehow I'm the one on my knees,' she said plaintively. 'Does anything ever slow Sheila down?'

Niall let out a grim little chuckle. 'Not so far. But if it's any consolation, she's been making most of the islanders feel inadequate for more years than I care to count. Welcome to the club.'

It was some solace to know she wasn't alone in being intimidated by Sheila's incredible vitality and determination, Merry decided as she sank her aching body into a hot bath later that evening. But although the knowledge soothed her pride and comforted her ego, it was absolutely zero help with her blisters.

Chapter Fifteen

Merry read the email from her agent, Phoebe, three times before it sank in.

I can't believe you kept me up until two o'clock in the morning, turning the pages! The story is wonderful, the plotting perfect and the writing feels effortless, although I am certain it was not. An absolute triumph – no wonder the LA studios are fighting to turn it into a film. Brilliant, brilliant, BRILLIANT!

Now, are you ready for it to go to your editor? I think it makes sense for them to have read it before the meeting next week – what do you think?

It was more than Merry had dared to hope for when she'd sent the manuscript to Phoebe at the end of April. How long had it been since she'd had an email full of such effusive praise for a new book? It must be over two years – the length of time she'd been struggling with her writer's block. And for a long time, Merry had been terrified she'd never write again, let alone complete another novel, so Phoebe's compliments were even sweeter. She'd just have to hope her editor felt the same way, despite the fact that this novel was not the one Merry's publisher had been expecting.

Phoebe had broken the news to them once Merry had finished writing, and although Merry suspected it hadn't gone down as well as her agent implied, the fact that the story had already been optioned for a movie had definitely helped to smooth over any problems. Merry herself was still sceptical that the film would happen – she'd been on that particular ride before – but Sam Silverton appeared to be a producer who got things done, and several studios were said to be interested. And it was all thanks to a chance meeting with Helen at the Italian chapel, who'd shared her grand-parents' real-life love story. The romance had struck a chord in Merry's writerly brain and encouraged her to learn more about Orkney's involvement in the Second World War. She could scarcely believe it when, some three months later, she'd typed those magical words: *The End*. And now that she had the thumbs up from Phoebe, she could think about sharing it with another reader whose approval mattered to Merry: Helen's grandmother, Morag Rossi, who had inspired Merry to create a grand fictional love affair to match the real one between Morag and her Italian POW husband, Giovanni. Morag had been so generous with anecdotes and snippets from their courtship that Merry couldn't help feeling the older woman's praise was almost as important as Phoebe's.

And, of course, Jess needed to read it too. Merry had kept her secret project under wraps even from her best friend, so unsure of her ability to write it that she'd only confessed once the book was completed. It had taken a moment or two for Jess to adjust, both to the idea that Merry hadn't confided in her and that she'd branched out into a genre that was so different from her usual work.

'It's still a love story,' Merry had said, into the silence on the phone. 'It just happens to be set seventy-five years ago, that's all.'

The silence had lasted for another few seconds, then Jess had laughed. 'You're a dark horse, Merina Wilde. How does Phoebe feel about it?'

Merry had taken a deep breath. 'That's the other thing,' she'd said, and explained about the film deal. 'I'm coming down to London in a few weeks to see my publisher, and so Phoebe can meet the producer guy who's made the offer.'

Jess whistled. 'Anything else you've neglected to tell me? You've eloped to Reykjavik with the hot Viking? You've signed up to climb Everest?'

And Merry had smiled, because Jess was well aware that while she'd had a couple of excellent dates with Magnús, she was determined not to fall in love with him. 'No, but I'm hiking to the Old Man of Hoy with Niall on Sunday. Does that count?'

'Not unless you're planning to snog him on the way. Niall, that is, not the Old Man.' She paused. 'Unless he's hot.'

'Jess!' Merry exclaimed, laughing even as she felt herself blush. 'I've told you, he's practically a colleague. Don't you think my life is complicated enough?'

'Just putting it out there,' Jess said, sounding unrepentant. 'It's always good to have options.'

Except that Niall *wasn't* an option, partly because he thought Merry was in a relationship with Alex, but mostly because she only considered him in a professional light, in spite of his superhero looks and thoughtfulness.

She was very aware that ensuring her time as Writer in Residence went smoothly was part of his job, although she'd started to think of him as a friend too. In fact, it was this friendship that bothered Merry every time she had to field Niall's well-meaning enquiries about Alex; she didn't like lying and really ought to come clean. But she had no idea how to even broach the subject – she'd pretended for so long now that the mere thought of revealing the truth made her cringe inside.

To make things worse, Jess had no idea Merry had been less than honest about her relationship status, although she knew Merry's reasons for wanting to avoid romantic entanglements. It was something else Merry had to address, and sooner rather than later. But maybe not on the same day as dropping the book and movie bombshells.

'Options, right,' she'd echoed down the phone and crossed her fingers. 'I'll keep that in mind.'

Now, here she was, two weeks on, and she still hadn't done anything to resolve either problem. Her trip to London was looming, but admitting she'd used Alex as protection wasn't the kind of thing she wanted to explain via messaging or email; she'd tell Jess over a few drinks at the George and hope the fallout was lessened by gin and the presence of other people. Maybe that would give her the impetus to tell Niall the truth too, when she returned to Orkney. Maybe . . .

Sunday dawned bright and clear, one of the beautiful blue-skied Orkney mornings that Merry knew she'd miss terribly when the time came for her to leave the croft and return to London permanently. She took a moment before Niall's arrival to stand on the clifftop overlooking Brightwater Bay and gaze down at the seething sea below. Even on a calm day, the waves of the Atlantic Ocean crashed against the cliffs with a roar that Merry found soothing in its constancy. Coupled with the cries of the birds, which she'd learned to recognize as mostly guillemots, razorbills and kittiwakes, and underpinned by the gentle bluster of the breeze, it provided a soundtrack that was unlike anywhere else Merry had lived. If only she could bottle this peacefulness, she thought as she closed her eyes and let the sounds of the natural world wash over her. Recording the sound just wasn't the same, some-how. She needed to feel it.

The sound of an engine told her Niall was drawing near. She turned to wave at him as he parked alongside the croft. 'Good morning,' she called. 'Did you arrange the weather?'

He grinned through the open window. 'I wish I could take credit. Should be a lovely day to visit the Old Man, though.'

The comment reminded Merry of Jess's joke, which in turn made her recall the context in which it had been made, and she almost blushed. 'Let me just grab my rucksack and we can be on our way.'

The drive to pick up the ferry from Houton took thirty minutes, which gave Merry and Niall plenty of time to firm up their route plan. Once they'd reached Houton, they'd take the ferry to the island of Hoy and park at Rackwick. From there, they could walk the few miles to the lone sea stack that was known as the Old Man of Hoy, pausing to take in the views and then making their way back to the car. It wasn't a long or especially strenuous hike, but Merry was hoping it would be the perfect way to stretch her muscles after the previous Saturday's half-marathon. At least this time there'd be no sprint finish. She hoped not, anyway. Not unless they wanted to end up tumbling down the steep slope to the foot of the Old Man.

'There's a decent pub in Houton,' Niall said, as they waited in the car to board the ferry to Lyness, 'if you fancy a drink to celebrate our victory.'

Merry laughed. 'I think I could be persuaded.'

The ferry ride took a further forty-five minutes and sailed them over the water of Bring Deeps and past several uninhabited islands and Niall explained there was another ferry that took passengers on a longer route to the isle of Flotta. When they reached Hoy itself, the ferry docked at Lyness and Niall guided the car off the ferry. Emerald fields stretched along either side of the narrow grey road, dipping gently to the sea on the right-hand side and sloping into undulating black hills on the left, curving beneath the cloudless blue sky. The occasional farm or tumbledown cottage flashed by as they drove, but for the most part the panorama was uninterrupted and, once again, Merry was struck by the beauty of Orkney's landscape; she might have expected to become inured to the way the view seemed to stretch forever, but its ability to take her breath away showed no sign of dimming.

And long may that continue, she thought, watching a gull circling over the bay to her left.

She hoped she'd never get used to the incredible scenery.

Niall glanced across at her, then out of the driver-side window to where the sunlight sparkled on the grey-blue water. 'That's the Bay of Quoys,' he said. 'Quoy is a pretty commonplace name here – it means cattle pen.'

'The Bay of Cattle Pens,' Merry echoed. 'Doesn't have quite the same ring, does it?'

'English has its charm as a language, but I find Orcadian place names work best if you don't bother to translate,' Niall said, smiling. 'And the area past this junction is a designated RSPB nature reserve, so keep your eyes peeled for puffins, hen harriers and stonechats.'

Merry had learned to identify several species of birds since her arrival on Orkney, mostly because some of them nested around the cliffs of Brightwater Bay. Magnús had claimed there was a colony of puffins at the base of the cliffs, although she'd only seen one or two hopping around the grassy clifftop and had to take his word for it. She assumed more must be nesting in the sandstone cliffs surrounding Hoy, rather than among the purple heather that rolled across the greenery here, although she was pretty certain she wouldn't recognize a stonechat if it pecked her on the nose.

The road spanned a few streams, or burns as Niall called them, and wound into the low hills. They met no other cars on the single-track road and the view was almost timeless; only the occasional electricity pylon reminded Merry they were in the twenty-first century rather than the eighteenth. It was only when they reached the parking area at Rackwick that they saw other cars – a camper van and a minibus that suggested they might not be the only walkers set for the Old Man of Hoy that morning.

'They might be visiting the beach,' Niall conceded as he stopped the car beside the camper van. 'It's quite a popular spot – we'll be able to see it behind us as we get a bit higher.'

Their own destination was just over three miles away, and Niall had predicted it would take them around two and half hours to walk there and back, depending on how long they lingered to admire the dramatic sight of the sandstone sea stack outlined against the sea and sky. He set a brisk pace that Merry was content to match; three months ago, she might have felt differently, but her legs were used to the demands of running along the cliffs after Sheila these days. Niall pointed out various flora as they followed the signs marked 'Old Man' and turned to show her the sandy expanse of Rackwick Bay as they climbed. And eventually she saw a narrow fingertip of rock pointing upwards from the greenery.

'That's him,' Niall confirmed when she asked. 'The Old Man himself, soon to be reclaimed by the sea although it's impossible to know exactly when that will happen.'

It was an impressive sight, Merry thought as they carefully

descended the stony path that led to the viewing area of the solitary column of rock some distance from the cliff. Sunlight played across its reddish-grey surface and she could see the layers of strata that made up the rock; she knew from the small amount of research she'd undertaken that the sandstone was comparatively soft and therefore vulnerable to the relentless erosion of the waves. Around two hundred and fifty years earlier, it had been part of the cliff – in another hundred or less, it would probably have collapsed into the sea. Daredevil climbers loved the challenge it posed but Merry was more than happy to admire it from the safety of the clifftop, even as she pondered how she might fit it into a story.

'Allow me to introduce you,' Niall said as he opened his rucksack to pull out a flask. 'Merry, meet the Old Man of Hoy.'

She smiled and inclined her head towards the majestic tower of rock. 'Delighted to make your acquaintance.'

The only response was the crash of the waves below as they ebbed and flowed across the base of the stack. After snapping some photos which Merry had to admit failed to do the spectacular view justice, she and Niall sat to drink the coffee he'd brought. There were no signs of any other walkers, which he said was rare on such a clear day. 'This place usually attracts a few twitchers, especially at this time of year when the great skua are breeding.'

'Maybe they know something we don't,' Merry said, scanning the azure blue sky for the merest suggestion of clouds that might herald rain or a storm.

'Or maybe we just got lucky,' Niall replied. 'Let's appreciate it while we can, anyway.'

They lingered for another fifteen minutes, tucking into the pastries Merry had bought from Rossi's bakery in Kirkwall the day before, although Niall warned her to keep an eye out for rampaging great skua. 'They're not scared of humans – they've been known to dive-bomb anyone who gets too close to their nests, and I wouldn't put it past them to snatch food right out of our hands if they liked the look of it.'

Merry watched the birds circling around the Old Man, hunching over her pastry until there was nothing but crumbs left. Protecting the wildlife was one thing, but anything from Rossi's was much too good to share.

Once Niall had finished his own snack, he stretched and fixed Merry with a speculative look. 'We've got some time to spare before we need to catch the ferry back. We could go and take a look at Rackwick Beach ... unless you're up for a wee bit of tragedy?'

Instantly, he had her full attention. 'Always,' she said, as her writer's instincts began puzzling over what he might mean. She knew the Old Man of Hoy was considered a serious challenge among climbers – had someone lost their life trying to scale its summit? 'What kind of tragedy?'

His expression became mysterious. 'Not what you're thinking. Why don't we see how long it takes us to get back to the car and maybe I'll explain then.'

The return hike was uneventful, although steel-grey clouds rolled in and stole both the blue skies and the sunshine, making

Merry glad she'd brought a few warmer layers of clothes. She did her best to prise more information about the tragedy from Niall but he remained tight-lipped and enigmatic. They walked for just over an hour and found the car alone in the car park. Once back in the passenger seat, Merry turned an impatient look on Niall. 'Okay, I'm dying here. What's the tragedy?'

Shaking his head, Niall focused on checking his phone. 'Let me take a look at the weather before I make any promises I can't keep. I'm not sure I like the look of those clouds.'

He meant the glowering bank of purple-grey that crouched over the darkening landscape in a way that reminded Merry of a bruise. 'Trouble?'

Peering at the screen for a few more seconds, Niall frowned. 'Heavy rain seems to be blowing in from nowhere. But I think we should just make it before the worst of it hits us. If we hurry.'

He started the engine, but it wasn't until they'd retraced their route through the nature reserve and turned south that he gave in to Merry's demands to spill the beans. 'Has anyone told you the story of Betty Corrigall?' he finally said.

Merry racked her brain but the name was unfamiliar. 'I don't think so, no.'

Niall's eyes lit up in a way Merry recognized; he had a real passion for Orkney history that somehow made everything come to life for his audience. She settled into the passenger seat and prepared to listen. 'It's something of a cautionary tale,' he began, 'although I'm happy to say times and attitudes have changed.'

Betty was a young woman who lived in Greengairs Cottage on Hoy in the late eighteenth century, Niall explained. She wasn't married, but had fallen in love with a local man, whose flattery encouraged her to give in to his advances before they made it to the church. When Betty discovered she was pregnant, he refused to take any responsibility and ran away to sea.

'Typical,' Merry interrupted, rolling her eyes.

'Oh, he was quite the coward,' Niall agreed. 'He abandoned her to face the scandal alone and, by all accounts, her neighbours were vicious in their condemnation. The shame was so great that Betty tried to drown herself.'

Merry couldn't prevent a gasp of horror. 'No!'

'She was rescued from the waves in the nick of time,' Niall said. 'And you'd think the shock of near disaster might have jolted people into finding some compassion, but if they did, it was too little too late.'

A heavy weight settled in the pit of Merry's stomach. 'What happened?'

Niall sighed. 'She hanged herself a few days later.'

He'd been right to describe it as a tragedy, Merry thought unhappily. Mother and baby both lost. 'Poor Betty.'

'To make matters worse, because she'd taken her own life, both the church and the local lairds refused to have her buried on their land. She was placed in an unmarked grave on unconsecrated ground and soon forgotten.'

Niall pulled the car into the side of the road and turned to face Merry. 'But she didn't stay that way forever. In 1933, some men were digging for peat near the Water of Hoy. Their pickaxes hit a wooden coffin.'

Suddenly, Merry knew where the story was going. 'They found Betty's grave,' she breathed.

'After checking with the postmaster, they decided to open the coffin. And inside, they found—'

A sudden spattering of rain hit the windscreen, causing Merry to jump and squeak. She gave a self-conscious laugh. 'Sorry. I've read too many Stephen King novels.'

He smiled. 'It's not a million miles from something he might have written, actually. Inside the coffin, they found the body of a woman, as fresh as the day she'd died, with lustrous dark hair curling around her shoulders.'

Merry gave him a shrewd look. 'If you're about to tell me she had unnaturally pointy teeth . . .'

'You, me or Mr King would probably have thought to check, but nobody else did,' Niall replied as rain continued to patter at the windows. 'The authorities decided she should be reburied in the same place and left in peace.'

'Why do I think that isn't quite what happened?'

Niall tapped his nose. 'Your spider senses are correct. In 1941, some soldiers stationed on Hoy were digging for peat again and found the coffin. Once they'd opened it and realized what it was, the men decided to cover Betty's remains once more, but word of her remarkable preservation spread among the soldiers' peers. Before long, others came to dig her up and take a look.'

Merry felt a rush of sorrow and anger at the further

indignities Betty had suffered in death. 'Please tell me she rose from the grave and inflicted a terrible revenge on them for disturbing her.'

'Not as far as I know. But we could go and check if you like?'

She gaped first at him, then out of the rain-lashed window at heather and grass landscape beyond. 'You mean—'

He nodded. 'She's buried not far from here. Once the soldiers' commanding officers found out what was happening, they arranged for her body to be moved out of temptation's way. Eventually, a little tombstone was placed as a marker, and a fence was put up to make sure everyone knew not to disturb her again.'

Merry grabbed her waterproof jacket and started to pull it on. 'What are we waiting for? Let's go before the rain gets any heavier.'

The temperature had dropped significantly and they'd only taken a few steps from the car before Merry began to question the wisdom of her suggestion. But the rain was already dripping from her coat and spattering her face by then, and besides, there was no way she was going to turn back. Betty's story had been so unfair – so desperately and furiously sad – that Merry somehow felt the least she could do was pay her respects.

By the time she and Niall stood at the small, slightly neglected rectangle of picket fencing, the sky was almost black and the rain was torrential. Merry wiped her face and shook the water away. 'If this were a horror story, now would be the perfect moment for Betty to rise up for revenge.'

Niall pursed his lips. 'I've always felt there was something more Brontë-esque about her story,' he said, shielding his eyes with one hand. 'I can imagine poor Betty's ghost wandering the peat moors along the water's edge, driven by despair and misery, calling for the lover who'd abandoned her. Can't you?'

She could, Merry realized, and it was exactly the sort of story Emily Bronte might have written, if her own life hadn't been cut so tragically short. There was such a correlation with *Wuthering Heights*, in fact, that Merry could almost visualize a figure materializing out of the rain right now . . .

'Shall we get back in the car?' she asked Niall, before her imagination could get the better of her. 'In case we get washed away?'

'Good idea,' he said. 'And with a bit of luck, we'll still have time for that drink in Houton.'

Chapter Sixteen

The rain and wind worsened overnight and by Monday morning had been officially designated as Storm Elsa.

Merry and Niall had made it back across the water to the Orkney mainland, although it wasn't a crossing she looked back on with fondness. The water had been choppy and the rain driven by gusts of wind, so that the ferry rolled as it cut through the waves. Merry had been grateful to reach land without losing the contents of her stomach, and even regular sailor Niall had looked relieved. They'd agreed to forego a visit to the pub and instead had driven to Brightwater Bay. Seeing Merry shivering in spite of the car's heaters on full blast, Niall had insisted on coming into the croft to get the fire started while she dried off.

'But you're drenched too,' she objected when he knelt before the fireplace and piled up the logs.

'Then I'd better hurry up and get this lit,' he said, and she couldn't argue with his logic.

She'd put the kettle on before heading to the bedroom to change. By the time she was wrapped up in warm, dry jeans and a jumper, Niall had made a pot of tea and poured two steaming mugs. Merry took one gratefully and sipped at the scalding liquid. 'Thank you for today,' she said. 'It was fascinating – almost a perfect day until the rain hit.'

Niall shook his head. 'I don't know where that came from – even the guys on the ferry were surprised. It wasn't on the long-range radar.'

'Maybe it was Betty,' Merry said solemnly.

'Maybe,' Niall replied, smiling. 'Or maybe it was just a freak rainstorm. It happens on Orkney.'

And of course it hadn't been Betty – it had been Elsa, the news had declared later that evening, and she'd grown in fury until most of Scotland was being battered by downpours and gale-force winds. Merry had lain in bed, shivering a little as she listened to the winds tear across the roof of the croft, and hoped the cottage would survive the onslaught. This wasn't the first storm to hit the islands, she told herself logically, and it wouldn't be the last. But logic was hard to appreciate when it felt as though you might be blown away at any moment . . .

Merry woke on Monday morning with an ache in her bones and skin that felt too hot. Paracetamol helped dull the headache but, by lunchtime, her throat was on fire and she had to concede she was ill. She did her best to sleep, sipping water and dozing on the sofa while the wind and rain raged across the cliffs. Jess wanted to know she was safe from the storm, and Merry sent a reassuring reply to her faintly anxious message, while Niall had texted to make sure she had everything she needed, including power to the croft. It was only Magnús she was unable to fool. And that was because she'd slept through three of his messages, which prompted him to ring her.

'You sound terrible,' he said, when she'd croaked a hello into the phone. 'What's wrong?'

Merry considered lying – the last thing she wanted was for him to feel honour-bound to drive over to the croft – but her bone-weary exhaustion meant she didn't have the energy. 'I've got a cold.'

His tone was immediately concerned. 'How ill are you? Is there anything you need?'

Her gaze came to rest on the cold, blackened fireplace and the barely touched cup of tea on the coffee table before it. The croft had central heating and her fever was still high enough that she was sweating beneath the blankets she'd draped over herself while she'd been shivering earlier, but that didn't mean she wouldn't find some comfort in the glow of a real fire in the grate. She couldn't ask Magnús to drive through the storm just for that, however. 'I'm fine.' She pressed the back of one hand against her too-hot forehead and closed her eyes. 'Honestly, don't worry.'

'You don't sound fine,' Magnús persisted. 'Why don't I come over? You shouldn't be alone in weather like this if you're ill.'

'Please don't,' Merry said, her eyes snapping open in alarm. 'I don't want you to risk driving in this wind.'

'I have a big truck,' he replied. 'I'll be perfectly safe. And besides—'

But she never got to hear what he was about to say next, because the light above her head went out and Magnús's voice was cut off abruptly.

'Hello?' she said and looked at the screen to see the call had failed because her Wi-Fi connection had vanished. She tried calling back, but the phone stayed stubbornly silent, with no signal to suggest she was still connected to the outside world. And then she forced herself to get up, wincing at the pain in her shinbones as she shuffled over to the light switch. Nothing happened when she flicked it on and off, just as the lights in the kitchen and bedroom remained dead. Merry pulled the blanket tighter round her shoulders and groaned as her head swam. A power cut was the last thing she needed, she thought, and made her way slowly back into the darkened living room. She'd have a little rest on the sofa, gather her strength, and then she'd light the fire.

Merry had no idea how long she'd slept when she heard someone banging on the door. The living room was almost completely dark, but that didn't mean anything; the sky was so heavy outside that there was very little natural light to brighten the room. But there was no mistaking the urgency of the knocking and even in her feverish, sleep-addled state, Merry knew who it must be. Keeping the blankets close, she pulled herself upright and went to let Magnús in.

His truck was parked right outside the croft but he still seemed to be drenched to the skin as she opened the door.

Rain gusted inside, splattering Merry's face in a way that was both pleasantly cooling and shiver-inducing at the same time. Magnús took one look at her and hustled her back inside, shutting the door firmly after himself.

'You shouldn't have come,' Merry said. 'It's awful out there.'

Water glistened on his face as he looked her up and down, worry evident in his eyes, and then glanced past her into the cold, dark living room. 'I definitely should have. The power lines are down and you're ill.'

She swallowed painfully. 'I might be contagious. And even you can't single-handedly restore the power if the lines are down.'

'No, but I can get the fire going,' he said, stripping off his waterproof coat and shepherding her back to the sofa. 'And I brought supplies.'

Merry sank onto the cushions and feverishly wondered if he would set the logs roaring by firing a lightning bolt from his fingertips. But he reached for the matches and, a few minutes later, orange and yellow flames were licking greedily at the wood, sending some warmth into the room.

'Do you have any oil lamps?' he asked, glancing around. 'Or candles?'

'There are some in the kitchen,' she managed. 'I was going to get them when the power went off but I think I dozed off instead.'

Magnús frowned and placed a blissfully cool hand against her forehead. 'How long have you felt like this?'

It seemed to take Merry an age to answer the question; yesterday's visit to Hoy felt almost like a dream. But she pulled her woolly thoughts together long enough to tell him it was less than twenty-four hours, and to describe the soaking she and Niall had endured.

'I must have been coming down with something already,' she said slowly. 'And getting half drowned made it worse.'

He shook his head as he lifted her feet onto the sofa and tucked the blanket carefully around her. 'First, I'll find the candles. Then we can discuss your treatment.'

She wanted to protest that all she needed was more paracetamol and rest, but he'd gone so Merry closed her eyes and let her head lean against the cushions. When she woke up again, it was to the inviting smell of vegetable soup and the sound of the storm still howling outside. Magnús was sitting in the armchair opposite her, lit by candlelight.

'How are you feeling?'

She blinked slowly, and gazed around, taking in the blazing fire in the hearth and the overall peacefulness of the room, despite the wind battering at the walls. Her headache seemed to have lessened and her skin felt less like it might spontaneously combust. 'A little better, I think,' she said cautiously.

'Are you hungry?' he asked. 'I made you some soup but didn't want to disturb you.'

Merry considered the question; the scent of the food was making her stomach growl but she didn't feel in the least bit hungry. 'I should probably eat something,' she admitted. 'I think I skipped breakfast – lunch too. In fact, I don't even know what time it is.'

He stood up. 'I'll warm the soup and you can try it.'

It took a few moments after Magnús had left the room for Merry to wonder just how he was going to heat anything up when the kitchen had no electricity to power it. Perhaps he'd hung a pot over the fire and cooked the soup that way. Glancing across the back of her shoulder, she tried to see into the kitchen and thought she could just about make out a faint blue glow. Either he'd brought the Tesseract back from Asgard or he was using a camping stove.

Several minutes later, Magnús reappeared with a piping-hot bowl on a tray, which he laid across Merry's lap. 'Thanks,' she said. 'You didn't need to do any of this, but thank you.'

He settled back into the armchair and shrugged, his long hair glistening like burnished gold in the light from the fire and the candles. 'You know, even the Valkyrie accept help sometimes.'

It wasn't the first time he'd referred to her that way but it still made her want to remind him that the comparison couldn't be more wrong; even at the best of times, she was a soft-hearted novelist, not a legendary warrior with the strength and courage of a hundred mortal women. And it wasn't that she didn't want his help now – she was pathetically grateful that he'd driven over to take care of her – but she hadn't wanted to need it. She hadn't wanted to need *him*.

'I'm fairly sure the Valkyrie don't let a bit of rain slow them down,' she pointed out, and took a sip of the soup, which was hot and delicious. 'They definitely don't take to the sofa the moment they have a bit of a sniffle.'

Magnús raised an eyebrow. 'Merry, your temperature was thirty-nine degrees. That's more than just a sniffle.'

She swallowed another mouthful of soup. 'I'm too tired to argue. But please don't feel you have to stay with me. I can keep the fire going, can use it to make toast if I need to, and I'm sure the power will be back on soon.'

'Perhaps. But you need to rest and you can't keep the fire alight when you're sleeping.' He gave her a level look. 'Why don't we pretend we have had this conversation and you've accepted that I'm not going anywhere until you're better?'

Merry ate in silence for a few seconds as she considered her options. It wasn't as though she could make him leave and the truth was that he was right – she could barely keep her eyes open for more than half an hour. And, underneath all her pride and self-reliance, there was a tiny part of her that was glad he was there. That part of her wanted to lean into his arms and fall asleep, safe in the knowledge that she'd be taken care of. It wasn't who she was, and she hated having to acknowledge it, but it was there, nonetheless.

'Thank you,' she said eventually and glanced at the rivulets of rain running down the window. 'And I suppose it's better than sending you back out into that.'

He smiled. 'Exactly. And it's not as though I am short of books to read.'

Merry followed the line of his gaze towards the croft's bookshelves, curated by Niall to cover a wide range of genres and subjects. 'True,' she allowed. 'You should try something by my best friend, Jessie. Sheila and her friends are already big fans.'

'I might just do that. She's coming to visit, after all – I feel as though I should read some of her work before then.'

Jess would probably explode when she heard the hot Viking was reading one of her novels, Merry thought, and hid a weary smile behind the last few spoonfuls of soup. When she'd finished eating, Magnús took the tray away and returned moments later with a glass of water. 'Try to drink this and get some rest,' he suggested. 'I'll be here when you wake up.'

And Merry, whose eyelids felt suddenly hot and heavy, nodded and allowed herself to drift off.

The storm blew itself out overnight, but it took until late in the afternoon for the croft's power to be restored. Clare Watson, from the neighbouring farm, had dropped by just after nine o'clock that morning. Merry was still in bed and hadn't even heard anyone knocking, but she caught the exclamation of surprise in the other woman's voice when the door opened to reveal someone who was very clearly unexpected.

'Oh, she's not well?' Clare said loudly. 'Hugh and I thought we'd better bring some emergency supplies, but we had no idea she was ill or I'd have come last night.'

A low rumble told Merry that Magnús had replied, but she didn't catch the words. Her head still felt thick and woolly as she swung her feet out of bed and pulled her dressing gown on to shuffle to the hallway. 'Thank you so much, Clare,' she called, causing Magnús to turn and study her. 'That's really thoughtful of you.'

'It's no trouble at all,' Clare said, beaming, and held up a jute bag. 'Just some bread and milk and cheese, but I can see you've already got Magnús here looking after you.'

It was a good thing she must look a fright, Merry thought as she resisted the temptation to flatten her sweat-sticky hair, otherwise Clare would be putting two and two together and coming up with something north of a billion right now. 'Yes, he drove over when the electricity went off yesterday. Brought a camping stove and made some soup.'

The blonde-haired woman nodded approvingly. 'Just what you need when you're under the weather.' She thrust the bag towards Magnús and her bright-eyed gaze slid back and forth between him and Merry. 'Well, don't let me get in your way. I just wanted to make sure you were okay, that's all.'

'Thank you,' Merry and Magnús said, both at the same time, and Clare grinned, nodding once more before she turned away.

'See you soon,' she called. 'Don't forget you promised to come up to the farm for tea!'

She climbed into the Land Rover and was gone, leaving Merry to lean against the wall of the croft's hallway with the sinking feeling that she was about to become the subject of some very hot gossip indeed.

'How are you doing this morning?' Magnús asked. 'Did you sleep well?'

Merry glanced into the living room, at the sofa where he'd spent the night and to the flames which still roared in the hearth. 'Probably better than you,' she said. 'Please tell me you didn't wake up every hour to put more logs on the fire.'

'Of course,' he said. 'But it was a worthwhile sacrifice to make.'

Merry felt her mouth drop in dismay, until a faint twinkle in his eyes told her he wasn't being serious. 'You didn't.'

'No, I did not,' he said, much to her relief. 'One of the first things you learn in Iceland is how to bank a fire so it stays alight while you sleep. We'd never get through the winters otherwise.'

Merry felt a wry smile tug at her lips. 'And there I was thinking you'd have central heating.'

He raised the jute bag enquiringly. 'Hungry? I could make some scrambled eggs if you like?'

'I need a gallon of water first,' Merry said, suddenly aware of her own thirst. 'And then maybe a little bit of something to eat.'

Magnús nodded. 'Perfect. Go back to bed, I'll bring you the water.'

The thought of him being in her bedroom seemed too intimate somehow, Merry decided, and wondered how she could frame an objection without sounding like a Victorian prude. And then it occurred to her that she had no memory of waking up from the sofa and taking herself to bed the night before. Which probably meant Magnús had carried her there as she slept and tucked her in under the covers. And if that was what had happened, it seemed a little redundant to object to him coming back in with a glass of water . . .

'Sure,' she said, feeling a flush of heat that had nothing to do with her illness. 'Thanks, I'll just—'

She escaped back into the bedroom and covered her over-heated face with both hands. Jess was going to have a field day when she heard about this, Merry thought as she shook her head and burrowed deep into the now-cool covers on the bed. She'd probably want to book the hen party venue and start buying bridal magazines. And Clare Watson would be right behind her.

Chapter Seventeen

Hey, stranger, how are you?

Merry stared at the message for a long time, wondering if she was still feverish. It was Thursday morning and she'd woken early to pack the last few things for her trip to London; the last thing she'd expected to see when she checked her phone was a message from Alex, sent at 10.57 the previous night. It had been months since he'd last tried to contact her and she'd followed Jess's stern advice to ignore the attempt. She didn't even have his number saved. Her finger hovered over the delete button but then the screen showed the word *online*, followed by *typing* . . .

She waited, staring at her phone as though paralysed. What was the etiquette here? He must have seen she was online too – could she simply close the message app and pretend not to have seen he was typing? Of course she could, she thought, and locked the screen. But the thought nagged at her and she found it hard to focus on wedging the last few items into her case. A moment later, her phone was in her hand and the message from Alex was on the screen.

I still have a few things at the flat. Seems silly after all this time but I need them. Any chance you could arrange for me to get access?

A deep frown creased Merry's forehead. What could he possibly have left that he needed now, more than seven months later? Whatever it was, the likelihood was that Jess had thrown it away when she'd undertaken the Alex Purge just after Christmas. And Jess would almost certainly tell her to ignore this message too, that whatever it was Alex wanted, it was far too late. But Jess hadn't been his childhood sweetheart, hadn't spent fifteen years loving him . . . Taking a deep breath, Merry began to type.

Hi. What is it you need? I'll get it posted to your work.

There was a brief pause and she saw he was typing a reply.

Books, mostly. I won't know until I see the shelves – you remember how your books and mine were always snuggled up together. I can picture them but I can't tell you the titles.

The words raised a sad smile, because that was exactly how they had always been – her romances cosied up with his spy novels. They'd used to joke about the baby books they might have together. Then she remembered the way he'd looked as he'd told her out of the blue that he didn't love her anymore, in a restaurant so she wouldn't make a scene, and she hardened her heart. Whatever game Alex was playing, he'd lost the ability to manipulate her feelings a long time ago.

No idea if they'll still be there – I threw a lot out. I'm staying there for a few days from today but maybe Jess will meet you with the key next week.

He read the message immediately.

Great – thanks. Speak next week x

She gazed at that kiss for a moment, wondering all over again what the hell he was playing at, then reluctantly deleted the whole thread. If Alex really wanted his books, it was up to him to ask her again.

The view from Duck and Waffle was nothing short of spectacular. London seemed to have pulled out all the stops for Merry's return: sunlight sparkled on the rooftops below the fortieth floor restaurant and the sky was so blue that she felt the floor to ceiling windows must have some kind of filter. And even if the panorama hadn't been so distracting, Merry suspected she'd have had difficulty concentrating on the no-nonsense negotiation that was pinging back and forth between producer Sam Silverton and her agent, Phoebe Marsh. It had been a whirlwind twenty-four hours. Since arriving in London the day before, Merry hadn't stopped. She'd been reunited with Jess for drinks in the George on Thursday evening, followed by a breakfast meeting at her publisher's offices first thing the next day. Merry's nerves had been fluttering going in, but Phoebe had been with her and she needn't have worried; her editor admitted she'd fallen in love with Orkney in the Second World War almost before they'd sat down at the meeting table. And the marketing team were equally enthusiastic, laying out their vision for the best way to handle the change in direction for Merry's writing. She'd left the meeting with her head swimming, but generally feeling positive. And then the next message from Alex had arrived.

Why don't I pop round to the flat while you're here? Saves bothering Jessie x

She wondered if Jess's poorly hidden dislike was the reason Alex was so keen to avoid her – she couldn't think of any other reason he'd prefer to see Merry. After the break-up, he'd blocked her; that wasn't the action of a man who wanted to spend time with his ex. And it had taken her a long time to come to terms with that, but finally, thanks to Jess's constant encouragement and the residency on Orkney, she'd accepted that she didn't need Alex to be happy. She could certainly do without seeing him while she was in London, but perhaps it was easier to do things this way. Once he'd got the books or whatever it was he wanted, she could close the door on him, satisfied that she'd been the better person.

A lull in the conversation caught her attention. Merry looked up to see both Phoebe and Sam watching her and she realized they must have asked a question – a question that needed an answer only she could provide. Mentally, she spooled back through the conversation; she'd only been half listening, but it seemed Sam wondered whether she had any particular actors in mind as she'd written the main characters. And, of course, she had been able to picture her characters perfectly as she'd written but not because they were famous actors. It was because they were based on real people who lived and worked on Orkney. 'Not really,' she said. 'The setting is the real star.'

Sam nodded, as though that was exactly the answer he'd anticipated. 'Well, the good news on that score is that we should be able to get permission to film there at a time that suits our schedule. Are you going to want to watch?'

And that wasn't something she'd considered, mostly because she hadn't really allowed herself to believe the movie would ever get to the stage of filming. But she didn't have to think too hard before answering that question either. 'Absolutely,' she said. 'I'd love to have a reason to go back to Orkney. It's the most amazing place.'

Sam held up his hands in mock surrender. 'You're preaching to the choir here, Merry. I already know how wonderful it is.'

And Phoebe looked back and forth between them. 'I think I need to visit and take a look for myself. No one who has been seems to stop raving about it.'

An image of Niall popped into Merry's head, his face glowing as he described some detail of the land of his birth, and she smiled. 'Believe me, you'll understand why when you get there.'

Sam nodded and raised his glass. 'To Orkney, and the beginning of another incredible adventure for all of us.'

'To Orkney,' Merry echoed and wondered exactly when the islands had started to feel more like her home than London.

*

Merry had an hour spare before she was due to meet Jess for dinner that evening so she took a deep breath and told Alex to come to the flat they'd once shared in Chiswick. She didn't know quite what she'd been expecting – that he'd have changed in the seven months they'd been apart – but he looked almost exactly the same as he had the day he'd casually smashed her heart into tiny pieces and walked out of her life. And she felt a surprising level of satisfaction when his jaw literally dropped at the sight of her. He recovered fast and tried to smooth it over with a yawn, but Merry had known him a long time. Perhaps he'd been expecting her to be where he'd left her, still pining for the past.

'It's good to see you,' she said, stepping back from the front door to allow him into the flat. 'I hope you're well?'

He cast another covert look her way and then gave up any attempt at pretence. 'Not as well as you, I think. You look amazing, Merry. Have you ... have you been hitting the gym?'

The last word was tinged with disbelief and she understood why: in the fifteen years they'd been together, Merry had joined the gym a total of five times, mostly as New Year resolutions that she'd broken almost instantly. Whatever else she'd been during their relationship, she'd never been one for working out.

'Not exactly,' she said politely. 'But you're not here to talk about my exercise regime. What is it you need to find?'

He blinked and ran a hand through his blond hair, a gesture she knew he only did when he was off-balance. 'Sure.

Right. It's the Mick Herron books – the ones about Jackson Lamb. I think you bought me the first one.'

Merry knew the series he meant, just as she remembered buying a first edition as a birthday gift and getting it signed by the author at some event or another. She'd downloaded them all on audiobook after Alex had dumped her, partly as a distraction from her misery and partly in a desperate attempt to still feel close to him. And the paperbacks had survived Jess's cull; sending a signed first edition to the charity shop felt like a betrayal of the author somehow, and if she was keeping one it made sense to keep its companions. But Merry had no intention of letting Alex see she remembered.

'Oh, okay,' she said, waving vaguely at the bookshelves. 'I don't know if I hung on to them. Why don't you have a quick look?'

His eyes lingered on her for a moment, then he nodded. 'Thanks.'

The temptation to be polite and offer him a drink was strong; she had to clamp her mouth shut to stop the words escaping. But Jess had been adamant.

'I don't know what his game is, but he's up to something,' she'd said the night before. 'Don't get sucked in, babes. He's history, remember?'

It was hard to keep that in mind now he was right in front of her, Merry thought, watching as his hand trailed across the spines on the bookshelf. She wanted to ask how he was, what he'd been up to, but Jess had been clear on that too.

No small talk! Get rid of him as soon as you can.

'How's life in the frozen north?' he said, as though reading her mind. 'Do you have to chop wood for the fire every day – is that why you're looking so well?'

The words were innocuous, but there was something about the tone that suggested he was having a dig at her decision to take the residency. She summoned up what she hoped was a bland smile. 'Of course not. I have a Viking who does that for me.'

He didn't turn around, but she did detect a slight stiffening of his shoulders and knew she'd hit the mark. It was petty – she wasn't trying to make him jealous – but that hint of disparagement had nettled her.

'Good for you,' he said and this time he did glance at her. 'But I bet you'll be glad to come home in August. Back to civilization.'

Leaving Brightwater Bay wasn't something Merry had let herself think about lately. She'd got so used to her routine, to the peace and quiet that allowed her to plot and brainstorm and – most importantly of all – to write, that she felt an unsettling buzz of anxiety when she contemplated returning to the hustle and noise of London. No doubt she'd get used to city life again, and the creative block that had almost destroyed her seemed to have lifted so she hoped she'd be able to continue to write once she was back home, but there'd be a definite period of readjustment. And no matter how fast she settled into her old life again, she knew she'd never stop missing Orkney.

'Maybe I'll stay there,' she said, and the words were out before she'd even had time to consider them.

Alex stopped browsing and stared at her. 'Really?'

She didn't know why she'd said it, the possibility hadn't ever occurred to her until that moment. 'Yes, maybe. It's helped me focus on writing and I've made friends.'

'You've got friends here,' he said. 'I can't see Jess being happy if you move away permanently. And what about your publisher? Your events?'

He sounded almost accusing. 'It's Scotland,' Merry replied, 'not Antarctica. I can be in London in five hours.'

The look he gave her was disbelieving, and suddenly she wanted him out of the flat. Out of her life again. Stepping forward, she pointed to the row of black-spined paperbacks that bore Mick Herron's name. 'These are what you're look-ing for. Did you bring a bag, or shall I get you one?'

She found a cloth bag – a freebie from another signing – and tried not to mind the gap on the shelves once Alex had removed his books. He stood for a moment, the full bag weighing heavily from one hand, and studied her as though there was something more he wanted to say. But then he produced the boyish, rueful smile she'd known since school and shook his head. 'Thanks for being so good about this. The books, I mean.'

'No problem,' Merry said. 'Was there anything else?'

She could almost hear Jess groaning in her head. *Don't give him another opening!*

'No,' Alex said, after a moment's pause. 'Just these.'

She followed him to the door, a weirdly formal gesture that underlined the fact that they weren't much more than acquaintances now, and waited as he adjusted the bag on his shoulder.

'It's really good to see you, Mer,' he said, his eyes warm. 'Take care of yourself, okay?'

He kissed her cheek before she could stop him. She took an involuntary step back, restoring the distance between them, and she saw him notice.

'You take care too,' she said swiftly. 'Bye, Alex.'

She shut the door fast, adding the chain for good measure although there was no danger Alex might come back in; he'd returned his key months ago. And then she turned and leant against the cool white wood, closing her eyes for a moment.

She was tired; the day had been long and she suspected she wasn't quite over her illness from the start of the week. Seeing Alex had been more difficult than she'd expected too – her stomach was still churning – and she'd quite like to curl up on the sofa for a nap. Except that it wasn't this sofa she longed for – it was the one in front of the fireplace in the croft, where she might glance out of the window and see the guillemots soaring over the cliffs. She sighed and opened her eyes, taking in the familiar yet unfamiliar décor of the flat.

Had she meant it when she'd told Alex she might stay on Orkney?

She didn't know, but the thought soothed her jangling nerves at least. By Sunday, she'd be back in the croft again and perhaps she'd be thinking of London with this same longing. It was impossible to tell what her true feelings were, especially since seeing Alex seemed to have stirred up emotions she'd thought were settled. But it wasn't something she had to decide today, she reminded herself. All she had to do right now was meet her best friend for dinner.

'And that is why revenge is a dish best served cold, with a double side of regret,' Jess said, when Merry told her how Alex had reacted at the sight of her. 'Good. I hope he realizes what a monumental prick he was, now that it's far too late to get you back.'

Merry sipped her margarita. 'It's weird – all those times I dreamed about seeing him again, hoping he'd look at me the way he used to . . . and today that happened, sort of, and I didn't really care.'

Jess drained her own glass and signalled to the waiter for a refill. 'Of course you didn't, because you are *over* him.' She paused and fixed Merry with a meaningful gaze. 'And besides, you have someone new who makes Alex fade into nothingness. How could he possibly compete with Magnús? Did you tell him you're dating an actual Viking? Please tell me you did – and showed him a photo.'

Which reminded Merry uncomfortably that she still hadn't told Jess about letting everyone on Orkney believe she was still with Alex. She'd wait until the waiter turned up with Jess's refill, she decided, and then she'd order a bottle of sauvignon blanc. This wasn't a conversation she wanted to have entirely sober.

'So, let me get this straight,' Jess said, when Merry finally felt she was fuzzy enough around the edges to confess. 'You told the sexy librarian you were with Alex so you wouldn't be tempted into snogging him.'

Merry started to interrupt but Jess held up her hand. 'Don't argue – it's the only thing that makes sense. And then you told the hot Viking the same thing so you wouldn't be tempted into snogging him. But then you snogged the hot Viking anyway.' She glanced over at Merry for confirmation, who nodded in mortified silence. 'Have you also snogged the sexy librarian?'

'No!' Merry exclaimed. 'I told you, we work together. Apart from anything else, it would be unprofessional.'

Jess gave her a sideways look. 'It's pretty unprofessional to lie to the people you work with. Which technically includes me, I might add.'

'Besides, Niall's good-looking, but he's not sexy,' Merry went on. 'He's funny and kind and really interesting—'

'But not hot,' Jess cut in. 'Got it. So Magnús knows you're not with Alex, but Niall doesn't. And Magnús knows Niall doesn't know you're not with Alex, but Niall doesn't know you're dating Magnús.'

Merry took a moment to unravel the words, then nodded again. 'Yes. I think.'

'So, the question is,' Jess said, holding up a slightly unsteady finger. 'If Niall isn't sexy, why are you worried about being tempted into snogging him?'

'I'm not,' Merry insisted with a groan. 'He had the wrong end of the stick about Alex, back when I first arrived, and it seemed like the safest thing at the time to go along with it. I didn't know I was going to meet Magnús and things would get so complicated.'

Jess took a long swig of wine and gazed at Merry over the top of her glass. 'I genuinely don't understand how you've got yourself into this mess, babes, but there's one thing I do know. It's a bloody good thing I'm coming up there next month to sort everything out.'

Chapter Eighteen

There was a beach at the base of Brightwater Bay.

It couldn't be seen from above, only from the sea, although Merry suspected she might just about glimpse the narrow strip of pale gold if she ever stood right on the edge of the cliffs, and it was flanked on either side by an outcrop of vicious-looking rocks. In the autumn, Magnús said it was where grey seals came to give birth to their pups; he assured her the slender shelf of land was never submerged by the tide, making it the perfect place for mother seals to bond with their babies before introducing them to life under the waves.

'No one bothers them here,' he said, leaning on the steering wheel of the boat as the engine fell silent and gazing at the now-empty beach. 'There are much easier places to spot them around Orkney, so the tours don't come this way.'

Merry leaned back in her seat and craned her head upwards. The cliffs seemed even more immense from the water, making Magnús's boat feel like a toy as it bobbed on the white-crested waves, and she was amazed to see they weren't as sheer and barren as she'd imagined. The mottled brown and grey rock was sprinkled with yellow and lilac and pink flowers, their roots burrowing deep into the strata and taking hold wherever they could. Vibrant green leaves and grasses burst out around them, producing a kind of floral wallpaper effect that Merry loved. Birds soared on the thermals created by the warm mid-afternoon sunshine and perched on the flowery ledges; others chose rockier shelves and Merry wondered if they might have nests there. It was evidently breeding season for some, if not all, of Orkney's bird population.

Magnús rummaged under his seat and pulled out a pair of binoculars. 'Use these if you want a closer look. You might even spot some puffins if you are very lucky.'

She took the binoculars and trained them on the cliffs. Over the last few months, Merry had learned to recognize a number of the birds she could hear as she awoke each day: the guillemots, with their distinctive black and white plumage, the kittiwakes, who looked so very like the gulls she knew from London, and the razorbills, with their funny blunt beaks that were anything but razor-like. She sat for a few moments, enjoying the close-up view of her feathery neighbours as they soared and jostled over the blue-grey water; if there was a better way to enjoy the late May sunshine then she couldn't think of it right then.

Eventually, she lowered the binoculars to glance across

at Magnús. 'How do they raise their chicks on the cliffs? There doesn't seem to be room for a perch, let alone to incubate an egg.'

'Evolution,' he said, shrugging. 'Guillemots in particular have adapted to cliff-face breeding – they protect their eggs from predators by nesting as close together as possible and their eggs are specially designed not to roll off the edge.'

Merry stared at him in disbelief. 'Specially designed?'

He tipped his head. 'I'm guessing you've never seen a guillemot egg. They're very distinctive in colour – usually a beautiful shade of turquoise – but it's the shape that's the best feature. One end is round and the other is pointed, so that they grip better on the stacks and make things easier when the parents need to swap places for incubating duties. It's really very clever.'

She trained the binoculars on the cliffs again and saw that he was right: the guillemots were huddled together like commuters in the rush hour. 'I hope they all get along.'

Magnús grinned. 'Not always. My zoologist friend studies them and she says it's like watching *Game of Thrones* sometimes. Lots of family drama, fights and infidelity.'

'Wow,' Merry replied, with another glance at the crowded rock face. 'I hope it's less bloodthirsty.'

'Things can get pretty brutal,' Magnús conceded. 'The puffins are quite boring by comparison, although they're cute, so everyone wants to see them.'

She scanned the cliffs, searching for the distinctive orange-beaked birds and found none. But there were so many birds – the cliffs really were teeming with them – that she thought she might easily miss the puffins.

'Let me have a look,' Magnús said, when she told him she hadn't been able to spot any. 'There's definitely a colony a little further north, so if we don't see them here, we can head up the coast a bit.'

He retrieved another pair of binoculars from beneath a seat and studied the skies above Brightwater Bay. After a moment or two, he nodded in satisfaction and made his way to sit next to Merry. 'See that outcrop there?' he said, pointing at the top of the cliff to her left. 'Train the binoculars on that, then move them slowly upwards.'

Merry followed his suggestion, trying to ignore the lazy flip-flop of her stomach at his sudden nearness. It had been years since she'd experienced this constant fluttering in the presence of a man – the buzz that made it hard to focus on anything but him. Had it been like this with Alex at the beginning? It must have been, although what she mostly remembered about the early days of their relationship was the excruciating awkwardness of being fifteen. The way she felt around Magnús was an all-grown-up version of that self-conscious but intense attraction, especially in comparison with the utter lack of desire she'd felt when she'd last seen Alex, in London. She'd told Magnús about her trip, of course, and mentioned seeing Alex but hadn't revealed her fleeting idea of possibly extending her time on Orkney. The thought had taken hold in her subconscious, however, and it had grown. Now, with Magnús so close she could hear him breathe, Merry was starting to wonder whether it was time to invite him to spend the night at the croft again.

For the moment, however, she tried to concentrate on following his directions to find the puffins. And then suddenly, as her gaze roved towards the grassy top of the cliffs, past the hundreds of other birds, she saw the small cluster of snub orange beaks and cheeky markings that made them so popular.

'Oh,' she breathed, watching the distant birds with a thrill of delight. It didn't matter that she was too far away to see them in detail; that could wait for another day. What mattered was that she'd seen her first puffin in the wild.

She lowered the binoculars and turned to Magnús, only to find he was gazing at her. Before she could move, he bent his head and kissed her.

All rational thought flew from her head when his lips met hers. Even the caws and cries of the birds seemed to fade into mere background noise and she was sure the waves had stopped crashing against the cliff base. Magnús placed a hand on her back to urge her nearer and her arm snaked around his neck as the kiss grew deeper, her fingers twisting into his hair.

Then the pocket of his jacket vibrated against Merry's ribs and she realized his phone was ringing.

At first, she thought he was going to ignore it – the pressure on the small of her back increased, as though he was expecting her to pull away. But then his mouth broke with hers and he let out an audible sigh. 'Sorry,' he said. 'I'm a volunteer on the lifeboat. It might be important.'

And when he put it like that, Merry felt bad for wishing he'd let it go to voicemail. But it soon became clear that it wasn't the lifeboat station on the phone; Magnús answered whoever it was in what sounded to Merry like Icelandic. Frowning, she watched as he stopped speaking to listen, and then his face turned grey beneath his light golden tan. He rattled off a few more sentences, his tone urgent and abrupt, then she saw his eyes shut as though he'd just had the worst news possible. Merry averted her gaze then, and tried hard not to eavesdrop, even though she didn't understand a word in any case. She studied the beach, the birds, the cliffs – anything to avert the quiver of unease that was now rippling through her body. Something was wrong: she could tell from the tense set of his jaw and the stiff, hunched shoulders, but it wasn't until he ended the call and lowered the phone that Merry discovered how bad it was.

'My mother has had a heart attack,' he said numbly. 'She's been taken to hospital in Reykjavik.'

Merry gasped in horror. 'No! I'm so sorry, Magnús.'

'That was my sister,' he went on in the same dull mono-tone. 'She says everything is under control but I should get there as soon as I can.'

'Of course, you must,' Merry urged. 'Are there direct flights from Aberdeen?'

Magnús got to his feet and dithered for a second or two. And that was when Merry realized just how worried he was; she'd never seen him anything less than solid and purposeful. 'From Edinburgh, maybe. I need to check the times.'

He gave her a regretful look but she sensed he was only half there. 'I'm sorry – I need to take you back to Kirkwall.'

'Don't be sorry,' Merry said swiftly. 'Let's get going.'

The journey seemed to take forever, although Merry thought Magnús was pushing the engine harder than he had on the journey out. When they reached Kirkwall harbour, he'd helped her disembark and kissed her cheek in a distracted fashion. 'I'll call you,' he said, once his boat was securely fastened to the harbour.

Merry shook her head. 'Please, don't give it another thought. I hope it's not serious and that your mother makes a speedy recovery.'

'Thanks,' he said as he checked his phone again. 'I really enjoyed spending time with you today and I'm sorry to be cutting things short.'

His expression was so sincere that she was very tempted to kiss him again, except she knew his mind was elsewhere. She settled for squeezing his arm once and stepping back. 'No problem. Have a safe journey.'

He nodded once and strode away, leaving Merry to gaze after him, hoping his fears would soon be laid to rest.

Merry didn't hear from him for another thirty-six hours. She tried not to worry, knowing he'd be busy with his family and speaking to the doctors, finding out how serious the heart attack had been and what his mother's prognosis was. But even so, she couldn't help fretting a little as the hours passed – even the notes from her editor couldn't distract her fully. In the end, she went for a run in the afternoon sunshine, north along the cliffs to where Magnús had suggested she'd have a better chance of seeing the puffins up close. And he was right; it took her several miles, but she eventually spotted a colony at the top of a grassy cliff. Some of the adult birds were hopping clumsily around the greenery of the headland; they didn't seem to mind her presence, although she took care not to get too close. Their movement was almost comical on land, but they became a different bird when diving into the sea, plummeting the vast distance to the waves and often emerging with a wriggling eel in their beaks. She spent some time watching them before retracing her steps to the croft and a long hot shower.

The strenuous activity helped to settle her anxiety, but she was still restless and found herself glancing at her phone more often than usual, its stubborn silence only making her more ill at ease. After another hour of unproductivity, she gave up trying to work and messaged Niall.

Up for a post-work pint?

It took a few minutes for her phone to buzz with his response, but the message made her smile:

How about dinner instead? You haven't seen the views from The Skerry yet – pick you up at 6.30?

Merry glanced guiltily at her laptop and imagined a long evening of staring at its screen, while trying to ignore her phone, and decided an evening with Niall would be infinitely more preferable.

OK, but it's my turn to drive. Pick you up at 6.45.

*

The Skerry turned out to be a modern, eco-friendly restaurant a few miles from Kirkwall, overlooking a flat wildflower meadow that sloped towards the glistening expanse of Scapa Flow to the south. The sun was still a long way from dipping below the land as Merry and Niall took their seats on the terrace outside the glass and wood building; she knew from experience that it wouldn't set until around ten o'clock. The temperature had begun to drop, however, and she was glad of the jumper she'd decided to wear. In London, Jess had reported their favourite rooftop bar in Trafalgar Square was hot enough to bring out a flurry of sandals and sundresses among the clientele – in Orkney, there was evidently no such rush to summer clothing and Merry was pleased she'd judged it right.

'You won't be surprised to hear I recommend the Orkney gin,' Niall said, as they studied the cocktail menu. 'The Rhubarb Old Tom is particularly good if you like a bit of sweetness, or the Johnsmas is more floral and summery.'

'Sold,' Merry said and she leaned back against the cushions of the wicker armchair, taking in the blue skies and meadow-scented air with a sigh. 'This was a wonderful idea – thanks for suggesting it.'

He smiled. 'Wait until you taste the scallops – you'll want to thank me all over again.'

The flirtatious vibe of the sentence caused Merry to blink but there was nothing in Niall's expression that suggested he'd meant it that way. *I've been spending too much time with Jess*, she thought, and pushed the observation away.

'I'm glad to be out and about, anyway,' she said, careful to keep any hint of embarrassment from her voice. 'I do love the croft but writers have a tendency to get lost in their own heads sometimes – it's good to be reminded that there's still a lot of the islands I haven't seen.'

As often happened, Niall somehow picked up on the things she wasn't saying. 'Rough day?'

She glanced at her phone, face down on the table, and forced herself to ignore it. 'Not for me,' she said. 'But ... a friend had some bad news and I'm waiting to hear from ... them.'

A frown creased Niall's forehead and Merry knew he'd noticed her clumsy attempt to pick her words carefully. 'I'm being melodramatic,' she said, with a self-deprecating shake of her head. 'Ignore me.'

He studied her for several long seconds, then nodded slowly. 'This would be Magnús. I heard he'd had to rush back to Iceland – something about his mother, I think?'

Of course he already knew, Merry told herself. This was Orkney, where people spoke to their neighbours and everyone looked out for each other. Magnús would have had work commitments to cover and friends to notify. He wouldn't have simply left with no word to the other people who cared about him.

'Yes,' she said to Niall, as a black-and-white clad waitress appeared to take their drinks order. 'This is about Magnús.'

Merry took Niall's recommendation and chose the Johnsmas gin with a matching tonic, while he ordered a bottle of the terrifying-sounding Skull Splitter. 'It's an Orkney ale, quite light and citrussy,' he explained when he saw her staring. 'The name makes it sound worse than it is. They also brew a beer called Clootie Dumpling, but that's more of a winter ale.'

'Of course,' Merry said, straight-faced. 'So, there's a brewery, a gin distillery and more than one whisky distillery on Orkney. You take your drinking seriously here, don't you?'

He grinned. 'We're mostly descended from Vikings. What did you expect?'

And that made her think of Magnús again. Niall must have realized because he cleared his throat. 'I didn't know you and Magnús had become such good friends.' He stopped and seemed to review the sentence in his head. 'I mean, obviously I knew you were *friends,* but I hadn't thought you were – well – *good* friends, what with you being ...'

He trailed off and Merry could see he was blushing. With her being what, she wondered. Only on Orkney for a few more months? Or apparently engaged to another man? 'Niall—' she began.

His cheeks turned an even deeper shade of crimson. 'You can tell me to mind my own business if you like.'

This was it, she realized, the moment she'd been dreading. It was time to tell Niall the truth. But then she spotted the waitress approaching with their drinks and decided it could wait, at least until after they'd ordered their meals. They sat in uncomfortable silence while the woman arranged their drinks and turned a friendly smile on each of them. 'Now, what can I get you to eat? The soup of the day is broccoli and Stilton, and the chef's special is sea bass with garlic and lemon.'

Merry chose the pan-seared scallops to start because Niall's recommendations had always been on the money when it came to island food, followed by the Scapa sirloin. Their waitress beamed in approval as Merry made her choices. 'The whisky cream sauce that comes with the steak is especially good.'

Niall went for the scallops too, after checking Merry didn't object to them both having the same starter. 'Some of my friends take a dim view of that sort of thing,' he said. 'They claim it removes the opportunity to try each other's food.'

Merry smiled, because that was very much the way Jess saw things. 'At least if we both have the same thing, neither of us will have food envy.'

Once he'd ordered the sea bass, the waitress left. Niall raised his glass of beer and held it towards Merry's gin. 'Cheers.'

She tapped her glass against his. 'Yes, cheers.'

The gin was good, she thought as she took a long cool sip. It might even have been very good, but it was hard to tell because the stress of what she was about to do next was enough to prevent her from enjoying the flavours as much as she might. But there was no backing down now. 'Niall, there's something you need to know.'

To his credit, Niall listened without a single interruption, not even when she got to the part where she'd misled him about still being in a relationship with Alex. When she finished the whole excruciating explanation, he sat in silence for a moment and then drained his glass in one movement.

'Suddenly, a lot of things make sense,' he said, meeting her gaze with a rueful expression. 'I could never understand why Alex hadn't come to visit – if you were my girlfriend, I'd have been here as often as I could. But I just assumed he was the sort of city idiot who was always working. Turns out he's an idiot for entirely different reasons.'

The urge to defend Alex was still there; even after all these months, her brain automatically lined up excuses for him and she belatedly wondered how long she'd been mentally excusing his lack of attention in all aspects of their relationship. But there was no point in raking over the coals of a stone-cold fire – Alex and his failings were most definitely part of her past.

'I wish I'd told you sooner,' she said to Niall. 'I don't really know why I didn't.'

She certainly wasn't about to advance Jess's theory for her reluctance; the evening had been embarrassing enough. But Niall seemed to accept the words at face value. 'Better late than never,' he said, his tone curiously cheerful. 'As I say, it all makes sense. You didn't seem like the type to cheat, either, but now I know you were always perfectly free to date Magnús.'

'Yes,' she said. 'I'm sorry if I put you in an awkward position. I didn't expect any of this to happen.'

He waved away her apology. 'Don't worry about that. I'm

more concerned with whether or not you're happy now. Has being here on Orkney helped?'

It was a question she could answer with total honesty. 'Yes, in so many ways.' She took a deep breath. 'In fact, I'd go so far as to say it's saved me.'

She expected him to flash his Superman smile, but instead he fixed his gaze on the still waters of Scapa Flow. 'You'd be surprised how many people feel that way,' he said quietly, after a few seconds had passed. His eyes met hers. 'Or maybe you wouldn't.'

She thought of the sense of peace she felt while running along the cliffs above Brightwater Bay, her hair streaming on the breeze and the birds calling across the endless sky, the way the words of her stories came more easily here, and the feeling of belonging she'd had almost from the first moment she'd arrived, the way her heart had been soothed over the last few months until it no longer felt fractured and was steady. All of that and more crowded into her mind as she returned Niall's gaze and she knew she'd never be able to say it all out loud. But she might just be able to capture it on the page.

'No,' she said, and realized with a sudden bloom of warmth that where Niall was concerned, she didn't have to explain a thing. 'I wouldn't be at all surprised.'

Chapter Nineteen

When Magnús finally rang her, it was after eleven o'clock. She and Niall had finished their meal at The Skerry around nine-thirty, and she'd dropped him home with her stomach full of good food and her mood considerably lighter. She'd settled in front of the fire with a glass of Valkyrie and the new *Rivers of London* novel, and was soon lost on the city's supernatural streets. She was so engrossed that it took her a moment to work out what the buzzing sound was and she half expected to see a magically enabled drone outside the window, like the one she'd just been reading about. And then her mobile vibrated against the wood of the coffee table and she picked it up to see Magnús's image on the screen.

'Hello from Reykjavik,' he said when she answered the call, and his voice sounded cracked and weary.

'How are you?' she replied. 'How's your mum?'

'I'm okay. My mother ...' he trailed off and cleared his

throat. 'My mother is in intensive care right now. Stable but serious, the doctors say.'

Pity clutched at Merry's stomach. 'I'm so sorry, Magnús. Have they been able to tell you what happened?'

There wasn't much to tell, he said. One minute his mother had been fine, eating breakfast with his sister, Lara, and laughing about something on the morning news, the next minute she'd been unable to breathe and clutching at her chest. She'd been unconscious when the ambulance had reached the hospital and hadn't woken since. The doctors said she'd suffered a severe heart attack and suspected there was significant damage, but it was too early to tell how badly the rest of her body had been affected.

'She's breathing on her own,' he finished. 'That's something at least.'

The sadness behind the words made Merry's own heart ache. 'I'm sorry.'

'So am I,' he said. 'But she's strong – a fighter. Lara and I both believe she will come through this.'

'Is there anything I can do?' Merry asked, although she knew the answer before he gave it.

'Thank you, but no.' He paused. 'But it's good to hear your voice. I'm sorry to call you so late.'

'It's no problem,' she said. 'I'm glad you got there safely, even if the news awaiting you wasn't quite as positive as you'd hoped. And you must be shattered now – why don't you get some rest? We can talk again when you get the chance.'

Coming Home to Brightwater Bay

'Okay,' he said, and she heard him stifle a yawn. 'Goodnight, Merry.'

'Goodnight,' she replied. 'Speak soon.'

She sat for a short while after the conversation had ended, staring into the glowing embers of the fire, her book forgotten. Magnús had sounded worried and exhausted, which was hardly a surprise, and she felt terrible for him. Both her own parents were gone. They had died within a year of each other, from different illnesses, but she sometimes thought her father had simply given up after he lost her mother. She hoped the doctors' suspicions were wrong. She hoped Magnús's mother was the fighter he said she was and would battle her way back from the seriousness of her condition. And most of all, Merry hoped he would be spared the pain of grieving for a parent taken too young. She knew from experience how much that hurt.

The days rolled by. May became June and Merry finished the changes to her book suggested by her editor. Sam Silverton asked for the latest draft because he'd found the perfect screenwriter to adapt it and Merry slowly started to believe that this time would be different. This time, perhaps, something might actually come from a movie option on one of her stories.

Meanwhile, she spent her non-writing time exploring Orkney. At first, she half expected to run into Magnús on her travels, the way she had so many times already, but he was never there and she started to grow used to his absence.

289

His phone calls and messages had been sporadic, snatched between what she assumed was an endless whirl of hospital visits and meetings with medical staff and whatever sleep he could get. She knew how draining it all was and didn't blame him on the days when she heard nothing. But when those days started to stretch to two or three, and her messages went unread, a cold feeling grew in the pit of her stomach.

'Don't read too much into it,' Jess warned, when Merry confided her anxieties over the phone. 'He's probably chasing around sorting out his mum's care. Didn't you say she'd regained consciousness?'

She had, Merry said, although the message from Magnús had been brief and scant on detail. 'And you're right – I'm sure he's horribly busy.' She hated the way complaining made her feel, like a demanding toddler who wanted her favourite toy. 'It's just that it reminds me a lot of how Alex was for the last year or so of our relationship – distant, like I couldn't reach him. And even when I could, I felt as though I was annoying him.'

'But this isn't Alex,' Jess reminded her gently. 'It's Magnús and he's got some pretty serious stuff going on. Have you had The Conversation yet?'

The implied capital letters told Merry she was asking if she and Magnús were still at the seeing each other stage or whether they'd pinned things down into an 'official' relationship. 'We haven't talked about being exclusive,' she said hesitantly. 'But I didn't think we needed to. Neither of us is dating anyone else.'

'Well, then,' her best friend said in a brisk tone. 'You've got nothing to worry about. He'll come back to you once things settle down, I'm sure.'

Merry nodded, knowing she was talking sense and feeling ashamed of wanting more than Magnús could possibly give at that moment. But how much time did it take to read a message? On the other hand, Jess knew much more about dating etiquette than Merry, who'd only ever had one partner.

'Okay, you're right,' she said and gave herself a mental shake. 'Now, hadn't we better plan this event? Niall has asked if there's a theme we'd like to focus on – something that's common to both our writing styles, or perhaps the different ways we approach creating characters and stories?'

Her best friend laughed. 'I spend a lot of time looking at Instagram photos of beautiful men. And then I imagine what it would be like to have sex with them, and write it all down as fast as I can before I forget.'

Merry grinned. She knew for a fact that a number of the men Jess had met through various dating apps had found their way into her books too, although names had been changed to protect the innocent, the guilty and the downright terrible in bed. The Argentinian rugby player she'd hooked up with in Cannes one weekend had formed the basis for several characters that her readers had fallen head over heels in love with. And then Merry thought of the book she had just delivered, of the characters who were loosely based on real people – people she knew from Orkney – and she wondered how she and Jess were going to find any common theme between their work.

'What about escape?' Jess asked slowly. 'You know – as in novels are a good way to escape from everyday life, especially when it sucks. Some people call my books guilty pleasures and I'm perfectly on board with that – as long as they're giving pleasure.'

Merry considered the idea. She used to think her books brought joy to readers, back when writing was easy and she'd taken enormous satisfaction in writing something her fans would love. But she wasn't sure her new book would have quite the same effect; some parts were bound to make them cry, despite her best efforts to lighten the mood where she could. It was a story about love, and all the ways love showed itself, set against the terrible losses of the Second World War. It featured no Argentinian rugby players with biceps the size of branches.

'How about happiness?' she said. 'Why do books make us happy, even when they make us cry? What kind of stories do we reach for when times are tough?'

Jess was quiet for a moment, and Merry could picture her thinking the suggestion over, a long strand of golden hair twisting between her fingers. 'You know, that might just work,' she said. 'Good job, Mer.'

The conversation moved onto the more practical aspects of Jess's upcoming visit: where she'd stay and who would meet her at Kirkwall Airport. Merry recalled her first impressions of the tiny plane that flew to Orkney and told Jess what to expect. Just before Jess signed off, she asked a question that caught Merry off-guard.

'Have you heard from Alex lately?'

'No,' Merry replied, frowning. 'Not since I saw him in Chiswick. Why?'

There was a brief pause. 'No reason. I just wondered, that's all.' She cleared her throat. 'Listen, don't worry about Magnús. It'll be fine.'

The call ended shortly after, leaving Merry to draw what comfort she could from the reassurance. Jess was right – he wasn't Alex and, besides, the situation was entirely different; a few dates, however wonderful, wasn't the same as a long-term relationship that spanned years and Magnús didn't owe her anything.

It was just that it had felt like the start of something, she thought wistfully. Something good. And she couldn't help wondering whether the distance she sensed in his messages was down to more than just the ocean between them.

On Tuesday, Merry returned from her run with Sheila to find a scene of devastation at the croft. The washing she'd carefully hung out to dry in the sunshine that morning was strewn across the grass; her favourite blouse was draped over the bench that overlooked the bay, one sleeve snagged on the wood was all that had prevented it from floating away on the breeze. A pair of jeans were making their way inland and several pairs of knickers were adorning the roof.

'Shit!' Merry exclaimed, dropping her water bottle and

hurrying forward to collect the scattered clothes. She cast a suspicious look at the clothes airer, which now only held a few lonely socks and a tea towel, and then up at the sky in search of an explanation. There wasn't enough wind to explain the mystery, not when she'd taken care to pin everything securely with clothes pegs. So how had it happened?

The answer became apparent when she ventured around the back of the croft to make sure she hadn't missed anything – and discovered Gordon the goat placidly munching on her best La Perla bra.

'Hey!' she yelled and ran towards him. 'That's not for eating, you monster!'

Gordon regarded her quizzically for a moment, then dropped the bra and ambled a few steps to one side. Merry reached for a soggy, grass-flecked strap and groaned. Just as she'd suspected, the bra was ruined. The gauzy material, delicate at the best of times, had not coped well with the machinations of a goat's teeth, which were famously designed to grind anything the animal ate into pulp. One underwire was poking out, like an antenna. The other was completely gone and Merry could find no trace of it anywhere around the croft.

She turned to gaze at Gordon, who was now tearing up mouthfuls of grass to round off his lingerie main course, and a horrible thought occurred to her: what if he had swallowed the missing underwire? Goats had a notoriously robust digestive system but surely even they couldn't cope with twelve centimetres of curved metal. And as much as Merry was furious with Gordon, she wasn't angry enough to ignore the potential consequences of his crime.

She was going to have to call Clare Watson.

The call went straight to voicemail and there was no answer on the landline Clare had given Merry for emergencies. Placing all the washing back into the machine, Merry dithered for a few minutes, Googling the effects of animals eating metal objects and not liking what she found: a perforated gullet or stomach was a serious risk. And although Gordon didn't seem to be showing any signs of distress, Merry wasn't about to take the chance that he might deteriorate. She found a length of rope in the shed that housed the Mini and tied it as firmly as she could around the goat's neck.

'You and I are going for a walk,' she told him, in a firm tone that she hoped transcended the language barrier. 'I'm taking you home.'

It was not like walking a dog.

At first, Gordon had seemed to understand what she wanted him to do, although that might have had more to do with the bag of snacking seeds she'd brought to encourage him to come quietly. But the further they got into the two-mile journey, the slower the goat walked. He stopped often to tug grass from the fields they crossed and refused to move when Merry tugged on the rope in careful encouragement. At one point, she resorted to placing her hands on his flanks and pushing, but that only made him dig his hooves into the ground more. There was still no reply from the farm; Clare and Hugh must be out with the llama stock, she decided, pushing her sweaty hair from her forehead and glaring at the goat. She couldn't shake the impression that he was laughing at her.

'You are a bloody pain in the arse,' she snapped. 'I'm going to write you into a book and feed you to a dinosaur.'

He opened his mouth and let out a bleat that sounded a lot like a string of expletives. Then he trotted off, leaving Merry to stare after him before breaking into a jog to keep up. Maybe he did understand her after all, she thought.

She hadn't given much thought to what she would do if she arrived at the farm to find no sign of the Watsons, but luckily she met Hugh in the Land Rover at the bottom of the lane that led to the farmhouse. He leaned out of the open window, taking in her warm-cheeked, sweaty appearance with obvious surprise. 'Hullo, Merry. Out for a walk?'

Then he saw the goat, and the length of rope in Merry's hands, and understanding dawned. 'Oh dear,' he said with a sorrowful shake of his head. 'What's he done this time?'

She glossed over the details of the crime. Apart from anything else, she wasn't sure she wanted to discuss her expensive lingerie habit with someone she barely knew. When she mentioned the missing underwire, Hugh's expression had grown serious.

'It's unlikely he ate it, but you never know with goats,' he said. 'Hop in the front and I'll drop you at the house before I call the vet.'

Merry hesitated, aware that she was dripping with

perspiration and almost certainly smelled of goat. It wasn't the kind of professional image a Writer in Residence should project, she felt, especially not to the always perfectly groomed Clare Watson.

But Hugh picked up on her reticence and grinned. '*Och*, don't fret. Clare's just back from shearing the llamas. She smells worse than you.'

It wasn't the most reassuring thing he might have said, but Merry suddenly felt desperate for some water. She'd left her bottle back at the croft, not realizing how long it would take her to walk Gordon to the Watson farm, and her throat was dry and sore. She needn't stay long, she told herself. Just long enough to quench her thirst and make sure Gordon would be okay.

Clare Watson did not look or smell as though she'd spent the morning among the llama flock; in fact, she looked impossibly glamorous for a farmer's wife. She insisted on making tea and fussing around Merry while Hugh went off to call the vet, showing her to the bathroom and pressing fluffy towels into her arms, telling her to use anything she wanted.

'I've got some trousers and a jumper that will fit you if you want to take a shower,' she said, and Merry looked at her glossy blonde hair and fresh-faced complexion and was almost tempted.

'No, a good wash will do for now,' she said after a momentary hesitation. 'Thanks, though.'

Ten minutes later, she felt more human, if not quite up to

Clare's standard of grooming. Several long gulps of strong tea helped, as did a slice of featherlight angel food cake from Rossi's.

'Do I even want to know what Gordon did to make you frog-march him over the fields back to us?' Clare asked, once Merry was sitting at the long wooden table in the light and airy kitchen. 'Is it going to be very expensive?'

Merry explained and the other woman's hands flew to her face. 'Not La Perla! Oh god, I'm so sorry – we'll replace it, of course. The last time he did something like this, it was a pair of M&S boxer shorts and the writer threatened to call the police.'

'Really?' Merry said, and she couldn't suppress a smile at the image of Gordon with a pair of boxers in his mouth. 'I'm not going to do that. I was worried about the underwire, that's all. Google suggested it might cause serious problems.'

Clare gave a little snort. 'That goat has more lives than a cat – I'm sure he'll be fine. But thank you for bringing him to us. It was really kind of you.'

'I tried calling, but Hugh says you've been out with the llamas this morning,' Merry said.

'Every day is a shearing day in summer,' Clare replied. 'We rotate the flock so that we have a constant supply of fibre to spin into wool. Would you like to go and meet them?'

Merry sipped her tea, privately wondering whether she'd had enough of livestock for one day, but there didn't seem to be a polite way to refuse. Besides, she never knew when she might need to know about llama farming for a book. 'Okay,' she said, smiling. 'That would be lovely.'

'I'll lend you some wellies,' Clare said, glancing down at Merry's running shoes. 'Things can get a bit agricultural, if you know what I mean.'

The llamas were dotted across four fields, each with a modern-looking barn at one end. There was a concrete yard in front of the nearest barn and that was where Clare said they did the shearing.

'Do the llamas mind?' Merry said, studying one slender-nosed animal whose fringe was flopping across its long-lashed eyes, giving it the look of a sulky teenager.

'They're used to it,' Clare said. 'Most of our flock has been with us for a few years now and we're careful about breeding so there aren't a lot of youngsters.'

It was clearly a well-managed operation, Merry thought as Clare showed her the inside of one barn. They kept cows and sheep too, Clare explained, plus chickens for their eggs. 'Having the llamas around deters the foxes too,' she said. 'They're better than guard dogs.'

It wasn't until they were back in the farmhouse, with more tea and a packet of chocolate Hobnobs, that Clare asked outright if Merry was sleeping with Magnús.

'No!' Merry exclaimed, feeling her face flush right to the roots of her hair. 'That would be very difficult, given he's not on Orkney right now.'

Clare tipped her head to concede the point. 'True enough.' She leaned forward, her eyes sparkling. 'But before he went – had you sealed the deal?'

It was an incredibly personal question, Merry thought,

but somehow she couldn't hold it against Clare. It wasn't the first time she'd shown interest in Merry's relationship with Magnús, and she had discovered him at the croft the morning after Merry had fallen ill. It wasn't a total surprise she was curious about what had happened.

'No,' Merry said, and couldn't prevent a sigh from escaping her. 'And after the conversation we had yesterday, I'm not sure we ever will.'

Magnús had called just after lunchtime, when Merry had been on her way to Kirkwall. Knowing he might not find the time to ring back if she didn't take the call, she'd pulled the Mini over beside the tranquil Loch of Stenness and answered.

'Hi,' she said cheerfully. 'How are you?'

But it soon became clear that Magnús had more on his mind than just catching up. His voice was subdued as he told her his mother was out of intensive care.

'But that's good news,' Merry said, her brows knitting together in confusion. 'Isn't it?'

'It is,' he replied. 'But she's still very weak. The doctors say it will take months for her to recover and she'll need a lot of care in that time. And it doesn't feel fair that my sister should have to do that on her own.'

Merry felt as though a stone had settled in the pit of her stomach as she absorbed his meaning. 'Right,' she said softly. 'So, you're going to stay there.'

He sighed. 'It's the proper thing to do. Lara needs to work – she can't spare all the time our mother needs. If I'm here, we can split the care between us.' There was a short pause. 'But I'm afraid that causes difficulty elsewhere.'

Difficulty was something of an understatement, Merry thought. The distance between Reykjavik and Orkney wasn't huge in terms of miles, but it was a difficult journey whichever way you travelled. It certainly wasn't a quick commute, nor was it cheap; Magnús wouldn't be able to keep his boatbuilding business running, or his summer tours around the islands. But perhaps – perhaps – they might still be able to make a relationship work, if they both committed to the idea. It wouldn't always be like this, after all.

'Don't think I haven't considered it,' he said when Merry made the suggestion. 'I've been racking my brains, trying to think of ways to make things easier. But . . .'

He trailed off and panic dug its claws into Merry's insides.

'It could work,' she said, before he could finish the sentence. 'I could come to see you for the weekend, you could come here. Or even to London, once I'm back – there are loads of flights between Reykjavik and the London airports.'

'The trouble is that I know it wouldn't be enough,' Magnús said, and his voice was so yearning that Merry thought she might cry. 'I don't want half a relationship with you – I want all of it. I want to wake up with you in the mornings, without the constant pressure of the clock ticking in the background. I want to be able to drive over to see you if the mood takes me, to invite you on a spontaneous picnic or go and catch a band one evening. You deserve someone who can give you all of that, Merry, especially after the way

Alex treated you. And ... I'm sorry that I can't be the one to make you believe in love again. Not right now, anyway.'

Merry's head whirled. This couldn't be happening ... not again. 'But—'

'I can't do it – not now. And not for a long time,' he went on gently. 'I've watched you mend your heart after the pain Alex caused you – I like to think I've even helped put the odd piece back in place, here and there. But it would be wrong of me to stand in your way now, when I can't offer anything more than half my attention and even less of my time. It's not the kind of man I am.'

He'd been so determined, so implacable in his belief that this was the right thing to do, that eventually she had been forced to accept it. She'd driven to Kirkwall, had called in at Rossi's to see Helen and Morag, and visited the library to finalize the details of Jess's visit the following week. And, throughout, she'd held it together, hadn't let even a shred of the disappointment and sadness that was dragging at her heart to show. It wasn't until she was back at the croft, gazing out across Brightwater Bay, that she allowed herself to mourn. Then she'd phoned Jess and let her no-nonsense common sense soothe away the hurt.

'I know it feels shit,' Jess had said. 'And it's a bloody awful situation. But at least he was honest.'

Merry sniffed and felt her lip wobble. She wouldn't cry. She *wouldn't*. 'Yeah, I know.'

'And thank god for a man with the emotional intelligence to step back when he can't give a woman what she needs,'

Jess went on. 'At least you know where you stand, babes. That's something.'

And now Clare Watson was reaching across the table to squeeze Merry's hand and saying almost exactly the same thing. 'It sucks. And it doesn't matter how much you can see it's the right thing, it still hurts.'

Merry nodded. 'It feels a bit better today. I went for a run along the cliffs and that helped me get a few things straight in my head.' She took a Hobnob and dunked it in her tea. 'And in a funny way, Gordon helped too. Took my mind off things, anyway.'

Clare laughed. 'There's nothing quite like a goat eating your designer lingerie for that. Sorry again.'

'Don't apologize,' Merry said and shook her head. 'It's not as though I'll be needing it any time soon.'

Hugh appeared a few minutes later, with the vet right behind him. 'No trace of the wire,' he said in answer to Clare's question. 'I bet the attention-seeking little bugger hid it somewhere.'

His wife snorted. 'Sometimes I wonder what Gordon actually brings to life on the farm.'

'Good looks, charm and a cracking personality,' Hugh said, deadpan. 'A bit like me.'

The laughter that followed lifted Merry's spirits a little bit more and she decided it might almost have been worth losing her precious lingerie for – although she'd already decided she would be drying the Agent Provocateur set indoors from now on. Once was more than enough to teach her a lesson.

Chapter Twenty

There was no mistaking the look of trauma in Jess's eyes when she walked into the Arrivals Hall at Kirkwall Airport on Friday afternoon, but Merry suspected it wasn't the flight from Aberdeen that had caused it. Jess was followed by a cluster of other passengers, mostly women, who were looking at her as though she were Beyoncé. And they showed no signs of going about their own business now that they'd reached their destination; in fact, they seemed intent on sticking close to Jess as she spotted Merry and sped up.

'Uh oh,' Niall said as he clocked the group too. 'I think Jess might have been recognized.'

'I'll leave you to handle them,' Merry murmured and strode forward to hug her best friend. 'Hello. How was your journey?'

Jess didn't let go, holding Merry close. 'What is this place? They knew who I was before we even got on the plane,' she whispered. 'They demanded selfies.'

Merry smiled as she stepped back. 'Welcome to Orkney, where writers are pretty much treated like rock stars. You get used to it after a while.'

Whatever Niall said to the group of women who'd been following Jess worked, because they hurriedly dispersed, albeit with several excited glances at her as they went. He came to stand beside Merry and held out a hand. 'I'm Niall Gunn, the librarian here on Orkney. Lovely to meet you at last.'

Merry watched as the impact of his smile registered on Jess. 'You have no idea how pleased I am to meet you,' Jess said, flashing her own killer smile. 'Merry's talked so much about you that I feel like I already know you.'

And now Merry saw Niall notice Jess properly, watched him take in her wavy blonde hair, tanned skin and dimpled cheeks. It wasn't the first time she'd seen her best friend's charms have this effect, but it was the first time she'd felt a tiny stirring of something resembling unease deep in the pit of her stomach.

What's that about, she wondered, even as she squashed the feeling flat.

'Only good things, I hope?' Niall said, his cheeks growing faintly pink.

'Of course,' Jess said. 'She's done nothing but rave about Orkney since she got here. I actually think you might have trouble getting her to leave.'

As usual, Niall seemed delighted to hear that Merry spoke well of the islands. 'Well, we try our best.' He waved an arm towards the doors, exactly the way he had when Merry had first arrived four months earlier. 'The car is this way. Can I carry your case?'

Jess allowed him to take the pull-up handle and waited until he'd turned away to mouth, 'Oh my god!' at Merry.

She waited until he was a further few metres ahead to lean in close. 'He is insanely gorgeous. Why aren't you banging him?'

Merry's gaze shot forwards to ensure Niall was definitely out of hearing. 'Jess, he's right there!'

'Believe me, I know,' Jess said emphatically. 'I can't take my eyes off him. Please tell me he doesn't still think you're with Alex.'

Merry's cheeks burned. 'No, he doesn't. Now can we drop this? He's going to hear you!'

Jess gave her a look that was entirely unconcerned. 'We can drop it for now. But at some point over this weekend, you and I are going to have a serious conversation about this. Because he,' she pointed at Niall's retreating back, 'is too fine an opportunity to pass up.'

For a fleeting moment, Merry felt panic at the thought of all the damage her best friend's well-meaning interference might cause. And then she remembered that this was Jess, who would never do anything to hurt her, and the panic was washed away by a wave of happiness that she was on Orkney at last. 'I'm so glad you're here,' she blurted out, and was surprised by the sudden prick of tears at the back of her eyes.

'Me too,' Jess said, looping her arm through Merry's. 'We're going to have a blast.'

Niall had been all set to book Jess into The Harbour Lights Hotel in Kirkwall but she was having none of it.

'What's the point in coming all the way up here to see you and staying twenty miles away?' she'd asked Merry, when they'd been planning the visit. 'I'll sleep on the sofa at your place – it'll be like old times.'

Merry, who'd been sitting on the sofa of the croft at the time, had looked doubtfully at its two-seater capacity. 'I don't think that's an option. Not unless you want to wake up with sciatica.'

But Jess hadn't been deterred, not even when Merry sent her a photo of the sofa. And now she was standing in the living room of the croft, gazing at the sofa with undisguised suspicion. 'Yeah, I'm not sleeping on that.'

Merry nodded. 'I thought you'd say that. So, either I can ring Niall and ask him to book you into a hotel in Kirkwall for the next few nights or we can share the double bed.'

'No brainer,' Jess said, grinning. 'The bottle of tequila I brought isn't going to get drunk if you have to drive back here every evening.'

The bottle of tequila wasn't going to get drunk even if Jess was staying at the croft, Merry wanted to point out, but she knew better than to risk throwing down a gauntlet like that. 'Why don't I give you the grand tour?' she said. 'It'll take all of ninety seconds.'

Once she'd shown Jess the inside of the croft, she took her out to the bench overlooking the bay. It was early evening and the sun still hung high in the sky, warming the air and bathing the cliffs in golden light. The birds had yet to settle and were wheeling overhead on the thermals, calling to each other as they wove lazy circles across the cloudless blue sky. Beneath them, the Atlantic crashed its steady beat against the rocky shoreline.

'I can see why you've fallen in love with this place,' Jess said, after a few minutes of silence. 'It's beautiful.'

Merry remembered the first time she'd stood where Jess was now; it had been February then, and the sun had been dropping below the horizon when she'd arrived at the croft. She'd had her breath stolen by the sunset and she had known right then that she'd found somewhere special. And what made it even more special was sharing it with her best friend. 'Yes,' she replied. 'It's not bad, is it?'

Jess turned to look at the croft, with its ancient stone walls and living turf roof, and she let out a sigh of appreciation. 'If you tell me there's Deliveroo, I might just stay here for ever with you.'

'Not that I know of,' Merry said. 'But I know a great restaurant with views that are almost as amazing as this. Shall we go?'

'Sure,' Jess said but she made no effort to move. 'How are you feeling about Magnús? Has he been in touch?'

It was a good question, Merry thought. The first day or two had been tough – there had been moments when she'd almost asked him to reconsider, and others when she'd been filled with anger at the unfairness of the situation. But there hadn't been anything close to the all-consuming emptiness she'd felt after Alex, which wasn't a surprise given she and Magnús had only been dating a short while. She was disappointed at the way things had worked out and mournful of what might have been, but her heart hadn't been broken. Bruised a little, perhaps, but she'd survive.

'We agreed to leave it for a while before messaging,' she told Jess. 'Just to let the dust settle.'

The other woman gave her a hard look. 'That's fine, but how are you feeling about it? Don't avoid the question.'

'I'm okay,' Merry said. 'And much better now you're here.'

'Good,' Jess said, apparently mollified. 'I'm sad I'm not going to meet the man who could put Niall the sexy librarian in the shade, but you can't have everything. Now, how do we get to this restaurant and have we got time for a cocktail first?'

Merry awoke the next day with only the slightest of headaches. Mindful of their event on Saturday evening, both she and Jess had taken care not to overdo it with the tequila or the whisky once they'd returned from a delicious meal at the Skerry. It had still been light enough for them to take their full glasses out to the bench; they'd sat wrapped in blankets, and watched the sun go down while putting the book world to rights. Then they'd gone inside and called it a night.

'Plenty of time for a wild one after the event tomorrow,' Jess had said, unable to hide a deep yawn.

And so it was that Merry found herself clear-headed and ready for whatever the day brought. She glanced over at the still-sleeping Jess and smiled. It was good to have her here.

Slipping out from under the covers, Merry headed for the kitchen to make coffee and, by the time Jess joined her an hour later, she'd already caught up on her social media and jotted down the bare bones of a short story. It was incredible to think that she'd been barely able to look at her laptop when she'd arrived at Brightwater Bay back in February, Merry thought as she saved the outline and got to her feet to brew more coffee. She'd never be anything less than grateful to Niall for choosing her to be Writer in Residence. It had most definitely changed her life.

She treated Jess to a tour of some of her favourite Orkney places during the day, stopping by Rossi's for lunch, to introduce her to Morag and Helen and their incredible tiramisu. And then they'd returned to the croft to freshen up before heading to the library for their event.

Niall greeted them both with obvious pleasure, but Merry thought she observed an extra sparkle in his smile for Jess and she wasn't entirely sure how she felt about that.

'All set to wow our audience?' he asked.

'If one turns up,' Jess answered with a self-deprecating quirk of her eyebrows.

Niall's smile deepened as he led the way to his office so they could leave their bags and collect their radio microphones. 'Oh, I think they'll turn up. As you discovered on the plane, you've got quite a fan club here. We've sold around three hundred tickets.'

Merry took pleasure in seeing Jess's jaw drop. 'I told you, we're practically rock stars here. Wait until you see the signing queue afterwards.'

The talk was being held in the large hall that Merry's previous two events had used. This evening, it had a comfortable-looking armchair facing a velvet sofa on the raised stage, with many rows of seats for the audience. They'd begun to trickle in long before Niall escorted Merry and Jess to the hall, so by the time six-thirty arrived, there was a sense of expectation in the air.

'This is going to be fun,' Merry whispered as they took their seats on the stage.

Jess grinned back. 'Of course it is. And to think we call it work!'

The applause was thunderous once Niall had introduced them. Once it had died down, he turned to them both and smiled. 'I can't believe how lucky we are to have not one but two incredible authors with us tonight,' he said, his gaze roving from Merry to Jess. 'But as well as being authors, you're also best friends. Can you tell us how you met?'

'Believe it or not, we took a residential writing course together,' Jess said. 'It wasn't long after I'd arrived in the UK from New Zealand, and I remember feeling pretty nervous about spending a week with a bunch of people I didn't know. But then I got chatting to Merry over the welcome pastries and knew right away we'd be friends.'

Merry smiled. 'It was like a romcom – we both reached for the last maple pecan Danish, our eyes met and BAM! We've been friends ever since.'

'Who got the pastry?' Niall asked.

'I did,' Jess said. 'It might have been a totally different story if Merry had demanded we split it.'

'Even then, I knew better than to ask you to share cake,' Merry said, which got an appreciative laugh from the audience.

'And who got the first book deal?'

'Jess did,' Merry said. 'We were both writing women's fiction – or at least, the kind of novels that publishers considered to be for women – but that was where the similarities ended. Anyone who has read one of Jessie's books knows that they're sharp, sexy and fun. Mine were gentler, more traditional love stories and there was a big demand for the kind of fiction Jess was brilliant at, so she landed an agent and then a book deal before me.'

'Not long before you,' Jess cut in. 'I think it was only a few weeks. And our books might be different in style, but they do have a few things in common – we both write stories that readers love to get lost in. I've lost count of the number of times people have told me they read one of my books really fast, that it was really easy to read.'

Niall nodded. 'It's something I hear a lot as a librarian. How do you feel about it?'

Jess shrugged. 'I love it, of course. Easy reading doesn't equal easy writing but if someone enjoys one of my books so much that they forget they're even reading, it means I've done my job properly.'

She glanced at Merry, who picked up the conversational baton. 'Having a light touch also allows us to explore some tricky themes and ideas, without the story being laden down by the issues our characters might be facing. It's a bit of a balancing act.'

'And one that both of you manage with great style and talent,' Niall said. 'As I'm sure anyone in the audience who's read your books would agree. And one of the reasons Orkney Library invited you here, Jessie, is because you've got quite a fan club among our readers. Can you give us an insight into your writing process? How do you come up with such memorable characters?'

Jess grinned wickedly. 'Some of them are actual people. But others are purely products of my imagination. Take Oscar, the hero of my third novel – he was based on someone I met on holiday on the Cote d'Azur and readers loved him so much that I brought him back for Book Five . . . and Book Seven . . .'

The conversation flowed seamlessly between the three of them, often causing ripples of laughter to spread across the audience, and Merry was genuinely sad when Niall checked his watch and said it was time to open the floor to questions. She wasn't surprised to see her neighbour, Sheila, with her hand in the air, alongside her best friend, Bridget McGinty, and a couple of other older women she recognized as being from the same book club; they were all huge Jessie Edwards fans. Niall had obviously spotted them too because he homed in on them straight away. 'Yes, Sheila, what's your question?'

Sheila got to her feet and Merry saw with some amusement that she held a clipboard. 'This is for Jessie,' she said. 'In *Lola's Lolly*, you described a film star who gets caught in an indelicate position by the paparazzi. Was that based on anyone real, and if so, who?'

Jess smiled in a way that Merry had seen a hundred times before. 'I couldn't possibly say,' she said, in a tone that left no doubt the character was absolutely based on a well-known A-lister. 'But let's just say if he were real, he'd be famous for his licence to thrill as much as anything else!'

A murmur went through the audience as they tried to second-guess who she meant and Merry had to hide a smile. Jess was a master at hinting who her characters might be based on, without ever revealing the truth. By the time questions had finished, she had the crowd eating out of her hand.

'I hope you're ready for this,' Merry said, once Niall had wrapped the evening up to thunderous whoops and cheers. 'You're going to be signing for hours!'

She wasn't wrong; Jess's queue was twice the length of her own. But she didn't mind – Merry wasn't exactly old news to the readers of Orkney, but many of them had been at previous events and had at least one of her signed books already. Jess was fresh meat and therefore naturally attracting the bigger queue. Merry still had plenty of fans in front of her signing table, however, and she spent a busy forty minutes working her way through them, chatting and signing while Jess did the same beside her.

When Merry had signed the last book in her queue, she looked up to see Niall on the far side of the room, wiggling his hand in a gesture that suggested a drink. She was about to nod gratefully when she saw something that made the breath catch in her throat.

Walking towards her was the last person she'd expected to see. In fact, she had to blink twice to make sure she wasn't imagining him.

'Shit,' she muttered. 'Shit, shit, *shit.*'

Jess gave her a sideways look but was too busy signing to ask what was wrong.

Merry glanced helplessly around, but it was far too late to try to escape – he was almost at the table. She was going to have to face him.

'Hello, Alex,' she said, once he stood in front of her. 'What the hell are you doing here?'

She heard what sounded like a pen clatter onto the table-top beside her and guessed Jess had overheard.

'Hello, Merry,' Alex said, and flashed the smile she knew so very well. 'It's good to see you.'

Jess had stopped talking to her fans now and Merry could almost feel her bristling. Niall seemed to have realized something was going on too, because he was striding across the hall. Merry's heart thudded uncomfortably in her chest as she stared at Alex, so incongruously out of place that it made her ears roar. He was part of her London life, or had been. He didn't belong on Orkney.

'Seriously, Alex, what are you doing here?' she repeated, and saw Niall's face drop in dismayed astonishment when he heard the name.

Alex spread his arms in boyish appeal. 'Isn't it obvious? I'm playing the romantic hero for once in my life.'

He reached down to take both her hands and draw her to her feet.

'I've come to get you back, Merry.'

Part Four

Sunset over Brightwater Bay

Orkney Literary Society invites you to a

Summer Ceilidh
with Merina Wilde

To celebrate the end of a successful tenure of our
current Writer in Residence,
we invite you to dance the night away as we travel
back in time to
Orkney in the 1940s.
Dress up or dress down, it's up to you, but wear your
dancing shoes!

Friday 31st July
7pm until 11pm at Orkney Library
Booking essential.
Email Niall.Gunn@Orkneylib.gov.uk

Chapter Twenty-one

'Merry? Are you okay?'

Merina Wilde didn't turn at her best friend's words. Instead, she kept her gaze trained on the spire of St Magnus's Cathedral, reaching up towards the still-light night sky even though it was long after nine o'clock in the evening. Behind her stood Orkney Library, its sleek modern design a stark contrast to the centuries-old cathedral that towered over Kirkwall. And, between the bench where Merry had been sitting for the last forty-five minutes and the library, was Jess.

'I'm fine,' Merry said, in a voice that sounded nothing like her own. 'Just taking a moment.'

She heard the tap of Jess's heels as she crossed the courtyard that had been filled with enthusiastic readers just an hour earlier. Then there was the faint rustle of fabric on stone as Jess settled next to Merry.

'You've been out here alone for the last fifteen minutes,' she said, draping a jacket around Merry's shoulders. 'You must be cold.'

She was, Merry realized, and the observation caused a belated shiver to ripple through her. What she'd mostly felt until now was numbness. It had started the moment she'd looked across the crowded library hall and seen her ex-boyfriend watching her, had gone on throughout his earnest apologies and heartfelt declarations of his own stupidity, and had lasted right up to this very second, when she couldn't even find the words to reply to Jess. It was exactly how she had felt the night Alex had ended their sixteen-year relationship, back in November, when she'd stared at him with stunned incomprehension as he'd told her he no longer loved her. Except that tonight he'd reversed that painful assertion by saying he'd never *stopped* loving her. And Merry couldn't even begin to get her head around the implications, much less figure out what to tell Jess.

'Thanks,' she managed, pulling the jacket close beneath her chin. 'It is a bit chilly.'

Jess nodded patiently, as though a chat about the weather was precisely what she'd come outside for. 'So, what did the weasely little prick have to say for himself? No, wait, don't tell me – I bet I can guess.' She adopted a sorrowful expression. 'I'm going with "I had to leave you to find myself, but all I discovered was that I can't live without you, babe."'

It was such a perfect line that Merry smiled in spite of herself. 'Isn't that from one of your books?'

'Might be,' Jess said, shrugging. 'But I reckon that's the angle Alex took. Am I right?'

There was no point in trying to deny it, Merry thought.

Jess had been her best friend for more years than either of them cared to count and she'd been there throughout the devastating aftermath of the break-up; she had a pretty well-formed opinion of Alex's behaviour, before, during and since. And, on this occasion, she was absolutely bang on the money.

'Pretty much,' Merry conceded. 'He said that when I changed, that made him change too and he lost sight of how good we were together.'

'Okay, let's just unravel that . . .' Jess frowned. 'So, what he means is, your mental health issues made him decide he could do better.'

Merry blinked. That was blunt even for Jess. She opened her mouth to object but her friend held up a hand. 'Don't argue, that's exactly what happened. And now that you're back on your feet, looking smoking hot and with a shiny new movie deal in your back pocket, he's suddenly afraid you've moved on.' Jess paused and shook her head. 'I bet he even had the audacity to say he didn't want to lose you!'

Merry said nothing, because Alex had indeed said he didn't want to lose her, and Jess slapped a hand against the stone bench. 'You know who he is? Jasper Bloom, from *The Holiday* – the mealy-mouthed arse who gives poor Kate Winslet just enough attention to make her hope, but not enough to mean anything. It's only when she kicks him to the kerb that he goes chasing after her. Sound familiar?'

Another shiver chased its way down Merry's spine and she felt the dull thud of a headache beginning at the base of her skull. She rubbed the back of her neck and sighed. 'I know you don't approve, Jess. But what was I supposed to do – send him away without even listening to what he had to say? He travelled a long way to see me.'

Jess let out a snort of derision. 'It was his choice – you didn't ask him to.'

'No, but that doesn't mean I can pretend he's not here.' Merry paused as another of Jess's comments came back to her. 'You're wrong about the movie deal, by the way – it hasn't been announced so he doesn't know it's even happening. As far as he's concerned, I could still be struggling with writer's block.'

And now Jess laughed. 'Have you looked at yourself in the mirror lately, Mer? You don't look like you're struggling with anything. In fact, you look like you could take on the world.'

The words made Merry remember something Magnús Ólafsson had said not long after they had first met, that she reminded him of a Valkyrie. She'd assumed he was joking at first, but once he'd made it clear he wasn't, she'd gradually begun to feel flattered by the comparison. If only he hadn't been called back to his native Iceland to nurse his sick mother, Merry thought wistfully. She'd have felt much less unsettled by Alex's sudden appearance if Magnús had been at her side.

'I don't feel like I could take on the world,' she admitted to Jess. 'Right now, I'm not even sure I can handle the drive home.'

'That's easily fixed at least,' Jess replied, getting to her feet. 'I should probably tell Niall his writer is still in residence, anyway – I think he was worried Alex might sweep you off your feet and whisk you back to London.'

A moment later she was gone, leaving Merry to cringe inwardly with embarrassment. Niall Gunn was the link between her and the Orkney Literary Society, which funded the Writer in Residence scheme, and she couldn't help wondering what he thought of this latest twist in her tangled love life. Surely none of the previous incumbents had caused this much drama, she thought with another rush of mortification. He'd probably let out a long sigh of relief when her residency finished at the end of July.

Those fears were exacerbated when Niall arrived with Jess a few minutes later.

'Is everything okay?' he asked. 'Jess says you're not feeling too good.'

His manner was as professional as ever but Merry was certain there was an unfamiliar coolness in his blue eyes. She dredged up what she hoped was a reassuring smile. 'I'm fine, honestly. It's just—' Her voice wavered and she felt the smile slip as an unexpected gush of emotion bubbled up inside her. 'It's just been a long and slightly overwhelming evening.'

He nodded. 'Yes, I can appreciate that. Why don't I drive you both back to Brightwater Bay? The Mini will be fine in the staff car park – we can sort out collection tomorrow.'

'I grabbed your bag,' Jess said, holding up Merry's battered but much-loved Mulberry. 'Was there anything else?'

'No, just that,' Merry said. She took the bag gratefully before turning her attention back to Niall. 'There's really no need for you to come all the way to the croft. I'm sure I can manage the drive.'

'It's no trouble,' he replied, a slight frown creasing his forehead. 'As you said, it's been a long evening and it's my job to get you home safely, so I'm afraid I'll have to insist.'

And that made Merry feel even worse. Of course, he was just doing his job but seriously, just how much of a liability did he think she was?

As usual, Jess read her mind. 'You've had a shock, Mer. I'd drive if I could but, obviously, I'm not insured for the Mini. Let's get back to the croft and we can chill out over a glass of whisky and some cheese.'

Weariness washed over Merry again and she realized she was too worn out to argue. What she wanted most was the solitude of the bench that overlooked Brightwater Bay, where the sea-faring birds would be settling down for the night as the sun finally sank beyond the Atlantic Ocean. That, coupled with the whisky Jess had suggested, might help her come to terms with the turn her evening had taken. And if all else failed, she'd undoubtedly feel better in the morning. As long as she and Jess didn't get carried away with the drinking . . .

'Okay,' she said, and did her best to smile. 'Thank you.'

'I'll just make sure Callum is happy to lock up,' Niall said. 'Why don't I meet you in the car park?'

Whether by accident or design, neither Jess nor Niall spoke much on the journey back to the croft. Usually, Niall would point out interesting features of the landscape or tell stories about the landmarks they were passing, but this evening he was quiet. Merry allowed her eyes to close as she rested her head against the passenger seat and let the steady thrum of the engine soothe her. Before she knew it, Niall was turning down the narrow lane that led to Brightwater Bay.

'Thank you,' Merry said as he pulled up beside the croft. 'Both for delivering a brilliant author event and for bringing us back here.'

'As I said earlier, it's no trouble,' Niall reassured her. Then his gaze flickered to Jess in the rear-view mirror and he half turned. 'See you tomorrow, then. About ten?'

Merry frowned. Tomorrow? They didn't have any plans involving Niall for tomorrow. Had she forgotten an event? But Jess didn't seem confused; Merry twisted in her seat just in time to see her best friend bob her head.

'Sure,' Jess said. 'Can't wait.'

Niall smiled. 'Great.' He gave Merry an enquiring look. 'Maybe I can take you into Kirkwall once I've brought Jess back, so you can pick up the Mini.'

'Maybe,' Merry echoed, now thoroughly bewildered. Brought Jess back from where, exactly? But whatever their plans were, they didn't seem to include her and it felt oddly intrusive to ask. Instead, she gathered up her bag and reached for the door handle. 'Anyway, thanks again.'

She almost expected Jess to linger in the car but she hopped smartly out and followed Merry to the croft. Focusing on unlocking the door, Merry didn't turn to wave at Niall as he started to reverse away and stayed silent as she flicked on the lights and dropped her bag onto the sofa. It shouldn't bother

her that Jess and Niall had plans to do something without her; apart from anything else, she was due to go for a run with her neighbour, Sheila, in the morning. But there was a tiny, unreasonable part of her that was irritated. And she didn't understand why.

'Valkyrie?' Jess suggested, stripping off her jacket and hanging it on the hooks by the front door. 'Or do we need to bring out the big guns and go straight to the tequila?'

Merry glanced out of the living room window, towards the bench at the edge of the cliffs. There'd been plenty of nights she'd grabbed a cosy woollen throw and sat outside with a drink until the stars began to glimmer overhead. In fact, up until five minutes ago that was exactly what she'd planned to do, with Jess by her side. But now all she wanted to do was sink into bed and close her eyes.

'Do you mind if we skip the drinks and post-mortem?' she called, striving to keep her voice light. 'I think I need an early night.'

'Of course, I don't mind,' Jess said, following her into the room. 'Niall's showing me round Skara Brae tomorrow and you know I'm not normally a morning person. An early night suits me too.'

The words caused another barrage of little needles to prick at Merry's nerves. She did her best to ignore them. It made total sense for Niall to be taking Jess to Skara Brae, the way he'd taken Merry when she'd first arrived on Orkney. 'You'll have a great time,' she said, hoping her tone was less wooden than it felt. 'Niall really brings the history to life.'

But Jess was adept at reading between the lines. A slow frown creased her forehead. 'You don't mind us going without you, do you? I didn't think you'd be up for it since you've already been.'

It was the kind of place she could visit over and over and still see something she'd missed, Merry thought, especially when Niall was her guide, but she didn't say it. The last thing she wanted was for Jess to decide that she was – well – jealous or something equally ridiculous. 'No,' she said carefully. 'I don't mind. And I have a run planned, anyway – an eight-miler with Sheila. She'll hunt me down if I miss it.'

'Okay. We could all go somewhere for lunch when we're finished,' Jess suggested.

It was a nice idea, and just a few hours earlier, Merry would have liked nothing better. But now she just did her best to smile. 'Perhaps. Let's talk about it tomorrow.'

She still felt shivery when she got into bed fifteen minutes later, but the cotton sheets felt like silk against her skin and she'd never been more grateful to lower her head to the pillow. An epic yawn caught her by surprise; events were tiring at the best of times, she thought, but even more so when an ex-fiancé crashed the party and stirred up a whole host of feelings she thought she'd forgotten. It wasn't the time to think about Alex, she told herself wearily – the only thing that would do was ensure she lay awake all night. But in spite of her determination to give her exhausted brain some rest, it took Merry a long while to fall asleep. And just before the darkness came to claim her, a face flashed into her mind and almost jolted her into wakefulness. But it wasn't Alex who drifted in and out of her dreams until dawn. It was Niall.

'And I'll tell you something else: she's not quite what I expected.'

They were two miles into their regular Sunday morning run along the cliffs and Merry was starting to wonder whether Sheila might sing Jess's praises for the entire duration. It wasn't that Merry minded hearing how much her neighbour had enjoyed their joint author event the night before – far from it – but Sheila never usually talked this much on a run. In fact, by this point she had usually grown bored of Merry's slower pace and abandoned her to lope off into the distance. So it was something of a surprise that she seemed inclined to chat now, on a day when Merry was secretly craving the silence and headspace that running normally gave her.

'I mean, I thought she'd be sharp,' Sheila went on conversationally. 'It's obvious from the way she writes that she's very clever. But she's funny and charming with it, so you don't notice her mentally running rings around you, and then there's the way she looks. I imagine she stole a few hearts last night.'

Merry concentrated on navigating the springy, heather-laden ground beneath her trainers. It wasn't anything she hadn't heard before – Jess was never short of admirers – but she couldn't help wondering if Sheila had noticed any hearts in particular being stolen. Nevertheless, she stored the comments away to pass on to Jess later. 'I'll tell her you said so.'

Sheila nodded, almost to herself. 'Aye, she's got a good head on her shoulders, that one.'

Merry considered some of the awkward scrapes she and Jess had got themselves into over the years and tried not to smile. Her best friend's famous sense of adventure meant she never held back but Merry couldn't deny she was equally good at getting herself out of trouble. 'Most of the time,' she said to Sheila.

They ran on in silence for a few minutes, settling into an even pace, and Merry began to think her companion had finally grown tired of talking. But it appeared she was wrong – Sheila had something else on her mind.

'So was that the infamous Alex last night?'

Merry wanted to groan. The crowds had begun to thin by the time Alex had made his sudden appearance and she'd hoped Sheila and the rest of her eagle-eyed friends might have missed it, but no such luck. There was no point in pretending it had been someone else; news travelled fast on Orkney and Sheila had probably already tapped into the community network to establish where Alex was staying, how long he was staying and how many eggs he'd had for breakfast.

'Yes.'

'I thought it must be,' Sheila replied, managing to sound satisfied and disapproving at the same time. 'I said to Bridget, he looks like the type to break a woman's heart. Eyes too close together, I told her. Untrustworthy.'

The last word rolled off her tongue with such emphasis that it seemed to linger in the crisp morning air. And as always, the criticism evoked an instant desire in Merry to defend Alex. 'Really? I've always liked his eyes.'

Sheila threw her a sideways look. 'Clearly, since you were prepared to marry him. But he's no Magnús, is he?'

It was on the tip of Merry's tongue to point out that Magnús hadn't proved to be a good long-term romantic prospect either, but she couldn't bring herself to say it. The circumstances of his departure from Orkney had been out of his control and he'd left to do the honourable thing, to care for his ailing mother; there was no way Merry could fault him for that, no matter how disappointed she'd been when he'd gone.

'Or Niall, for that matter,' Sheila went on with barely a pause. 'I've known him his whole life and I can tell you now, he's steadier than the stones at Stenness.'

Steady. That was exactly the right word for Niall. He'd certainly been her rock since she'd come to Orkney, although she was more aware than ever that it was his job to support her. But Alex had been steady too, for the best part of sixteen years.

'Not that Niall is boring, mind,' Sheila continued. 'I know it can seem like he's married to his job but that's just his passion for Orkney.'

'I can certainly understand that,' Merry said. 'It's the kind of place that inspires passion.'

It most certainly was, she thought, watching a cluster of

guillemots soar across the cornflower sky. She'd done plenty of research before her residency had begun but nothing could have prepared her for just how beautiful the islands were and there was still a lot that she hadn't seen. Orkney had worked its magic on her, encouraging her creativity to flow and teaching her to believe in love again. She'd hoped to find the peace and quiet to get over her writer's block; she hadn't expected to find serenity.

'You'll miss it when you go back to London.'

Merry felt the same hard knot in her stomach that had become familiar whenever she thought about leaving Orkney. How would she cope without her view of Brightwater Bay each morning? Without the wild, exhilarating freedom that came when she ran along the cliffs? London had plenty of parks, and her flat in Chiswick wasn't far from the river, but it couldn't offer the same spectacular views that blessed her running here. And what if her rediscovered ability to write depended somehow on this remarkable place? Even so, she knew she couldn't stay – the residency was coming to an end and the rest of her life lay in London. She had to go back.

She squashed the knot down and summoned up a smile. 'I will miss it. Maybe even Gordon.'

The glance Sheila tossed over one shoulder was speculative. 'I daresay Alex knows that too. Which is why I imagine he's turned up now, to remind you where your home is.'

He hadn't said it in so many words but it had definitely been there in the subtext, Merry thought. *It'll be just like it was, Mer – you and me with London at our feet.*

'Look, you can tell me to mind my own business if you like,' Sheila began, with the kind of placid confidence that suggested no one ever had. 'But when you get to my age you realize it's better to be blunt and it seems to me that Alex is part of your past, not your future. And it doesn't matter where you're actually living – you've moved on.'

'That's pretty much what Jess says,' Merry conceded, remembering all the times her best friend had expressed the same sentiment in the months following the break-up.

'Well, then,' Sheila said. 'Great minds think alike. Do yourself a favour and tell Alex that ship has sailed.'

Merry opened her mouth to reply but the other woman wasn't finished. 'And make sure you don't miss your own ship,' she said, with another shrewd look. 'There's nothing worse than a lifetime of regret because you didn't quite have the courage to reach for what you want. Believe me, I know.'

With that final cryptic comment, she lengthened her stride and began to pull away from Merry. 'Say hullo to Jess, won't you?' she called as the distance between them grew. 'Remind her she promised to put me in her next book!'

Merry watched her go, then checked her watch; if she wanted to go for lunch with Jess and Niall, she should turn back now. But that would mean a six-mile run rather than eight, and her head was still a jumble of thoughts and emotions that she was struggling to untangle. Perhaps another mile might give her some much-needed clarity, she pondered, although she'd be cutting it fine for making herself presentable enough for lunch. Then again, it was unlikely

Jess and Niall would finish early at Skara Brae and altogether possible they'd be late themselves. Turning her face to the sun, Merry began another mile.

Chapter Twenty-two

There was no sign of Niall's car when Merry puffed into view of the croft. Wincing at the ache in her legs, she leaned against the door, first gripping one ankle and then the other to stretch her tired muscles. She had run further than she'd intended – over ten miles – and now it was almost midday and she had very little time to shower before Jess and Niall returned. But she felt better for the longer run, clearer-headed, at any rate, and she was more than ready for lunch.

By the time she'd taken a hurried shower and dressed, there was still no sign of Jess and Niall. Merry reached for her phone, expecting to see a message from Jess explaining they'd been held up. Instead, she found a message from Alex.

Dinner tonight? I'd love to see you if you're free x

She stared at it for several long seconds, trying to work out how she felt. A significant chunk of her run had been spent sifting through her emotions over Alex's surprise appearance and Sheila's advice had lingered long after the older woman had vanished over the horizon. *Tell Alex that ship has sailed*, she'd said, and Merry had arrived at the inescapable conclusion she was talking sense. But that was before this message, with the single kiss that he'd only taken to adding since their break-up. Merry's finger hovered over the screen. Should she reply with a bright and breezy *Thanks but no thanks*? Or accept the invitation so that she could give Alex the news in person? She probably owed him that much. The trouble was that dinner with Alex would mean abandoning Jess for the evening, which hardly felt fair; Jess was only on Orkney for a few days, after all. But Alex wasn't going to be around for long either – maybe she should deal with him first. Merry sighed and rubbed her temples. Life seemed suddenly a lot more complicated than it had twenty-four hours earlier.

She was saved from sinking further into the agony of indecision by the sound of a car drawing up outside. Stuffing her phone into her bag, she got up and hurried to the door, only to meet Jess on the doorstep.

'Sorry, need a wee,' Jess gasped, squeezing past her. 'Long queue – thought I could wait but we got held up on the way back.'

Merry winced in sympathy. 'Poor you. Take your time – I'll see you in the car.'

Niall smiled as she opened the rear passenger door and slid along the back seat. 'Hello. How was your run? Has Sheila talked you into the London Marathon yet?'

'Not yet,' Merry said, knowing he was only half joking. 'I

think she's biding her time, waiting until my guard is down. How was Skara Brae?'

'As awe-inspiring as ever,' Niall replied. 'I think Jess enjoyed it, although the journey here was a little bit fraught.'

Merry glanced across at the door of the croft, where Jess had just reappeared looking a lot happier. 'Jess mentioned a hold up. What was the problem?'

'A coachload of tourists arrived just as we were leaving, so the queue for the ladies was longer than usual,' Niall explained. 'And then we ran into the aftermath of an accident on the road – nothing serious but enough to cause a delay. Which had an – erm – knock-on effect on Jessie.'

Right on cue, Jess opened the car and swung herself into the passenger seat. 'That's better. I can honestly say I've never been so happy to see you, Mer.'

Merry couldn't help laughing. 'Thanks. I think.'

Jess grinned over her shoulder. 'Any time. What do you want to eat? I'm starving – who knew travelling back in time thousands of years gave you such an appetite?'

'Me,' Niall said. 'How about the Aurora, just along from the harbour in Kirkwall?'

'Yes, please,' Merry replied. 'You have to try the Orkney crab, Jess.'

'Sold,' Jess said promptly. 'Let's hope that busload of tourists hasn't had the same idea.'

Kirkwall was busy, its streets thronging with the usual crowds of summer visitors, and Merry was secretly wondering whether they'd be able to get a table at Aurora.

But she should have known Niall would have everything under control; they were greeted at the door by the owner himself.

'Hullo, Niall,' Rory said, clapping him warmly on the shoulder. 'It's always good to see you. Especially when you bring my favourite author.'

Merry smiled. She'd met the restaurant owner several times now and he seemed to up the charm with each meeting. 'Hello, Rory. How are you?'

'All the better for seeing you,' Rory replied, his dark eyes twinkling. His gaze moved to Jess. 'And you must be Jessie Edwards. My wife went to your event last night and she's had her nose in one of your books ever since.' He shook his head and sighed. 'I had to get my own breakfast this morning.'

Jess's delight was evident. 'I wish I could say I'm sorry but I'm not.'

Niall laughed. 'Rory used to be head chef at the Savoy. He's perfectly capable of making a bit of toast.'

'Just about,' Rory conceded cheerfully. 'Now, I saved you one of the window tables. It's not often we have celebrity diners and I want to make sure everyone gets a good look at you.'

'Merry's the superstar, not me,' Jess said. 'I'm just hanging onto her coat-tails and basking in the reflected glory.'

'I'm not the most stolen author in Orkney Library,' Merry pointed out. 'You are.'

'Really?' Jess said, her jaw dropping in astonishment.

'Really,' Niall confirmed with a sigh. 'I've had to replace *Ball Boys* three times in the last few months. *Gorgeous* is also proving very popular with our more light-fingered readers.'

'I don't know whether to feel flattered or furious,' Jess said, although Merry thought she looked pleased.

'If it helps, it's a distinction you share with Ian Rankin and Diana Gabaldon,' Niall told her.

'There you go, then,' Rory said with a wink. 'Definitely a celebrity.'

He led them over to a table that was bang in the centre of a large floor to ceiling window. Merry exchanged a wry look with Jess – Rory hadn't been kidding about making sure they were seen. But it did at least give them a panoramic view of the harbour, and of the sunshine sparkling on the water beyond.

'Now, what can I get you to drink?' Rory asked once they were all seated. 'This round is on the house.'

Merry eyed the wine list wistfully. 'Just a sparkling water for me,' she said, turning to the page of non-alcoholic drinks. 'I'm driving.'

'A glass of prosecco, please,' Jess said, without hesitation.

'I think I might join you,' Niall said.

Jess grinned. 'Thank god for that – I hate drinking alone.'

'Me too,' Rory said. 'I'll bring you a bottle and then you can keep each other company throughout lunch.'

Jess cast a moderately apologetic look Merry's way. 'Sorry, babes. Next time.'

'It's fine,' Merry said, trying hard to ignore a niggle of

something she couldn't quite put her finger on. 'I'll have to drive later, anyway.'

'Oh, where are we going?' Jess asked, her eyes gleaming. 'Is it the whisky distillery? Please say yes!'

Too late, Merry realized she should have kept her thoughts to herself. Now she'd have to explain that her plans didn't involve Jess, or a visit to Highland Park. She shifted uncomfortably in her seat. 'Alex wants to meet for a drink.'

Jess eyed her in silence for a moment, then sighed. 'I suppose it's too much to hope that you told him to shove it?'

'Well, I haven't said yes yet—'

'But you're going to,' Jess cut in bluntly. She sighed again. 'I know you said you can't just ignore him but I still don't really understand why. He had his chance, he blew it and now he needs to move on.'

Across the table, Niall cleared his throat. 'I've just remembered there's something I need to sort out. Will you excuse me?'

He stood up. Merry's cheeks burned as he made his way across the restaurant but she kept her gaze fixed on her best friend. 'It's one drink, Jess. And I'm planning to tell him there's no hope of us getting back together.'

The news seemed to mollify Jess. 'Good,' she said, sitting back. 'In that case, I might forgive you for abandoning me.'

'It's only for an hour or so,' Merry replied. 'And I'll pick us up a takeaway on the way back – how about that?'

'Okay,' Jess conceded. 'As long as you promise you won't let Alex talk you into anything else. Like a wedding.'

Merry laughed. 'I think I can safely say there's no chance of that.'

A few moments later, Niall reappeared. He glanced at Jess as he retook his seat. 'Were you serious about visiting Highland Park? I gave them a call and they'd be happy to offer you an informal, after-hours tour this evening if you'd like. It won't be as grand as the one they laid on for Merry but you'll get to see how things work and taste a few of their whiskies.'

Jess blinked. 'Sounds amazing – where do I sign?'

He laughed. 'They close at five so it would mean hanging around Kirkwall until then. Does that sound okay?'

'No worries at all,' Jess said. 'It'll give me a chance to check out the shops.'

'Great,' Niall said warmly. He nodded at Merry. 'We'll sort out a taxi back to the croft, so you can enjoy your evening out.'

Merry fought to keep her expression neutral as she felt her stomach twist. 'It's hardly an evening out.'

Niall tipped his head. 'It means you can keep your options open. If you need to.'

'Unless you'd rather come and drink whisky with us,' Jess said innocently. 'I know which I'd choose.'

In other circumstances, Merry would have loved to visit the distillery again, especially with Jess and Niall. But the shadow of Alex was looming over her and she knew she had to deal with him, for both their sakes. Besides, Niall's invitation hadn't extended to her – he'd only asked Jess. And why should he have invited Merry? She'd just revealed she was thinking of meeting Alex, after all, and Niall was simply being his usual professional self in making sure Jess wasn't left at a loose end. Just like he had that morning, Merry reminded herself. Which was part of the problem, if she was honest; the idea of Jess and Niall hanging out together made her uneasy. It shouldn't but it did.

'No,' she said slowly, fighting an irrational desire to say she would join them. 'I really ought to meet Alex.'

'I'll still be up for a takeaway later,' Jess said. 'Unless Niall gets me too drunk to stand up.'

Niall grinned. 'It's not me you have to worry about – it's Andrew. He could drink Valhalla dry and still navigate his way home. Isn't that right, Merry?'

Merry forced herself to smile. 'So the legends say.'

'Sounds like my kind of man,' Jess said with approval and reached for the menu. 'I think I'm going to need a bigger lunch.'

'So, this is where the magic happens.'

Alex was standing in the middle of Merry's living room, gazing around with an expression she couldn't quite decipher.

'I suppose you could say that,' she replied. 'It's where I write, anyway.'

'You weren't kidding when you said it was small.'

'It's perfect for me.' Merry resisted the urge to fold her arms defensively across her chest. She was already regretting allowing him to come to the croft but his obvious curiosity had been hard to deflect as they'd discussed the plan for that evening.

'I just want to see where you've been hiding away all these months,' he'd said down the phone. 'That's not too much to ask, is it?'

He had sounded so reasonable that she hadn't felt able to say no. And naturally that had led to his suggestion that he pick her up in his hire car, rather than her drive to meet him. But now that Alex was here, in the refuge she'd fled to in the aftermath of their break-up, she wished she'd stuck to her original plan and met him at the pub.

He glanced at her now and smiled. 'It's not a criticism – I can see it suits you.'

The genuine warmth behind his words surprised Merry. 'Oh. Well, thanks.'

'In fact, I understand why you're tempted to stay,' he continued and gestured towards the window, with the bay beyond it. 'Who wouldn't be, waking up to that view?'

Here comes the part where he reminds me where I really belong, Merry thought, just as Sheila predicted. But Alex surprised her again. 'What I'm trying to say is that I think you did the right thing, coming here. But since that's a conversation we should probably have over a glass of wine, let's save it until we're in the pub. Are you ready to go?'

His comments were so unexpected that she nearly forgot her resolve to take her own car. But the thought of Alex driving her home once she'd told him there was no hope of a reconciliation was enough to make her draw in a deep breath. 'I was thinking I might take my own car, actually. It seems silly to make you drive all the way out here again later – you might as well stay in Kirkwall.'

'I don't mind bringing you home,' he said. 'You must have to drive most of the time – why don't you give yourself the night off?'

'I'm supposed to pick Jess up later,' Merry fibbed.

'I'm sure she can get a taxi.' He fixed a steady-eyed gaze on Merry. 'Unless the issue here is you can't bear to be in a car with me.'

Merry felt warmth begin to rise in her cheeks and she fought to keep herself from blushing. 'No, of course not,' she said, crossing her fingers where Alex couldn't see. 'It's just less hassle for everyone if I take my car.'

'Everyone except you,' he said, frowning. 'But I don't want to make you uncomfortable. The offer is there if you want it.'

His gaze remained level but she knew him well enough to know he must be growing impatient. The trouble was, she could see it made sense from his point of view – why take two cars when one would do? And the pub they were going to was in Kirkwall, at least; she could ring Jess when she left Alex and maybe they could share a cab back to the croft. Assuming Jess was ready to come home by the time Merry had finished breaking the bad news to Alex, that was . . .

'Okay,' she said, aware she'd been silent for too long. 'I'll leave my car here.'

A wide smile appeared Alex's face, as though he'd never doubted his ability to talk her round. 'Great. You can explain those big stones by the side of the road – I assume they're Orkney's answer to Stonehenge.'

'Something like that,' Merry said, recalling Niall's detailed description of what archaeologists thought the Stones of Stenness might have represented. 'They're pretty amazing, aren't they?'

Alex looked at her, shaking his head in obvious admiration. 'Not as amazing as you.'

'Ha ha,' Merry said, hiding her discomfort behind an awkward smile. 'We should probably get going. I'll grab my coat.'

She couldn't tell whether it was because Alex was making a concerted effort, or whether she'd simply forgotten how charming he could be, but Merry found herself reluctantly enjoying his company on the journey to Kirkwall. He kept the conversation light, filling her in on various things he'd been doing in the months following the break-up. She was amazed to hear he'd booked on the National Three Peaks Challenge in September.

'I know,' he said when he caught her looking at him in open astonishment. 'I surprised myself, to be honest. But Georgie from Accounts has raised over a thousand pounds for charity and I thought why not join her?'

'But you've always hated walking,' Merry pointed out. 'Even when there was a pub at the end.'

'And you've always hated running,' Alex countered. 'Yet here you are doing marathons.'

Merry shook her head. 'Half-marathons.'

'Still bloody impressive,' he said. 'And my point is that

346

people change. As evidenced by the fact that I'm going to be climbing three mountains in twenty-four hours when the nearest I've ever been to one in the past is Space Mountain on our Year 10 trip to Disneyland Paris.'

Merry couldn't repress a smile at the memory. 'And you threw up immediately afterwards.'

'Too much Cherry Tango,' he replied solemnly. 'I won't make that mistake again.'

The pub they'd agreed on was the Fisherman's Rest, tucked away behind the busier main streets. Merry had suggested it partly because it wasn't one of her regular haunts and partly because she knew there was no live music, unlike a number of other pubs in Kirkwall, so there would be no temptation to stay longer than necessary. She and Alex would also be able to hear each other speak, which was important. She didn't want the horror of having to repeat herself when she told Alex he'd had a wasted trip in coming to Orkney.

For all his enthusiasm to meet up and talk things through, Alex seemed in no hurry to raise the subject of their relationship, however. After getting drinks at the bar, he asked after Merry's brother in Australia, and answered her questions about his own family, who still lived in the same Surrey town where he and Merry had grown up. That led to more reminiscences of their school days and, almost inevitably, memories of how they'd got together.

'I fancied you for ages,' Alex said with a rueful smile. 'But you always had your nose in a book – I had to join Mr Tumelty's book club to make you notice me.'

He was wrong, Merry thought wistfully; she'd been aware of Alex in the same way that a moth noticed a flame. But, unlike the moth, she'd had a sense of self-preservation and had known better than to give in to the attraction. She had been bookish and quiet, while Alex had been cool and funny. She'd thought they had nothing in common at all, apart from being in the same year, and had admired him from afar for a long time. Then he'd materialized in the book club and her world had been turned upside down. At the time, she'd had no idea he was a reader and had expected him to stick around for one session and then get bored. But he'd returned, week after week, and had surprised everyone with his perceptive comments. Merry had fallen head over heels almost from the moment he walked into the library after school and had scarcely believed her ears when he'd asked her out. It had taken him three attempts to convince her he was serious; she'd felt like the heroine of a teen novel as he refused to give up. But there was no point in reminding him of any of that, she told herself sternly. It hadn't stopped him from ending their relationship, sixteen years later, and it wasn't enough to bring them back together now.

'I never understood what you saw in me,' she said, as briskly as she could. 'But it's all water under the bridge now.'

'You were mysterious,' Alex replied. 'And you loved reading. Sometimes, I'd see you with a book I'd already read and I really wanted to ask what you thought of it.' He paused and sighed. 'With you, I didn't have to be funny or loud. I could just be myself.'

It was true that the Alex she'd got to know was different

to the one he displayed in class. No one had expected them to last more than a few weeks but they'd surprised them all. And no one had been more surprised than Merry herself; she and Alex had been more alike than she'd dreamed possible. The weeks had turned into months, then years, and books had been the cornerstone of everything, especially when she got her first publishing deal. Alex had been thrilled to meet some of his favourite authors and loved being part of the literary scene, although he'd never wanted to write anything himself. She couldn't pinpoint the exact moment things had begun to change but she guessed it was when she'd started to struggle with writing. When she'd actually needed him, as Jess had often pointed out.

Merry took a long sip of her gin and tonic and reminded herself that the past was the past. Straightening her shoulders, she mentally prepared to let Alex down but before she could speak, he leaned across the table. 'Do you remember the first book we read after I joined the book club?'

'*Wuthering Heights*,' Merry replied before she could stop the words from tumbling out. 'Mr Tumelty almost threw you out of the library for calling Heathcliff an arsehole.'

'I stand by that opinion,' Alex said. 'In fact, I'm pretty sure he'd be considered a psychopath these days. But you didn't agree.'

Merry was embarrassed to recall that her teenage self had thought Heathcliff's brooding desire was the pinnacle of romance and she'd defended him furiously against Alex's outrageous accusation. It wasn't until she'd re-read the novel, years later, that she'd realized he'd been absolutely right. 'I agree now.'

Alex nodded. 'Like I said earlier, people change. It took me losing you to see what an arsehole I'd been.' He held up a hand to stop Merry from interrupting. 'Walking away is the last thing I should have done but I'm here now. And I always will be.'

His face was alive with passion, reminding her of the boy she'd fallen in love with. She bit her lip, pushing the memory away. She had to stay strong, do what she'd come to do. 'Alex, I—'

'We were so good together,' he went on, as though she hadn't spoken. 'And we'll be even better when you come back home, especially now you're over your health issues.'

'Home,' she echoed. 'You mean London?'

'Of course,' he said impatiently. 'Where else? It's not as though there's anything to keep you on Orkney – I thought maybe you'd met someone else but there's no way that cottage is big enough for two.'

She remembered the way he'd looked around the croft, sharp-eyed and inquisitive. What if it hadn't been curiosity that had made him insist on driving out to pick her up, she thought with growing uneasiness. What if it had been naked self-interest?

'We're a great couple, Merry, everyone says so. Imagine us on the red carpet – you and me, dressed up to the nines with the world at our feet.'

The words resounded in her head like a thunderclap.

'The red carpet,' she repeated slowly. 'Why would we be on the red carpet?'

'When your book gets made into a film,' Alex said, a little frown creasing his forehead. 'There'll be a premiere, right?'

Acid swirled in Merry's stomach, causing an ache that had nothing to do with hunger. 'I didn't know you'd heard about that. The producer hasn't gone public yet.'

Something shifted in Alex's eyes, as though he realized he'd said the wrong thing. 'Oh, right. I ran into Nick Borrowdale a few weeks ago – he asked me to pass on his congratulations and said to remind you that you owe him a drink.'

And suddenly everything made sense. Jess had been right: he knew all about the film deal. That was what had really brought him back – the chance to bask in the lights of Hollywood – and everything else was just window dressing. For a moment, Merry wanted to cry. And then the anger hit – furious, white-hot rage that she'd almost been fooled. 'I owe Nick more than a drink – I think I need to buy him a whole bottle,' she said and was amazed to hear her voice was calm and level. 'To think I believed you when you said you still loved me.'

He gaped at her, colour rising in his cheeks. 'What are you talking about? Of course I still love you. Would I have come all this way if I didn't?'

Merry stood up, gin in hand, and reached for her bag. 'The only person you love is yourself, Alex. And for the record, you're still an arsehole.'

Alex tensed, clearly braced for her to throw the drink in his face, but instead she raised it to her mouth, drained it in one go, and swept from the pub.

Chapter Twenty-three

'I can't believe you didn't throw the drink.'

Jess leaned against the grey stone wall beside the door that led into the Highland Park distillery and shook her head in wonderment. 'You're more merciful than me.'

Merry managed a half-smile. 'It wasn't mercy. I just didn't want to waste the gin.'

'Good point,' Jess conceded. 'That snake isn't worth the energy or the alcohol. But at least he made things easy for you, even though I know it hurts.'

The astonishing thing was how much lighter Merry felt. It was as though a weight had been lifted, one she hadn't even realized she'd been carrying. And in its place there was a weariness, which had always been her reaction to stress, and anger that Alex had tried to play on her feelings, but she couldn't say she was hurt. In fact, the overwhelming emotion she felt was relief. 'You were right all along,' she told Jess. 'You're always right, about everything.'

Her best friend laughed. 'Don't give me too much credit. It's easier to see what's going on when you're outside looking in.'

Merry reached out and squeezed her arm in grateful thanks. 'Where would I be without you?'

'In a nearby hotel room, having mediocre make-up sex, I expect,' Jess said, and glanced towards the half-open door to the distillery. 'Why don't you come in and celebrate the fact you've escaped that terrible fate?'

The thought of facing Niall, who knew she'd been to meet Alex, was more than Merry could stand. 'No, I couldn't. I've already interrupted your tour.'

Jess waved a dismissive hand. 'Don't worry about that – we'd finished the tour. Andrew was just about to open a bottle of the good stuff.'

The good stuff being the forty-year-old single malt Merry had tried the last time she'd been to the distillery, which had in turn led to her accidentally drunk-dialling Magnús and belting out a belligerent accompaniment to Destiny's Child. But that wouldn't happen this time, she reminded herself. Apart from anything else, she'd deleted his number from her phone in case the drunken temptation to call had arisen again.

Even so, she shook her head at Jess. 'I can't. Niall will work out what's happened.'

'So?' Jess was looking at her as though she was crazy. 'He'll probably figure things out when I casually drop it into the conversation after you've gone.'

Merry was aghast. 'You wouldn't.'

'We both know I would,' Jess replied serenely. 'So you'd better come inside and keep an eye on me, hadn't you?'

'One drink,' Merry said. 'And then I'm getting a taxi and a takeaway, okay?'

Jess held up her hands. 'Absolutely, babes. Trust me, I'm your best friend.'

'Ohhhh, I am never drinking again.'

Merry looked up from her laptop to see Jess framed in the doorway of the living room, her blonde hair tousled and a delicately pained look upon her face. 'Morning,' she said. 'Or should I say afternoon?'

'I don't care what time of day it is, just make this hammering in my head stop, will you?'

Pressing her lips together in sympathy, Merry patted the empty side of the sofa. 'Why don't you come and sit down? I'll make you a coffee and find the painkillers.'

A few minutes later, Jess was tucked up on the sofa with a mug of coffee on the table and two round ibuprofen in her hand. She tossed them down carefully, as she was worried her head might fall off if she moved too fast, and let out another heartfelt groan. 'How come you don't have a hangover?'

'Because I learned my lesson last time,' Merry answered. 'I did try to warn you – Andrew's measures are about a mile north of generous.'

Jess winced. 'There's generous and then there's reckless endangerment. I think I might need a new liver.'

'You'll feel better after a fry-up,' Merry said. 'I popped up to the Watson's farm earlier to pick up some bacon and eggs, if you fancy it?'

'Maybe in a little while,' Jess said, reaching for her coffee. 'Once I'm sure I'm not actually going to die.'

Smiling, Merry returned her attention to the piece she was writing for the Orkney Literary Society website. Part of her remit as Writer in Residence was to promote reading and writing among the island communities and, so far, she'd managed to produce a short story set on each of the islands she'd visited.

'Was I very bad?' Jess asked, after a few minutes had passed. 'I remember singing along to something – that can't have been good.'

There had been singing and even some dancing, when they'd locked up the distillery and headed to Wrigley and the Reel, a nearby pub. The music was already in full swing when they arrived but they managed to squeeze in at the back of the hot and crowded room. Andrew had eventually been persuaded to join the musicians on guitar, and Merry had been amazed to discover Niall was an accomplished flute player. Most of the songs had been instrumental – a mixture of rollicking reels to get toes tapping and slower, more delicate melodies that held the audience spellbound – but there'd been one or two songs Merry had recognized, including a couple of singalongs. Jess had joined in with enthusiasm. Inevitably, they'd finished up dancing, despite the lack of room. It had made Merry look forward to the ceilidh Niall had organised to celebrate the end of her residency. And best of all, they'd been so busy having fun that she hadn't thought of Alex once.

She gave Jess a reassuring nod. 'Oh, you were very good. It was a great night.'

'I do remember laughing a lot,' Jess said. She reached for her mug and managed a smile. 'I suppose that's worth the hangover from hell.'

'Of course it is,' Merry said. 'You and Andrew seemed to hit it off.'

Jess's smile grew warmer. 'Yeah, he was an unexpected bonus. I like a man who's good with his hands.' She took a sip of coffee. 'Speaking of which, did I dream Niall's fantastic fingering?'

It took Merry a moment to understand she meant on the flute. 'No,' she said, fighting a blush at her own imagination. 'He's a very good flautist.'

'I bet he is,' Jess replied, arching an eyebrow. 'Is there no end to the man's talents?'

Trust Jess to somehow make that sound rude, Merry thought wryly, and cleared her throat. 'Do you remember meeting the presenter of Radio Orkney?'

Jess squinted thoughtfully. 'Young, dark-haired, extremely Scottish?'

'That's him,' Merry confirmed. 'He's keen to record an interview with us, for broadcast one day this week, if you're up for it?'

'As long as it's not today,' she said with a shudder. 'I don't think I can be sparkling and professional while I'm wondering if I am going to throw up.'

Merry pulled a sympathetic face. 'No, not today. He gave me an email address so we can schedule something in for when you're feeling better.'

'Excellent.' Jess grimaced. 'Sometime next year should be fine.' She paused and fired a direct look at Merry. 'Speaking of feeling better, you seem pretty chilled this morning. No regrets about telling Alex where to shove his red carpet?'

It was a good question, and one Merry wasn't entirely sure she could answer. She'd replayed last night's scene over and over in her head, and each time she had felt a resounding sense of rightness. But she'd be lying if she didn't admit there was also a sadness, some lingering regret at the way things had turned out. Her feelings for Alex had changed but they had still been together a long time. And they'd been happy for at least some of it.

'No,' she said cautiously, picking her way through her own jumbled emotions. 'I almost messaged him this morning, to check he was okay, but decided against it.'

'Good,' Jess said. 'He doesn't deserve your concern. Forget him.'

It wasn't the first time Jess had told her to put Alex out of her head – she'd been adamant for months that the break-up was a blessing in disguise. Meeting Magnús had helped Merry to believe she might fall in love again but he'd left just as things were heating up between them. And despite knowing the reasons he'd ended their burgeoning relationship were sensible and fair, there was still a tiny part of her that wondered whether there was something wrong with her. It had left a tiny chink in her armour, one Alex had managed to find and try to exploit but catching him out had given her the strength to close the door on him for the last time.

'Believe me, I'm done,' she said emphatically. 'With men in general too.'

'Let's not go that far.' Jess flashed her an encouraging smile and then lifted a hand to her temple. 'Now, where can we find a time machine? I want to warn Past Me to beware of Orcadians bearing whisky.'

The BBC Radio Orkney studios were on Castle Street in Kirkwall. It wasn't Merry's first visit – she'd recorded several interviews with the station's main reporter, Fraser Ferguson, and he'd always been warm and friendly, with the kind of dry sense of humour that would have fitted right in at the Edinburgh Fringe. She'd encouraged Jess to listen to an episode of the daily news bulletin, *Around Orkney*, so she'd know what to expect but Jess had raised her eyebrows.

'I've done loads of regional radio interviews,' she'd said. 'I know the drill.'

'That's what I thought,' Merry had answered with a rueful smile. 'I guarantee none of them have been quite like this one will be.'

On Tuesday morning, Fraser greeted them in the reception of the old bank building, which still had its original safe on display, and led them upstairs to the broadcast studio.

'We've finished today's show so we have the run of this studio until it's needed for the news update at lunchtime,' he said, ushering them into seats on the other side of the mixing desk. 'If you pop those headphones on, we'll just do a quick sound check.'

'So far, so normal,' Jess murmured to Merry, after Fraser had offered them water and made sure they were comfortable.

'Wait,' Merry whispered back.

'Ready?' he asked, glancing back and forth between them.

'Absolutely,' Jess said, and flashed her most charming smile. 'Ready, willing and able, as Doris Day used to say.'

Fraser pulled his headphones over one ear and grinned. 'Then let the games begin.' He swiped a hand across the mixing desk and leaned into the microphone. 'Love is in the air today as I'm joined in the studio by not one but two Queens of Hearts. Regular listeners will remember hearing from Orkney's current Writer in Residence, Merina Wilde, but today she is joined by her close friend, fellow romance writer Jessie Edwards. Good morning, ladies, and welcome to BBC Radio Orkney.'

Both women returned the greeting and Merry barely had time to register a wide-eyed glance from Jess before Fraser was posing his opening question.

'So, Jessie, how does it feel to be the most stolen author in Orkney Library?'

Jess didn't miss a beat. 'It feels pretty amazing, to be honest,' she said in a tone that held a definite under-current of amusement. 'Obviously I don't condone any criminal activity but I must admit it's quite gratifying to be so – well – desirable.'

Fraser nodded, his eyes dancing with delight. 'You certainly seem to be that,' he said, and glanced at Merry. 'I understand from our esteemed librarian, Niall Gunn, that library borrowing and reader engagement have both significantly increased in the five months you've been Writer in Residence, Merina. What do you think you've done to have such a dramatic effect?'

Merry took a deep breath. 'I can't take all the credit but I think it's a combination of different things – a range of interesting events and workshops at the library, plus I've tried to get out and about as much as I could, to meet people and get to know them.' She paused. 'And, of course, the community here on Orkney is wonderful. I've never felt more welcome – I count myself very lucky to have got the gig.'

'I think we're the lucky ones, if Niall's numbers are to be believed,' Fraser said. 'Now I know the two of you are best friends – how did you meet?'

Merry let Jess recount the familiar story. Anyone who'd been at their event on Friday evening would know the details already but *Around Orkney* had a whole raft of listeners who wouldn't have been at the library to hear the tale. Fraser nodded along, then smiled at Merry. 'It's no secret you've been inspired by some of the local real-life love stories you've heard, Merina. How useful has it been from your point of view, being on Orkney?'

'It's been wonderful,' she replied, without hesitation. 'I

don't know what I'd be writing now, if I hadn't come here. In fact, I don't know if I'd be writing at all.'

'There's definitely something magical about Orkney,' Jess chipped in. 'I don't know what it is, but I want more of it!'

Fraser looked pleased. 'Perhaps you should apply to be our next Writer in Residence, Jessie. You've certainly proved a hit with readers already.'

He steered the conversation expertly around to their writing habits and then asked what they were working on now. Jess gave her standard vague answer about pulling together new ideas and Merry explained she was waiting for the copy-edits on the novel she'd written set on Orkney.

'That's the historical love story inspired in part by Morag and Giovanni Rossi, is that right?' Fraser said, checking his notes.

'That's right,' Merry said, smiling. 'I'm hoping to come back to Orkney nearer to publication and perhaps have a little celebration.'

'And since you both write about romance, would it be fair to describe yourselves as romantics?'

Jess's gaze flicked sideways to Merry, who understood why: where was Fraser going with this?

'Definitely,' Jess said. 'It's hard to write about love if you don't believe in it.'

Fraser tipped his head. 'So, would it be impertinent to ask if either of you have found romance on Orkney?'

Merry fought the urge to groan into the microphone. The trouble with a close-knit community was that news travelled;

Fraser must have heard about her and Magnús, she guessed. Which meant she couldn't dodge the question, or even fib. 'There was someone special for a while,' she said, choosing her words carefully. 'But not all romances are for ever – some are as short as a single kiss on a starlit night. And that makes them all the more unforgettable.'

'It does indeed,' Fraser said, offering her a sympathetic smile. 'Poetically described. How about you, Jessie?'

She winked across the mixing desk. 'I've only been here a few days, Fraser. Give me half a chance!'

He laughed as she went on. 'But I do have my eye on a certain someone. Whether it will develop into anything more than a crush remains to be seen.'

'He'll be a lucky man if it does, whoever he is,' Fraser replied solemnly, then shifted slightly in his seat, indicating the interview had come to an end. 'Thanks to Jessie Edwards and Merina Wilde for coming in to chat to us here on *Around Orkney*. If you're inspired to try their books, you can borrow them at Orkney Library and they're on sale in all good bookshops.'

He wrapped up the recording and thanked them both again. 'I hope you didn't mind the wee curveball at the end,' he said, getting to his feet. 'Our listeners love to feel they've got the inside scoop.'

'Not at all,' Merry said politely, and Jess nodded her agreement.

Fraser seemed relieved. 'That's good. It'll go out in tomorrow's broadcast, so do have a listen. And thanks again for taking the time to come in.'

It wasn't until they were outside that Jess gave Merry an incredulous look. 'I see what you mean about it being different from any other interview. I don't think I've ever been asked if I fancy any of the locals before.'

'It's a first for me too,' Merry said wryly. 'But I suppose if it helps to sell a few books . . .'

She trailed off as Jess's comments replayed in her head. *I do have my eye on a certain someone . . .* Any other time, she'd demand to know who it was but this time she was afraid of the answer. Surely it couldn't be Niall, not after all her best friend's encouragement to pursue him herself. But Merry had insisted she didn't see him that way and, as Jess had pointed out, she'd only been on Orkney for a few days – the possibilities were limited. If it wasn't Niall, who could it be? And if it was Niall . . . how did that make Merry feel?

'Come on,' Jess said. 'Let's find somewhere decent for lunch. My treat.'

Merry forced herself to smile. What did it matter if Jess had a crush on Niall? It wasn't as though he was off-limits – he was fair game, the same as any other single man on Orkney. But she still couldn't bring herself to ask Jess who she'd meant. Some things were better left unsaid, she decided, and pushed the thought firmly out of her head.

'Good idea,' she told Jess, linking her arm through hers. 'I think it's time I introduced you to the joy that is Eviedale's sourdough pizza.'

Chapter Twenty-four

Loved the interview today! Are you busy tomorrow night?

The message from Clare Watson was one of many Merry received on Wednesday morning, after *Around Orkney* had finished its thirty-minute broadcast. She shared them all with Jess, who shook her head in wonderment.

'This place is amazing,' she said. 'So much love for books and authors.'

'I told you – writers are like rock stars here.' She smiled a little wistfully. 'I'm going to miss being a minor celebrity.'

Jess leaned back into the sofa and gazed out of the window at the clear blue skies over the bay. 'At least you've got another month of it. I have to go back to grey old London on Friday.'

There were worse places to live, Merry thought dryly, but she knew what Jess meant. London could be breathtakingly beautiful, especially in the summer, but it didn't have the islands' endless skies and ethereal golden light. She didn't know whether it was the landscape or its people or both, but Orkney seemed to wrap itself around the heart and make the thought of leaving impossibly hard.

'You could always come back,' she suggested.

'I could,' Jess said, and stretched with cat-like grace. 'You know, I might just do that.'

Merry's phone vibrated, indicating another message. She picked the handset up and swiped the screen. 'Clare wants to know if we're up for a dinner party tomorrow night, at their place.'

Jess frowned. 'Remind me – who is Clare again?'

'You met her briefly on Friday,' Merry said. 'Blonde hair, beautiful smile, owns the farm up the road and keeps llamas. You'll like her, I think.'

'Ah, yes, I remember,' Jess said. 'I thought we might go for a drink in Kirkwall, since it's my last night here. But a dinner party could be fun, as long as she's not the type to try and match us up with her terminally single friends. Who else is going to be there?'

'I'll ask,' Merry said and tapped at her phone.

Moments later, the screen lit up again. 'You, me and Niall,' she said. 'Plus Clare and her husband, Hugh, of course.'

Jess visibly brightened. 'That's fine, then. And it would be great to see Niall again before I go – let's do it.'

Pushing aside a faint needle of irritation, Merry typed in their acceptance. 'Done. Sheila says Clare's a fantastic cook. You might even get to meet Gordon the goat.'

'The master criminal himself,' Jess replied, grinning. 'I can't wait!'

Hugh insisted on coming to pick them up on Thursday evening.

'I've got to be up at the crack of dawn tomorrow anyway,' he said, when Merry and Jess thanked him. 'And I think Clare wants to impress you with her fancy wine list. It's all wasted on me – I'm a whisky man through and through.'

Clare met them at the door of the farmhouse. She hugged Merry, enveloping her in a cloud of sea salt and freesia, and then stood back to smile at Jess. 'Lovely to see you both, thanks so much for coming.'

'Thanks for inviting us,' Jess answered. 'I can't think of a better way to spend my last evening on Orkney.'

'We'll try to give you a good send-off,' Clare promised. 'Niall's through in the living room. I hope you won't mind but he's brought a friend.'

Jess sent an accusing look Merry's way and she had to bite her lip to fight down a sudden giggle. 'Anyone I know?'

'Oh, I think you've met,' Clare said enigmatically and led them down the hallway.

'If it's anyone over fifty, I'm running for the hills,' Jess hissed, grabbing Merry's sleeve. 'Unless he's George Clooney, obviously.'

The mystery guest turned out to be Andrew, which allowed Merry a sigh of relief. Clare wasn't matchmaking – she'd simply invited guests Merry and Jess knew and liked.

'Hullo again,' Andrew said and grinned at Jess. 'How's the head?'

'Better, thanks,' Jess replied. 'I hope you're not mixing the drinks tonight.'

Clare laughed. 'No fear. I've been slaving over a hot oven for hours – you all need to be sober enough to appreciate the results!'

Merry and Jess both accepted her offer of prosecco and settled onto the comfortable-looking sofas in the heart of the oak-beamed room.

'Great interview yesterday,' Niall said. 'Fraser was on good form, I thought.'

'He was nosy, you mean,' Clare sniffed, coming back into the room with a champagne flute in each hand. 'But Merry and Jess handled it perfectly.'

Andrew shook his head. 'He's a journalist – they're always on the lookout for a good story.'

'But I bet he didn't ask the same question when he interviewed the last Writer in Residence,' Jess pointed out.

'No idea,' Andrew replied. 'He was so boring that I think I fell asleep.'

Niall shifted on the sofa. 'I do try to choose authors who'll appeal to different readers on the islands,' he said mildly.

'But you've got to admit you struck gold with Merry here,' Clare said. 'I don't think I've ever seen such consistently big crowds over the six month residency.'

Merry felt her face start to burn with mingled pride and embarrassment. 'I don't get anything like those numbers back in London,' she protested. 'Orkney clearly has a lot of dedicated readers.'

'And you've done a brilliant job of engaging them,' Niall said with a warm glance. 'Our next Writer in Residence has some big shoes to fill.'

'Speaking of shoes,' Clare said grimly. 'Did Hugh tell you Gordon ate my favourite pair?'

'No!' Merry said. 'Honestly, is there anything that goat won't eat?'

'Not that we've found,' Clare replied with a sigh.

'It was your own fault,' Hugh rumbled. 'You left them outside the backdoor and you know he's partial to a daisy.'

Clare rolled her eyes. 'The kind that grow, not the ones attached to my expensive sandals!'

Everyone laughed and the conversation moved on to some of Gordon's even more outrageous crimes. Clare flitted in and out, checking on the food, and announced ten minutes later that their starters were ready.

'I hope you like scallops,' she said to Jess as they took their seats around the long kitchen table. 'Hand-dived this morning and straight from the boat.'

'Love them,' Jess replied. 'And they smell amazing.'

Merry found herself facing Niall, with Andrew on her left and Jess diagonally opposite. Hugh and Clare sat at the head of the table and conversation flowed easily as they ate. The scallops were expertly cooked, and every bit as delicious as they smelled. Then there was a main course of crispy salmon fishcakes, topped with a glistening poached egg and drizzled with an exquisite beurre blanc sauce. It was as good as anything Merry had been served in a London restaurant and she told Clare as much.

'Oh, bless you, I don't know about that,' she said, her cheeks pink with pleasure. 'But it's hard to go wrong when the raw ingredients are so fresh.'

Niall glanced across at Hugh. 'I don't know how you're not the size of a house if you eat like this all the time.'

Hugh let out a snort of amusement. 'You think she goes to this much trouble when it's just me?'

Clare glanced at him, unperturbed. 'You do all right, Hugh Watson.'

Merry tried not to watch the way Jess reacted to Niall as the evening wore on. Clare had chosen excellent wine – Hugh had been right – and Jess grew more tactile with each course of the meal. By the time the spectacular rhubarb crumble sundae was served, Merry was finding it hard not to grit her teeth every time her best friend laid a hand on Niall's arm, or laughed a little too hard at his jokes. It was the wine, she told herself firmly. Jess was just being Jess after a few drinks – expansive, charming and a tiny bit over-friendly. But it grated on Merry's nerves all the same.

Determined not to let it spoil her evening, she turned to Andrew. 'So how long have you played the guitar?'

'As long as I can remember,' he answered. 'Niall and I used to be in a band together when we were teenagers but you know how it is – artistic differences and all that.'

Niall glanced across the table. 'What Mr Handsome over

there means is that he used to get all the girls and the rest of us had to stand around and watch.'

Jess raised her eyebrows. 'I can believe that Andrew was popular with the ladies but surely you got more than your fair share too?'

'You're forgetting one crucial thing,' Niall said gravely. 'I'm a librarian. There's nothing sexy about that.'

'Oh, I don't know,' Jess said, aiming an innocent look at the ceiling. 'I think it kind of depends who you ask.'

Niall laughed. 'It helped that Andrew was a double Ba' champion, man and boy. He's practically Lionel Messi by Orkney standards.'

'Ba'?' Merry repeated, looking back and forth between the two men. 'What's that?'

Clare grinned. 'I can't believe you've been here this long and no one has described the madness that is the Kirkwall Ba' Game. You've been lucky.'

'Don't listen to her,' Hugh said. 'The Ba' Game is a feat of skill and strategy that happens every Christmas Day and New Year. Basically, all the men in Kirkwall are split into two teams—'

'The Uppies and the Doonies,' Andrew cut in.

'Aye, you're either an Uppy or a Doony, depending on the family you belong to or which part of town you were born in,' Hugh agreed. 'It's one huge football match, played for the honour of our ancestors. The Doonies are trying to get the ba' into Kirkwall Bay and the Uppies have to touch the ba' against a wall in the southern end of town.'

'Football,' Clare said, with a snort. 'It's more like a cross between rugby and a mass brawl. And it goes on for hours. I've known it take more than eight hours for someone to get the ba' across the metaphorical line.'

'Hardly anyone gets injured,' Andrew objected. 'In the teams, at any rate. The spectators are sometimes collateral damage.'

'Sounds like the kind of sport my fellow Kiwis would love,' Jess said. She looked at Andrew. 'And you've won it twice?'

He nodded. 'There's a boy's match in the morning and a men's match in the afternoon. I've been lucky enough to be on the winning side in both matches, although a few years apart.'

'Only because you carried the ba' over the rooftops,' Niall observed, then sighed as he glanced at Jess and Merry. 'Which is entirely within the rules and got him presented with the ba' itself at the end of the match.'

It sounded exhilarating and terrifying in equal measure, Merry thought, and she couldn't imagine anything she'd like to do less. 'So which team has won the most?'

'The Uppies,' Andrew said, pride evident in his tone. 'Obviously the better team.'

Hugh nodded his agreement but Niall shook his head. 'I think, if you check with the Orkney Archive offices, you'll find that the Doonies have won more.'

Andrew took a deep breath, obviously preparing himself to argue, and Clare cleared her throat meaningfully. 'If we've all finished eating, why don't we take this *fascinating* discussion through to the living room?'

'Good idea,' Hugh said. 'That's where the whisky is, after all.'

But by the time they'd thanked Clare for the outstanding meal, and taken themselves through to the sofas, the fire had gone out of the argument and the conversation moved onto other subjects. Eventually, Merry found herself hiding two consecutive yawns and glanced at her watch to discover it was almost midnight.

She glanced over at Jess, who was sandwiched between Andrew and Niall. 'We should probably make a move,' she said.

'Us too,' Niall agreed. 'We'll drop you back at the croft if you like. Save Hugh from having to go out.'

'That would be great,' Merry said. 'If it's not too much trouble.'

'None at all,' Niall replied, smiling. 'We're heading that way.'

They thanked Clare and Hugh for their hospitality, and Jess promised to send Clare a copy of her new book as soon as it was available.

'That'll make Sheila grind her teeth with jealousy,' Clare said, grinning in delight.

Then they climbed into Niall's car and drove down the track that led to the main road. A few minutes later, they were outside the croft and Jess was saying goodbye.

'So good to see you again,' she said to Andrew, throwing

her arms around him before turning to Niall. 'And you —
thanks for taking such good care of me.'

She hugged him too, and Merry saw her whisper something into his ear before she stepped back. Whatever she'd
said, it caused Niall's face to turn pink. And that caused
the glowing embers of Merry's irritation to burst into
sullen flames.

'Thanks for the lift,' she said, aware of the brusque-
ness in her tone but unable to prevent it. 'Nice to see you
again, Andrew.'

She caught Jess looking sideways at her but ignored her
friend. Instead, she turned and went into the croft.

Jess stayed outside and Merry guessed she was waving the
car off. No sooner had the front door closed, however, than
Jess was confronting her. 'Okay, Mer, what gives?'

Merry pressed her lips together, determined not to give
in to her annoyance but Jess wasn't letting her off the hook.
'Don't pretend there's nothing wrong,' she went on. 'You've
been giving me daggers all evening and you were downright
rude to Andrew and Niall out there. What's going on?'

And just like that, Merry's temper broke. 'I'll tell you
what's wrong – you don't seem to understand the concept of
acting professionally.'

Jess's jaw dropped. 'Come again?'

The words tumbled from Merry's mouth before she could
stop them. 'You know what I'm talking about. You've been
draping yourself over Niall for the past four hours, flirting
with him like we were in a nightclub instead of my friends'

house. I know you have a crush on him but you're going home tomorrow, Jess. I have to work with these people – it's just not professional.'

'So that's it,' Jess said quietly and took a deep breath. 'For your information, I wasn't flirting with Niall and I don't have a crush on him.'

'Don't bother denying it,' Merry snapped. 'It was obvious to everyone in the room. And whispering in his ear when we got back here – what was that about if you weren't flirting?'

'That's between me and Niall,' Jess said evenly. 'But I promise you it wasn't anything close to flirting. I'm your best friend, for god's sake – I'd never behave that way around someone you're interested in.'

That made Merry's blood boil even more. 'I'm not interested in him,' she said furiously. 'How many times do I have to tell you that? It's our working relationship I'm worried about.'

Jess tipped her head. 'So you keep saying. But I've got to be honest, Merry – if the thought of Niall with another woman gets you this bent out of shape, perhaps you need to think about why.' Turning on her heel, she headed for the bedroom. 'I'm going to pack my case for the morning. And after that, I'll sleep on the sofa.'

The words took some of the fire from Merry's anger. 'It's too small.'

'That's right, it is,' Jess said, pausing in the doorway. 'But I'd rather take my chances on there than have you try to stab me in the back while we sleep. Goodnight, Merry.'

Her tone was so final that Merry knew better than to argue more. She locked herself in the bathroom, splashing water onto her flushed face and staring at herself in the mirror. She hadn't been imagining it, had she? Jess had definitely been all over Niall – even Hugh must have noticed. Maybe she'd ask Clare in the morning, she decided, once she'd taken Jess to the airport. The last of her fury drained away as she rested her head against the coolness of the mirror, leaving an empty uncertainty in its place. She and Jess had never argued like this, not even once in their long friendship, and she had no idea how to make it right. She'd just have to hope a good night's sleep would provide the answer.

Merry woke up the following morning to an uncharacter-istically silent croft. She padded through to the living room to find the sofa empty and a hastily scrawled note on the coffee table.

I got a cab to the airport – seemed like the best idea. Let's speak soon when our tempers have cooled. Love, Jess.

Merry sat on the sofa for several long seconds, staring at the scrap of paper torn from Jess's notebook. And then she put her head in her hands and sobbed.

Chapter Twenty-five

'Did Jess get to the airport all right?' Clare asked, when Merry stopped by to see her on Friday afternoon.

Merry's shoulders drooped. 'I assume so. She – er – took a cab and left before I got up.'

Clare lowered her mug of tea to the table and stared. 'That doesn't sound good. What happened?'

The whole sorry story spilled out: Merry's gradually building suspicion that Jess was attracted to Niall, the argument that had resulted when they'd returned to the croft and Jess's furious denial.

'And the worst of it is, I don't know how much of it was my imagination,' Merry finished wretchedly. 'I can't decide if I'm losing the plot.'

'Why would it matter if she was attracted to Niall?' Clare asked, frowning. Her eyes widened 'Unless— oh.'

'Exactly,' Merry said. 'She's got it into her head that I'm jealous.'

Clare regarded her steadily. 'Right. Are you jealous?'

'No!'

'Okay,' Clare said, pursing her lips. 'Well, I can't say I noticed her flirting with Niall but I was in the kitchen a lot of the time.'

Now it was Merry's turn to stare. 'She was all over him, especially in the living room after dinner.'

Clare shook her head, smiling sadly. 'That's not what I saw. But whether she was or she wasn't, she is right about one thing. You need to work out why it's such a problem for you.'

Something heavy settled in the pit of Merry's stomach as she absorbed the meaning of those words. Her feelings for Niall were purely professional, weren't they?

Weren't they?

It felt odd not to be in contact with Jess over the weeks that followed. Merry lost count of the number of times she'd reached for her phone to send a message or share a joke with her best friend, before remembering that they didn't do that anymore. She'd received a single message to say Jess had landed safely, and that they'd talk soon, but there'd been no further communication. Merry took refuge in her work, delving into her copyedits with a grim determination to lose herself in the story she'd created, but the moment she resurfaced, her silent phone reminded her of Jess's absence.

She kept her distance from Niall, too, claiming she was busy wrapping up the last of her Writer in Residence projects when he asked if she was okay. But she should have known she wouldn't be able to fend him off for ever. He turned up at the croft early one Saturday morning in mid-July, dressed in hiking gear and carrying a hefty rucksack.

'Get your hiking boots on,' he instructed, in a tone that was unusually businesslike. 'I'm taking you island hopping.'

The sky was bright blue over his shoulder and Merry realized with a start that it had probably been days – no, weeks – since she'd left the croft, other than for her regular runs with Sheila. And, suddenly, she longed for a different view.

'Where are we going?' she asked, but Niall refused to be drawn.

'You'll need layers, as always, but try to bring as little as possible,' he said. 'And make sure you bring some ID.'

It wasn't until they turned down the road to Kirkwall Airport that Merry understood why she needed some identification: they were catching a plane.

'Seriously, Niall, where are we going?' she asked, as he led the way towards the Departure gates.

He pointed at the boards. 'North Ronaldsay. There are a few people there I think you need to meet.'

The Loganair flight reminded Merry of her arrival on Orkney, back in February, when she'd thought she might actually die mid-air. But it was easier this time as Niall kept her talking, pointing out the towering red and white lighthouse of North Ronaldsay as soon as it appeared, and she'd barely got used to the fact that they were airborne before the pilot was instructing them to prepare for landing.

The landscape of the island was typical of Orkney: flat and green. Niall took a moment to get his bearings, then headed towards a building not far from the airport. As they got closer, Merry could see that it was a garage.

'Are we hiring a car?' she asked.

Niall shook his head. 'Not a car. I suppose I should have checked this before, but I hope you know how to ride a bike.'

'We're cycling?'

'Over to the lighthouse. I thought you might like a tour. But first, we're going to meet a friend of mine.' He paused to smile. 'I guarantee you won't have met anyone like her before.'

It had been some time since Merry had been on a bike and that had been in London. She doubted she'd have to contend with inconsiderate commuters and oblivious buses on North Ronaldsay but those weren't the only things concerning her. 'How far is it exactly?'

'The lighthouse is a couple of miles north. But the island is only three miles long from tip to tip.' He gave her an encouraging smile. 'We can have lunch at the lighthouse café and I've brought plenty of snacks for the journey.'

'Sorry, I sound like a toddler,' she said, embarrassed at her own ingratitude. 'Okay, I'm game. Is your friend's house on the way?'

'Not exactly,' he said. 'We're going to see her at work. Which today means a detour to the southernmost tip of the island.'

Merry did the maths in her head. 'So that's a six-mile round trip, right?'

'We can leave the bikes at the lighthouse if you think your leg muscles aren't up to it,' Niall said. 'I'm sure I can persuade someone to drive us back to the airport later.'

And that made Merry feel even more like a child. 'It's not my legs I'm worried about,' she replied. 'Without wishing to be indelicate, it's the seat that's the issue. My flabby writer's bum isn't used to spending six miles on a bike – it might protest.'

Understanding dawned on Niall's face. 'Ah, I see. Well, without wishing to be indelicate myself, you ran the Orkney half-marathon a few weeks ago. Your bum doesn't look flabby to me.'

His ears turned pink the moment he'd stopped talking and Merry felt her cheeks start to flush. 'That's – uh – good to know,' she said, hoping she sounded less awkward than she felt. 'Shall we get the bikes?'

Ten minutes later, Merry was astride a sleek grey-and-black bicycle, with a helmet firmly clipped onto her head. She was sure she looked ridiculous as she wobbled along the road after Niall but it didn't take long for her to remember how to ride. And the roads were flat and quiet, which was a blessing. Merry found she was able to take in the lush green fields on either side of her and listen to Niall as he talked more about the island.

'As you might have guessed, it's not the busiest of places,' he told her. 'The population has been steadily falling and

I think there are only around sixty residents now, mostly older people. But they're trying to encourage families with children to come and live here.'

Merry tried to imagine living somewhere so remote that she'd need to catch a plane to go to a supermarket. 'Is there a school here?'

'There was,' he replied. 'The only pupil started secondary school a few years ago, so it's currently closed. There's a bird observatory, though – there's obviously an abundance of the usual suspects but I'm told the opportunities for spotting a peregrine falcon or a merlin are pretty good too.'

Merry smiled. She'd never been much of a twitcher but watching the birds over Brightwater Bay had been one of her unexpected pleasures during her time in the croft and now she could easily identify a wide range of Orkney's bird population, from gulls to puffins. She wasn't sure she'd like to see a bird of prey among them, however. That sounded altogether too stressful. 'Is that where your friend works – at the observatory?'

Niall gave a shake of the head. 'No. She's – well, it's probably best if I let Kirsty explain it. I don't want to spoil the surprise.'

It wasn't long before Merry caught the distant sparkle of sunshine on waves. A few minutes later they arrived at a dry-stone wall, beyond which the North Sea gently lapped at the rocky shore, and Niall came to a stop. 'This is Nouster. Do you see the pier over there?'

Merry gazed across the blue-grey water and saw a narrow finger of stone jutting out into the bay. She nodded.

'If we'd caught the ferry from Kirkwall, that's where we would have disembarked,' he explained. 'But it takes two hours and forty minutes and I thought it made more sense to fly. Especially after Hoy.'

Merry shivered. The last time she and Niall had taken a ferry to one of the smaller islands, the weather had taken a turn for the worse and she'd caught a fever that had knocked her off her feet. 'Good idea.'

He checked his phone, frowning. 'Kirsty said she'd be somewhere around here this morning.' Wheeling his bike to the side of the road, he propped it onto its stand. 'We can leave these here while we find her. I seriously doubt anyone will move them.'

He set off along the course of the stone wall. Merry looked around. Apart from the pier and a couple of isolated houses overlooking the bay, there didn't seem to be anywhere for Niall's friend to work. Unless she was a fisherman. Which was entirely possible, Merry supposed.

She became aware of the sheep after they'd been walking for around a minute. It was on the other side of the dry-stone wall, head down and nibbling at something on the rocks. As Niall and Merry drew level, it raised its head to stare at them, chewing methodically as it did so.

'Shouldn't that sheep be on this side of the wall?' she asked Niall.

'No,' he said, glancing across the layer of vertical stones that topped the wall. 'If it were on this side, we'd have a problem.'

Frowning, Merry peered at the sheep again. It seemed to have a string of something brown and distinctly seaweedy hanging from its mouth. 'Are you sure?' she said. 'It looks a bit lost, all on its own.'

'It's not alone,' he said, pointing further along the shore. 'There are more over there.'

And there were, Merry saw, a small cluster of creamy white animals with brown faces and neat little horns. Others were dotted along the shoreline, in groups or alone. Some were brown, others were black, but they all had one thing in common: every single one appeared to be enjoying a tasty mouthful of seaweed.

'Ah, there she is,' Niall exclaimed and raised his arm to wave. 'Kirsty! We're here!'

Merry followed his line of sight and saw a woman's head peeking over the other side of the wall, some fifty metres away. She looked up when Niall called and waved cheerfully back.

'Stay there,' she called. 'I'll come to you.'

A few moments later, she was standing in front of them and Merry noticed she wore heavy-duty workmen's dungarees and thick sturdy boots, all of which looked practical and waterproof. Her auburn hair was pulled back into a neat ponytail and she wasn't wearing a scrap of make-up; then again, she didn't need to, Merry thought as she took in the other woman's bright eyes and healthy glowing complexion.

'Hello, Niall,' she said, nodding at him. 'Good to see you again.'

'And you,' Niall said before turning slightly. 'Merry, can I introduce you to Kirsty Tallantyre? And Kirsty, this is Merina Wilde – our current Writer in Residence.'

Kirsty wiped a hand on her dungarees then held it out to Merry. 'Lovely to meet you, Merina. Niall's told me a lot about you.'

'Oh, call me Merry,' she replied, wondering what exactly Niall might have said. 'He's been very mysterious about you and your job.'

'Not mysterious,' Niall corrected mildly. 'Discreet. I wanted to let Kirsty tell you herself. But I'll give you a clue – it's got something to do with the sheep you were so worried about.'

Merry thought for a moment. 'You're a farmer?'

Kirsty grinned. 'More of a builder. And the sheep are the reason I'm here.'

'A builder?' Merry repeated, looking round for evidence of construction and finding none.

'I'm in charge of the sheep dyke,' Kirsty said, waving a hand at the stone wall beside them. 'It runs around the whole of the island – around thirteen miles – and it's been here since the nineteenth century.'

Finally, Merry understood. 'Of course – the wall. To keep the sheep away from the sea.'

But Kirsty shook her head. 'Not quite. To keep the sheep *beside* the sea.'

Niall grinned. 'Meet the famous seaweed-eating sheep of North Ronaldsay,' he said, with the air of a magician presenting a trick. 'Their digestive systems are specially adapted to get nutrients from it – they live on the shore for most of the year and the wall is to stop them from coming ashore and eating the grass.'

Kirsty saw Merry's confused expression. 'I know, it sounds weird, doesn't it? But they're a rare breed only found on the island – their bodies are used to seaweed,' she explained. 'If they eat too much grass, they don't absorb the correct nutrients and can suffer from copper poisoning. Part of my job is to make sure they stay on the shore where there's plenty of the right food.'

'Got it,' Merry said. 'You're responsible for maintaining the wall.'

'That's right. My official job title is Sheep Dyke Warden and I travel around the island, repairing and rebuilding the parts that have been damaged by the winter storms or just the passage of time.'

Merry gazed at her in fascination. 'That's amazing. How long have you been doing it?'

Kirsty tipped her head. 'Only since last November. The dyke was being maintained by volunteers but, despite their best efforts, it's been slowly falling into disrepair for a while. North Ronaldsay Trust decided to create a permanent role for someone to take care of the upkeep full time and I got the job.'

'Wow,' Merry said, thinking that it must be the kind of thankless task even Hercules would have blanched at. 'And how's it going so far?'

'It has its up and downs,' Kirsty admitted wryly. 'The

bad weather earlier this year meant several stretches of dyke were damaged. And the ferry was cancelled a lot, which made getting food interesting. But things are easier now the weather has improved.'

'And it's the Sheep Festival soon,' Niall said encouragingly. 'That's always a high point.'

Kirsty's eyes twinkled. 'So I've heard.' She turned to Merry. 'The festival is when loads of volunteers arrive on the island to help repair the dyke. It lasts for two weeks and there's a whole raft of music and entertainment that runs alongside it, to thank the volunteers for giving up their time and energy to help out.'

'It's a wonderful couple of weeks,' Niall said, then raised his eyebrows at Merry. 'You should think about volunteering. It might be good book research.'

Merry laughed. 'I'm pretty certain dry-stone walling is a highly developed skill. Any section I worked on would fall down in a gentle breeze.'

Kirsty smiled. 'I understand we get volunteers from all walks of life – you'd be very welcome if you wanted to join us. The more the merrier, in fact.'

'You wouldn't say that if you'd seen me playing Jenga,' Merry answered, laughing. 'But I know where to come if I ever need to write a character who builds walls, though. Thanks for talking to me.'

'My pleasure,' Kirsty said, her gaze warm. 'Niall's got my number if you need to ask anything, or you can always pop back over. And if all else fails, I'll see you at the ceilidh.'

'I'll look forward to it,' Merry said. 'Thank you.'

Beside her, Niall checked his watch. 'I suppose we'd better get going. We don't want to keep Bobby waiting.'

'You're going up the lighthouse?' Kirsty asked and grimaced at Merry. 'I hope you've got a good head for heights.'

'Don't try to scare her,' Niall said. 'It's only a hundred and seventy-six steps to the top.'

'One hundred and seventy-six!' Merry said, as her jaw dropped in dismay. 'That's almost as many stairs as Covent Garden tube station and they nearly killed me the last time I walked up them.'

'Ah, but that was before you started running half-marathons,' Niall replied. 'You'll have no bother jogging to the top here.'

'One half-marathon,' Merry corrected. 'And I'll have cycled three miles to get to the lighthouse.' She gazed at Niall through narrowed eyes. 'I'm starting to wonder if you're actually running a writer's boot camp instead of a residency.'

Kirsty laughed. 'It does sound a lot like that. Good luck, anyway!'

They waved goodbye to Kirsty and walked back to their bikes. Niall rummaged in his rucksack and handed Merry a bottle of water. 'I've got home-made flapjack, courtesy of Sheila, and fruitcake from Bridget. I don't know why they think I need feeding up but they dropped them into the library this week and I thought they'd be good for boosting our energy today.'

Merry smiled. Sheila often brought her baked goods too

and they were always delicious. She opted for the flapjack and savoured the syrup-coated oats before climbing onto her bike once more. But they hadn't gone more than half a mile along the road when Niall stopped again. 'Are you up for a detour?'

Privately, Merry was up for anything that put off the moment she'd have to tackle the stairs of the lighthouse but she didn't say so. 'Of course.'

Once again, they left the bikes by the side of the road but this time, Niall led Merry across a gently sloping meadow covered in wildflowers. She took a moment to appreciate the quiet air around them, broken only by the buzz of bees and the occasional call of a bird overhead. As they neared the summit, Merry saw a solitary column of grey stone reaching towards the sky and knew it must be the reason Niall had brought her here.

'Behold the Stan Stone,' he said with a dramatic sweep of his arm. 'Said to be the sister of the Odin Stone, originally part of the Standing Stones of Stenness.'

Merry was used to seeing the stones at Stenness, silhouetted against the Orkney sky. This stone was lonelier but no less impressive, although there was one noticeable difference. 'Is it supposed to have a hole in the middle?'

Niall nodded in approval, as though she was a promising student. 'I'm glad you asked – it gives me an excuse to bore you with yet more island history.'

Merry laughed. 'You're never boring. Tell me.'

'Okay, since you insist. As I said, the Stan Stone is thought to be sister to the Odin Stone, which used to be one of the

Stones of Stenness although it's no longer standing. Odin's Stone had a hole in the centre too, and people used to think that gave it healing properties. But, more interestingly, the hole allowed them to clasp hands through the heart of the stone, and legend said that anyone who did so while swearing an oath to Odin would create a binding agreement – say, for example, a promise to be faithful to a lover or even a marriage vow.'

'And what happened if they broke the oath?' Merry asked, imagining lovestruck couples plighting their troth among the stones.

Niall sighed. 'I know you want me to say lightning bolts and terrible vengeance were delivered by Odin himself but there's no evidence to support it. That said, most people took it very seriously and tried not to break the oath. The community elders took a dim view of anyone who reneged on a deal made on the stone.'

Merry studied the stone before them, with its much smaller hole. 'You couldn't clasp hands through this one.'

'No,' Niall agreed. 'Although some people still believe this stone has magical powers too. It's meant to grant wishes.'

'Really?' Merry said. 'What do you have to do?'

He shrugged. 'Touch the stone and swear to honour Odin, then silently make your wish.'

She threw him a sceptical look but his expression gave nothing away. 'What have you got to lose?'

It was exactly the kind of scene she might find in countless novels but Merry still felt foolish as she took a deep breath and reached out a slow fingertip towards the hole. She opened her mouth to start her oath but the moment her skin made contact with the cool stone, she felt a jolt run through her shoulders as though she'd been struck.

'Raaaaah!' Niall bellowed in her ear and then broke into helpless laughter. 'Got you!'

Shaken, Merry stepped back and glared at him, flexing her shoulders. 'That wasn't funny.'

'It – was,' he gasped, as tears appeared in his eyes. 'I'm sorry but it was!'

She tried to stay cross but his laughter was so contagious that Merry couldn't help joining in. It started with a tug at the corner of her mouth, followed by a snort that finally descended into full-on belly laughter.

'Sorry,' Niall managed, placing his hands on his knees after a minute or two. 'I couldn't resist.'

'I'm never believing anything you tell me again,' Merry said, trying unsuccessfully to still sound annoyed.

'I'm sorry,' he said again. 'But you looked so totally convinced. It was mean of me.'

'It was,' Merry agreed. 'And now I'm going to put you in a book and do something horrible to you.'

He grinned. 'Please do. Infamy at last.'

Merry shook her head; he looked like a little boy whose prank had exceeded even his own wildest dreams. 'If you've quite finished terrifying me, didn't you say we needed to get to the lighthouse?'

Sobering a little, Niall checked the time. 'Yes, we probably should. But it's okay, the roads are flat. We'll just have to cycle a bit harder.'

Merry swallowed a sigh and straightened her shoulders. 'Remind me to say no next time you turn up on my doorstep and demand I go island-hopping with you.'

'You're going to love the lighthouse,' Niall said, setting off for the road. 'More importantly, you're going to love Bobby, the lighthouse tour guide.'

'Am I?' She glanced back at him. 'Are you about to spin me some story about him being descended directly from Odin himself?'

'No, but he's what you might call an interesting character,' he said. 'Believe me, you're definitely going to want to put *him* in a book.'

Chapter Twenty-six

Up close, the lighthouse was even more impressive than it had been from the air. As promised, they were met at the base of the red and white tower by Bobby Murray and Merry instantly knew why Niall had been so certain she'd want to write him into a story: if someone had asked her to picture a salty sea-dog of a lighthouse keeper, Bobby was exactly what she would have imagined. All that was missing was a thick black pipe poking out from his bushy white beard.

'Ah, if it isn't our trusty keeper of knowledge and his esteemed writer friend,' he said as they approached, in a voice that was richer and louder than the stillness around them warranted. 'I hope you had a pleasant journey here?'

'Very smooth, thank you,' Niall said, allowing the older man to pump his hand with more enthusiasm than necessary. 'Can I introduce you to Merina Wilde?'

Bobby took Merry's hand and shook it with the same vigour he'd used on Niall. 'Charmed. Absolutely charmed.'

'Lovely to meet you too,' Merry said, surreptitiously wiggling her fingers to make sure they still worked. 'Thank you for taking the time to show us around.'

'It's no trouble at all,' Bobby insisted. 'I'm grateful to you for coming – we don't get as many visitors as we used to and it does me good to climb the stairs. There are quite a few, in case you didn't know, so I hope you've had a decent breakfast.'

Merry flashed a meaningful look at Niall, who smirked but said nothing.

Bobby raised his voice a little as he slipped into what Merry assumed was his work patter. 'This beauty is the tallest land-based lighthouse in the United Kingdom. She was built in eighteen fifty-two and stands at a hundred and thirty-nine feet, giving unrivalled views across these beautiful islands. Of course, she's not just a pretty face.' He nodded proudly at Merry. 'She plays a vital role in keeping ships from foundering on the treacherous shoals beneath the sea around the island. But more of that later.'

He waved a hand towards the door of the lighthouse and beamed at his visitors. 'Shall we begin our ascent? It's such a clear day that I think we might even see all the way to Fair Isle.'

He kept up a steady stream of facts and figures all the way to the top, his voice booming off the smooth painted walls, while Merry tried to keep up and wondered how he could even talk, let alone bellow.

'Are you familiar with Peppa Pig?' Niall murmured as they climbed.

Distracted, Merry nodded. Alex's nieces had been big fans and Merry had watched more than a few episodes while babysitting them. She had no idea why Niall had chosen this particular moment to mention the show, however.

'Do you remember which character lives in the lighthouse?' he asked.

And then it made sense, because Merry had a sudden flashback to an episode featuring a white-bearded rabbit with a booming voice who lived in a lighthouse. The resemblance to Bobby was striking and the thought caused Merry to snort with laughter.

Bobby paused on the stairs above her. 'Are you quite well?'

Merry waved a hand. 'Fine. Just a little cough – carry on.'

'Sorry,' Niall whispered, once Bobby had set off again.

'You are behaving very badly today,' Merry said, in a tone of mock severity. 'What's got into you?'

He grinned. 'Must be the North Ronaldsay air.'

At the top, Bobby tactfully gave them a minute to catch their breath and went on to explain that this was the second lighthouse to be built on the island. 'You can still visit the remains of the old beacon and a very sturdy old lady she is too.'

Beside her, Merry felt rather than heard Niall trying not to laugh. 'Did you say we might catch a glimpse of Fair Isle?' she asked quickly, before she could catch the giggles too.

Bobby beamed at her. 'I should have known you'd be interested in distant lands. Writers and poets always are.'

He pointed to the north, where Merry could just about

make out a shape that looked a little like another island. 'And of course, they can see the light sweeping the waves most nights,' Bobby went on. 'It's a fully automated flash every ten seconds these days but back in the eighteenth and nineteenth centuries, they used burning oil.'

After explaining more about how the lamp worked, Bobby gave them some time to themselves. 'This is when most people want to take a selfie or two, as a memento of their trip,' he said. 'Although I'm always happy to act as photographer if you prefer?'

Niall and Merry both shook their heads and Bobby retreated, although Merry noticed he stayed on hand, presumably because there wasn't really anywhere for him to go, other than down the stairs, and she assumed even Bobby wasn't enthusiastic enough to climb the spiral steps twice in the space of an hour.

The wind was much stronger than it had been at the base and Merry found her dark hair whipping around her face as she snapped a few photos on her phone. She'd normally send one or two to Jess, she thought, and the observation caused some of her good mood to drain away.

Niall seemed to read her mind because he asked, 'Heard from Jess lately?'

'Not much,' Merry replied, wondering whether he had any idea that they'd fallen out. 'Why?'

He leaned on the parapet and shrugged. 'Just wondering. You've been tucked away in the croft for weeks so I haven't had a chance to ask you whether she enjoyed her visit.'

'Oh,' Merry said and took a moment to gather her thoughts. 'Yes, I think she did.'

Niall kept his gaze fixed on the shifting waves below them. 'Any particular highlights?' he asked, his tone casual.

Frowning, she turned to study him. 'Not that she's mentioned. Why, do you need some official feedback?'

'No, nothing like that,' he said, and managed an awkward smile. 'I wondered if she'd said anything, that's all. Mentioned anyone in particular.'

Merry felt her heart begin to thud in her chest and a horrible suspicion loomed in her mind. 'Like who?'

Now Niall's expression grew even more awkward. 'I'm not supposed to say. Forget I mentioned it.'

Merry shook her head, trepidation building. 'You can't leave it like that. What's this about?'

He sighed and looked over his shoulder, as though checking Bobby was out of earshot. 'It's no big deal, I suppose. Andrew was asking after her. He took a bit of a shine to her and asked me to find out if she felt the same way.' He paused, looking wretched. 'And I know it's a wee bit unprofessional but he's my best friend, so I said I'd try to find out.'

The relief that flooded over Merry was so strong that she had to grab hold of the railing along the parapet. 'Andrew likes Jess?'

Niall nodded. 'You can't tell her. And you can't tell Andrew that I told you. He made me promise to be discreet.'

She felt the corners of her mouth edge upwards into a smile. 'Well, I think it's safe to say you don't have a career as a spy in your future,' she said, still reeling from her own jumbled emotions. 'But if I'm speaking to her any time soon, I'll see what I can find out.'

'Would you?' he said gratefully. 'I'd really appreciate it. He's been mooning around like a lovesick puppy ever since she left and I know she's probably forgotten all about him but if you could find out for sure, one way or the other . . .'

'I'll see what I can do,' Merry promised, and decided not to explore her relief at Niall's revelation.

Bobby loomed in front of them. 'Are you sure you don't want a photo? I thought all you young folks put this kind of thing on Instagram these days.'

Niall raised an eyebrow at Merry. 'Shall we? Might be handy for the library newsletter.'

She raised a hand to smooth her tangled curls and then gave up. 'Sure,' she said. 'Why not?'

It was much easier descending the stairs than it had been coming up, although Merry still marvelled at Bobby, who almost skipped down like a man half his age. At the bottom, he directed them to the shop and café, where they could buy authentic Fair Isle jumpers and get a decent cup of tea. Merry and Niall thanked him profusely for the tour but he waved away their thanks. 'Just make sure I get a copy of your new book when it's ready,' he said, eyes twinkling. 'It sounds like just my thing.'

'Of course,' Merry said, and made a mental note to be gentle if she ever wrote Bobby into a story.

They were on their way out of the door when the loudest

horn Merry had ever heard reverberated around the base of the tower.

'What the hell was that?' Merry asked in alarm, covering her ears with her hands.

Niall shook his head, mystified until Bobby reappeared behind them, grinning at their shocked expressions.

'And that's what the foghorn sounds like,' he bellowed, and his voice seemed to reach even higher decibels. 'Sorry if it made you jump.'

'He's not sorry,' Merry muttered, after she and Niall had laughed politely and begun to make their way towards the café. 'I bet he does that to everyone.'

'Probably,' Niall said, pressing a finger against his earlobe and jiggling it. 'Although I'm pretty sure he could just stand at the top and shout to warn ships on foggy days.'

Merry couldn't help laughing. 'Maybe that's what he does. Come to think of it, isn't that the plot of a *Peppa Pig* episode?'

He threw her a sympathetic look. 'Damn. It's true what they say – there really are no new ideas in the world.'

'See?' Merry said. 'Being a writer is harder than it looks.'

'Never mind,' Niall said, pushing open the door of the café. 'I'll buy you some cake to make up for the disappointment.'

Merry let out a loud sigh. 'And that is why Writer's Arse is a thing.'

It wasn't especially late by the time Niall stopped the car outside the croft, but Merry was finding it impossible to hide her yawns.

'I'd invite you in for coffee but I don't think I'd stay awake long enough to drink it,' she told him with a rueful smile.

'I'm pretty exhausted myself,' he admitted. 'It's all that cycling.'

'Not to mention the stairs,' she reminded him. 'But despite all the exercise – or maybe because of it – I had a really great time.'

'Me too.' His eyes rested briefly on hers, then he fixed his gaze on the sea. 'They've gone fast, these six months. It hardly seems like yesterday that I brought you here for the first time and watched you become utterly mesmerized by the sunset over the bay.'

Merry felt her smile widen at the memory. 'It was a pretty spectacular effort, even by Orkney standards. And I still find the sunsets mesmerizing. I'm going to miss them so very much.'

That wasn't all she was going to miss, Merry wanted to say, but she was more aware than ever of the professional line between her and Niall. It might have blurred a little today but it was still there, and it felt to Merry like a tangible barrier. It was certainly enough to stop her confessing that the idea of leaving Orkney in a few weeks' time caused her heart to ache every time she thought of it. There was nothing to be gained from telling Niall how she felt; he couldn't offer her an extension of her residency – it wasn't within the terms of the agreement to do so. Besides, she was certain she must have been a particularly troublesome writer for him to wrangle; as far as she could tell, none of the others had let their personal lives intrude upon their work in quite the way she had. Niall was probably counting down the days even as he sat with her right now.

'You'll have to come back and visit,' he said. 'If you want to, that is. If you have time.'

His tone was oddly stiff, she noticed, which suggested he was being polite. But it didn't matter because she knew once she went back to London, and fell back into the cycle of her old life, the spell would be broken and it was unlikely she'd return to Orkney.

'I might have to,' she said, striving to keep her tone light. 'I need an idea for my next book, after all.'

'Of course,' he agreed. 'You bring your laptop, I'll supply the whisky.'

The idea of a dram or two of whisky sounded like heaven, Merry thought as another yawn crept up on her. 'Sorry,' she said, with some embarrassment. 'I think I'd better call it a night. Thanks for a great day.'

'Thank you for coming with me,' Niall responded. 'I love travelling around the islands but it's always more fun with a partner in crime.'

Merry smiled and reached for the door handle. 'Goodnight, Niall.'

'Goodnight, Merry.'

She watched the tail-lights of his car until they blinked out of sight. Then she went inside, collected a bottle of Highland Park, a glass, and her favourite yellow woollen blanket, and took both out to the bench overlooking Brightwater Bay.

Sunset was still a few hours away but in a few short weeks she'd lose the opportunity to sit here for ever. She had to appreciate it now, while she still could.

And a tiny voice in her head suggested that the view wasn't the only thing she'd lose when she left Orkney. But there was nothing she could do about either.

Merry thought she was hallucinating when she drove back to the croft on Thursday morning to find Magnús's Ford pick-up truck parked outside. She blinked, wondering who could have borrowed it and why they'd driven out to see her. And then she got out of the Mini, just as the driver of the pick-up pushed open the driver's side door. She recognized him long before he'd unfolded himself to his full height; there was no mistaking Magnús Ólafsson. What he was doing outside the croft, when he should have been in Reykjavik, was another matter entirely.

'Surprise,' he said, as the sun appeared from behind a cloud to turn his long golden hair into a halo. 'How's my favourite Valkyrie?'

She reached into the car to gather up her shopping and slowly walked towards him, her heart thudding. 'Hello, Magnús. I didn't know you were back on Orkney.'

'I was reminded of some urgent business that needed my attention,' he said, slamming the car door. 'Can I help you carry your shopping?'

Merry still wasn't a hundred per cent sure she wasn't imagining him – all six foot five of him – but her gut seemed convinced; it had begun tying itself in knots the moment she'd spotted the truck. 'I can manage.'

His gaze was level. 'I know you can manage. I'm asking if you will permit me to help.'

A cynical part of Merry's brain suggested that it would be much harder for her to get Magnús to leave if he'd already gained access to the croft; for example, by carrying her shopping into the kitchen. But that wasn't Magnús's way. If he wanted to come in, he'd simply ask. And Merry was pretty certain her treacherous mouth would say yes, so she might as well save them all some time and invite him inside now.

'Thank you,' she said, handing over the heaviest bag. 'There are a couple more bags in the Mini, if you don't mind.'

His fingers brushed hers as he took the bag handle and she felt an all-too-familiar stab deep inside; apparently, he was real. She focused on finding her keys and pushing the right one into the door lock. What she needed was the kind of mental boost only coffee could give, and she needed it fast.

Merry left the shopping where Magnús had placed the bags, in the middle of the kitchen floor, and put some coffee on. Then she carried two mugs through to the living room, where Magnús now sat, looking as relaxed as ever, in his usual armchair. He took the drink she offered with a grateful tip of his head and placed it carefully on the table in front of them.

'You look well,' he said. 'It's very good to see you.'

Merry ignored the swarm of butterflies released in her stomach by the compliment and sat on the end of the small sofa, as far away from Magnús as possible. 'You look great too,' she replied, because anything else would have been a lie. 'How are things back at home?'

'Slowly improving,' he said. 'To the point where I felt comfortable enough leaving my mother and sister alone for a couple of days, at any rate.'

'That's good,' she replied. 'I'm glad she's getting better.'

He looked around, taking in the pile of books stacked up beside the bookshelf. 'I see you've started packing. Have you decided what you will take and what you'll leave behind yet?'

She'd found it hard to decide on anything when it came to leaving Orkney but she wasn't about to explain that now. Taking a deep breath, Merry decided on the direct approach. 'Not really. What can I help you with, Magnús?'

He nodded, as though the blunt question had been exactly what he'd been expecting. 'I heard your interview on Radio Orkney. You and Jess work well together – I can understand why you are best friends.'

Which was very nice but didn't answer her question, Merry thought. She waited.

'As you know, it's been a difficult few months for me,' he went on. 'I don't mind telling you that my mother's illness scared me. It reminded me that our time on earth is short and the thought of losing her sent me into a panic. I made some choices that seemed right at the time but that I now regret. And one of those regrets is breaking up with you.'

Merry's head began to whirl the moment Magnús finished his last sentence. She had always admired his decision to put his family first and return home to Reykjavik to care for his mother, even though it had hurt at the time. But his absolute determination to do the right thing, by both Merry and his family, had been so undeniably *him* that it had somehow made it easier for Merry to let him go. And now here he was, telling her that he regretted his decision to end their relationship, that perhaps it hadn't been the right thing after all. It was almost enough to blow her mind.

'I'm not sure you had much option,' she managed, surprised by how even her voice sounded. 'We went over this at the time, remember? You had no idea how long your mum would need you, and decided it was better to make a clean break of things between us rather than keep me dangling. Which I am very glad for, by the way.'

Magnús watched her carefully. 'I do remember. And I am certain, at the time, that it seemed like the most logical and sensible thing to have done. But what I am saying now is that I was wrong.'

She nodded slowly. 'When did you realize?'

'Almost immediately,' he said. 'But I was not selfish enough to disturb your peace of mind, plus I was afraid you might have moved on, so I buried the thoughts and got on with the task of nursing my mother.'

'What changed?' Merry asked, even though she already knew the answer.

'Hearing you talk on the radio,' Magnús said simply. 'You mentioned a kiss on a starlit night and I knew you meant the night we spent watching the Merry Dancers. And it gave me hope that perhaps it was not too late, that I might be able to put right the mistake I had made.'

The memory of kissing Magnús underneath a blanket of the aurora made Merry's cheeks burn. 'But the interview was weeks ago,' she said, trying to get her racing heart under control.

Magnús sighed. 'I know. It has taken me this long to summon up the courage to come and see you. We are not all brave Valkyries like you, Merry. I knew there was a good chance you would say no, and then my hopes would be dashed.'

Merry stared at him for what felt like an eternity. How many times after he'd left had she longed to see him again, dreamed of a moment just like this when they could fall into each other's arms. Now here he was, a few metres away from her, his green eyes fixed solemnly on hers, and the desire to kiss him was almost overwhelming. All she had to do was get to her feet and cross the room.

All she had to do was say yes.

Chapter Twenty-seven

'I don't know.'

The words were out of Merry's mouth before she could stop them. Part of her brain recoiled incredulously – the part that was urging her legs to move – but another part was replaying everything that had happened with a much more objective eye. And it was that considering, sensible part of her brain that had confessed that she didn't know how to react to Magnús's revelation.

A wary expression crossed his face, although Merry didn't think he was surprised. 'Of course, this is not something I expect you to decide now,' he said. 'You should take your time and be guided by what you want, as much as what I want. But just as I regret the decision to break off my relationship with you, I know I would also very much regret it if I didn't ask for another chance.'

Merry watched as he drained his coffee and stood up. 'You're leaving?'

He nodded. 'For now, to allow you the time and space to think. But I will be on Orkney for another day, at least. If you want to talk more, or decide you would also like to try again, then you know how to contact me.'

He moved towards the front door. Merry followed him, feeling strangely light-headed and confused. 'And if I decide I don't want to try again?'

'Then I will be very sorry but at least I will have the satisfaction of knowing I tried,' he said and paused in the doorway. 'And just in case you have forgotten how that kiss felt . . .'

Cupping her cheek with one calloused hand, he lowered his head to hers and planted the softest of kisses on her lips. Instantly, Merry felt heat rush through her veins and every part of her seemed to burn at once. But no sooner had the kiss begun than it ended and she was left longing for more.

Magnús stepped back, his eyes stormy, and she knew he'd been just as affected as her. 'Be well, Merry. I hope to hear from you soon.'

He walked away, leaving her leaning against the doorframe, weak-kneed. So that was the kind of kiss that left the recipient trembling, she thought, as the engine of the pick-up truck roared into life. And even as she stepped back and closed the door, her mouth still tingling and her body still yearning for more, the part of her that was a writer was storing the sensations away for use in a story someday.

Maybe that was the way to approach this, she thought as she wandered back to the sofa; maybe she should think it through as though Magnús was the hero in one of her stories. Except that in the world of romantic fiction there was no decision to be made; her readers would be shouting yes even before the kiss. The trouble was that this was real life and emotions were not as easily rewritten. And Merry's feelings were as tangled as it was possible to be.

What she needed was a friend to offer steady but impartial advice. But all she had was herself.

Merry spent a sleepless night tossing and turning, replaying the scene over and over in her mind until she wanted to cry with bewilderment. More than anything, she wished she could message Jess, to reap the benefit of her forthright but trustworthy wisdom. But that wasn't an option now and she'd deliberately left her phone in the living room, so that she wouldn't be tempted to contact her. This time, she had to work out her path alone.

Or did she? She might not be able to talk to Jess but she did have friends on Orkney. When she arrived at the farmhouse just after eleven o'clock, Clare took one look at her pale face and puffy eyes and ushered Hugh from the kitchen. He took the dismissal in his stride, glancing from Clare to Merry without comment and pausing only to squeeze Merry's shoulder as he left the room.

'Don't take this the wrong way but you look like hell,' Clare said the moment the door closed. 'What's wrong?'

'Everything,' Merry said dully. 'Or maybe nothing. I actually can't tell.'

Clare eyed her sharply, then reached for the cake tin. 'Right. You cut the Battenberg, I'll make the tea and let's see if we can't sort this out.'

She listened while Merry poured everything out: the ongoing silence from Jess, Niall's revelation about Andrew, Merry's mixed feelings about returning to London. When she reached the part about Magnús, Clare's eyes became saucers but she didn't interrupt, not even when Merry described the kiss. She waited until Merry had finished speaking, then sat back in her seat and puffed out a long breath.

'I don't know where to begin,' she said, with a small shake of her head.

Merry sighed. 'Me neither.'

Clare took a mouthful of cake and chewed in an absent-minded way. 'And you've heard nothing from Jess? Not even when you apologized?'

Merry shifted on her chair. 'Well, I haven't exactly apologized.'

'Okay,' Clare said carefully. 'Do you think maybe that might be a good place to start? It's pretty clear now that there's nothing going on between her and Niall.'

'Is it?' Merry replied, raising her chin. 'Obviously, Niall doesn't see her that way but that doesn't mean Jess doesn't fancy him.'

The other woman stared at her. 'You know her best, of course. But she's been back in London for a few weeks now – is it really likely she's still carrying a torch for Niall when they live seven hundred miles apart?'

The answer was no, Merry knew. When it came to dating, Jess had the attention span of a goldfish and rarely maintained interest in one man for more than a month. And it seemed unlikely she and Niall were still in touch, given his questions to Merry the day they'd visited the lighthouse. So even if Jess had been interested in Niall, that interest had almost certainly faded by now.

'What I'm getting at here,' Clare went on in a gentle tone, 'is whether it's worth potentially losing your best friend over something that probably isn't true. Especially since you know there's no way Niall sees Jess as anything more than a friend.'

She was right, Merry knew, and the realization made her want to groan. 'I'm such an idiot.'

'No, you're a human being,' Clare said. 'We all make mistakes and I'm sure Jess will understand. But I think you need to say sorry if you want to repair the damage to your friendship. The sooner the better.'

Merry nodded gratefully. 'Okay. I will.'

'As for whether you're ready to go back to London, who says you have to?'

'I'm only meant to be here for six months,' Merry said. 'I'm sure the Literary Society would take a dim view if I refused to leave at the start of August.'

Clare shrugged. 'We've got a spare room – you could stay with us until you find somewhere else to live. But, actually, the croft stays empty for half the year – the Writer in Residence scheme only runs from February to August, so it's not as though someone else will be moving in when you vacate. You might find the Literary Society is open to you extending your stay, if you offer to pay rent and don't mind the long winter nights.'

Merry's jaw dropped a little. It was such a simple solution – why hadn't she thought of it? 'But why hasn't Niall suggested it?' she asked, still trying to get her head around the idea.

'Maybe he doesn't know you're thinking about staying,' Clare said. 'Have you ever actually told him?'

It was another good point, Merry acknowledged – had she? She'd certainly said she'd miss Orkney when she left, and Niall had always been so good at reading between the lines that perhaps she'd expected him to understand without ever expressly mentioning that she might stay. 'I don't know,' she told Clare. 'It's possible I haven't.'

'So that's another conversation you need to have,' Clare said with some satisfaction. 'And with a bit of luck, you can sort something out and then that problem will be solved. Which leaves us with Magnús.' She stopped and took a long sip of tea, watching Merry over the top of her mug. 'What are you going to do about him?'

'Honestly? I have no idea.'

Clare pursed her lips and lifted her hands as though ticking off options. 'Let's think it through. One, you stay on Orkney and restart things with Magnús, seeing each other when he comes here or you go to Reykjavik.'

That had been the suggestion Merry had made to Magnús when he'd first announced he was moving back to Iceland to look after his mother. 'Okay,' she said. 'It's not the easiest journey but it could work if we put the effort in.'

'Option two, you go back to London and restart things.'

'That could work as well,' Merry said. 'In fact, getting to Reykjavik from London might be easier than from here. But it would mean leaving Orkney ...'

She trailed off as the familiar bubble of reluctance rose up inside her.

'That's true,' Clare said. 'And I think we've established you're going to stay. So that means the final option is staying on Orkney and not restarting things with Magnús. How does that make you feel?'

Wrapping her hands around the mug of tea, Merry gave it some thought. Seeing Magnús had certainly reminded her of the physical attraction between them and she knew there'd been much more to their relationship than that. He was kind and thoughtful and generous and caring ... In short, the perfect boyfriend. Dating him again would be no hardship, even if it had to be long-distance for now, and she had no doubt she could fall in love with him, given time. So, what was stopping her from accepting his offer, she wondered yet again. Why wasn't her heart singing a big joyful *YES*?

She sighed and met Clare's eyes. 'I think he's too late,' she said slowly, feeling her way around the admission for the first time. 'I think maybe there's someone else I like more.'

Her friend watched her for a moment, then nodded. 'I think so too. Although just for the sake of clarity, I have to check you don't mean Alex here.'

The comment was so unexpected that Merry let out an involuntary snort of laughter. 'No,' she said, blinking. 'I definitely don't mean Alex.'

Clare sat back in her seat. 'Good, because I didn't want to have to slap you. And for what it's worth, I think the someone you like likes you too.'

But Merry shook her head. 'No, he doesn't. He's made that pretty clear.'

'Has he?' Clare asked sceptically. 'Or have you just decided he's not interested because that meant you didn't have to confront your own feelings?'

Ouch, Merry thought as the observation hit home. She grimaced at Clare. 'Have I ever mentioned you have a lot in common with Jess sometimes?'

'I'll take that as a compliment,' Clare said, grinning. 'But seriously, I've known Niall a long time and I've never seen him as obviously smitten as he is now. I don't know why he hasn't told you how he feels – maybe it's a work thing, because you're our Writer in Residence and that makes you somehow off limits. But I bet if you stay on after the residency ends, you'll discover how he really feels.'

The thought of having a conversation like that with Niall, of perhaps going on a date and maybe even kissing him, unleashed a fury of butterflies in Merry's stomach. 'But what if you're wrong?'

Clare spread her hands. 'Then I'm wrong. But here's the thing – do you want to go through life regretting the chances you didn't take?'

Merry thought back to Magnús, and what might have been if he'd taken a risk on their relationship. 'No,' she said quietly. 'I don't want to regret anything.'

'Well, then,' Clare said. 'I think my work here is done. Do you feel better?'

'I do,' Merry said, smiling. 'A tiny bit terrified but definitely better. Thank you.'

Clare returned her smile. 'Good. And in return, you can help me muck out the llamas. What size wellies do you take?'

Chapter Twenty-eight

Merry was unaccountably nervous when she arrived at the library for the ceilidh on the last Saturday in July.

It wasn't that she was anxious about the dancing; everyone had assured her there would be a caller giving clear instructions on what to do and when. And it wasn't because the night represented the official end to her duties as Orkney's Writer in Residence, although she was sorry her tenure was coming to an end – but not as sorry as she might have been if she was heading back to London on Monday morning. Thanks to Clare's sensible suggestion, she'd raised the idea of staying on at the croft with Niall and he'd been delighted to negotiate an extension to her tenancy lasting until the end of the year. But despite the lack of a tangible reason, there was no denying the pins and needles in Merry's fingers, or the rapid thud of her heart, as she stepped from the taxi and approached the library.

She paused for a moment in the courtyard, taking in the

fairy lights that adorned the walls and listening to the buzz of conversation and laughter that floated from the library itself. She'd done so many public events here over the past six months and none had made her feel as unsettled as she did now. But there was no backing out – the whole evening had been arranged in her honour – so she straightened her calf-length red dress and smoothed her 1940s-style curls behind their rose-covered clips and went inside.

The lobby was thronged with people, all dressed in Forties finery. The women had really made an effort, Merry noted with delight; the dresses were a kaleidoscope of vintage colour and the hairstyles covered every style from victory rolls to pin curls. Many of the men had opted for traditional dress, in kilts and sashes and knee-high socks, but a few were dressed in suits and ties. It was a sight to gladden Merry's heart and she was pleased she'd gone to town on her own outfit.

The first person to catch Merry's eye was Sheila, who wore an elegant tea dress that Merry suspected was genuinely from the wartime era.

'Don't you look lovely!' her silver-haired neighbour exclaimed, looking Merry up and down with evident satisfaction. 'I can't take all the credit, of course, but those runs along the cliffs have put roses in your cheeks to rival the ones in your hair.'

Merry laughed. 'It's definitely all down to you, Sheila. I'd have sat on my sofa all year if you hadn't encouraged me to join you.'

Sheila beamed at her. 'And now that you're staying on, the best is yet to come,' she said. 'I'll have you running a marathon before you know it.'

Niall appeared beside them. 'Don't scare the poor woman, Sheila. She might decide to go back to London on Monday after all.'

'We wouldn't want that,' Sheila observed, raising a knowing eyebrow at Niall. 'But I'm sure you two have official business to discuss now, so I'll leave you to it.'

She raised her glass and moved towards another group, which Merry saw contained Bridget and several other members of Sheila's book group.

'How are you feeling?' Niall asked, smiling at Merry. 'Ready to celebrate?'

She tipped her head. 'Sort of. I'm weirdly nervous, to be honest.'

'You don't look it,' he said. 'In fact, you look beautiful.'

He blushed slightly as he said it but Merry noticed his gaze was steady. 'Thank you. You look great too. Very dapper.'

Glancing down at his kilt, he nodded. 'It's kind of you to say so but I think we can both agree I don't have the knees for this. Still, it's tradition and I don't mind sacrificing my dignity in honour of you.'

It wasn't true, Merry thought. There was nothing wrong with his knees or any other part of him, as far as she could tell. But she felt some of her anxiety slip away as she smiled. 'I'm suitably grateful. What's the plan? I assume we'll do the talking bit before the dancing starts?'

He nodded. 'We'll open the doors to the hall shortly and let people take a seat. Then, once the speeches are done, you'll be presented with a small token of thanks from the Literary Society and the readers of Orkney. And after that, you'd better be ready to dance. I suspect you're not going to be short of partners.'

'Poor them,' Merry said. 'I hope they won't mind me treading on their toes.'

Niall grinned. 'It's your own toes you should be worried about. We're not all Billy Elliott, you know.' He paused and looked around. 'Want to come and have a sneaky peek at the hall? The library staff have worked wonders getting it ready for tonight – it's like stepping back seventy-five years.'

Merry felt her face light up. 'Absolutely. I can't wait to see it.'

'Then follow me,' he said, and snagged two glasses of champagne from a passing waiter. 'I know you don't normally drink before an event but this is a very special occasion.'

She took the glass he offered her and sipped. 'Maybe one won't hurt. It might even help.'

As always, the hall had been set up with row after row of seats, all facing a small, spot-lit stage. But Merry barely noticed. She was too busy admiring the sumptuous decorations that lined the walls, the glorious art-deco bar that lined the back wall, and the perfect 1940s vibe of the seating on the stage. There were four winged armchairs, a Winchester rug and even a gramophone on a stand. A tall standard lamp stood behind one of the chairs and she spotted vintage tea-cups with saucers laid out on the table instead of the usual bottles of water.

'It's amazing,' she said, shaking her head in wonderment. 'What a transformation.'

'We'll move the chairs once the presentation is over, and bring in some tables for around the edges,' Niall said. 'And the band will take the stage, obviously.'

Merry marvelled at the hall again. 'This is incredible. Thank you.'

Niall shrugged. 'Don't thank me, thank the library staff. I'm just as blown away as you.' He paused and gave her a sidelong look. 'Now, there's someone I think you need to see before we kick things off. Wait here a minute and I'll go and find her.'

Merry frowned as he hurried away, wondering who on earth he meant. Perhaps there was someone on the Literary Society she ought to meet. She waited, sipping her cham-pagne as she found new details in the decorations to admire. And then there was a click as the door to the hall opened. Merry looked over and almost dropped her glass. Standing in the doorway was Jess.

'Hi, babes,' she said, her vintage shoes clicking on the wooden floor as she came towards Merry. 'Surprise!'

Merry's eyes flooded. 'Oh my god! What are you doing here?'

Jess threw her an innocent look. 'Oh, you know. I just happened to be passing and thought I'd drop in.' She stopped a few feet away from Merry. 'Are you pleased to see me?'

'Pleased?' Merry echoed and hurried forward to throw her arms around her best friend. 'I've never been happier to see anyone in my life!'

Jess hugged her back and Merry closed her eyes against the tears that were threatening to ruin her carefully applied make-up.

'You didn't reply to my message saying sorry,' she said, standing back and sniffing. 'I thought you hated me.'

Jess shook her head. 'Of course I don't hate you. I wanted to give you a bloody good shake to make you see sense but that's not the same thing. And when I thought about it, I figured it was better to sort things out face-to-face. Less risk of any more misunderstandings.' She hesitated, then sighed. 'And I owe you an apology too because I have a small confession to make. I might have slightly pretended to be interested in Niall to make you jealous.'

Merry's mouth fell open. 'What? Why?'

'I know, it wasn't my finest moment,' Jess said, with an embarrassed shudder. 'But I thought it might make you realize how you felt about him and – I don't know – snog him to within an inch of his life or something.'

'Jess!'

Her best friend eyed her slyly. 'It worked, though. Niall says you're staying on here for a few months – that's so you can have lots of hot sex with each other, right?'

She ought to be angry, Merry thought, but it was

impossible to feel anything other than relief and joy. 'Maybe,' she said, feeling the beginnings of a blush warm her cheeks. 'I still have no idea if that's what he wants.'

'He does,' Jess replied firmly. 'Trust me, he really, really does.'

Merry had no idea how she could be so certain and decided she didn't want to ask. But there was something she did want to know. 'So, you know when we did the Radio Orkney interview, and you said there was someone you had your eye on – was that part of your plan to make me feel jealous?'

Jess frowned. 'What? No, of course not. I meant Andrew, you idiot.' She rolled her eyes in mock exasperation. 'Anyone with half a brain could see that, let alone the person who's supposed to know me best.'

'Ohhh,' Merry said. It all made perfect sense. 'Oh, and he likes you too! Niall told me he's been asking after you – you should definitely speak to him while you're here.'

'Way ahead of you, Mer,' Jess said, her eyes sparkling with affectionate amusement. 'Unlike you, it doesn't take me six months to work out what I want. And maybe Brightwater Bay will have another Chiswick author for a tenant next year.'

'Really?' Merry squeaked and brought her hands together in a gesture that was half prayer, half applause. 'That would be so awesome.'

'It's not a done deal,' Jess warned. 'But you didn't leave me much choice – I'm not sure I can cope with another six months without you.'

Merry thought her face might crack if her smile got any wider. 'I'm so glad you're here now.'

'Me too,' Jess replied. 'Now let's get another drink. I intend to be very tipsy indeed by the time the dancing starts.'

Niall made a beeline for them as soon as they returned to the lobby. 'All okay?' he asked, his eyes resting on Merry.

'Everything is perfect,' she said, beaming at him. 'How long have you known she was coming?'

'About a week,' he admitted. 'I'm sorry I couldn't tell you – Jess swore me to secrecy.'

'No need to apologize,' Merry said. 'It was a lovely surprise. Thank you for helping to make it happen.'

Jess cleared her throat. 'Do you mind if I leave you to it for a bit, babes? There's someone I really need to see.'

Merry followed her gaze and saw Andrew, dressed in what looked an awful lot like a Viking version of a kilt, in amongst some of the other Highland Park gang. 'Go ahead,' she said. 'We can catch up later, after the speeches.'

'And talking of the speeches,' Niall said, as Jess headed towards Andrew, 'we should probably kick those off. Let me go and open the hall doors and make an announcement for people to take their seats.'

By the time everyone had filtered into the hall – among gasps of admiration, Merry was pleased to note – and filled up the rows of seats, Merry had begun to feel nervous again. But no sooner than her hands started to shake than Niall was beside her on the stage.

'One last job to do,' he murmured encouragingly. 'Then you can enjoy yourself.'

The other guests took their seats: Hamish Burns, the chair of Orkney Literary Society, and Morag Rossi, who Merry was going to present with a specially bound edition of her new novel. Niall stood up and raised his hands, and immediately the room fell quiet.

'Ladies and gentlemen, what a pleasure it is to welcome you here tonight, as we gather to celebrate another wonderful contribution from Orkney's Writer in Residence scheme.' He glanced around the room and smiled. 'As you know, our hope at the start of each residency is that the chosen writer will encourage people to read more. Judging from the incredible turnout tonight, and at every other event we've run this year, that hope has more than been realized.'

He turned to glance at Merry, eyes shining. 'We always try to choose an author who will appeal to as wide a demographic as possible, as well as someone who will help to show our beautiful islands in a positive light through their writing. I think it's safe to say that this time, we chose very well indeed. But you don't need to take my word for it – now I'd like to hand over to Hamish Burns, who is going to talk about some of the remarkable ways this year's Writer in Residence has promoted Orkney.'

Hamish got to his feet amid a smattering of applause. 'Thank you, Niall. I'll be the first to admit I hadn't read much of Merina Wilde's previous work before she came to Orkney.' He cast a sheepish look at Merry, who smiled. 'But from the moment Niall put one of her novels in my hands, I was hooked. And as Niall has just suggested, her work as our Writer in Residence has exceeded all expectations. Who could forget her electrifying short story about the fate of Skara Brae all those centuries ago? Or her haunting retelling of Betty Corrigall's tragic tale? But I'm sure you will all agree that the cherry on the cake – the one we never dreamed might be possible – is the novel Merina has written during her time here. A story set on Orkney, inspired by our very own islanders, and soon to be transformed into a major Hollywood movie starring Nick Borrowdale and Emily Martins.'

An excited murmuring rose from the crowd even as Niall gave Merry a stricken look. He got to his feet and whispered something to Hamish, who cleared his throat. 'I'm told that last piece of information is still a secret so – er – please keep it to yourselves. But regardless of that, I'd like to extend our warmest thanks to Merina, who has been everything we wanted in a role model and more. And as a token of our gratitude, we'd like to present you with a small gift.'

Niall stood up and motioned for Merry to join him as he handed Hamish a small box. Certain her cheeks must be bright red from all the praise the two of them had heaped upon her, Merry stepped forward.

'Many thanks for all your enthusiasm and hard work, Merina,' Hamish said and gave her the box. 'We're delighted that you'll be staying on in an unofficial capacity for a few months more.'

The crowd burst into applause as he shook Merry's hand. Beside him, Niall conjured an enormous bouquet seemingly out of thin air and presented it to Merry, grinning as it almost eclipsed her head. Then both men stepped back and allowed Merry to take the microphone.

'Thank you, Hamish,' she said, doing her best to juggle the flowers and the box until Niall stepped forward and took them both. 'And thank you, Niall. You're always there when I need you.'

His eyes met hers and, for a moment, she forgot where she was. Then reality crashed back in. Taking a deep breath to calm her nerves, she gazed out at the audience and tried to remember what she'd planned to say. A sea of faces returned her gaze, some now familiar and dear to her, others less so, but every single one seemed to wear a smile. The last of her nerves vanished as she smiled back at them.

'As some of you will know, I came to Orkney looking for magic. I'd lost my way with writing, was struggling to finish the novel I was being paid to write, and I wondered if I'd ever enjoy my work again. But I'm delighted to say I found everything I needed here and more. Everyone I've met in the last six months has given me something – a name, a story, a location or perhaps even a secret – and I couldn't have dreamed that I'd feel so inspired.' She turned to look at Morag. 'And some people gave me more than one single story. Some people, like Morag here, gave me their whole lives.'

Merry took a step back and reached under her chair, where Niall had left a white box inscribed with Morag's name.

'I'm incredibly grateful to Morag for letting me use her story as the inspiration to create one of my own. In this box is a special, one-of-a-kind edition of the novel I wrote after hearing Morag and Giovanni's love story. I'd like to present it to you now, Morag, along with my undying thanks. You'll also find the novel is dedicated to you and your husband.'

Once again, the crowd broke into applause, this time with deafening whoops and cheers, as Merry planted a gentle kiss on Morag's papery cheeks and placed the box in her hands. 'Thank you so much,' she said, surprised to feel tears pricking at the back of her eyes as she looked at Morag.

'Thank you for making our story live for ever,' Morag replied. She stood up and made her way slowly to the front of the stage. 'I know I'm not meant to make a speech but I've never been one for doing as I'm told.'

A wave of laughter rolled across the hall, then died away as Morag opened her mouth to speak again. 'Giovanni was never really one for romance but I reckon he'd have loved the story our Merry has written here. As most of you know, he came here as a prisoner of war, but he always used to say it was love that made him stay. And that's what you'll find in this book – love. Romantic love, family love, patriotic love but most of all, the capacity we all have to love each other. And I don't know about you, but I think that's something we all need to do more, no matter who we are. So, make sure you read it!'

The applause as Morag retook her seat was thunderous and went on for what felt like minutes, resisting all attempts to quieten it down. Merry leaned across to Niall. 'I need to employ Morag as my publicist. She's fantastic!'

Niall grinned. 'I know. I'd better double my order of the book for publication day – I think you're going to surpass Jess as the most stolen author in the library.'

Once the crowd finally fell silent again, Niall took the microphone once more. 'Thanks for that ringing endorsement, Morag. I don't think you could ask for a better review than that, Merry – "make sure you read it!" You should put that on the front cover.'

There was more laughter. 'You'll be glad to know it's almost time for the dancing,' Niall went on. 'If we can ask you all to move into the lobby area again, we'll clear this room and let you know when it's ready. But before you do that, can we thank Hamish, Morag and, of course, Merry, for being here this evening.'

It took a further ten minutes for the audience to disperse, during which Merry chatted to Morag and Hamish. But it wasn't until the two other guests had left the stage and the room was almost empty that she thought to open the box Hamish had given her. Inside, she found a delicate necklace: a glistening silver-cased oblong of polished blue and grey and green gemstone. And through the centre, there was a hole.

'Do you like it?' Niall asked, materializing at her side. 'I had it specially commissioned from a local jeweller in Dounby.'

Merry ran a gentle finger across the smooth surface

and swallowed. 'It's beautiful,' she said huskily. 'What's it made of?'

'Ocean Jasper,' he said, then paused. 'It's supposed to have healing qualities, especially where the heart is concerned.'

'Just like the Odin Stone,' she observed, touching the hole in the middle of the gem.

'Exactly like that,' he replied, and she looked up to find him watching her intently. 'In the same way that it represents vows made and promises kept.'

There was something in his voice, a depth that told her he was saying more than the words implied. 'I'd like to wear it,' she said. 'Will you help me?'

Niall's gaze didn't waver. 'Of course.'

She slid the fine silver chain from the box and laid the necklace in his hand, before lifting her hair from her neck. Niall passed the chain around her throat and he was so near that she could feel his breath warm on her cheek. His fingers brushed her skin as he fumbled with the clasp, and she shivered at his touch. Then it was done. Niall stepped back, leaving the pendant resting on her chest. Merry raised a hand to touch it and turned to smile at him. 'Thank you. I know this is really a gift from you.'

He inclined his head. 'I didn't pay for it. But yes, I suppose you could say it's from me.' He took a deep breath. 'From my heart to yours.'

Up until then, Merry had been aware that there were other people in the hall, chatting and laughing as they moved chairs and arranged tables, but at that moment everything else faded away. Her pulse sped up as she gazed into Niall's eyes. 'Are you sure you mean that? I don't have the best track record when it comes to love.'

He smiled and reached out a finger to touch her cheek, causing the breath to catch in Merry's throat. 'I've never been surer of anything in my life.'

For a second or two, she was certain he was going to kiss her. And then, with a whoosh of disappointment, she remembered where they were and knew he wouldn't; not here, in the place where he worked, surrounded by the people he worked with and half of Orkney besides. But, once again, he surprised her. With one swift movement, he placed a hand on the small of her back and pulled her near, dipping his head and kissing her with an assurance and thoroughness that took the breath from her lungs.

Heat flooded her body. She pressed against him, and he let out a soft moan that told her he'd wanted this to happen almost as long as she had, although she'd fought it from the start. And somehow, it felt different to any kiss she'd experienced before: deeper, more resonant, as though every other kiss had been preparing her for this one, the one that really mattered. It was, she thought as they finally broke apart to stare at each other in wonder, like coming home.

Niall spoke first, his voice low and gravelly. 'I know this is all happening too fast but I have to say this while I still have the nerve – I love you.'

For the third time that evening, tears burned in Merry's eyes. 'Oh, Niall. I love you too.'

They might have kissed again if the sound of loud cheering hadn't broken the spell. Feeling a wave of mortification wash over her, Merry turned to see they had an enthusiastic audience of onlookers that included Sheila and Bridget, Clare and Hugh, plus Andrew and Jess. Every single one of them was grinning and applauding with such gusto that both Merry and Niall couldn't help laughing too.

'About bloody time, babes!' Jess called, pumping the air with her fist.

'Absolutely,' Andrew bellowed. 'This definitely calls for a dram or two.'

On the stage, Niall turned back to Merry. 'Well, your official duties are done – can I interest you in some drinking and dancing?'

Merry wondered if her heart might actually burst with happiness. 'Only if you kiss me again first,' she whispered, and reached up to pull his head towards hers.

Acknowledgements

This has to begin with my unending thanks and gratitude to Jo Williamson of Antony Harwood Ltd, superstar agent and life-support system – I know it's often like herding cats but I really appreciate your perseverance. A massive thank you to Bec Farrell for helping to shape Brightwater Bay with skill, patience and humour (I'm really sorry about Magnús), and to Judith Long for taking over when Bec moved on to pastures new. Thanks to absolutely everyone on the Books and the City team for ensuring Merry's story is an irresistible package – special thanks to Pip Watkins for designing up an Orkney storm and giving me such gorgeous covers – they might just be my favourites.

A big hat tip to the real-life Jessie Edwards, who allowed me to steal her name and general gorgeousness for the character of Jess – I think we can all agree she has the best lines. Thanks to Nick Haslam for answering my running questions – you might just make a runner of me yet. And enormous shiny-eyed gratitude to Rowan Coleman, without whom this book might never have been written; you made Orkney come to life and your expert tips on incredible settings made putting the scenes together so much easier. Maybe we'll go there together one day.

A friend who sends encouraging Chris Evans pictures and GIFs is a friend worth having – I consider myself very lucky to have Miranda Dickinson to keep me going. I'm also blessed by Queen Clare Watson as my life coach, cocktail partner and total glamour inspiration – couldn't have got through the last 14 days/weeks/years without you! As always, thanks to Julie Cohen, Kate Harrison and Cally Taylor, who are as inspirational as ever. Cuddles to T and E for always, always, *always* being there to pick me up. And last of all, thanks to my readers – this book is for you. I hope you've fallen in love with Orkney as much as I have.

Last Orders at the Star and Sixpence

Holly Hepburn

**Roaring fires, cosy nooks and friendly locals,
welcome back to the perfect village pub ...**

It is September and the new season is bringing change to
the village of Little Monkham. Nessie has moved in with
the lovely Owen and his son Luke, leaving her sister Sam
next door in their renovated pub, the Star and Sixpence. But
is all change for the good? Sam and Joss have gone their
separate ways and he's left Little Monkham for good.

New chef Gabriel Santiago is causing a flutter among
the women of the village but Sam is determined not to
make the same mistake again and keeps things strictly
business between them. But an inconvenient attraction to
Gabe is the least of Sam's worries when an unexpected
visitor arrives at the Star and Sixpence. Who is Laurie
Marsh and what does he want from the sisters?

'Warm, witty and laced with intriguing secrets!
I want to pull up a bar stool, order a large G&T and
soak up all the gossip at the Star and Sixpence!'
Cathy Bramley

**SIMON &
SCHUSTER**

A Year at Castle Court
Holly Hepburn

Sadie is a single mum, nursing a broken heart. Her best
friend from childhood, Cat, is burned out from working long
hours as a chef in Paris. In need of a change, they decide
to invest in their dream – running their own handmade
biscuit shop in gorgeous Castle Court, a three-storey food
court tucked away behind Chester's bustling streets.

They soon discover that Castle Court has its own
community – a little haven of delight against the stresses
of the outside world. But not everyone welcomes the new
business: the patisserie owner is less than pleased by
what she sees as direct competition and Greg, who runs
the fancy bistro that dominates one end of the courtyard,
doesn't think Sadie and Cat have the talent or business
acumen to succeed. Luckily, there's support in the form
of the delectable Jaren, who owns the Dutch waffle
house opposite Smart Cookies, and Swiss chocolate-shop
owner, Elin. And if all else fails, the friends can drown
their sorrows in Seb's cocktail bar on the third floor!

**AVAILABLE NOW IN PAPERBACK
AND EBOOK**

**SIMON &
SCHUSTER**

The Picture House by the Sea

Holly Hepburn

The Palace at Polwhipple is a lovely art deco cinema,
nestled in front of azure Cornish seas. But it's long
past its heyday now. Its only saving grace is Ferrelli's,
the family run ice-cream concession in the foyer.

When Ferdie, the owner of Ferelli's, breaks his leg, his
granddaughter Gina drops everything to come and help
out. But when she arrives she is dismayed by the state of
the cinema, which she remembers fondly from childhood
holidays. Along with local renovation expert Ben, she
sets about reviving the Palace to its former glory.

But the cinema needs more than a lick of paint. Its very
future is under threat from a developer with greed in
his eyes. Can Gina save the place before it's too late?

'Fabulously feel-good, funny and fresh, it will
sweep you off your feet'
Rowan Coleman

**AVAILABLE IN PAPERBACK
AND EBOOK NOW**

**SIMON &
SCHUSTER**